CAR~~~~~~
TRILOGY

BOOK ONE

# BLURRED
# RED
# LINES

USA TODAY BESTSELLING AUTHOR
CORA KENBORN

# BLURRED RED LINES

*Obsession is the deadliest vice*

*Carrera.*
A word whispered in fear.
A name to avoid at all costs.
Until I come face-to-face with it.


Abducted.
Held against my will.
Prisoner of a war I know nothing about.
Captive to a ruthless cartel prince who wants more than my freedom...
*He wants me.*


I should hate him…
But the deeper Valentin drags me into his bloodstained world the harder it becomes to resist.
Until that stain? That blood?
It becomes mine…
And I'm no longer a prisoner of war.
*I am the war.*

*For those who have ever wondered how completely different your life would've turned out if only you'd closed your eyes and leaped. . .*

*This is for you.*

# PLAYLIST

Till I Collapse - Eminem, Nate Dogg
Bring Me To Life - Evanescence
End of Me - Apocalyptica, Gavin Rossdale
Gun In My Hand - Dorothy
Dark Nights - Dorothy
Mad Hatter - Melanie Martinez
Pony - Ginuwine
Criminal - Fiona Apple
I Put A Spell On You - Marilyn Manson
Closer - Nine Inch Nails
Creep - Radiohead
Stay - Shakespears Sister
Pretty Baby - Vanessa Carlton
Hands To Myself - Selena Gomez
Without You - Lana Del Ray
Bad Blood - Taylor Swift, Kendrick Lamar
Love On The Brain - Rhianna
Issues - Julia Michaels

# *Prologue*

## EDEN

*There's a fine line between love and hate.*

I'd heard that cliché all my life thrown around by half-interested adults who gave few fucks about either one. The idiom du jour served to placate me enough to remove my adolescent angst from blocking Monday night football and return to my room, where I belonged.

It wasn't until my heart blackened to a charred void that I understood the true meaning of the phrase. I found it amazing how much that fine line thickened while sweat dripped from the brow of someone I loved as I aimed a gun at his heart.

"Eden, you don't know what you're doing."

His image blurred although my hand held steady. "Yours is the betrayal I never saw coming...congratulations." In my head the words sounded cold, despite the wetness that trailed from the corners of my eyes. Crawling to my feet, I paced the small space in front of him before I realized I'd uprooted from my spot. Keeping my breathing shallow, I focused on inhaling only when necessary. The run-down house reeked of dank mildew and death.

The number of deaths that would be added to the stench remained to be seen.

"I never wanted to hurt you," he implored, begging me to recall what we'd meant to each other. When I vacantly stared at him, he licked his lips and attempted to reach me on another level. "After all we've been through, it ends like this?"

"You've left me no choice."

"There's always a choice."

Hatred burned my eyes, incinerating the man reflected in them. "Fuck you."

His sigh turned into a cough, rattling his chest. A knowing smile curved his lips. "There's my feisty girl."

I waved the gun in the air—a stupid move on all accounts, but his play on my emotions ripped at my soul. "I'm not anything of yours. You sold me out. You made me believe we were on the same side." Tears rolled harder, ignoring my commands to stop. "The whole time you had an end game, you son of a bitch!"

*One step. Two steps. Three steps.*

If I pulled the trigger now, it'd be point-blank range. I couldn't claim self-defense. True, it hadn't been his hand that'd pushed me off the step and sent me careening down a flight of stairs. But, in the end, it was his actions that brought me here.

And I wasn't the one looking down the barrel of a Colt 1911 .38 Super.

All this time I'd believed him. All this time I'd trusted him. In the end, I'd been a fool because all this time I'd been used.

"Eden," he pleaded, searching for a shred of the affection we'd shared. "I love you."

*There's a fine line between love and hate.*

Watching him grovel for his life, I suddenly understood the meaning behind the phrase. When I loved a person, I saw them through rose-colored glasses. Everything was perfect...until it wasn't. I walked the line until I got knocked off and opened my eyes to the person I'd been blind to. My heart became torn... desperate to recapture the first untainted moments where the line was straight and steady. Before I knew it, hate filled the space where the love vacated, and my heart battled with my head.

Like an addict who promised one more hit would be the last, I knew it was a lie but told it anyway. I knew I couldn't stop. The cycle always repeated, and I hurt myself until there was nothing left but hate for both of us.

*Unless the cycle ends.*

I thought the past eighteen days had hardened me to violence, so it surprised me when my chin quivered. Vengeance took my salvation, but apparently, a conscience still resided somewhere in the deep recesses of my mind. Maybe that was one thing he hadn't killed. Maybe that was the last shred of humanity I could hold onto as I burned in hell for the path I'd walked.

I would've done anything for him. He'd held me in his arms and promised to protect me.

I didn't bother to stop the lone tear as it rolled across my nose and fell onto my bottom lip, pausing briefly before tumbling down my chin. "I love you, too," I whispered as I unloaded the gun, my mask slipping as he stumbled.

It's funny how sometimes the people you'd give your life for are the ones who take it.

# Chapter One
## VALENTIN

The chair creaked as I leaned forward for the small glass, while seated at my desk. It pissed me off, and I made a mental note to have Mateo replace it tomorrow.

To most people, a creaking chair was a minor annoyance. At the very least, it wasn't worth the destruction of an eight-hundred-dollar piece of furniture.

However, in my line of work, the creak of a chair could mean the difference between life and death. The slightest sound determined whether my head rested on my pillow at the end of the night or splattered in pieces against the wall.

Silence was golden. There were no exceptions.

Wrapping my fingers around the stem of the short tequila glass, I sat back, controlling my temper as the hinges from the chair protested. I held the glass up to eye level, ensuring it remained at room temperature.

Without so much as a knock, my office door flew open and bounced against the wall behind it with a crash.

*"Quién te crees tú? Te calmas o te calmo."* Who do you

*think you are? Calm down before I calm you down.* My fingers tightened around the glass as I lifted an eyebrow at my first lieutenant. "You don't knock anymore?"

"Sorry, *jefe.*" Mateo lowered his gaze in respect. "May I come in?"

I waved my wrist, indicating my disinterest. "You already are, aren't you?"

He gave a quick nod and closed the door behind him. "We have a situation…"

"Do you know how old I was when my father gave me my first stem of tequila, Mateo?"

A deep line etched in his forehead. "*Jefe?*"

"I asked you a question."

He clutched a paper in his hands and shook his head. "I don't know…fifteen, maybe sixteen?"

A smile pulled at the corners of my mouth. "Nine."

His only answer was an immediate widening of his eyes. Not that I didn't expect it. I enjoyed a little shock value from time to time.

I lifted the stem between us and swirled the liquid against the sides of the glass. "Do you see how it sticks to the walls? That's called a string of pearls. It means it's good shit. My father taught me how to tell the difference as a boy. Now, most men would just shoot this and be done." I narrowed a stare at him. "What would you do, Mateo?"

His face flicked from the glass to my face, I assumed trying find the correct answer hiding somewhere between the two. Unexpectedly, his gaze shot across the room to the side table where the bottle of *Gran Patrón Burdeos Añejo* sat, half empty.

"I'd drink it in small sips, letting it touch every part of my tongue before swallowing."

My tug of a smile extended farther. "And why would that

be, lieutenant?"

"Because it's expensive shit, *jefe*. When tequila is three-thousand-five hundred pesos per shot, you don't drink it…you experience it." He stood straighter, radiating the strength of a man confident he'd proven his worth.

"*Buena respuesta*!" I laughed, approving of his answer, then raising the stem. Taking a sip, I set it down and clapped my palm down on the wooden desk. "What do you need?"

Mateo shook his head slightly and glanced at the paper in his hands. "There's been a situation, but we've contained it. I just wanted to inform you."

*Situations* were never good. If I had to be informed of their existence, it made them worse.

"Shipments or ranks?" I asked, studying his young face.

"Ranks." He lowered his head. "Another task force. This one slipped by us. They infiltrated through the lower ranks and pinched a lieutenant."

A red haze shifted across my vision. Task forces were as commonplace as waking up and taking a piss. By now, we'd learned every trick the DEA agents threw at us. It was always the same song and dance set to a different beat. Each time a hotshot agent rose to power, thinking they were the second coming, we'd knock them back down. It soon became my favorite game. Hearing that one slipped by my guarded lines fueled my anger.

"How the fuck did someone just slip by? Do you know what this could do to us?" My hands clenched and swept across the desk, sending the bottle and glass crashing to the floor. "*Pinches idiotas*!"

Mateo flinched as glass shattered at his feet. To his credit, he made no attempt to move from his spot. "It was pussy, *jefe*."

I paused my tirade. "I'm sorry, did you say 'pussy'?"

His chin dipped as his blunt fingers stroked the sparse hairs of his goatee. A momentary break in his armor exposed the nervousness on his face. "The DEA sent a female agent."

"A female DEA agent got to one of our lieutenants…and now we're fucked?" I arched my brow, not quite believing the words.

Mateo smirked. "Not as much as she was."

If the situation didn't screw us so much, I would've laughed. But nothing about a betrayal in a cartel's ranks warranted humor. "What do they have?"

"Our informant on the inside says three months of wiretapping. They're moving tomorrow."

Without thinking, I ran my hand through my hair, dislodging it from the carefully combed back style my father favored. I cursed as unruly strands dusted over my forehead. "Who?"

Mateo hesitated. "Nando."

My shoulders hunched as a dagger lodged deep in my back. Nando Fuentes sat next to me as we crossed the border six years ago. He'd been with me from the beginning, and to find out he'd sold my soul for his own tested my control.

"What has he told them?"

"According to our informant, just details about upcoming shipments." Mateo shifted the paper from hand to hand. "No names or chain of command, but…"

"But?"

He steeled his expression, holding my stare. "He's flipping."

Regaining my composure, I pressed my fingers together for a moment before reaching into my pocket for my phone. Hitting a coded button, I dialed the last number I wanted to call. It annoyed me to need a favor from anyone—especially him.

After several rings, he answered with a smirk in his voice. "Carrera, what a pleasant surprise."

I gripped the edges of my desk to calm myself and tempered

my voice. "Harcourt, we have a slight situation."

"Why doesn't that surprise me?"

I paused a moment to stop a knee-jerk reaction I'd regret. "How's the bid for the district attorney nomination coming?"

"Steady," he answered cautiously. "DA Garrison is all but out the door. Favorability polls are looking up."

"Good." I knew I'd hit him where it counted and went in for the kill. "As I said, there's been a situation. My lieutenant tells me it's with one of my men and a DEA agent. Is it a bluff or has he already made a deal?"

"It's not a bluff," he said after a long pause. "He hasn't talked yet, but they're coming for him tomorrow."

"I need a glitch in the paperwork to stall them."

A slow sigh preceded a hush in his voice. "Damn it, Carrera, this isn't the time to be sticking my hands in evidence."

He should have thought of that before he stuck his hands in cartel business for career advancement. Having Houston's first Latino governor's ear came in handy.

"Think long and hard, Harcourt. It'd be a shame for someone to be tipped off about a few grams in your car. No one would elect a junkie DA."

"Asshole," he growled. "You wouldn't. Besides, how do you know I'm not recording this whole conversation?"

"Because you're not a suicidal moron. You think an assistant district attorney scares me, Harcourt?" I leaned back in the noisy chair. "I've poured men like you down drains with nothing left but a bad smell. You want to take the risk? It's been a while since I've made soup."

Silence between us had a smile breaking across my face. The soup talk always clinched the win in an argument with Americans. They wanted to believe it was an urban legend but didn't want to take the risk to find out.

"Fine," he mumbled, clearly irritated. "Name?"

"Nando Fuentes. And hurry; I don't like to wait." I disconnected the line before he could respond. I'd learned the tactic from my father. Always end a conversation with the last word—by whatever means necessary.

I turned to Mateo. "Take care of him."

A slow blink indicated his acknowledgement of Nando's fate. "Fifty-five-gallon drum? The acid will leave no trace within three hours."

Hell, no. I wanted a trace. Pieces of Nando were going to trace all over the goddamn place for his betrayal.

"No," I replied calmly. "I want a message sent. Make it look like a murder-suicide. You know the *policía* around here. They'll claim that's what it was whether they believe it or not."

Mateo tilted his head. "Suicide?"

A wicked grin spread across my face. "He's been fucking some *puta* who's snorted more of our profits than he's moved. I'm sure his wife won't mind."

"*Está bien*," he nodded, accepting his task without argument.

After what was left of Nando was bagged and tagged, I'd have to reevaluate Mateo's place in my hierarchy. Although he and I hadn't known each other very long, he'd proved his loyalty repeatedly.

I briefly glanced at the destruction of my desk, now residing in chaos on the floor. "If that's all..."

Mateo shifted his weight and cleared his throat. "There's one more thing."

I sighed. "Make it quick."

He finally glanced at the paper he held in his hands and scratched his head. "One of our new dealers, Isabella, informed us that a repeat buyer in Maplewood has put four grams of our shipment up his nose. He's in for about ten g's and missed the last two drops. Do you want us to torch his place?"

I remained silent for a moment, processing the information. Normally, morons who snorted their paychecks meant very little to me. That's why I had a crew. But with Nando disrupting the trust in my organization, I needed to send a message to our associates that we weren't to be fucked with on any level.

"What would my father do?" I countered.

Mateo's face paled. "He'd have them beheaded and mounted on a stick in the family's yard."

"True," I said, the images I'd seen as a boy in Mexico giving me pause. "However, that's hardly our style." Shifting in my seat, the damn chair creaked, eliciting an involuntary clenching of my jaw. "But the debt makes us look weak, so it can't go unpunished."

I paused as my gaze roamed my desk and landed on the only thing that withstood my earlier mood swing—a framed picture of my father as a young man. His blackened eyes mocked me with silent words he'd ingrained into me before every beating: 'Mercy doesn't exist in our world. Mercy yields weakness, and weakness brings death.'

"*Jefe*?"

I met Mateo's stare. "Ten g's?" He nodded. "Have Emilio pay our friend a visit and see what he's managed to collect for a payment. For every grand he's missing, he owes us a finger."

"And if he has nothing?"

Leaning back, I loosened the top button on my collar. "I suppose our friend will need to find a new profession. I imagine it's hard to hold a hammer with two bloody stumps."

Without another word, Mateo nodded and left my office to handle business. It was half of what I liked about the guy. I gave orders and he shut his mouth and followed them. I needed more men like him in my operation.

"Fuck." Surveying the broken glass on the floor, I watched the expensive tequila soak into the carpet, making no move to clean it up. As usual, my thoughts wandered to an unwanted distraction who'd managed to invade my day-to-day business more and more lately.

When I arrived in America, I assumed everyone had my same tastes and high standards. The first time I ordered a shot of *Añejo* tequila in Houston, the bartender handed me a highball glass of chilled, *blanco* piss water garnished with a hunk of lime and a salt shaker. It was insulting. In Mexico, a man could get shot in the face for less. There seemed to be only one bartender in the entire Houston metro who could get it right, although I tried not to show my face there if I could help it.

Being there wasn't safe or smart. Regardless of what she looked like in those shorts.

# Chapter Two
## VALENTIN

*Six Months Ago*

I stood in the corner of the cantina watching her long before I sat down. She wore an expression of a caged animal that had been poked with a stick one too many times. Leaning my back against a corner wall, I studied a line that sank deep between her eyebrows and the line of sweat that trickled down the back of her slender neck. Fascinated, I followed her busy hands as she poured drinks with marked precision without giving a thought as to what she was doing.

That took skill. I appreciated skill.

It'd been a long day making sure I had the district attorney's office in my back pocket. Not that I couldn't run my business around them, but having someone on the inside of the legal system made life a hell of a lot easier. The young assistant DA had been resistant, but everyone in this town had a weakness—the challenge was simply to find it.

And I never backed down from a challenge.

I needed to unwind in the quiet of my own house, but as much as I told myself I should stay away from a business I cleaned cartel money through, curiosity won out over common sense.

Since opening Caliente Cantina, my lieutenant, Emilio, had gone through no less than four bartenders. They weren't particularly bad at their jobs; Emilio just had a problem with employer/employee lines. If he didn't calm the hell down, his proclivities would cost me a sexual harassment lawsuit.

I couldn't have cared less about paying the girls off—to hell with them. They were expendable and no great loss, as far as I was concerned. In fact, every bartender in Houston failed the simplest task of a drink order. That alone could be how I'd ended up here.

Maybe I'd come here to see if his new hire was as useless as the others.

Shouting diverted my attention to wild, animated hand gestures coming from an obviously not twenty-one-year-old male trying to order beer. The new bartender demanded identification, having none of his shit.

*Good girl.*

Even while he cursed at her and flipped his middle finger, she never wavered. Not one flicker of emotion clouded her face as she cocked an eyebrow, calmly held up her palm, pointed to him, and nodded toward the door. Cursing at her again, the punk shoved the drink menu across the bar and motioned for his buddies to leave with him.

An amused smile tugged at my mouth, stunning me. People rarely entertained me. Most often they annoyed me to the point of solitude. I needed a closer look at this girl; but first, I needed to show this asshole some manners.

He passed me on his way to the door looking like an over-privileged frat boy who knew nothing of the real world. His face was red with anger as he tugged on his overgrown, shaggy, brown hair.

"Bitch took my ID." He turned to his friend as he reached for the door. "Maybe she just needs to get fucked really good. Maybe I should wait for her outside and help her get rid of that shitty attitude."

I brushed his shoulder with enough force to make my displeasure known, locking eyes with him in a way that made grown men piss themselves. "And maybe I should wait outside for you and help you get rid of your shitty attitude."

Flushing, he opened his mouth to argue. When his eyes landed on my waist, he choked on his own cockiness. "I…uh, no, dude. I'm just joking. It's a joke. No harm."

No one would call me a huge man by any stretch of the imagination, but I had more than enough muscle to kick his ass before he had a chance to fight back. It didn't matter, though. I didn't have to lift a finger. I knew where his eyes were and what made him want to disappear into himself.

I didn't go anywhere without my pistol. To make my point, I pulled my jacket back to make sure he knew I wasn't fucking around. "If I ever see your face in this cantina again, I'll have dick fajitas on the menu so fast your fucking head will spin. Are we clear?"

He couldn't speak. I got a quick nod as he grabbed his friend and ran.

*God, I love power.*

Returning my attention to the bar, I strained to hear her conversation with the random drunks gawking at her. Loud Mariachi music blaring in the background and annoying yells of over exuberant patrons made eavesdropping almost impossible. Trying to act bored as hell, I slipped into a seat at the end of the bar and leaned forward.

"I'll be with you in a minute." Tilting her chin in my

direction, she kept her focus on the sugary frozen concoction she created. Puckering her red lips, she blew a piece of hair out of her face that escaped the sloppy bun on top of her head.

A sloppy, candy-red bun to match candy-red lips.

The kind of lips that could tell a man any lie they wanted and he'd gladly buy any shit they sold for just a taste.

My dick twitched, reminding me it'd been a few days since I'd gotten laid. It didn't help matters Emilio found it amusing to dress the bartenders in the tiniest denim shorts he could find, with black tank tops drawn across their chests so tight that the Caliente logo disappeared under their arms.

*Well played, Emilio.*

I'd never been one to chase women. I didn't have to. They fell at my feet, crawled in my bed, and blew my phone up with calls and texts I never returned. But I found myself intrigued and unable to turn away as I watched Emilio's new bartender flip through her texts, frown, and bite her lip, smearing the bright red lipstick that still had my pants in an uproar.

I watched her eyes glaze over as she muttered something under her breath and stared at the liquor bottles in front of her. With a long, drawn-out sigh, she snuck a sweeping glance around the bar. Immediately, I dropped my eyes down to my phone, suddenly engrossed in a blank screen.

*Do it. Be bad.*

Satisfied no one watched, she bent down and pretended to tie her shoe, taking a bottle of vodka with her to the floor. Tucked safely underneath the sink, I shifted over the bar to get a better view of the show as she reached up with a slim, milky-white arm and snagged a glass. Pouring two large shots, she downed them successively, grimacing at the eighty-proof burn.

Well, damn. She just became much more interesting to me.

I arched an eyebrow and fought a smile. "Bad day?"

"Bad life," she shot back, narrowing her eyes, then licking the remaining cheap vodka off her lips. Screwing the cap back on, she pushed off her heels and slipped the bottle back onto the counter.

"I would've gone for the Grey Goose myself. Drinking that shit is just asking for the day to get worse." I should've stopped talking. I considered small talk to be a waste of time.

She dragged the back of her hand across her mouth. "I don't remember asking your opinion."

"Can I get a gin and tonic, please?" A man two seats down from me wore a pissed off impatient look I didn't care for and waved a credit card in her face. My jaw ticked, but before I could put him in his place, pale blue eyes that could start a war pinned him to his seat.

"Here," she drawled in a marked Southern accent as she threw a basket of chips on the bar. "Fill your mouth so shit stops coming out of it. I'll get to you in a minute."

Normally, that'd be cause for termination, but she amused the hell out of me. I couldn't stand weak women, and this girl had enough fire for a room full of them. Plus, the asshole had it coming. I began to understand why Emilio spent so many nights at the cantina.

Catching my eye, a wicked smirk lifted the corners of her mouth as she placed her forearms on the bar and leaned in close enough for me to catch the scent of citrus and vanilla. It was a bizarre combination that lit a heated trail straight from my nose to my pants.

"So, what is it you want?"

*You. Naked and spread out on this bar.*

"I doubt you could handle it." I refused to blink, holding her stare, making sure she understood the double entendre. I wanted to push her to see how she'd react, but honestly, I knew the answer to both meanings.

Nobody had been worth a fuck yet. I didn't see why this would be any different.

My challenge seemed to piss her off and invigorate her at the same time. "Oh, I don't know about that. Haven't had any complaints yet." Spreading her fingers wide on both hands, she slid her arms out and narrowed her eyes. "Give me your best shot."

*I'd give you my worst. I'd wreck you and leave you broken.*

"*Añejo* tequila. Straight shot, in a stem glass—not a highball—room temp." With her bizarre, intoxicating scent still fucking with my head, I realized she was knocking me off my game. I didn't like it. So, being the ass I was, and remembering Emilio's tendencies toward cheapness, I leaned in close. "And if it hasn't aged at least three years, shove it up the owner's ass."

She brushed that damn stray hair out of her eye again and winked. "I'll do my best."

Swinging her hips all over the bar, she glanced my way a few times, making a big production of bending over unnecessarily to pick shit up off the floor. More than once, I promised my cock some uncomplicated pussy, if it'd calm the fuck down and stop trying to get a look at her ass, too.

Before it could accept my terms, a stem glass appeared under my nose just as I requested.

*That's a first.*

Raising a questioning eye up at her, she smirked and nodded to the drink. "Well? Are you going to drink that or wait until Jesus turns it back into water?"

A full-chested laugh I barely recognized came from my mouth as I reached for the glass. "I think that was wine."

She shrugged and waved her hand. "Whatever. Sunday School wasn't my thing."

26

As she watched me carefully, I hoped for the best and downed the shot with low expectations. The moment the liquid hit my tongue I knew I was fucked.

*Dios mío*, was I fucked.

By the smug look on her face, she knew it, too.

Twirling the empty glass in my fingers, I studied the captivating woman with renewed interest. "How is it that you're the only bartender in Houston who can get this drink right?"

Still grinning, she licked that damn lip again and returned the bottles to the shelf, the motion causing her tiny tank top to ride up and expose her flat stomach. "It's not rocket science. Hell, some people would say I'm a hit or miss on making anyone happy." Wiping down the counter, she shot me a look with untold pain hidden behind it. "Some people would even say I've never gotten anything right."

"Some people don't deserve to breathe your same air."

*Fuck, I meant that. What was wrong with me?*

Her face broke into the first genuine smile I'd seen from her all night not hidden behind a smirk or condescension, and my chest warmed. My fucking chest warmed, and it wasn't from the tequila.

"So, you got a name, Danger?"

"Danger?" I tried for a flat tone, but my voice raised an octave, betraying my interest.

*Damn.*

"Yeah, you know...as in, tall, dark, and dangerous?" She squinted her pale blue eyes and silenced an incoming text on her phone. "You look like you could get a girl in a lot of trouble."

I wanted nothing more than to wipe that damn grin off her face. She looked so smug. So sure I wanted her.

Fuck, I wanted her. "You have no idea."

Moments passed between us as we stared at each other in

silence. That shock of red hair grabbed my attention again, and I couldn't help but wonder who, or what, happened in her life to cause it. Nobody just did shit like that on purpose. Candy-red colored hair didn't just happen. It pissed me off that I even cared. I wasn't a good guy. I wasn't even a decent guy. I didn't ask girls their names, much less their stories.

"So, that's it?" she asked, chin tilted and one hand resting on a cocked hip.

Shit, had she been talking to me this whole time? "What's it?" I asked, trying to seem bored.

"You really have no name?"

I shot her a pointed look, mentally slamming the door on her inquisition. "Danger works. I like it."

I did. I liked it too damn much. And I hated nicknames. I thought they were childish and reserved for those annoying assholes who sat on the same side of the booth at restaurants.

"Of course, you do," she snorted in an unladylike, but oddly sexy way.

The bar started to get crowded, as patrons shoved bills toward her and demanded drinks. I watched them curiously, wondering what she'd do. To my pleasure, she held up a finger to them and kept her eyes on me.

Those eyes were what did it. Those pale blue eyes that tried to hide exhaustion exposed by the dark circles under them and sadness well beyond her years. They sucked me in and broke one of my cardinal rules. "What about your name?"

"Hey, what about my drink? You think you could take a break from your date over there to do your job, honey?"

Her eyes flickered relief for a moment, then darkened, becoming void of emotion. "Duty calls. Glad I could meet your expectations, Danger." She reached for the shot glass I held, and I grabbed her hand, my out-of-character reaction surprising both of us. Hesitating a moment, she lifted her eyes and met mine in a battle of wills.

I could tell we were both at war with what would happen next; I contemplated the consequences of fucking one of Emilio's employees. He seemed fond of this one, and the moment it was over, I'd have no choice but to have her fired.

Shifting her weight, she made the decision for both of us when she released her hand from my grip and pointed toward the douchebag two seats down, now glaring at us. "Let me know if you want another."

As she poured a gin and tonic for the asshole who cock blocked me, I pulled three, twenty-dollar bills out of my wallet and placed them face down on the bar. The exorbitant tip wasn't a handout, as I suspected she'd think after I left. I genuinely enjoyed her company. Which was exactly why I had to leave and never talk to her again.

She called me dangerous. If I was dangerous, she was fucking deadly.

My life revolved around the cartel, stray pussy, and money. I had no time for complications of anything else, and candy hair was a walking, talking complication. I knew in one touch I had no business being near her. A woman like that could cause the destruction of a man like me.

While she argued with the dickbag about the amount of gin she shorted him, I slipped around the long end of the bar, through the kitchen, and out the back door. I cut myself off like a junkie jonesing for his next hit of short shorts and a-size-too-small tank top. After tonight, I knew I couldn't afford the distraction.

Perfect drink or not, I was done with that girl.

So, I gave my business to every other bar in Houston and walked out of them pissed off and sober as hell for two months before I caved. However, I never returned to a barstool. Always sitting at one of the tables, I allowed young, annoying waitresses to serve me while I watched her flirt with a new man month after month until it got to be too much to take and stopped going altogether.

Some women were storms who blew into a man's life and ruined his plans for the night. That woman was a hurricane who uprooted and flooded the very foundation of everything a man thought he knew.

# Chapter Three

## BRODY

*Present Day*

After a third pencil lead broke on the Norris case deposition, I snapped the wood in half and threw it across the room. It hit the wall and skidded across the floor as I ran a sweaty palm across my unshaven chin.

When did shit get so out of control?

Everything piled on top of me, forcing my head underwater and my hand to the devil. I'd had no intention on bending to Val Carrera's will, but he'd backed me into a corner. I'd lived in Houston long enough to know that a corner was the last place anyone wanted to be with the Carrera Cartel.

Working in the judicial system, I saw, firsthand, what happened to men who crossed him. One day they were in our custody, the next, pieces of them fell out of a body bag. The constituents of Harris County elected me assistant district attorney to protect the community from men like Carrera. If they knew how much of my soul I'd sold to further my career, I wouldn't have to worry about the election. I'd be lucky to bus tables at the Waffle House for the rest of my life.

"Harcourt, you coming to lunch, or what?"

Glancing up from my curled fists, I settled a hardened glare on one of the prosecuting attorneys from the fourth floor. Dressed in a crooked blue tie and a missing suit jacket, he held my office door open as if I'd extended an invitation. His sloppy appearance grated on my last nerve, and my fingers twitched, searching my desk for another pencil to break.

"Too much work to do," I mumbled, rearranging the papers on my desk. "Get out."

Glancing up from surfing the web on his phone, he lifted a dark eyebrow and smirked. "Who pissed in your corner office?"

I leaned back, crossing my arms over my chest in a defensive gesture. On edge and in no mood for idle conversation, the last thing I wanted was to spend an hour trading locker-room stories and weekend plans with the subordinate assholes. I wasted little time under the illusion they were my friends. Every one of them had eyes on my job and only kissed my ass to stay in my good graces for when I became district attorney.

"No time for lunch. I've got press releases needing to go out. Some of us work for a living, Todd."

"Ted."

I honestly didn't give a shit. I'd wasted half the day trying to figure out a way out of the hole I'd gotten into with the Mexicans. I'd never been shady in my life, much less illegal. Everyone knew about the Carreras, but just like any sane person, I ignored them when they came calling. I sure as hell rebuked their offers of help. Their golden ticket came attached with strings tied to a lifetime of misery.

Then the stress of the upcoming primary resulted in a moment of weakness that solidified a hell I'd regret for the rest of my life. A fifth of Jack on a night she'd decided to grow a set of morals and a standard, and I found myself in the backseat of an Escalade signing my name in blood.

"If there's nothing else," I grumbled, sending a flat expression his way, "I trust you can see yourself out."

He answered with an eye roll. "Whatever." He laughed, nodding to a herd of fellow fourth-floor assholes as they grumbled about being late. "Maybe you need to take off early and get some ass, man. Might make you less of one, and you may have a few friends."

I waved his suggestion away as he laughed and joined the other hopefuls down the hall. Scowling at his audacity, I slammed papers onto the desk and swiveled my chair to stare out the wall of windows onto the city below.

*My city.*

The city that depended on me to keep them safe from the very people who bent me to their will and owned the next breath I took. How in the hell could I walk into a courtroom and look a jury in the face knowing I was no better than the criminals I prosecuted?

Rubbing my eyes with my thumb and forefinger, I mulled his words around in my head, letting them sink in. Dropping my hand, I stared down at the passing cars and congested lunchtime pedestrian traffic, the bright June sun reflecting harshly off the roofs of the buildings below my tenth-floor window. Closing my eyes, I cursed a string of late nights and insomnia, causing the attorney's words to make too much sense.

I didn't need more friends, but getting more ass sounded like the best suggestion I'd heard all day. Spinning back around, I picked my phone off my desk and hit the speed dial button, knowing the risk I took in calling her before two o'clock in the afternoon. The woman had two moods—ready to fuck, and ready to slice my balls off. At half past noon, I was just glad my boys were safely across town.

Five rings later, her throaty voice groaned along thinly held patience. "Somebody better be dead."

"I had a thought."

"Good for you. It'd better be about someone who's dead, or I swear to God, I'll rip your balls off, Brody."

"What do you say I come over tonight?" I continued, ignoring her threat.

She half yawned; half groaned my name. "You know I have to work."

Reaching for the metal nameplate, I polished it with the sleeve of my white dress shirt and moved it to the center of my desk. "I was thinking I'd swing by the cantina for a drink before you get off. I don't like you closing all alone that late, especially with the crime in that part of town. I can walk you to your car and come over afterward."

"Brody…"

"Come on, Eden," I argued, determined to win my case. "Do you have a better offer?" I held my breath as silence filled the line. Drumming my fingers on the arm of my chair, I waited for her response, only to be met with the typical stubbornness that kept me wondering why I kept coming back to a woman who opened her legs to me but kept her heart and mind closed.

"Fine." She reluctantly gave in, her sigh holding much more meaning than simple agreeability. That sigh was deadly. That sigh meant for the first hour after arriving at her townhouse, I'd need to cover my dick with a pillow and watch all sharp objects with a keen eye.

After disconnecting the call, I stared at the phone in my hand, flipping it over and over until the screen became foggy with fingerprints. I had no fucking idea what Eden Lachey and I were doing, but it wasn't a normal relationship that had any future—regardless of what I wanted. Eden had made that painfully clear on multiple occasions. After four months of sleeping together, I'd been the fucking girl in the relationship, wanting exclusivity and some sort of commitment out of her.

All I'd gotten was an eye roll and a warning to stop being a little bitch.

I lived in marked unreality when it came to Eden. I should've known better than to get involved with a friend's ex, but I'd known the woman before the scorn. She hadn't always been hardened. Once upon a time, Eden Lachey was rather demure, although she'd deny it with her dying breath. Somewhere underneath that cracked shell the woman who used to love to laugh and try to tell a bad joke still existed. For some reason, I seemed determined to find her. Something inside of me cared about her, even though the Eden that wore a perpetual scowl these days swore she was dead and gone.

She could argue with me and be pissed all she wanted. Until I won, I'd enjoy hatefucks while we battled. What was the worst that could happen? Great sex?

"Mr. Harcourt?" My heart rate sped up as my assistant's voice boomed unexpectedly from the desk phone intercom.

Pressing the two-way button on the phone, I dropped my phone in my pocket. "Yes, Nancy, what is it?"

"The jury has reached a verdict in the Salinas case, sir."

I raised an eyebrow. Already? Jesus. I'd expected them to reconvene for at least a few days. This could go either way for me depending on how sympathetic the women on the jury were to the tears that man had managed to squeeze out on the stand.

*Fucking tears. Gets women every time.*

Straightening the knot in my tie, I hit the button again. "I'll be right there."

With both palms flat against my desk, I stood over it, sweat beading on my forehead. One verdict. One man's life hung in the balance, and once his fate was sealed, I could end this miserable week and not think about mine.

# *Chapter Four*

## EDEN

Staring at the bare white walls of my bedroom, I held onto my pillow as the same thought ran in my head for over an hour. No one got ahead in life by bucking the system. I never bought into that crap, although Dad drilled it into my head my whole childhood.

I suppose my vehement dislike for rules played a role in the clusterfuck I awoke to as my steady friend-with-benefits faced the opposite direction in my bed. Forcing myself to remain quiet, I squinted the eye not squished into my pillow to verify I wasn't dreaming or, even worse, still drunk.

*Nope—sober as a judge.*

After meeting me at work as he promised, the lump of man snored softly as if he had every right to occupy my sheets in the daylight. His dirty blond hair twisted haphazardly behind his head, which I assumed was from a repeated invasion of my impatient fingers.

*Hell if I remember.*

It must've been good though, because his back looked like

an exotic trash panda nailed him. One corner of my mouth lifted in amusement but quickly faded as my hands dove for the alarm clock.

9:00 a.m.

"Shit!" I gathered as many discarded pieces of clothing as I could find and pulled them on, not caring if my shirt was backward or my shorts were buttoned incorrectly. They wouldn't be on long anyway.

The lump on my bed grunted as a ball of his clothes hit him in the face with laser accuracy. "Babe," he mumbled, shaking his jeans off his cheek, then burying his head into the pillow. "Why're you up so damn early on a Saturday? Go back to sleep."

This shit wouldn't do. He knew the rules.

This time his cell phone bounced off his forehead. "Jesus!" He shot straight up, rubbing the red mark it left behind.

I shrugged and disappeared into the adjoining bathroom, turning on the shower full blast. When I reentered my room, he sat up glaring at me, but he'd at least put on his pants.

*Good boy.*

"Now that I've got your attention," I said, collecting his shoes and depositing them on the foot of the bed, "I'm going to shower, and you can get the hell out."

He stared at me with a blank look. "You're kicking me out?"

"Nothing gets by you, does it?"

I was being a bitch, maybe more so than necessary. But I had no illusions about what had happened last night or in the past few months. I wasn't an idealistic teenage dreamer who held onto some fantasy of love and happily ever after. I'd lived life enough to know happily ever after existed only in fairy tales and cheesy rom-com movies.

Once you've danced close enough to the fire to get licked by the flames, you learned to adapt to the darkness.

He grasped my arm in a firm hold, smirking as if he didn't believe me. "C'mon, let's hit round two. I'll even get you there first."

What he *got* were his car keys flung right between his eyes.

"Fuck!" His head snapped back against the headboard with a thud. "You're crazy, you know that?"

For the first time since waking, a conflicted smile broke across my cheeks, and a twinge of regret pulled at my stomach. Turning away, I paused at the bathroom door and glanced over my shoulder. "I know," I said, the corners of my mouth gravitating downward.

"What's wrong with you, Eden?"

My mind drifted as I closed the bathroom door. "Everything."

"I'm sorry. It'll never happen again—yadda-yadda—you know the drill." I tore through the back door, throwing the dusty brown apron over my head in the middle of my usual apology.

"I know that look." Nash shook his head as I double wrapped the tie around my waist.

Furrowing my brows, I busied myself unpacking the new shipment of paint thinners that had arrived during the morning delivery. "What look? I don't have a look. There's no look."

*Well, that doesn't sound suspicious at all.*

"Uh-huh." My brother smirked, his trademark platinum blond hair falling in a chunk over his left eye. He leaned in front of me, pressing his hands over the box I frantically emptied. "That, dear sister, is the freshly-fucked look. It's a blinking neon light all over your face."

"Nash!" My mouth dropped open, heat staining my cheeks.

He chuckled and reached into the paint box to help me

unload. "Not that I want to hear about my little sister's sex life." His face twisted into a grimace as if he'd just smelled something rotten. "Actually, keep the details to yourself. But can you please send the booty calls home half an hour earlier? It's impossible to sign for deliveries and man the counter at the same time."

Guilt washed over me as we worked in silence. I wanted to say something to ease the tension, but anything I said would sound like hollow promises. If I was honest with myself, that's exactly what they were anyway. Every time I rolled into the hardware store late for my shift, I'd apologize and swear it wouldn't happen again. Every time, Nash would nod, knowing damn well I was full of shit. The one consistent thing my family could rely on was my unreliability.

I could handle most anything, except for Nash's silence.

He chewed on his lower lip, concentrating on holding as many paint cans as he could in each hand, as his forearms strained with the weight. The unruly chunk of hair fell into his eyes again, and he attempted to blow it away with a harsh breath. I laughed as it flopped right back down.

"Damn," he muttered, shaking his head.

Licking my palm, I reached across the box and slicked the pale chunk across his forehead. It was a move I'd done hundreds of times when we were kids.

*Old habits die hard.*

"You need a haircut, towhead."

He narrowed his eyes. "That's disgusting. Keep your spit to yourself, Cherry Pop."

Insulting each other's hair had been our thing since my ex-husband sent me running to the hair dye aisle, half-crazed. I smiled to myself, remembering the moment Nash first saw my shocking, bright red hair. He'd laughed himself to tears, claiming I looked like a cherry popsicle. The name stuck, and for the better part of a year, I'd been Cherry Pop.

Siblings were just assholes like that.

Everyone around me swore I'd lost my mind, going from a natural blonde to a very unnatural stop sign redhead. Nash just smirked and left a twelve pack of melting red popsicles in my mailbox the next day.

The morning passed into afternoon and while the hardware store saw enough foot traffic to break even, hoping for a profit seemed laughable.

Watching my brother repeatedly rearrange a wall of washers, I drummed my nails on the register. "Have you heard from Dad?" I asked, my eyes trained on his methodical movements.

He paused as if contemplating the weight of my question, then resumed straightening the impeccably straight packages. "He'll be in later this evening."

"That's not what I asked."

A hint of irritation seeped into his voice. "Let it go, Eden."

*Tap, Tap, Tap.*

I continued drumming my nails. "I *have* let it go. I let it go when you worked fourteen hour shifts all week. And the week before that...and the week before that." Nash's back stiffened as I pushed away from the counter and took a few steps toward him. "I let it go when you left the community center for a couple weeks until Dad could find some help to ease the load. How long ago was that, Nash? Three weeks? A month? Or has it been so long that you can't remember?"

"I said, stop."

My brain heard him. It sent a clear message to my mouth to shut up. However, my insatiable need to push the envelope informed my mouth that it was clear for takeoff, and it barreled down the runway on a suicide mission.

"And I let it go when that second job he's been so tired from working all the time called and asked why he hadn't bothered to show up for the past four days."

A growl rose from the depths of my brother's chest as his fist tightened around an entire row of washers. His knuckles whitened and the metal bar ripped from the display wall as he twisted toward me. "Goddamn it, Eden, I said that's enough! He's tired, all right? The man spent our entire lives doing right by us, by himself. Do you think you could stop acting like you're the only one that's ever had something bad happen and grow the fuck up?"

He might as well have slapped me across the face. I stared at him, my mouth opening and closing like a fish gasping for breath. Struggling for words, I reached out a tentative hand to him. "Nash, I…"

The chime of the bell over the door rang and a swoosh of air sucked the tension out of the room. Anger faded from Nash's face, and the consummate professional took over. I fell in line behind him as he made a sweeping welcome gesture with open hands.

"Welcome to Lachey Hardware, gentlemen. Is there anything in particular you're looking for?" He approached the two Latino men and engaged them in deep conversation, parading them from aisle to aisle.

I busied myself with counting out the money in the register, catching pieces of Nash's conversation with the two men. Their voices elevated as they argued about cable ties, rope, and duct tape.

I barely held in a snicker. It wasn't the first time men had come in with that supply list since *Fifty Shades of Grey* hit the big screen. It wouldn't be the last. They all pretended we didn't know exactly what freaky games they were playing in the sack, and we indulged them until they walked out with their bags of sin.

Glancing at my watch, I blew out a frustrated breath and untied my apron, knowing Emilio would kick my ass for being late for my shift at the bar. I hated leaving so soon, but my job at the hardware store didn't keep my lights on.

Before I got a chance to lift the apron over my head, four hands shoved a bounty of rope and duct tape on the counter in front of me. Jumping, I gasped as I covered my chest with my hand.

"Jesus. You scared the shit out of me." My shock suddenly turned to unease as the taller one with scarred fingers and a long black ponytail leaned in close.

"Many apologies, *señorita*." Something seemed off as he bared his yellowed, stained teeth. "*Señor* Lachey said you'd ring us up."

Hesitating at first, my fingers finally found the keys on the register. After bagging the merchandise, a shiver shot down my spine when his fingers lingered over mine as he took the bag.

"*Gracias*," he said, indulging himself in a slow perusal up and down my body. I swallowed slowly while the man laughed low in his chest.

As he turned, I nodded to the bag, and the words tumbled out of my mouth in a rush of impetuous nerves. "Big DIY project?"

Throwing a sharp and predatory look over his shoulder, he sneered with a wink that had my skin crawling. "I always do it myself, Eden. Otherwise, you have to go in and clean up someone else's messes."

I opened my mouth for a rebuttal, closed it, then opened it again. "Do we know each other?"

His dirty fingernail flicked the name tag on my apron. "We do now."

Confounded and more than creeped out by his plastic smile,

I watched them both walk out the door and disappear before being jarred out of my thoughts by a light hand on my back.

"Assholes," Nash explained, reading my thoughts. "They wanted to argue with me over everything. They even wanted to know what time we closed, because if it wasn't what they wanted, they said they'd be back." Rolling his eyes, he smiled and pushed me forward. "Get out of here. You slept through half your shift, and the local drunks will have my ass if you're late for their shitty beer and chips."

Balling up my apron, I sighed and logged out of the cash register. As I retrieved my purse from under the counter, something snagged on the top of the cabinet door, sending the contents flying across the carpet.

Bending down, I grabbed the strewn papers and stifled a second groan as I realized what had been shoved in my purse. Still squatting on the floor, I ran my fingers across the top of the University of Texas brochure.

"Nash," I warned, waving the brochure in the air. He grinned and held his hands up innocently, walking toward the front of the store.

I shook my head and tossed the brochure into the trash can beside the register. Seven brochures had found their way into my purse, car, and apartment. All seven had made their way into the garbage.

Humidity smacked me in the face as I kicked the back door open with more force than necessary. Turning the ignition, my little PT Cruiser purred to life, and I backed out of the parking lot on my way to the cantina.

Nash refused to give up hope that one day I'd fall in line and enroll in college. Maybe his head filled with visions of me graduating with some fancy degree, but at twenty-five years old, I didn't need to take Intro to Algebra with a bunch of pretentious teenage assholes to prove a point. I spent three years proving I could be what someone else wanted, and it destroyed me.

Nash had no clue he was slowly proving he could be what Dad always wanted him to be—a replica of himself.

I punched the gas out of frustration, and the car protested, lurching hard into a busy intersection.

I'd die before I'd let that happen.

# Chapter Five
## BRODY

Still aggravated at the morning's turn of events, I slammed the car door and straightened my red power tie. My closet overflowed with variations of tones and patterns, but all were red. Red symbolized power, and it used to inject a jolt of confidence through my veins by just wearing it.

Now those damn red ties made me sick to look at them. The power was a façade.

My agreement with the Carreras had been made rashly with the ambition of a hungry assistant district attorney with eyes focused on a man too old and sick to run for reelection. The candidate pool had been vast, and I knew the only way to rise above the pack was to sell my soul to the devil himself.

So, I did.

Aligning myself with the Carrera Cartel was the biggest mistake of my life. Had I known what singling myself out from honest men would cost me, I'd have never made the deal. Now, with her life literally in my hands, I had no choice but to play the devil's game.

I just hoped it'd be enough to spare myself in the process.

Exhaling a rough breath, I squared my shoulders and walked with an outward confidence toward the simple, wooden front door. Knocking again, I glanced around the perimeter, a move I'd learned from my time with Carrera.

The simple whitewashed siding of the ranch style house was blackened with weathered time and carelessness. Overgrown grass hinted at a recluse who had better things to do than lawn care, and long-dead flowers lay dark and flattened next to the porch. If I didn't know any better, I'd think the place had been vacated long ago.

But I knew he was in there.

And he knew I was outside waiting.

The question hung immobile in the air, waiting for one of us to relent. I sure as fuck wasn't going anywhere. Irritated, I pounded harder on the door again, raising my voice.

"Open up, Lachey. We both know why I'm here. You can talk to me, or you can wait for the Houston PD to drag you out." Letting my anxiousness get the better of me, I counted my steps as I paced the porch. Moments dragged by before the door cracked open, and the disheveled shell of Elliot Lachey's face appeared. To his credit, he didn't back down under my glare.

I couldn't decide if he was brave or stupid.

When he sniffed and rubbed his nose vigorously, I knew the answer. The base of his nostrils was caked with white residue.

He was high.

"What do you want?" he asked, wrinkling his nose at a rapid pace.

I smiled tersely and stepped over the threshold of his home. Before he could protest, I raised a hand, silencing him. "Don't ask me questions you already know the answer to. And wipe your damn face. It's not smart to greet the man who holds your life in his hands with cocaine all over your face."

Lachey wiped under his nostrils and stepped backward, his black athletic pants and Texas State t-shirt a far cry from the put-together look I remembered from a few years ago.

I placed my hands on the kitchen counter, grimacing as my palms touched a sticky substance I assumed had lived there for days. The entire house looked and smelled like shit. Pulling out a handkerchief from my pocket, I wiped my hand and pinched the bridge of my nose impatiently.

"You're pathetic." I shook my head at him as lines of surprise wrinkled his forehead. "You get caught buying that shit and you still snort it? What kind of moron does that?"

"You don't know anything about me, Brody," he countered, his eyes wild and dilated from the drugs. "You don't know what it's like to be me. Stress is killing me."

Opening the cookie jar on the sticky counter, I pulled out a fresh eight ball bag of cocaine and threw it at his chest. "No, *this* shit's killing you."

The old man's eyes were vacant. "What does it matter? I have nothing left. If I'm going to jail, I might as well go high."

"What about your kids?" Thoughts reverted to the morning and the sadness in Eden's eyes. She kept a shell tucked around her like an emotional shield in an invisible gender war. No matter how hard I tried to break through it, she kept me at arm's length, giving me her body but never anything more. I wondered if her determined distance had been caused by her bastard of a husband or the detachment of her father?

"He's much better off in San Antonio where he can do his charity work." He paused, rubbing his mouth as his eyes misted. "And Eden stopped caring a long time ago."

I could've argued with him. I could've forced him to see what he'd done to his family and business, but I didn't have the time or the desire. I'd come here for one reason.

"You don't have to go to jail today, Elliot."

His jaw clenched, and he eyed me with distrust. "Oh? Are you sending me on a vacation instead?"

I tried to hide an amused smile. "No, more like an adventure." Refusing to waste any more time, I pulled a box from my pocket and held it up. "Know what this is?"

"I may be high, Brody, but I'm not blind."

*Smartass.*

"Inside this box is a DEA grade tracker. You're going to call your Carrera contact and make another buy with this device on you. You're going to find out the warehouse locations and how they get their shipments through the Corpus Christi ports."

Elliot laughed, walking away then turning back with disbelief painted across his face. "You think they're just going to hand over that information to a buyer? Are you crazy?"

I'd passed the point of not giving a damn about his life anymore. Someone more important depended on what he did after I walked out of this house. "I don't give a shit how you get it," I said, shoving it in his hand, his fingers barely touching the edges as if it burned him, "just do it. It's either this or the Houston PD gets a delivery of a video starring you and known drug dealers doing some business in the second ward. It'll be out of my hands then."

The stunned look on his face might have made me feel a bit sorry for him if I didn't already know he'd bled the hardware store dry. His selfishness caused Nash to leave his job in San Antonio and Eden to work two jobs just to keep it alive.

He frowned and continued staring at the box. As I was about to hit him with another ultimatum, he set it on the kitchen table and took a step back. "I'm sorry, Brody. I can't."

"Excuse me?" My gaze snapped from the box back to his

face.

"I can't," he repeated, his chin trembling. "I've lost everything. The only thing I have left is my life. If I do what you're asking, they'll kill me."

"They'll kill you anyway." He had to know that. Drug cartels never let debts walk. Even I knew Elliot Lachey had gotten himself in over his head with the Carreras. My hands fisted by my side. His cooperation wasn't an option. I wouldn't leave here without the answer I came to get.

My attempt at intimidation fell short.

Lachey's upper lip twisted in a wistful snarl as he laughed without humor. "You stand there with your suit and tie and pretty boy blond hair and lecture me on what the fucking Mexicans will do to me?" He threw his head back and held his stomach with a loud roar. "Worry about yourself, son. You're more in bed with them than I am. If you're at my house, freaking out with sweat rolling down your forehead like that, they must have something on you, too."

I schooled my emotions. He knew his words hit home, but I wouldn't give him the satisfaction of seeing it on my face. "So, you've made your decision then?"

A low snort fell from his closed mouth, and his eyelids half closed as he looked away. "You tell the district attorney's office to kiss my ass. I've never seen these pictures you say you have, so I'm not even sure they exist. If they want the goods on Carrera, they can get it themselves. I'll take my chances in jail."

Fury filled my chest as fear hid close behind it. Everything inside me screamed to tell him what was coming for him tonight, but because ears were on me, I kept silent.

Tucking my morals behind a steel expression, I approached him and whispered low in his ear. "You just made a fatal mistake." Saying nothing more, I turned to leave the room.

My casual tone broke his confident attitude as he grabbed my arm. "Stay away from my daughter, Harcourt."

Shaking him off, I glanced over my shoulder one last time. "Screw you."

With Elliot Lachey's fate sealed, I slammed the door.

I'D BARELY PULLED MY GRAY BMW INTO MY DESIGNATED PARKING space at the courthouse when my phone rang. I didn't have to glance down at it to know who was calling. Timing was everything, and I'd been expecting a shrill ring to break through the silence the whole ride back.

Forcing myself to answer, I leaned back in the seat and hit the green button on my phone. "Harcourt."

"Didn't go well, I hear." With the heavy accent and dangerous lilt in his voice, the man on the other end was unmistakable.

Wrapping my fingers around my chin, I squeezed in frustration. "You have me bugged. I tried, but I can't force the man. If he wants to die in jail, so be it."

"You know what's at stake, yes?"

"I can't forget." The picture he'd sent of his men inside of her bedroom had given me more sleepless nights than I could count. My stomach churned as I recalled the video of them going through her panty drawer and holding them up to their dirty faces. Taking long inhales, they'd licked the lace and smiled into the camera.

"The deal was, you get us a mole into Carrera's camp, and we leave that sweet pussy alone. You've failed."

Panic gripped me as light swam before my eyes. "Don't fucking touch her!"

The low growl of a laugh fueled my hatred. "She looks

good enough to eat, Harcourt." He made a throaty moan that had my fingers gripping the steering wheel.

"I'll kill you."

"No, you won't," he sneered, breathing heavily over the line.

"Give me more time." I focused on the people walking in front of the parking lot, returning from their lunch breaks, laughing carefree as if my world wasn't crashing down around me. "I can change his mind."

"No need. It's time for plan B."

"There's a plan B?"

He laughed again, and the sound grated on my last frayed nerve. "Thanks to your call with Carrera, Mr. Lachey will change his mind about helping you after tonight."

"What are you going to do?" I demanded to know. The man was crazy. He made Valentin Carrera look like the Pope.

"Don't worry," he warned, his voice low. "Carrera has it all set up. We just have to stick our hands in and shake it around a little."

"What the hell does that mean?"

"Your junkie is getting a lesson he'll never forget. When it's done, I'll call. You make sure the police arrest Carrera and make the evidence stick. My men on the inside will do the rest."

"Wait, arrested for what?"

"Premeditated murder."

"Where does that leave—?" A dial tone hit my ear before I could finish. Pulling the phone away, I stared at it, praying to a god that seemed to have left the city to keep her safe.

Because if I tried to, we'd both be dead.

# Chapter Six

## EDEN

"**S**weet cheeks, I've been dry for hours. How about shaking that ass over here and wetting me down?"

Wiping down the distressed wooden bar, my fingers tightened around the wet rag as I scrubbed harder at the hardened glob of salsa. "I heard you the first three times you said it, Frankie," I said, releasing the sigh I'd been holding. "The answer is still no. You're cut off."

"Aw, c'mon baby," he slurred as the empty glass tumbled from his hand. "You're not my mother."

I picked at what remained of the salsa with my fingernail. "No, I'm not." Reaching behind me, I smacked his outstretched arm with the soggy rag. "I'm also not your wife, so unless you want me to make a really unpleasant call to her, keep your hands to yourself."

Frankie raised his hands in surrender. Holding his palms up for inspection, he leaned on the shoulder of his drinking buddy, his eyes half-lidded. "I don't know why, they're the only ones in town that haven't been up Cherry's skirt."

His words circled my ears and detonated into a hundred pieces of truth, but I willed the emotion back down to the place I kept it locked away. No man would bring me to tears again–in public or in private. Especially some drunk asshole who couldn't find his limit if he tripped over it.

Squaring my shoulders, I dropped the rag across the sink divider and reached for my cell phone to call him a cab. I'd just rattled off the address to the cab company when Frankie's hand swatted at my ass.

"Hey, I go when I want to go, sweet cheeks." He laughed low under his breath. "Unless you want to ride me home."

Ignoring them, I balanced the phone between my ear and shoulder, rolling my eyes as Frankie and his cohort snickered and high-fived each other. He wasn't the first drunk asshole to try to manhandle me near closing time. He wouldn't be the last.

"*Pídele disculpas a la, señorita.*"

My chin instinctively turned toward the coffee-liqueur voice sending shivers down my spine in the otherwise sweltering cantina. Without the pressure of my jaw holding it in place, the phone tumbled from my shoulder and clattered against the counter.

My ears heard his foreign words, but my eyes commanded a stronghold over my common sense, gawking like I'd never seen a man before.

But I had. I'd seen him once at the bar and a few more times occupying one of the bar tables served eagerly by one of the revolving door of underage morons Emilio employed. He was impossible to forget and played a starring role in a few of my more descriptive fantasies. Of course, my creative mind replaced whoever I happened to be screwing with my Mr. Danger on more occasions than I cared to admit.

Now, as we came face-to-face again, he looked even more

dangerous than I remembered. He stood confidently, wearing black suit pants that hugged him in all the right places and a white button-up shirt with the sleeves rolled up. I gawked shamelessly at him as if he'd walked in stark naked. I had a feeling he'd discarded his suit jacket and tie before entering the bar, and I couldn't decide if I was appreciative or a little bummed. On one hand, the casual look displayed his muscular tattooed arms, but the idea of that man in a suit did things to me I wasn't proud of.

I stared, fascinated at the intricate designs on his forearms, while inky, black hair tousled around his bronzed forehead as if worried hands had disrupted a carefully prearranged style. A beard, slightly heavier than a five 'o clock shadow, stretched from temple to temple and filled in across defined cheeks, circling the fullest lips I'd ever seen.

He still looked like pure danger.

Tightened chocolate eyes lasered across the bar at Frankie and his friend, the golden flecks around his pupils speaking loudly in the silence.

"Excuse me, Pedro?" Frankie mocked, cupping one hand to his ear while hooking his other thumb between himself and his friend. "See, this is America. We don't speak your dirty-ass language here."

"Frankie!" I chastised, shocked at his blatant ignorance. However, Danger simply lifted a hand, effectively silencing me.

"Then let me say it in the language of the American asshole," he said, his tone an even keel. "Apologize to the lady."

Frankie snorted. "To Cherry? Are you shitting me?" He raised his finger as if he were about to make a point before swaying on the barstool. "I'm not apologizing for trying to get a piece of what everyone else in this town has tasted, Pedro."

My face flamed. "I'm sorry," I whispered. Normally I didn't give two shits what people said about me, for the simple fact that most of it was usually true. But for some reason, the idea that Danger thought I walked around fucking until my knees gave out bothered me.

He pursed his lips, softly offering a *tsk* of his tongue as he slipped out of his chair. My eyes tracked every move as he stalked with the cunning of a panther and the eye of a wolf. Danger placed both palms on the bar and leaned into Frankie, whispering so low, when I strained to eavesdrop, I couldn't even catch a mumble.

As he spoke quietly in his ear, Frankie's lips uncurled, his face paled, and beads of sweat broke out across his greasy forehead. If I didn't know any better, I would've sworn he'd pissed himself, too.

Frankie mopped his brow, wiping the back of his hand on his shirt. "I'm...I'm sorry, Cherry. I meant no disrespect."

I tapped my index finger against my lips to keep from laughing. "It's okay, Frankie. The cab is outside. Just go home and don't be a dick to your wife, all right?"

Nodding, he grabbed his friend's arm. Together, they moved with speed I'd rarely seen out of those two fat fucks and slammed the door behind them. With the town drunks out of my hair, I turned to thank my dark knight, only to be met with a vast space of nothing.

Jesus, again? What the hell was with this guy?

Vowing to take the sting out of his rejection with a call to Brody after work, I concentrated on refilling drinks and restacking chip baskets. With only a few stragglers left in the cantina, my eyes roamed to the small flat-screen mounted in the corner. When rows of caution tape caught my eye, I grabbed the remote and turned up the sound as a pretty brunette anchor recounted the grisly details of what appeared to be the latest in a string of murder-suicides.

*"The Houston PD say a woman who killed her boyfriend and then herself late last night also had plans to murder his wife, according to a note she left next to their bodies. Luckily, the wife of the slain man wasn't in their Robindell home when the killer showed up with a gun. The investigation into the fatal shootings is ongoing, but prosecutors say it appears to be a jealousy driven murder-suicide. Allegedly, the woman, Daniella Morales, started an argument at thirty-four-year-old Nando Fuentes's apartment around six o'clock p.m. yesterday evening, only to return around midnight, shooting Fuentes in the chest and herself in the head."*

"Damn." Lowering the volume, I shook my head along with a lady at the end of the bar with long dark hair sipping a highball of whiskey. I grabbed the rag and wiped down the bar again as I turned around. "That shit is happening too often, don't you... *Jesus Christ!*" I jumped back, a scream lodged in my throat as chocolate eyes singed every piece of exposed skin, swooping down to devour what was left.

He folded his hands confidently onto the bar. "We meet again."

"Do you always make a habit of sneaking up behind girls in bars?" I pressed my hand over my racing heart. "I thought you left."

His lip quirked. "Your problem is taken care of. Those *idiotas* won't be bothering you again."

I placed a fresh napkin in front of him and snorted. "Those *idiotas* are harmless, especially Frankie. He's all talk, and I could probably kick his ass blindfolded." I noticed him still staring, and I couldn't shake the feeling I was being tested. "But thanks," I added quickly. "You saved me a chipped nail."

We stared at each other in silence, his hypnotic eyes seeming to bend me to his will. I hadn't been rendered speechless in four years, much less dazed by the mere presence of a man. It

59

unsettled me in a way that made me edgy.

Forcing a break in the intensity, I concentrated on restocking the freshly-washed margarita glasses from the bin to the overhead slider. "So, what'll it be?"

The same smile that played on his lips earlier curled into a devilish grin. "*Añejo* tequila. Straight shot, in a stem—"

My head snapped up. "Stem glass, not a highball, room temp, and if it hasn't aged at least three years, shove it up the owner's ass, right?"

"*Precisamente.*" He laughed, throwing his head back, baring his perfectly straight teeth. "A man should watch out for a woman who forgets nothing."

I poured his drink and set it in front of him. "A man should watch out for me, period." I watched him swirl the liquid, then take a sip, as if it would be disrespectful to the drink to shoot it. "I remember you," I confessed, tilting my head to the side. "You're very specific about your hooch."

He took another sip, licking an escaped drop of tequila from his plump lip. "A man in my position needs to be very selective about many things, *señorita.*"

Suddenly it wasn't just my face that flushed. Every crevice in my body seemed to burst into flames. A very illogical, depraved part of my brain wanted to vault over the bar and straddle him while he licked the rest of the tequila off my chest.

*What the hell is wrong with me?*

Taking a breathable step backward, I put some space between us and nodded as the pretty woman with long hair smiled and left for the night. "Well, does that selectivity finally include your name?" I asked with a smirk. "I mean, if you're going protect my honor and all, shouldn't I thank you properly?"

I'd just broken my cardinal rule of not asking names for the second time with the same man. This guy worked some serious voodoo magic on me.

He glanced around the empty bar, studying me a moment before extending a bronzed arm and answering. "Val."

Fine. So, I knew his name. That didn't mean he had to know mine.

"Cherry," I replied, shaking his hand.

*Fuck.*

In an unexpected move, he tugged my hand closer and kissed the tips of my knuckles. "Ah, *Cereza*. Perfect. *El color del fuego y pasión*."

I had no clue what the hell that meant, but my panties were begging to find out.

I must've looked confused because he chuckled again. "Your name, *Cereza*. It's the color of fire and passion. It suits you."

"Long time, no speak, big tipper." I kept my gaze lowered, busying myself with mindless side work. Fear refused to allow direct eye contact. I'd fought for almost a year to regain the upper hand when it came to men. I'd be damned if I'd give it up now.

"You really don't forget anything, do you?" he mused, folding his hands together on the bar.

My mouth opened to tell him he could find out for himself after my shift ended when the chime on the door jingled, and my stomach dropped to my toes. Snatching my hand from his hold, I smoothed it over my pinned hair and cursed the plain cut off jean shorts and black tank uniform. The look screamed anything but refined. It screamed "chip slinging bar bitch."

"We're closing in twenty minutes, Davis." I kept my voice calm and civil, even though every instinct implored me to slam a wine glass against the bar and hold the jagged edge against his mouse dick.

"The sign still says open, Edie, and you always did make

a mean margarita." Giggling ensued beside him, and I gripped the edge of the bar to keep my hands away from the glasses. "Chelsea had a craving for one after the movie and just wouldn't settle down until I gave in."

*Chelsea craved a lot of shit you had no business giving her, you cheating fuckwad.*

Val's face hardened as I glanced at him over my shoulder. "Excuse me, I need to deal with some unfinished business." I gave him a weak smile, and his chin dipped in acknowledgement. It was the only sign he gave that he'd heard me as his focus returned to his tequila.

So much for a night of casual sex and dirty Spanish.

Turning to face Davis, his annoying All-American hero good looks focused on my ex-best friend, and I wanted to throw up the chips I'd eaten. Chelsea had obviously been killing what brain cells were left in that vapid hole inside her skull by frying her skin into shoe leather at her mother's tanning salon. She sported a nice shade of Oompa Loompa from her peroxide blond hair down to her aerobicized ass. By the way her clothes hung, I'd wager a guess she'd been eating a steady diet of chia seeds and air lately. Of course, being with Davis, that was a given. Davis had a strict no chub policy. During our three years together, I chewed diet pills like they were Pez.

"One drink, you guys. Then I have to close up." The day couldn't possibly end any worse.

"I'll have a Bud Light in the bottle, not a glass," Davis instructed, as if I couldn't recite his order by heart. "And what kind of margarita do you want, baby?"

Chelsea giggled again, flipping her bleached hair over her shoulder. "Edie, can you make a sugar-free, skinny margarita made with just lime juice, no sweet and sour and no salt?"

I blinked at her. "Sure."

"Oh, goodie." She clapped wildly.

*Murder is illegal. Murder is illegal. Murder is illegal.*

Turning my back to them, I filled a shaker full of ice, tequila, triple sec, and a shit-ton of sweet and sour mix. Then, because the knife wound between my shoulder blades still hadn't healed, I dumped a good shot and a half of simple syrup in and shook the hell out of it. Grinning like an idiot, I poured it in the glass, sifted in half a handful of salt and served it up.

"Skinny margarita, enjoy."

I'd never enjoyed watching another person drink alcohol so much in my life. I'd heard people use the word "giddy" before, but I'd never experienced its full effect until Chelsea slurped down every drop of that nine-hundred calorie concoction with a smile on her face.

Was it retribution for sucking my husband's cock? Hell, no, but it was a start. Besides, I knew Davis just brought her in here to be an ass. He was still peeved over finding out about my fling with his fraternity brother and took great pleasure in being a jerk-off whenever possible.

As long as I bled his ass dry in court, he could parade his whore around as much as he wanted. Our divorce was final, but by the time my lawyer was done with him, all their dates would be at the drive-thru.

Sometime during my pissing match with Davis, Val slipped out. It was just as well. I needed to show more restraint with the men I took back to my apartment. Considering all the murder-suicides going on lately, a girl couldn't be too careful.

I meandered to the sideboard and lined freshly washed chip baskets with wax paper, stacking them for tomorrow's lunch crowd. I'd just gathered the lot in my arms when the house phone rang. Shifting the baskets to one elbow, I picked up the cordless receiver.

"Caliente Cantina, how can I help you?"

"Eden, leave the alarm off tonight."

"Emilio? Where are you?" My boss never called right before closing, and he never left the alarm off. Too many hoods in the neighborhood would see it as an open invitation.

"Don't worry about that, doll. I have a cleaning crew coming in first thing in the morning, and I won't be around to turn the alarm off. It'll be fine tonight."

I shrugged, as if he could see me. "It's your bar, boss."

"How were sales tonight?"

"Not bad," I answered, turning off the television. "Steady flow. Davis came in with his side-piece."

"*Odio ese pinche hijo de su puta madre pedazo de mierda! Que no mame!*" he yelled, his native Spanish coming out in a tirade of insults.

I giggled into the receiver. "I don't know what you said, but I'm assuming it had something to do with him being a piece of shit."

Emilio's low chuckle vibrated in my ear. "You're one of a kind, Eden O'Dell. If I wasn't married…" He trailed off, and I cringed at his use of my married name. It had been on my driver's license when I'd applied for the job, and it'd just been easier never to correct him.

I'd have to fix that soon.

"Yeah, yeah…you're too old for me, Emilio. You'd break a hip in the first two minutes."

He snorted with a chuckle. "*Hasta mañana*, Eden."

"*Mañana,* old man," I joked, hanging up on him.

A LITTLE OVER AN HOUR LATER, I'D SWITCHED OFF THE MAIN LIGHTS over the bar, leaving just enough on inside to deter would-be criminals. I closed the front door and turned the lock with thoughts of eviscerating Davis with the blunt end of the dead bolt key. The bite of the betrayal still stung as sharply as it did a year ago. Maybe it always would.

Even though it was close to one o'clock in the morning, the muggy thickness of the June air mixed with pelting rain hit me in the face as I power walked to my car. The summer would be intolerable if it was already this sticky. Southern humidity deserved its own special circle in Dante's Inferno. It stuck in your lungs, ruined your hair, and made even the primmest of debutantes sweat like a two-ton pig fucking a donkey.

The inside of the Cruiser was no less than sweltering when I turned the ignition, flipped the air conditioner on full blast, and dug in my purse for my phone. After a few moments, I cursed to myself, remembering I'd let it bounce from my shoulder to the bar while being hypnotized by Val's gold-flecked, chocolate eyes.

Groaning, I slammed the door and ran the length of the parking lot back to the cantina. Once inside, I shook off the droplets, scooped my phone into my hands, and dialed Nash's number. If he was awake, maybe he'd be up for some company. When the call went straight to voice mail, I glanced at the ceiling as another idea came to mind. Walking toward the front door, I scrolled through my preapproved list of non-clingers, deciding who would suffice for an early Sunday morning screw. If I closed my eyes tight enough, I knew whose face I'd see anyway.

*Damn you, Danger.*

As I was about to dial, a crash and a muffled grunt echoed from the back. An electric shock shot down my spine while anticipation and dread chased its trail. My fingers went numb, as if preparing the rest of my body for the same sensation. Every

65

instinct pleaded with my legs to turn and run in the opposite direction, but as if tethered to an invisible line, they moved toward the kitchen.

Locked somewhere between a dream-like state and morbid curiosity, my hands reached for the swinging doors. My pulse roared in my ears, my skin a vibration of energy ready to explode.

At the last moment, I glanced at a side table and grabbed a fork.

*Sure, fork them to death.*

Another loud crash masked the sound of the door being pushed open. Breathing heavily, I slipped through unnoticed, feeling my way around. The light was dim, and my eyes took a moment to adjust as I furiously scanned every corner for activity. They came to rest on a figure slumped in the corner, jeans tattered and stained, t-shirt darkened, hands behind his back and burlap sack over his head.

Gripping the fork until I lost feeling in my fingers, I quickly slapped the other palm across my mouth to stop the cries that threatened to tumble out. He didn't move. He didn't even seem to take a breath.

Before I could contemplate a strategy in my head, the back door opened again, and a man walked in, his boots making a loud clomping sound against the tile floor. Paralyzed by fear, I twisted my body into the shadows behind a chef's cart. Hunched over and trembling, I glanced between the metal bars of the rolling cart as a steel-toed boot landed a swift kick in the hooded man's ribcage. I closed my eyes, unable to stomach the seven that followed.

When the silence returned, I opened an eyelid a sliver as the steel-toed-boot man crouched down. "*Hola, Señor* Lachey. We finally meet."

## Chapter Seven

### EDEN

*L* *achey.*

As the words reconciled in my head, I opened both eyes and rose to my knees, leaning forward for a closer look. All I could see was the back of the intruder's head.

This wasn't real. Surely, I'd heard wrong.

"My men tell me you've had a problem paying us our money. You should know we don't tolerate outstanding debt."

Debt? What debt? Oh, God, what had my father done?

A muffled voice rumbled from inside the burlap. "Fuck you."

The steel-toed-boot man laughed maniacally. "No, fuck you, Lachey. See, the *jefe* is getting his ten one way or the other." He pulled a knife out of his pocket and pressed a button, releasing the blade. "So, you can count them out on your stealing fingers, or we can just count your fingers." He jerked the sack off the limp man's head, as he proudly displayed his blade.

I clamped my hand over my mouth again. Time slowed as a fog drifted into my brain, distorting the connection between what

I witnessed and what I could process as reality. As my vision swam, one word repeated on a tongue that never moved.

*No, no, no, no, no.*

His face was bloody, broken, and so familiar that I saw it in my own reflection.

*Nash.*

It took everything inside of me not to call out to him. My brother barely hung on, and I hid behind a chef's cart like a fucking coward. As I leaned against the metal, it shook with tremors from my body that refused to listen to reason or rationality.

What meaning did those two words hold when my brother lay broken no more than eight feet away from me, and I couldn't help him?

The platinum blond chunk that always hung in his face lay matted and soaked in his own blood. His eyes were swollen and purple, his lip busted open and bleeding onto his shirt. Open cuts on his cheeks marred his skin. I could see the labored breathing from his chest rattling with each exertion.

Broken ribs.

Terror ate at my soul as I crouched in my confinement, tears rolling down my cheeks. My brain was a jumble of prayers, divided by shuddered breaths.

*Please let him go. Please let him go.*

"Let's have some fun, shall we, Lachey?" The steel-toed-boot man knelt beside Nash and in that moment, my world stopped. The voice connected with the face, and the tears rolled harder.

Emilio.

My boss. My friend. The man I trusted everyday as I sat alone with him in a darkened office of a dirty bar had beaten my brother near death.

"Screw you." Nash coughed, blood creating a splatter

pattern on Emilio's white t-shirt. "I've had enough fun for one day, thanks."

Emilio laughed, seemingly amused. "I have to admit, you put up more of a fight than most of my junkies." He scratched his chin with the tip of his knife. "I like that, Lachey. You've got balls."

"I'm no junkie, asshole."

"That's what they all say."

"I told you," Nash wheezed, his breath coming out weaker by the minute. "You've got the wrong guy. I never touched your damn drugs."

"They all say that, too." Emilio chuckled, his laugh hollow with impatience. "But see, Lachey, the problem is that I'm bored with you, and I've got other shit to do. So, let's get this over with so we can both get back home, all right?"

The lump in my throat grew the minute Emilio wrapped a hand around Nash's wrist as he struggled against him. Garbled curse words fell from my brother's mouth as his hold on his mask of indifference slipped. The moment Emilio dragged him to the wooden chopping block and held the blade against the tip of Nash's right forefinger, reality set in his eyes.

This was no mistake.

This was no joke.

This was real, and the only person left to protect him hid in the corner crying for her own pathetic life. I willed my feet to move, but the signal from my brain to my feet short circuited, leaving me paralyzed.

As the blade slammed down on my brother's fingertip, the cry of intolerable pain filled the kitchen, bouncing from the walls and piercing my already broken heart. I wanted to vomit, but like a coward, I removed my hand from my mouth and covered my ears. His screams shattered me.

"Two digits for two g's. That's the trade, Lachey. Think about that next time you decide to arrange a deal for blow and disappear when we collect." The clank of the knife hit the stark white tile floor, and my eyes popped open as Emilio moved toward the sink to wash the blood off his hands.

He could wash with bleach until his skin peeled off. The stain of my brother's blood would never leave his fingers. My eyes would never forget.

# Chapter Eight

## VALENTIN

By the time I reached the heavy ornate door, it was technically Sunday morning and the humidity had me sweating so much I looked like I'd gotten caught in a freak rainstorm.

I'd given up a long time ago trying to fight it with undershirts. Somehow mother nature centered a bubble around Houston with a climate siphoned straight from hell. Even as a boy living in Mexico City with high temperatures reaching one-hundred degrees, I couldn't remember anything so sticky and disgusting.

*Dios mío.*

Entering the pretentiously decorated Irish pub, I silently chastised myself for my momentary lapse in judgment in going back to Caliente. Being there had been reckless and stupid. With what I knew to be occurring in only hours, I'd shown my face in a place I should never have risked visiting.

Not only was being there dangerous, engaging the bartender was suicidal.

One moment I sat in my office poring over the profits from the last commodities investment we'd exported, the next, I found myself sliding onto a dirty barstool in the shittiest cantina in downtown Houston.

"Can I get you something, handsome?"

I glanced up, still lost in thought. Somehow, I'd made my way through the front door of the darkened pub to an even darker wooden bar. As I took in the bartender's tight, black Lycra shorts and half-tee that boasted the phrase "Naughty Irish Girl," I was sure turning the wheel into oncoming traffic would've been a better option.

"Probably not, but you can give it a try," I told her, absentmindedly flipping my phone from end to end between my thumb and forefinger.

Her toothy grin faded a little as a tinge of annoyance crept into her voice. "I'm pretty talented with my hands, sugar," she quipped, offering a smirk. "Why don't you try me?"

Any other time, I might have taken her up on her implied offer. She was attractive enough, but tonight my mind swam with swirls of red and streams of snappy banter.

"*Añejo* tequila. Straight shot, in a stem glass, room temp"—I glanced without interest at her nametag—"Tiffany." I had low expectations, but for the sake of drying my soaked shirt, I gave her a shot.

Giving me a wink, she clomped off in heels way too high for her uncoordinated legs to handle and began rummaging through a wasteland of bottles. I took the opportunity to evaluate my surroundings. Observation was a valuable skill my father instilled in me early in life.

A man could never be surprised if he was aware of danger before it struck.

The small room was dimly lit, brightened by only low watt overhead bulbs encased in terra-cotta shades. I found it strange décor for an Irish pub, but with the almost caricature Ireland memorabilia tacked to the walls, I had a feeling the place was anything but authentic.

My gaze bounced from man to man, inconspicuously searching for telltale signs of a shoulder holster, the outline of a gun protruding from a waistline, a nervous hand twitch, or a repeated glance toward the door. Every man in my father's inner circle, at one time or another, had brought me to a cantina since I was fifteen years old. They taught me to notice the unnoticeable, see the unseeable, and recognize the markings of a guilty man.

"Here ya go, sweets." Tiffany slid a highball glass in front of me, sloshing half the liquid on my hand. I didn't have to taste it. I could smell it on my skin.

*Blanco.*

Shit tequila. Aged less than a month…maybe two.

I'd rather die of dehydration. Grabbing a drink napkin, I wiped my hand and pushed the offending glass toward her. "Just a water, thanks."

A confused look crossed her face, followed by annoyance. "You still have to pay for it."

"Of course."

"Whatever, dude." Insulted, she moved down the bar, working her pathetic charm on some other unsuspecting man.

I should've known better than to order a drink no one in this town could seem to manage.

Except for her.

*Cereza.*

It was a dangerous move to know her name and even more so to give her mine. I had every intention of denying her request or even making up one. It wouldn't have been the first time I'd lied to a woman about my name. Since I never fucked the same woman twice, I never saw a need for such triviality as the exchange of names. My discretion was for their safety as much as mine.

Aside from the fact that she was the only bartender in Houston who could make a drink without fucking it up, I thought too much about her the past few weeks. I found myself gravitating toward women with long red hair and blue eyes. I'd fucked each of them, hoping to screw her out of my head.

It never happened. A man couldn't crave quality steak… salivate for it…then satiate his hunger with a cheeseburger from a drive-thru.

American women usually failed to hold my attention, but her strength and dominance surged all the blood in my veins straight to my cock. She was flashy, but her eyes hid a world of pain behind them. The pale blue color made a man want to break down her walls and discover her secrets while burying himself deep inside her body.

The same thin black tank top she wore did nothing to hide the curves that dipped into a trim waist, highlighting an ass I could sink my fingers into from behind.

That candy-red hair. Those smoky rimmed eyes.

Just thinking about her made me hard as a rock.

Immediately regretting the images flashing through my head, I almost excused myself to the restroom when a buzzing in my pocket distracted me. Pulling my phone out, I glanced at the number before answering in a hushed tone.

"*Si?*"

"Situation is handled, *jefe*," Emilio said, his voice slightly out of breath, and the sound of traffic roaring in the background.

"*Bien.*" Ignoring my intuition, I abandoned my native tongue and broke into English. "So, what have I gained tonight in assets?"

Emilio paused, as if choosing his words were of the upmost importance. "We got eight g's between the safe, register, and night deposit bag, so we took two fingers, and—"

"Why do I hear hesitation in your voice?" I scanned the perimeter of the bar again. Something didn't feel right in my gut. Experience taught me that my gut never betrayed me, but men did.

"Lachey isn't what I expected," he explained, waiting for me to respond. When I remained silent, he continued. "My crew, who knew him, talked like he was a junkie and scared of his own shadow. You know, set in his ways…real *pendejo*."

I grew tired of his hesitation. "For fuck's sake, what happened?"

"He didn't seem high. I don't know, *jefe*. Something just felt off."

With a single nod of my chin, I threw a twenty-dollar bill down on the bar. The shitty tequila wasn't worth the spit it would take to disgrace it, but it wasn't the bartender's fault she was a moron.

As I pushed open the door to the pub, I growled into the phone, my patience gone. "Of course, it felt off, *pendejo*. Cutting off a man's fingers isn't supposed to feel like hitting a piñata and watching a fuck-load of candy fall out. Go back in there, clean it up, and get him back where he belongs." Jerking the phone away, I strode to the car before hauling it back to my ear, confident he'd still be there. "And stop calling me for stupid shit."

Hitting the disconnect button, I glanced around before tossing the burner phone into a trashcan on the side of the street and slamming the car door.

DROPPING THE KEYS TO THE LEXUS ON THE SMALL TABLE LINING THE hallway, I watched them skid across the polished wood and crash to the tile on the other side. Exhaustion pulled at every muscle in my body, reminding me it'd been weeks since I slept a full night without interruption. I barely cast a glance at them as I rounded the corner toward my bedroom.

*Fuck it.*

They could stay there for all I cared.

With three million dollars spread strategically in offshore bank accounts, and another two million stashed in a safe underneath the baseboard of my house, I was still forced to drive around in an ordinary Lexus. A man of my wealth should be able to pay cash for a Bugatti or Maserati—not a family car that carted a family of five around for afternoon picnics. But those were the unwritten rules of the business, and they were followed, or you got taken out. Stateside cartel members weren't allowed to draw unnecessary attention to themselves.

I understood the rules. It didn't mean I had to like them.

Anyone driving by my house wouldn't give it a second glance. That wasn't by accident. I came to this country with specific instructions from my father on where to live, what type of house to buy, what to drive, how to dress, who to surround myself with, and who to trust. No decision was my own. It should've bothered me but taking orders from Alejandro Carrera was nothing new. The moment I'd decided enough was enough and demanded entrance into his world, I forfeited the right to an opinion.

Sitting at the small desk in my bedroom, I tried for over an hour to find a new unloading drop to distribute the next shipment, but fatigue kept me unfocused. Nando's fuck up and untimely demise left a major hole in my well-orchestrated hubs. The extra work it left for me made me want to raise Nando from the dead just so I could kill him all over again.

Resigned to the fact that my productivity was shot, I'd just exited out of my computer when a ring pulled my attention to the end of the desk. The nondescript, black phone had sat there undisturbed for weeks, quiet and gathering dust.

I stared at it, rubbing my eyes as if that had anything to do with the sound. Only one number would call on that burner phone. One voice on the other end of the line would answer. There could only be one reason why he'd call.

Running a hand down my face, I let my palm hover over my mouth as my thumb and fingertips dug into my cheeks. I listened to it ring again and again, while the sound pierced my ears as if he were already screaming his tirade. There'd be no voice mail to pick up and no end to the ring. It'd continue as a game of wills until one of us cracked.

It wouldn't be him.

Swearing under my breath, I slid my palm from my face and slammed it down on the phone, pressing the answer button with force. "What?"

"What took you so long?"

I fought to control the tone in my voice. "I wasn't aware I was being summoned."

"Show respect, boy. Family doesn't matter in business."

My fingers tightened around the phone as blood pounded in my ears. "I know that more than anyone, *sir.*"

A rare pause of silence passed between us before a rumble of laughter filled the line.

"When were you going to tell me that you allowed someone to flip a lieutenant?" he asked with accusation sharp in his tone.

"I wasn't." My jaw ticked from holding back anger. "I handled it."

"You handled nothing. I handled Nando's betrayal," he hissed.

The words sent a chill down my spine and a swirl of acid

in my stomach. I knew what he meant, but for some reason, my mouth asked the words I didn't want to hear the answer to.

"Father, he's gone. Why?"

The ice in his words bit through the line. "A narco lives and dies by the code. When he joins our family, so does all of his blood."

I didn't respond. I couldn't. I knew the code. I hated the fucking code. The code was the reason there were hundreds of movies in Hollywood about Italian mafia wise guys and Corleone bullshit. *Omertà* was a joke. Capos got pinched by the Feds and turned state's witness in a heartbeat to save their own skins. I could wipe my ass with their *omertà* pledge. The reason Americans rarely saw a movie about a true cartel or saw headlines about one turning against their own family was simple. It didn't happen. We had no need for a code of silence when we faced a code of death.

It was beaten into every low-level cartel runner that if they were busted and talked or cooperated with the DEA, their family and friends back in Mexico would be killed. There were no made men or ceremonies or pledges in our world. A simple threat of beheading your wife, children, mother, father, or multiple generations of your lineage, kept your mouth shut.

I hoped Nando's blow job was worth the death that would soon come for his wife in Houston and his family back home.

"Did you hear me, boy?" My father's voice carried a twinge of annoyance. I'd missed half of what he'd said.

"*Claramente*," I lied. I didn't hear him clearly. I didn't give a shit. I just wanted off the phone. The less I talked to the man the better.

"Watch for the Muñoz Cartel," he warned. "They just shipped new men across the border."

"I've got it under control. Don't worry." I had nothing under control, but I wasn't about to tell him that.

"*Eso espero.* I'll call soon." He disconnected the call before I could mention another word.

My father thought I was a moron, but I'd been aware of the Muñoz Cartel sniffing around my operation for a while now. It was because of that knowledge that Nando's betrayal couldn't have come at a worse time. I needed all my men close and vigilant. Shipments were being intercepted and it wasn't by the Feds. With Mateo, Emilio, and Nando, I'd been able to always stay one step ahead of them. With one man down, I was crippled. I couldn't afford to lose another fifty-two kilos.

Squeezing the phone in my hand, my father's words rolled around in my head, and I couldn't help thinking of Nando's sister and her two small daughters back in Mexico City. Were they already dead? Would my father make it a clean kill with no suffering, or would he be a bastard and mount their heads on a stake, leaving it in their front yard as a warning to the rest of the runners' families?

"Motherfucker!" Twenty-four years of resentment exploded as I hurled the phone across the desk. It skidded across strewn papers, knocking a glass and pictures over in its wake until it finally came to a stop against the wall.

Rising from the chair, I ran my fingers over the small, three-by-five pewter picture frame lying on the floor. I didn't give a shit about anything else. It could stay a clusterfucked mess for all I cared. Picking up the frame, I wiped the spilled water from the glass with the tail of my shirt, taking care to dry it before it could leak through to the photo.

As I crashed into bed, my vision blurred. The woman in the photo faded from a smiling, onyx haired image, to a clouded memory. The toothless boy wrapped in her arms grinned, innocent and blissfully unaware of the life that awaited him on the other side of destiny.

# Chapter Nine

## EDEN

**M**y stomach roiled as my gaze shifted from the sink that washed the evidence from my boss's hands to my brother, draped over the butcher's block. His face had drained of all color, and his lips turned a bluish hue. Blood poured from almost every crevice of his body. Gripping the steel rods of the cart, I sat up on my knees and forced myself to see what the man I trusted had done to him.

Bile crawled up my throat, burning a hole in the delicate tissue. The tips of Nash's middle and forefinger on his right hand were gone. The digits were scattered across the block, tossed like meaningless scraps from today's special ready for tomorrow's garbage pickup.

I couldn't take it. Blackness crowded the outer edges of my vision, and my grip tightened.

My big brother. My hero. Nash always saved the day and made sure I didn't screw up everything in my path. He never did anything wrong. He spoke the truth. He wasn't a junkie. He dedicated his life to getting inner city kids off drugs.

The shaking intensified, and the more Nash bled, the more I panicked. I couldn't pass out. He needed me. His eyes fluttered, and a slow trail of blood seeped out of his nose.

I'd already lost everything that meant anything in my life.

If I lost Nash, they might as well kill me, too.

Releasing one hand from the metal cart, I swiped the tears and pressed the back of my hand to my lips. The pressure was the only thing that quelled the cries of his name from bursting from my chest.

My brother wouldn't die alone. I was getting him the hell out of here.

Just as I twisted to crawl from behind the cart, my knee caught the end of the bottom tray. The move was enough to cause it to roll forward into the prep table in front of it with a metal clang. Only a slight noise pinged through the air, but to my own ears, it sounded like a gunshot.

Nash rolled his chin toward me, lacking the strength to lift it any higher. His sullen blue eyes blinked, narrowed, then focused in the dim light. In a split second, I knew he saw me, and everything happened before I could react.

Emilio returned from outside and must've heard the noise, too, because he immediately turned toward me. Furrowing his dark brows, he wiped the knife on his jeans. He took three steps toward the chef's cart and paused a few feet away from me. I held my breath, curling my fingers into my palms until my nails pierced my skin.

I wondered what it felt like to have your fingers cut off. Was it quick and painless, or was every slice of tendon and muscle pure torture, until the bone cracked? Vomit curdled in my stomach again, and I let out a small squeak, preparing to run to my brother.

At the same moment, Nash inhaled a rattling breath and

yelled across the kitchen. "Hey! Are two fingers enough? You need more? I mean, don't you need five to jerk yourself off?"

*What the fuck is he doing?*

Emilio jerked his head around. Darkness glinted in his eyes as his face twisted in anger. "What did you say, asshole?"

Now was my chance to move. Nash gave me the opportunity to take Emilio out. Sneaking a hand to the top of the cart, I curled my fingers around a cast iron skillet. It'd be loud, but if I got a running start, he'd go down before he could turn around.

As Emilio charged toward Nash, I reached for the handle. Out of the corner of my eye, I watched Nash's eyes bounce from his attacker to my movement. With a pained grimace, he shook his head forcefully.

"Gumshoe! Gumshoe, damn it!" The exertion spewed more blood out of his mouth, and he collapsed onto the block, his eyes half closed from pain.

I froze mid-movement.

Emilio did as well, pulling Nash up by his hair. "What the fuck? Get a grip, Lachey! You're going *loco*."

With his head wobbling, Nash held it suspended in midair, and our eyes locked. Mine pleaded with him not to hold me to a pledge between two teenage kids, who thought they knew everything. His demanded I honor a trust we once held more sacred than any promise.

*I OPENED THE CELLAR DOOR AND IT CREAKED WITH THE LOUD MOAN OF a dying man. I might as well blow an air horn announcing my late arrival. The darkness creeped me out, and shadows wrapped around foundation pillars, making my eyes see things that weren't there. It was the thing horror movies were made of.*

*The stairs creaked as my sneakers touched them, each one sounding like a gunshot.*

*Shit! Why were sneakers so loud?*

*Turning the knob, I slowly stuck my face through and peered through the mud room. It seemed quiet. Dad was in bed or passed out on the couch. Either option worked for me. Taking a deep breath, I opened the door wider and stepped into the bright room.*

*"Where're you going, boy?"*

*I froze with one leg in the mud room and one still stuck in the cellar. My father's voice carried from the kitchen, and from the trajectory I knew he was headed my way.*

*"Gumshoe," Nash yelled, much louder than necessary. "Damn gum on my shoe. Stay there, Dad, I've got it. I think I tracked it in here. You don't want it on yours." His voice elevated louder. "Damn, gumshoe."*

*Our code word clicked. Gumshoe.*

*The stupid word from our childhood we used to use during freeze-tag. As teenagers, we morphed it from its original detective meaning, into a code word alerting each other to, "stop what you're doing and hide." No ifs, ands, or buts.*

*Gumshoe had saved my ass more times than I could count.*

*I climbed back down and waited until Dad had fallen back to sleep to sneak upstairs.*

"Gumshoe." Nash whispered again as Emilio backhanded him. His eyes never wavered from my face. They were serious and hard, as if begging me to do this one thing for him.

Nodding, I slowly crouched back behind the cart. The relief on his face was something I knew I'd never forget. I felt shameful in watching my brother's pain, yet helpless to stop it.

Mercifully, Emilio ended his torture, dropping his knife back in his pocket. "You know, lucky for you, I've reached my limit for today, Lachey." He checked his reflection in the chrome refrigerator and smoothed back the sides of his greased hair. "My crew will stop by in a few minutes to take you back to your store." He glanced at the floor and smirked. "Try not to bleed too much on my floor."

I held my breath as he walked out of the kitchen, and I didn't release it until the cantina door closed. As soon as the chime rang, signaling his exit, I threw the chef's cart aside and scrambled on all fours toward my brother. I reached out to help him, then stopped. I didn't even know where to touch that wouldn't cause more pain.

"Nash," I whispered as my voice broke. When he didn't open his eyes, I panicked. "Nash, answer me!" My fingers clamped around his bleeding wrists, shaking against cold and clammy hands. The more I touched him, the more hysterical my voice became. All the pent-up fear I'd harbored behind the chef's cart came spilling out in a tirade of anger. "What the fuck have you gotten yourself into? Drugs? Fucking drugs, Nash? Jesus Christ, are you mixed up with a fucking drug cartel? They cut off your damn fingers, Nash!"

As if my asinine statements of the obvious woke him, Nash cracked one eye, and his tongue darted out to lick his cracked lips. "Is that what happened? I thought he was doing… *cough*… my nails."

"I'm not arguing with you," I whispered harshly into his ear. "You can explain later why you're doing fucking coke. We're leaving."

He nodded weakly, allowing me to wrap his torso around my shoulders. I'd heard stories of adrenaline rushes that allowed mothers to lift cars off their children. I never believed them until I hoisted my two-hundred-and-five-pound brother over my shoulder and prepared to carry him out.

His hand skimmed my back. "Cherry, I don't do drugs. They got the wrong guy. I swear."

I knew his words to be true. If there was one thing I believed in my life, it was that Nash Lachey didn't lie.

"Then what's this all about, Nash?"

His breath wheezed harder with forced exertion. "Dad."

It was the last word he spoke.

With him draped over my shoulder, I headed toward the back door when the knob turned. Nash's cheek twisted against my back to face it, and my heart knew my brother wouldn't let me put myself in between him and what was behind it.

The moment the door cracked open, Nash used his last thread of strength and flung himself off my shoulder and against the butcher's block. With mangled hands, he pressed his palm against my chest and shoved me hard into an open pantry door. The impact sent both of us flying backward. My ass landed on top of a huge bag of cornmeal as Nash crashed to the floor.

I barely breathed as I waited for Emilio to taunt Nash again. Instead, two new men, clad in jeans, green bandanas, white tank tops, and dirty long ponytails surrounded my brother. I assumed they were the men Emilio said would take him back to the hardware store and breathed a sigh of relief.

As they moved closer, my heart sped up. The older man's long ponytail caught a fleeting memory of a bag of cable ties, rope, and creepy innuendos.

I knew them.

"This is the same one?" the shorter one asked, raising an eyebrow.

"That's what *jefe* said." The taller one circled Nash, coming to rest behind him. With a slow smile, he leaned back and spit on him. *"El Muerte."*

The words were spoken with such contempt that they imprinted themselves into my memory. The snarl in which he said them, and the hatred in his eyes as he glared at my brother sent a chill up my spine.

The darkened pantry turned into my own personal confessional as the taller man pulled a long-barreled gun out of his back pocket and aimed it at the back of Nash's head. A silent voice inside of me screamed at my brother to run. It begged him to open his eyes and move.

As if hearing my pleas, my brother, who'd always protected me, stood by me, and never made me feel any less than worthy of his love, opened his eyes. Sadness glazed them and ripped an irreparable jagged hole in my heart.

His mouth silently formed the word that meant everything.

*Gumshoe.*

With a flash of light, and a deafening blast from the gun, my brother was gone.

I awoke to my name being called. Well, not necessarily my name. I'd taken enough high school Spanish to know what a *puta* meant, and it wasn't complimentary. It wasn't the first time I'd been called a whore, but disorientation had me frantically trying to come to grips with the situation.

My head hurt. I ran my fingers over the back of it and felt a big knot. Taking stock of my surroundings, I realized I sat in the middle of a pantry closet with a thick wooden shelf behind my head.

Nash had thrown me inside after the back door rattled and…

*Oh, God.*

I'd passed out after they…

Tears tumbled down my cheeks with reckless abandon. I squeezed them to block out the images that flashed through my head on constant replay.

The bright light. The crack of the gun. The vacantness in my brother's eyes as he fell.

The men from the hardware store murdered my brother, and now they were coming for me.

With a jolt, I remembered my car sat parked behind the cantina. My license plate shone like a beacon. All they had to do was look it up and they'd see who it was registered to. They'd know it was mine and that I worked for Emilio.

*Emilio.*

I'd accepted that murdering bastard as my friend. I'd never make that mistake again. I'd never allow any man that close to me. I'd honor that vow until the day I died.

I remained quiet as the voices moved from the kitchen into the main cantina. My skin crawled with fear, but I'd made a dying promise to my brother.

As low to the floor as I could get, I belly slithered across the tile on my elbows toward the back door. Every instinct pulled at me to go to Nash. I couldn't just leave him here. But as my body instinctively twisted toward the right, his voice boomed loud and clear in my head.

*Gumshoe, Cherry. You promised.*

Swallowing my heart, I commando crawled, forcing my mind to think of nothing but the door. I didn't look back. The voices from the cantina turned around, and I was running out of time. I reached for the door on my hands and knees and flung it open into the darkness.

Once outside, I pulled my keys out of a cross body bag slung around my chest. My chest burned, and my thighs screamed as adrenaline surged through my veins. Fumbling with the keys in the rain, I dropped them, cursing as my tears fell. The reality of the situation started to crash down on me as I tried to hold it together. Flinging the door open, I dove in and slammed on the accelerator.

Every part of me shook. I drove erratically, swerving across yellow lines, passing in no passing zones, and driving at least thirty miles over the speed limit. If I got pulled over, fine. They could just follow me back to Caliente and arrest the men who'd ended my brother's life.

Eventually, the adrenaline would fade, and the shock would wear off. I'd have to deal with the cold reality of what had happened, but right now, everything seemed surreal. The whole thing almost felt like it happened to someone else, and I'd played a movie role I'd never prepared for. How would I go on living tomorrow when the numbness wore off, and pain destroyed what little humanity I had left?

Tonight, however, I had one thing on my mind.

I needed answers, and there was only one man who had them.

# Chapter Ten

## VALENTIN

After an early morning of hitting the punching bag and splitting my knuckles, I'd worked out enough aggression to walk through the doors of RVC Enterprises and not throw punches. Tugging the sleeves of my dress shirt over my knuckles hid the destruction of the bag. I'd punched the hell out of it, imagining it was my father's face.

As I rounded the corner to my small office, incessant heels clicked behind me. Clenching my jaw, I inhaled slowly before coming to a complete stop. "What is it, Janine?"

She barreled into the back of me, papers flying everywhere. "Oh, goodness, I'm sorry Mr. Carrera." Her red framed glasses slid down her nose as she vomited apologies. "I didn't mean to wrinkle your suit or upset you…"

I glanced over my shoulder and let her squirm.

Stammering, she nervously pushed the glasses back into place with her forefinger four times before working up the courage to look me in the eye.

My silence made me a giant asshole, but I enjoyed watching

her anxiousness. I'd practiced my entire life at being intimidating as fuck. Unfortunately for my secretary, her skittishness around me made her my primary source for daytime entertainment.

"I'm not upset, Janine." I ran my hands down my red tie, straightening it. "You're my secretary. If you need me, that's fine."

"Oh, good. Then you probably—"

I held up my hand, silencing her. "But, let me walk into my office first, all right? I don't need a shadow."

Her lips tightened as she nodded quickly. Janine was efficient and knew her way around real estate, but if I walked up behind her and yelled "boo," she'd probably hug the ceiling fan.

Strange girl.

My office boasted the same extravagance as my home, moderate but adequate. The lone brick building stood unassuming and dull. Each agent had a tiny cubicle, and I insisted technology be kept at a bare minimum. The less opportunity for the Feds to bug our office or hack into our computers, the better. Not that I'd ever left a trail the DEA could find. Mateo outfitted the entire office with wiretap detectors, data scramblers and closed-circuit television.

Once seated, I folded my hands in front of me and leaned forward. I learned the power play move from watching my father during meetings. "So, what's so urgent?"

She rubbed her palms over her mouth. It was a move I'd come to know as her telltale sign of anxiety. "Well, sir, Rob called in sick early this morning, so I assumed there was no way you'd want to miss a chance at the Toller property."

Rob Young needed to be knocked down a few notches. He had an overextended sense of self-worth I found irritating. However, he'd proven to be my best flipper, so I'd let his attitude slide. All my house flippers were men. I'd never send a woman to a job site. It wasn't sexist; it was good business.

I was still alive, because I took nothing for granted. No situation was safe.

I didn't like where this was going. "I don't care about Rob. What happened?"

Janine wrung her hands while shuffling the papers in her hand. "When I got to the site, the house was a total wreck, as we expected. No one was there yet, so I thought I'd walk around the perimeter and check out the foundation."

A coldness filled the space where my soul used to be. I had no feelings one way or the other for Janine, but I'd hate to see ambition end her life. Only an American civilian would do something as stupid as wander a foreclosure in the second ward, alone and unarmed.

The lengthy conversation began to lose my focus, and I clenched my fingers around the edge of my desk. "For fuck's sake, what happened, Janine?"

Bristling from my comment, she hugged her chest, as her chin trembled. "As I rounded the back of the house, a man came up behind me. He scared me at first, because I thought no one else was around." She paused, dabbing at her eyes.

*Tears. Wonderful.*

I raised an eyebrow, then waited, my stare fixated on her.

"Yes, well," she continued, sniffling, "he grabbed my shoulder and asked me what I was doing. I know I shouldn't have responded, but I was so scared, Mr. Carrera."

"What did you say?"

She finally looked me in the eye. "I told him I was looking at the property to buy for my boss. He asked who you were, so I told him."

Blood pulsed against my temple. "You told him my name?"

She winced. "I said I represented RVC Enterprises."

At least she didn't use my name. That may've saved her life.

"Go on," I encouraged, my knuckles turning white.

She sniffled again. "He dug his fingers into my shoulder and told me the place was already under contract. I told him I'd just looked at the MLS listings and there'd been no update. That's when he got in my face and yelled at me."

Getting information out of this woman frayed all my thinned nerves.

"Words, Janine," I bit out between clenched teeth. "What did he say?"

She nodded her head. "He said he didn't give an f-word about my listing, and to back off and tell *El Muerte*, it's not over." She slouched forward, her earlier poise vanishing. Worried lines coated her eyes. "Who's *El Muerte*, Mr. Carrera? And what's not over?"

"Shit!" It pissed me off how quickly things derailed when my mind was consumed with flame-haired bartenders. I'd allowed the worst breach of my cleanest sanctum, and I had only myself to blame.

And maybe Janine for being stupid.

I stood and stormed to my office door. Throwing it open, I motioned to the cubicles lined outside of it. "Go, Janine. I need to think."

She paused, halfway out of the chair, her doe eyes rounded. "Who's *El Muerte*?"

I hardened a steeled look, my eyes informing her that we were done. Nodding her head, she hugged the papers to her chest. Her face held a mix of concern and fear as she exited my office.

Locking the door behind her, I tugged at my meticulously combed back hair until it hung disheveled in my face. I needed to be careful. Every decision I made from here on out affected everyone I met.

Janine wasn't in danger. Janine was a message. Muñoz enforcers were following an order.

Punching the wall, I rested my forehead against the molding. "I'm *El Muerte*," I whispered to an empty room. "The Reaper."

AS THE OFFICE CLEARED OUT FOR THE DAY, I OPENED MY DESK DRAWER and pulled out the gun from the hidden back compartment. Holding it up to my face, I marveled at the intricacies, definition, and power behind it. One small squeeze of a man's finger could extinguish another man's life. It was simple to think about but devastating on the psyche of a young man eager to find his place in a world he wasn't wanted.

*THE ROOM SMELLED OF METALLIC RUST. I MAY HAVE ONLY BEEN SIXTEEN; however, I knew blood when I smelled it. It singed my nose and gagged my throat, but I'd never show it.*

*I steeled my expression, showing nothing on the outside, just as I'd been taught. One solitary overhead light swung, and my eyes followed it back and forth. Somehow it gave the room more of a death shadow than what already hung over it. One chair rested in the middle of the dusty floor, and the rest of the room stood bare. I assumed the reasoning was for easier clean up, but what did I know...*

*This was the first time I'd been brought inside. Every other time, I'd stood guard outside the door, hardening my soul to the screams for mercy. Eventually, the begging stopped tearing at my insides.*

*Eventually, I'd become him.*

*A man, not more than twenty, sat bound in the chair with his face beaten and his eyes swollen shut. My two friends had worked him over good. I didn't ask what he'd done. Sometimes no one knew. Sometimes the one in the chair didn't even know. Strangely, no one questioned it.*

*That's how you knew power ran deep.*

*When you sat tied to a chair, bleeding and waiting for the hammer to fall on your execution, and you didn't ask why. You'd crossed the wrong people.*

*I smelled him before I heard him. My father had a distinct permanent scent of gunpowder and charred wood that roiled my stomach every time he drew near. Standing in that small room, I stood straighter. I squared my shoulders. I showed no fear.*

*"Take it, son," he commanded, handing me a black .22 caliber handgun. Curling my fingers around the trigger, I stared at it as a frenzied war raged quietly inside of me. I knew what he wanted. He'd been warning me that I'd be expected to prove my loyalty to the cartel.*

*I just didn't expect it to be so soon.*

*My father walked over to the weakened man with a sadistic smile, removed the cigar from his mouth, and pressed the lit end into the man's exposed shoulder. His tortured cries forced my eyes downward, the stench of burnt skin filling the room.*

*Alejandro's voice echoed against the bare walls. "Pon atención, Valentín!"* Pay attention, Valentin.

*My head snapped up in time to see the smile curl my father's mouth, his dark mustache curled heavy at the ends from weeks of moving locations.*

*Usually a very meticulous man about his appearance, his dishevelment gave him a sinister look I had no desire to push into a corner. We locked eyes, and he nodded to the victim, showing off by sliding into broken English.*

*"This man. He's committed a crime. Take him out."*

*Knowing this was a test, I stared at my father. If I failed, I could be in the chair next. Blood ran deep in cartel lines, but loyalty ran deeper. Steeling my breath, I raised the gun and aimed it at the man's heart. A clean shot seemed the most humane. I was a killer, but I wasn't an animal.*

*The dark side of me wanted him to curse me or spit at me. I wanted anything to provoke me into a rage. Instead, his eyes bore into me with a finality of acceptance. No fight remained inside of him.*

*At some point, I must have lowered the gun because my father's voice boomed from across the room. "Valentin!" Our eyes met, and as always, his coal black stare burrowed its way into my head. "This man, he raped his sister."*

*Bright white light burst across my vision. I no longer saw a defenseless man resigned to his own death. Rage welled beneath a bubbling surface of hate. I didn't hesitate.*

*I blinked and pulled the trigger. One clean shot between the eyes. The back of the man's head blew across the room, and my father laughed maniacally.*

*"Valentin," he said, clapping me on the shoulder. "It is done now. A new life for you, yes?"*

*It was a new life. One that would turn me from a boy with a shred of decency into a man with nothing but twisted black regret.*

*The man I killed was an only child.*

*He had no sister.*

I RAN MY FINGERS ACROSS THE SMOOTH METAL. I SUPPOSED SOMEWHERE deep inside a sliver of a soul remained, but beatings and threats ripped most of it away years ago. Now, most all I felt was a sense of relief when I killed.

Relief that it was them and not me.

Kill or be killed.

Shoot or die.

At the end of the day, I'd trained myself to wipe their last gasp of breath from my memory and forget their empty eyes over a glass of tequila and a willing woman.

Live by the sword and die by the sword.

Eventually it'd come for me. Because of my solitude, there'd be no innocent family members to suffer my same fate. At least I'd learned that valuable lesson from Alejandro.

Shoving the gun in the back of my pants, I pulled my suit jacket from the back of my chair. My head swam with ways to navigate shit, now that the Muñoz cartel made the first move against a civilian employee of mine.

That kind of thing didn't happen on American soil. That was a practice from home that'd specifically been left there.

As I adjusted my collar, my office door burst open, causing me to rip the gun from my back and aim it at the dark head that emerged.

"Shit! *Jefe*, it's me!" Emilio stood crouched in the doorway with his hands held high and his chin ducked, as if that would stave off a bullet to his brain.

"Jesus, Emilio, knock! How many times do I have to tell you people to fucking knock?" I shoved the gun back in my waistband. "I could've blown your head off."

Emilio stood frozen in the doorway, with matted hair and bloodstains splattering his shirt and pants. The sight alone would've sent most people screaming for their phones to dial the police, but the scene was nothing new in our world.

Nothing new except for the ravaged look of regret on his

face.

That look concerned me. Not because I particularly cared, but because regret had no place in our lives. It had to be checked at the door, along with a conscience if a man was to survive.

"Emilio?" I asked with an annoyed tone. I'd had a long day and was in no mood for this.

Emilio ran a shaking hand over his oily, slicked back hair, repeating the move as he mumbled. "I don't know what happened. We never get it wrong. Never wrong. And so, what if we do? It happens. It's the way of home, right? You play, your family could pay."

"Emilio?"

"But they pay with torture. That's the way you taught us, *jefe*. There are no mistakes. Never admit mistakes. But I didn't look in the side lot. I never thought…"

"Emilio!" I yelled, fed up with his incoherent ramblings.

He looked up, his eyes rimmed red. "We got the wrong guy."

"I thought you said it was done?" Alarm crawled up my spine as I ran over every order I'd given in the past few days.

"Lachey. The debt he owed us." He stopped and shook his head as if remembering something unpleasant. "We got him and took him to Caliente after hours. I did just as you ordered, but…" He trailed off, tugging at his collar. "I just found out my crew were taken out. The men who dropped off Lachey at Caliente weren't our men, and they didn't get the man who owed us. They got his son."

I walked past him, pulled him inside, and slammed the door. Circling him, I crowded right beside him and growled in his ear. "What the fuck? What son?"

Emilio visibly swallowed. "Lachey had a son who worked at his store. The old man has been MIA for weeks. My men wouldn't have gotten it wrong. This had to be Muñoz work. I swear, *jefe*, I only took his fingers and roughed him up. That's when I went outside to call you."

Emilio's normal commanding presence shriveled as he shook his head violently. A sense of dread filled me that I couldn't explain. I motioned for him to continue.

"I saw her car after we hung up. The cantina was empty. She told me she'd gone home. I don't know what happened."

My fists curled inward at my side. "Who?"

He closed his eyes as if blocking out the sight of me would block out the punishment he knew would come. "My bartender, sir. She was there. I went back to take Lachey home." He paused, his face growing pale. "But men came in after me and put a bullet in the back of his head."

Recognition fueled me. "Was there a message?"

He nodded fiercely. "Carved into his chest. *El Muerte*."

I vibrated with anger and pushed past him. Scaring my secretary was one thing. Brewing a war by interfering in my business was on a whole other level of uncharted territory. I wouldn't sit by and wait for another message from the Muñoz Cartel.

I'd almost stepped over the threshold when Emilio's bloodstained hand stopped me.

"Let go," I demanded.

"*Jefe*, my bartender is an innocent. When I went back out, her car was gone. If they have her, you know what will happen."

I knew all too well what happened to innocents who'd seen too much.

"Name?" I had no time for conversation.

"Eden," he sighed. "Eden O'Dell."

Whether driven by lust, fear, or revenge, my body stiffened, and my blood boiled as I made the connection. I had no idea why, but I just knew.

*Cereza.*

# Chapter Eleven

## EDEN

After stopping three times to throw up, the car barely stopped moving before I threw it into park and tore out of the driver's side, almost taking the door off its hinges.

Blood roared in my ears, and I knew a momentary break in my stride would snap the control I held onto by a thread.

Climbing the stairs to the front porch of my childhood home, I opened the glass door and pounded on the huge, paneled door with my fist.

*Nothing.*

I pounded harder, each slam of my skin against the wood timed with the slam of my heart against the wall of my chest.

*Still nothing.*

"Dad, open the door. I know you're in there!"

The night replayed in my head as if looped on an eight-millimeter film. "Dad!" I screamed, the adrenaline starting to fade, and reality setting in. "Open the damn door!"

A slight movement inside caught my attention. Desperation took hold, and a cry gurgled out as I pounded one last time with my hand flat against the door. "Dad," I pleaded, my voice breaking as I fought to breathe. "It's Nash. He's... God, Dad…" I couldn't say the words. Saying them aloud made them real.

Slowly the door creaked open, and I stumbled to regain my footing. My father stood in sweatpants and a T-shirt, unshaven and unkempt, his graying beard overtaking his round face. He looked like he hadn't slept in days. His eyes were rimmed red, with dark circles smudging the skin underneath them.

"What's wrong with your brother?" he asked, moving aside, and motioning me in. "Eden, what are you doing here so early?"

The minute I stepped inside my father's house the air changed. Tension filled the room, and apprehension practically vibrated off him.

Sticking his head out of the door, he quickly glanced around before shutting it and twisting two locks and a deadbolt.

I rubbed my chest, trying to relieve the suffocation that had built since running from the cantina. I leaned against the kitchen table, taking weight off my shaking legs.

"You're drenched," he commented, inching toward me. "Eden?" Almost hesitantly he reached for my arm, wiping off the smattering of rain that still clung to me like a second skin.

Flinching, I ran my hands down my face and stared at him as Nash's words flashed through my head.

*"Cherry, I don't do drugs. They got the wrong guy. I swear."*

*"Then what's this all about, Nash?"*

*"Dad."*

As a tear escaped, I let out a slow breath. "What's going on, Dad?"

He gave me a chagrined glance before turning his eyes away. "I don't know what you mean."

His face told me everything. My father was a shitty liar. Me? I was a pro. I'd crafted evasion into an art form, but my father couldn't look anyone in the eye and lie.

That's how I knew.

Catapulting myself off the table, I grabbed handfuls of his T-shirt and screamed in his face—all the anger, fear, and anguish inside of me releasing at once. "You're lying! Goddamn it, Dad. Do you want to know what happened to Nash tonight?" I released my hold on his shirt and twisted around to show him my back. "This is what happened tonight. This is Nash's blood."

I turned back around in time to see him pale, and his chin quiver. "God, is…is he okay?"

"No, he's not okay!" I bellowed, my body shaking violently. "He's dead! Drug runners shot him in the head!" Hysterical, tremors in my voice became audible as every word I spoke felt like acid on my tongue.

It was real. My brother was gone. The only constant in my life.

Dad stumbled backward, his eyes filling with unshed tears as his knees buckled. Running one hand across his mouth repeatedly, he pulled at his wayward hair with the other. "Jesus. It doesn't make sense. Nash had nothing to do with…" A mask of clarity blanketed his face. "Oh, Jesus."

His words took root in my head and exploded. One second later, I was on him. My father had a good eight inches on me, but grief rendered me unstoppable.

"Nash had nothing to do with what, Dad? What the fuck are you into that Nash got mixed up in, huh? Those men said something about Lachey owing money for cocaine. Why would…" My words trailed off as a closed suitcase and duffle bag perched on the couch caught my eye. Spinning back around, I wiped tears with the back of my hand and pointed to it. "What the hell is that? Going somewhere?"

He lowered his head, blinking back emotion as he walked

past me. Wrapping his shaking fingers around the handle of the suitcase, he dragged it over the top of the couch. "My life is over, Eden," he said, hugging it to his chest. "Everything's over."

"Fuck this," I muttered. He could spout his philosophical bullshit all he wanted. I'd had enough. My brother deserved more. If nobody else gave a damn, I'd call someone who would. Reaching into my purse, I grabbed my phone and started dialing.

"Who are you calling?"

"Not that it's any of your business, but I'm calling Brody. I care about catching the sons of bitches who murdered your son, even if you—hey, what the hell?" He snatched the phone out of my hands, staring at me as if I'd said I was calling the moon.

"Are you crazy?" he shouted, dropping it in his pocket. "We'll both be dead before you end the call."

"What's that supposed to mean? And answer my question."

"I'm a shamed, broken man," he replied, looking to the side as if an invisible vision of the past had appeared. "May God have mercy on my soul, but I have to leave."

"You do that," I hissed, clenching my arms by my side so I wouldn't take a swing at him. "You run like a little bitch while your son lays on a cold kitchen floor. Go hide, but I won't. I watched my brother die, and I'll take my last breath getting justice for him."

"Don't be stupid, Eden."

I felt his impatience but refused to budge. "I'm going after them. Every one of them will pay." My body shook as anger tore through me. Vengeance replaced the last traces of my humanity. "I don't know how I'll do it, but I can't go back to my same life after what I saw. That life is gone. It died with Nash. I'll live revenge, breathe it, and crave it until it's served."

We stared at each other, each of us unrelenting in our resolution.

Dejected, he reached into his pocket and pulled out a silver necklace. Closing his eyes, he let out a long breath and extended his hand, holding it by the chain. "Here. Take this."

"What is that?" I blinked furiously, trying to rid my eyes of falling tears.

"Take it," he repeated with finality, nodding once.

I couldn't explain why, but I took the medallion out of his hand and squeezed it. The rough metal and smooth porcelain contrasted starkly in the dim light.

Studying the face, I glanced up quizzically. "St. Michael?"

He dipped his chin. "The Archangel. The guardian of souls who triumphed over hell. He was a spiritual warrior in the conflict against evil."

Earlier images flashed in horrific sequence. "It's a little late for a triumph over hell, Dad. I'm in it."

Taking it from my hand, he draped it over my neck, and the chill of metal rested against my chest. "Never take this off, Edie. You're a warrior, and so much stronger than your old man. You can win this war, but you have to be smart and vigilant at all times." Finally looking at me, he stared at my face as if he were trying to imprint it into his mind. "Save yourself, Eden. Don't get involved with that man. They're watching you."

My brows creased. "What man? Who are you talking about? Stop talking in riddles!"

Without another word, my father grabbed his suitcase, kissed my forehead, and headed out the back door. My feet felt planted in concrete. Even as my brain commanded them to move, I stood rooted to my spot, watching him as he closed the door and walked out of my life.

*Fuck him.*

I'd spent most of my adult life on my own. Today would be no different. My face had been the last thing Nash had seen. I knew he saw the promise in my eyes. I wouldn't fail him.

Dropping the medallion from my hand, it landed with a thud against my chest. I never looked back as I stormed off the front porch, waking up the sleeping neighborhood. Children would be waking for breakfast in a few hours, and normal families would be making their way to church.

And I'd be plotting my next move.

With my keys firmly planted in my hand, I stomped to the driver's side of my car. I'd just moved my thumb to press the button on the keyless entry when a rough hand snaked around my cheek and covered my mouth. Shocked, I tried to scream, but the pressure on my lips stifled any sound.

A familiar voice, muffled by my own jerky movements, hovered over my ear. "Stop fighting and it'll be over soon."

The words seeped into my mind, and my heart pounded.

*It'll be over soon.*

I'd stayed here too long. They'd found me.

I had to make noise. I had to scream. The neighbors had to wake up. They'd come outside to investigate if they could just hear me. Inhaling hard, I mustered what little voice I could get out and squeaked a pathetic plea for help.

The gravelly voice behind me slithered in my ear once more. "I don't want to hurt you, but if you don't shut the fuck up, I'll do what I have to."

His overbearing weight lifted me off my feet, and I caught a strong metallic scent as he held me against him.

*Blood.*

My stomach roiled at the all too recognizable stench as I struggled harder, throwing elbows while trying to use my feet and legs to kick him. I'd almost gotten leverage when a sharp sting in my neck sent a seeping warmth through my skin and a thick haze across my vision.

The world swam and a black cloud overtook the morning light until nothing remained but hollow silence and a cold darkness.

# Chapter Twelve

## EDEN

*T*he room smelled of mildew and damp rain. I blinked to focus in the darkness, but even squinting, I couldn't make out the form sitting in front of me. Confusion set in as I tried to replay the events that led me to this dank hole, but my mind blanked. A fuzzy film coated my memory, prohibiting clarity.

"Don't be scared, Cherry."

My heart slammed against my chest. "Nash?" I couldn't remember why it hurt to hear his voice, but the slow cadence of his words tore a jagged hole in my heart. "Where are we? Why can't I see you?"

A low rumble of laughter filled the room. "You're feeling better. Already with the rapid-fire questions, I see."

I rubbed my neck where a stinging burned my skin. "What happened?"

"This isn't your fight, Cherry. You're going to get hurt. There's no game here. It's real."

Frustrated, I tried to move, but my limbs felt stuck in quicksand. "Why can't I see you?"

*"Listen to me," he instructed with a serious voice. "There's two sides to everything, and the key is in the middle. The guard will be your downfall."*

*"What does that even mean?"*

*"I love you. Be strong and keep your eyes open."*

His words finally broke through my muddled brain. *"No! Don't leave me!"*

Now barely a mist, his voice echoed in my ears over and over. *"Wake up, Eden."*

*"Don't go!"* Throwing myself forward, I landed on the hard, concrete floor, busting my lip and tasting blood.

His voice continued to echo in the small room.

*Wake up, Eden.*

*Wake up, Eden.*

"Wake up, Eden."

My head turned as my brother's voice took on a distinct Latino accent. "Wake up, Eden."

Worlds collided as the voice became louder. More blood filled my mouth, and I gagged as I swallowed it to breathe.

"Wake the fuck up, Eden."

Brightness burned my eyes the minute they cracked open. My body felt heavy as if I'd been asleep for days. Focusing on the voice, I turned my cheek from the hard floor toward his face, fighting the urge to fade back into darkness.

His form seemed familiar as he crouched down beside me. I realized I was lying on the floor, but my arm ached beyond reason. One shift of my eyes, and I knew why.

My left wrist was handcuffed to the base of a rusty iron bed.

Suddenly wide awake, I frantically jerked on my restraints while fear crept inside of my panicked thoughts. My bare heels scraped the cold concrete as I pushed away from him, crowding against the white sheets hanging off the side of the bed.

"Welcome back, Eden. You've been out since yesterday. You were starting to worry me."

My name. He kept calling me by name. I closed my eyes, recalling a memory from outside my father's house.

Someone said my name beside my car.

With blurred eyes, my lips cracked as I fought for my voice. "What…?" I cleared my throat, my tone hoarse and rough. "What am I doing here? What do you want?"

The man's outline moved closer. Crouching down, he reached out a finger and wiped it across my chin. I drew back, stiffening for a blow that never came.

"Relax," he said, wiping dark liquid from his hand onto his jeans. "You busted your lip when you fell. I told you if you calm down, we won't hurt you."

My body may have been restrained, but my antagonistic nature couldn't be. "Well, if you uncuff me, we'll be sure both of those things will happen, won't we?"

Dark eyes blazed with annoyance and mild respect. "You're one of a kind, Eden O'Dell."

I stiffened. "What did you just call me?"

Only one man called me by my married name.

He sighed heavily, and my vision finally cleared, adjusting to the dim light silhouetting his face. My head pounded, and dozens of spots plastered my vision. The fear that should have had me cowering under the bed hid behind an avalanche of rage and launched my body forward. Within inches of his chest, my wrist restraint jerked me backward and I banged my head against the iron railing of the bed.

Trapped, I let out a primal scream, yanking on my restraint again. "Murderer!" Nash's vacant eyes filled my head, and I shook it violently, desperate to rid it of the image.

"Whoa, *cálmete*!" he bellowed, raising a hand. "What the

113

hell are you talking about?"

"Fuck you!" I spat, throwing myself at him again. The cuff dug into my wrist, and I winced as it sliced my skin. Pain shot down my arm, but with adrenaline pumping, it only fueled my anger. "I saw you! I watched you cut my brother's fingers off. You walked out and sent those bastards in to finish him."

I continued battling against the restraint, blood pouring down my arm. My boss, the man I trusted completely, lifted off his heels and grabbed me by the shoulders, pinning me against the bedframe.

"Would you calm the hell down?" Emilio moved one arm and braced it horizontally against my upper chest while holding my wrist immobile with the other. "I didn't kill anyone. And what the hell are you talking about? Who's your brother?"

Unable to move and weakened with fading energy, my head wobbled on my shoulders as I lowered my forehead against his. "Nash Lachey, you asshole."

His face blanched. "Your name is O'Dell."

"You're a shitty businessman, Emilio," I taunted. "Do you always take everything at face value?"

The lines around his mouth deepened as his eyes narrowed inches from mine. His body leaned forward while his hold on my wrist tightened. I could see the confusion melt into irritation.

A wise woman would shut her mouth. I'd never been particularly wise.

"O'Dell was my married name. My name is Lachey. I was in the kitchen at Caliente." A dark glaze blackened his already coal eyes. "I saw everything."

The confession wasn't smart by any stretch of the imagination. In fact, it gave him every reason to kill me right there. I braced for it. I expected it.

But I'd never back down from it.

Nash left this world protecting me, and I'd be damned if I'd beg his tormentor for anything.

"I could've left you there."

I pulled on my bleeding arm again. "Because this is *so* much fucking better!"

Angered, he shook me, my head slamming against the bedrail. "You have no idea what was coming for you, do you, Eden *Lachey*?" He said my name with such contempt, I instinctively recoiled. "Being cuffed to a bed is a goddamn vacation compared to what waited behind me."

Emilio's anger overtook him. He'd all but climbed on top of me, pushing his face against mine, and barking words with disgust as sweat dripped from his chin onto my blood-caked skin. My chest heaved with terror, but only my widened eyes displayed any emotion to his aggression.

His hand released my wrist and fisted the back of my hair, lifting my face. Warm breath faintly reeking of alcohol filled my nostrils.

The threat of being killed spurred venom inside of me. Fear sat back and let vengeance ride shotgun. I twisted, desperate to get away from him, but his hold tightened.

A door slammed and an angry voice shouted behind him. "What the hell is this?"

Emilio stiffened, his furious glare becoming submissive. "She was out of control."

"Get your hands off her. Now!" the man growled.

Winking, Emilio released his hold and stood up. "Try to behave, Eden Lachey, and you might make it out of here."

As he walked away, I released the breath I'd held and sank to the floor.

"Lachey? Your name is Lachey?"

My head snapped up. With one glance, my breathing

became erratic, and my thoughts went haywire. Chocolate brown eyes flecked with gold stared back at me. Taking in my bloodied wrist, his own hands tightened into fists by his side.

"Val?" It made no sense, but the relief at seeing him outweighed my need for logic. He appeared as a contrast of darkened danger dressed in black slacks and an angelic white button-up shirt rolled up at the sleeves.

His jaw ticked as he spoke slow and deadly. "What did he do to you?"

I relived the last few moments and shook my head. "Nothing. I got angry."

"I saw him on top of you, *Cereza*." He shifted forward, and his face hardened. "If he touched you…"

"He didn't," I assured him.

Val glanced toward the closed door then knelt next to me, crooking a finger and running it down my cheek. Inexplicably, I leaned into his touch. In the quiet moment, I almost forgot where I was and why. Without thinking, I grabbed his hand and held it steady against my face.

"We have to get out of here."

"*Cereza*…"

"Listen to me. You don't understand." My voice rose, distraught at his calmness. "I was drugged and brought here against my will. Emilio, that man who was here"—I pointed toward the closed door—"he's my boss. He helped kill my brother. I was there." The words fell out at rapid succession, desperate for his help. "I don't know everything, but I think I heard the name Carrera. I know they're a drug cartel. My brother isn't an addict, Val. They fucked up, but I think I've got enough to go to the police."

"*Cereza*…" He lowered his head with a blank expression.

"Stop saying that and listen," I yelled, frantic and growing hysterical. "We have to get out of here. You have to find a key. We're not safe."

He remained quiet, pulling his hand away, with a tormented mask painted across his face. I could see his mind working, but mine refused to piece the unconnected puzzle together. His brows furrowed, and the deep line that etched between them severed my hope.

"I don't want to hurt you, but I can't let you go."

I splayed my hands against the cold metal of the bed. "Why…why can't you? I don't understand." He had to be here to help me, but there was an uncertain air around him I couldn't put my finger on.

"You're a danger to me and to yourself." Val rocked back on his heels, running a tanned hand across his full lips. "You have no idea what you've gotten into, and because of that, I can't trust you."

*I'm a danger to him? To* him*?*

Just as quickly as the fear had come, it exited, replaced by fury and understanding. "You can't trust *me*?" I clenched my hand and pressed it against my forehead. "Who's chained like a dog, here?"

Val's eyes hardened, and I waited for rage to follow. Instead, his lip twitched, lifting into a one-sided smirk. "You're bleeding pretty bad."

"Oh? I hadn't noticed," I sneered, narrowing my eyes.

"That mouth, *Cereza*… It's going to get you into trouble one day." Reaching for the buttons on his shirt, he opened them one by one. My eyes watched, fascinated, as he removed the shirt, revealing smooth bronzed skin covering a hard, toned chest marked with more tattoos.

"What the hell are you doing?" I wet my dry lips, unable to look away.

He lifted a dark eyebrow. "Cleaning your arm and stopping the bleeding before infection sets in. I assume you value your limbs."

"I highly doubt your shirt will stop gangrene."

Trailing his hand across my bloodstained skin, he scowled. "It may scar, but it won't be too deep." He finished cleaning the fresh blood and wrapped the shirt around the wound, tying it off. "How do you feel?"

"How do you think? I've been drugged, dragged, dropped, and sliced up. I fucking hurt."

Val ran his hand through his tousled hair, and his face turned an angry red color at my contempt. "I can't give you anything for the pain until the drugs Emilio injected are out of your system." He glanced at me with a glint in his eyes. "That may be a while longer."

The world spun around as betrayal thickened the air. Stunned, I looked deep into his eyes for the first time, seeing what his handsome face and sexuality blinded from me since the beginning.

I swallowed the lump in my throat. "Jesus, you're one of them." Pushing away from him, horror filled my vision at the bare-chested god of a monster crouched in front of me.

"Don't be so self-righteous," he whispered, leaning forward and boxing me against the bed once more. "I saved your ass."

"What did you give me?" I cringed, turning my chin away from his penetrating gaze.

"A little M99 combined with sedatives and opioids to counteract the side effects with some diprenorphine afterward to ensure you actually woke up."

I cut my eyes at him. "How very serial killer of you. *Dexter* fan, are we?"

"You're very mouthy for a half-naked woman cuffed to a

bed."

"How the hell did you even get that drug? So, you're a criminal *and* a practicing vet?"

"Ah, *Cereza*, I do love that mouth, but at this point, I'd suggest you shut it before you cross a line you don't want to." The gold flecks in his blackened eyes glittered with an underlying ruthlessness I'd yet to see.

I jerked on the cuff. "Fuck you."

He smiled a wicked grin that lit my skin on fire, infuriating me at my body's duplicity against my mind. "Not today. But if you cooperate and beg just the right way, who knows what might happen?"

Every stream of blood in my body pooled south at his seductive words. I closed my eyes, summoning images I'd forced in the dark. "I could never want you."

He cocked his head to the side. "What *do* you want, *Cereza*?"

"I want my brother back, you son of a bitch."

His lips twitched. If I didn't know any better, I'd swear it was out regret. But if the last half hour taught me anything, it was that nothing was as it seemed. People I thought were friends were enemies, and no one could be trusted. I was alone to save myself.

I didn't think. My hand flew to my chest and rubbed the St. Michael medallion. My father raised us Roman Catholic, but other than the required holiday mass and forced attended service, I'd never bought into religion. Maybe my mother walking out right after my birth had something to do with my issues with her god.

However, sitting in the small, dark room, I found myself repeatedly touching the symbol of the religion I'd turned my back on, hoping the courage and protection my father promised it'd bring would save me.

*Something had to …*

Val watched me with curious eyes. Leaning closer, he raised a hand to my face. Instinctively, I flinched, convinced a blow to my cheek was coming for my insolence. Gently, his thumb traced a wetness trailing from the corner of my eye down the side of my hairline.

I hadn't realized I was crying.

I'd promised myself I'd stay strong for Nash. Vengeance would be my comfort until I saw his killers suffer. My failure caused more tears to fall. Val's eyes softened, and before I could stop him, he tilted his mouth and pressed his damp lips where his thumb had been.

A shudder tore through me as his lips caressed my cheek, then as quickly as they warmed my skin, they were gone.

He stood silently and walked toward the door.

Mesmerized at the grace of a man who had evil running through his veins, my pulse sped up as I focused on his defined back. The most magnificent and nauseating tattoo spanned the entire width of his back from shoulder to shoulder and the length from his neck to his lower back. Numbers, dead flowers, swords, a demonic-looking bird, along with a lot of Spanish I'd never understand swirled in bright colors and harsh black lines. Without asking, I knew none of it got there on a drunken whim, each needle purposeful and full of meaning.

Part of me wanted to know, and the other was afraid to hear the answer.

Disgust for my lustful thoughts consumed me. How could the man responsible for the torture and murder of the one person who'd protected me my whole life, elicit such a reaction?

Nash had barely been gone twenty-four hours, and I'd already been disloyal to his memory. With my free hand, I untied his blood-soaked shirt off my cuffed wrist and balled it up.

"Hey, Danger…"

Paused at the door, Val glanced over his shoulder and lifted an eyebrow. I threw the shirt, hitting him in the face.

"Just so you know, I'm getting out of here with or without you."

Fisting the shirt, his nostrils flared as he unlocked the door with a key from his pocket and slammed it behind him. I slumped against the bedframe as the lock reengaged.

My head pounded in pain. My skin still bled. My body shivered with cold. My stomach growled with hunger, and my heart ached with sorrow. The stark reality that this was bigger than what I initially thought sobered me.

My revenge had become a suicide mission. I'd avenge Nash's death, but I wouldn't make it out of this alive as the captive of a drug cartel. I'd keep my promise to avenge my brother's death with my own.

Even if I was attracted to the one man I should hate more than anyone.

# Chapter Thirteen

## EDEN

I woke up shivering, but it wasn't from the damp air. I'd fallen asleep on the floor, leaned against the bed with my cuffed wrist behind my head.

How much time had passed since Val left?

I had no idea, but my fingers were numb from the unnatural angle of my hand, and my lips cracked with dehydration.

I didn't expect him to walk out on me, although I kept myself under no illusion that he'd let me go. I wasn't stupid. The man I thought could be my savior was one of my captors. I just didn't know how he ranked in the hierarchy.

Still, I thought maybe he'd turn around when I threw his shirt and at least give me some form of common comfort.

A real room.

Fresh clothes.

Another caress of his hand.

His touch had been the only thing in the past twenty-four hours that remotely came close to easing the ache where my heart used to be. The thought totally mind fucked me, because his hand had a part in its removal in the first place.

Every time I thought of being in the cantina, I felt sick, so I forced myself to concentrate on pumping life back into my cold and pale skin.

Wiggling my fingers, pins and needles shot through my arm, and I winced at the sensation. I'd never been so uncomfortable in my life as I sat upright, my stiff body screaming in protest. A quick glance at my wrist confirmed that the bleeding had stopped, so at least I knew I wouldn't die of blood loss.

*Small favors.*

The sound of keys rattling in the door pulled my attention away, and I balled myself up, not sure who'd be walking into the room. Out of the two, I'd prefer Val over Emilio. The dynamics of my relationship with my boss had been forever altered. Besides that, he seemed more of a loose cannon.

I held my breath until the door creaked open, and a young man about my age with a strong muscular build and shoulder-length, dark hair slipped through carrying a plastic tray. He eyed me curiously but glanced away once our eyes met.

"*Jefe* says you need to eat," he said, placing the tray in front of me.

I ground my teeth and turned away from him. "I'm not hungry."

That was a lie. I was starving. I couldn't remember the last time I'd eaten.

He ignored me and shoved his hands in his pockets. "I'd eat, if I were you. You don't want to piss him off."

I shifted a glare toward him. "Who is 'him'? Emilio? Val? Some other Carrera man hiding in this house who's yet to make sure I'm being a good prisoner? Tell me."

His fingers tightened in his pockets, and he paused a moment before answering. "You really don't get it, do you?"

"There's not much to get. Chains. Blood. Inhumanity. It's pretty self-explanatory."

"What?" His handsome face contorted in disgust. "No. You should be thankful he didn't leave you to those assholes. You'd definitely get a taste of inhumanity then."

I pulled on my cuffed wrist for emphasis. "Gee, thanks."

Shaking his head, he walked the few steps remaining from the door to the bed and arranged the plastic cup of water next to the tray.

No glass.

*Smart.*

I watched carefully as his gaze shifted to my wrist, the lines in his forehead deepening. Something in this man struck me as more rational than the other two. He seemed more human and more easily manipulated.

"Do you have a name, or do I just call you my personal chef?"

He chuckled and scratched his temple with his index finger. "*Jefe* said you were a handful. Nice try, but your trick isn't going to work, lady."

"No tricks. And my name is Eden. Do you have one?"

"I don't need to throw tricks. I'm not the one cuffed to a bed." He grinned, his smile fully amused at my expense.

"Nice." Turning inward, I closed my eyes and waited for him to leave. Moments passed with only silence in the room.

"Mateo."

Popping an eye back open, I stared at him. He still stood in the same spot regarding me curiously, with a smile tugging at one corner of his mouth. I had no idea why he hadn't walked out, but I wasn't about to let the opportunity pass.

"Excuse me?" I asked, raising an eyebrow.

"Mateo," he repeated. "My name? You asked my name."

"I didn't think you'd answer."

"I didn't either."

I waited for him to say more, but his lips pressed in a tight line. Obviously, Mateo had no intention of extending our conversation or providing me with any more answers.

However, sitting in one place for so long had restricted blood flow, and my legs were killing me. Beyond that, basic human function had taken over, and a full bladder took precedence over stubbornness.

I'd be damned if I'd beg Emilio or Val for anything, but for some reason, it didn't wound my pride so much to ask Mateo.

"I don't suppose you have a key on you anywhere?" I asked, tugging on my wrist restraint.

He narrowed a hard stare in suspicion. "Why?"

"Nature, Mateo. I need to go to the little prisoner's room."

*Totally petty but warranted.*

"I don't know…" His gaze bounced back and forth between sympathy and distrust.

*Wise man.*

"C'mon, dude," I whined. "Unless you want to mop up piss, I suggest you let me go. I know there's one in that room." I motioned toward a closed door adjoining the room.

Mateo twisted his face in horror. "Fine. Just don't piss on the floor, for Christ's sake."

Hurriedly, he fished in his pocket and produced a silver key that hung around a black key ring. I held my breath as he took hold of my wrist in one hand and unlocked the cuff with the other. The moment my arm was freed, I jerked it to my chest, rubbing it to force circulation back into my fingers.

We stared at each other like squirrels crossing a highway, both of us unsure of which direction to turn or what move to make.

Finally, I cleared my throat and pushed myself up on my knees, nodding toward the closed door. "Is that it?"

He followed my gaze and pursed his lips. Taking the opportunity, I pushed off my knees and sat on the bed, stretching my legs. Pain from sitting in the cramped position radiated down my back, and I winced.

I must've whimpered, because his eyes shot back to me as I leaned backward and fully extended with my arms behind me.

"What're you doing?"

I lifted a brow. "What does it look like I'm doing? I'm stretching like a normal human being instead of a caged animal." I nodded toward the bathroom again and repeated. "Is that it?"

My sarcasm seemed to throw him. "What? Oh, yeah…yeah. Go ahead, I'll wait."

"Super…a chaperone." Rolling my eyes again, I stood and walked toward the door.

"Eden?"

I glanced over my shoulder with a bored look, determined not to lose the ground I'd gained. "What?"

"Not too long or we'll take the door down."

Pausing at the bathroom door, I glared before slamming it shut. Once inside, I blew out a long breath and walked to the sink. Holding on to the edges with both hands, I lowered my head. Lack of sleep, an empty stomach, and the lingering effects of drugs in my system left me weak, but I couldn't let it show.

Licking my lips, I drew air in until my lungs filled and raised my head until my reflection stared back at me in the mirror. Familiar blue eyes were hollow and no longer held emotion that wasn't found in a lower circle of hell.

A slow, purposeful smile made its way across my lips as I reached behind my back, and underneath my tank top. Pulling out a long silver fork from the inside my shorts, I held it out in front of me and watched the fluorescent light flicker off the prongs.

I wondered how they'd feel piercing flesh.

After using the bathroom, I shoved it back into my pants, covered it with the hem of my tank top and flushed the toilet for emphasis. Washing my hands, and running them through my matted hair, I turned toward the door.

*Show time.*

•

# Chapter Fourteen
## VALENTIN

"**G**oddamn it!" My fist pounded into the cheap door as my foot kicked it from the bottom.

She infuriated the hell out of me. I didn't have to coddle her. I could leave her in there to rot or shove warm, day-old water and crusty bread at her until she choked.

Leaving her for the crew would've been easier. It'd been risky to show my face to her. I should've just left the logistics to Emilio like he wanted, but for some reason, I wanted to see for myself that she was all right.

How in the hell did *Cereza* turn out to be Lachey's sister? How'd I manage to bring the one woman who caught my eye into the middle of a cartel war?

My arrogance would get me killed one day.

I closed my eyes and paced the stark white bedroom. Blindly bumping into things posed no danger. Safe houses were anything but homey. A metal bed with sheets as soft as the needles on a porcupine was all that stood between my fist and the wall.

And God, she made me want to plow through plaster.

Pacing the room, I stopped occasionally to shove my hands through my hair, tearing at the strands until they fell around my temples. I ripped at the collar of my new shirt, buttons flying, and not giving a shit.

She made me crazy. No, she made me more than crazy. I wanted to grab that smart fucking mouth and squeeze until she shut it, and no words came out. I craved to have those pouty lips under my command, kneeling before me with her hands bound until she stopped her incessant talking.

I needed to see a moment of fear in her eyes…just a passing of uncertainty glaze her pale blue eyes, fearing my power over her. Then the fire would return. The cold power that lined her veins and steeled her jaw would demand her retaliation. She'd pull away, glaring at me with a mix of hatred and unwanted desire.

All that raw hate and vengeance inside one woman set something alive inside me that lay dormant for years. I could satiate carnal desires with any woman, but Eden Lachey was a sparked live wire for the taking.

The choice was mine to touch her and burn from the inside out or step away and die from nothingness.

Opening my eyes, I found myself at a dead-stop, leaned against the plain metal dresser. Hard as a rock, my slacks barely contained my erection.

*Damn this woman.*

Cursing, I pushed my palms away and stalked to the attached bathroom, stripping what was left of my suit off as I went. A trail of clothing followed my path until the tiny, stark white bathroom met my scowl. A single basin sink with cheap chrome faucets lined a dirty countertop, and I took care not to touch anything as I turned the shower on.

I'd kill Mateo for choosing this place.

Stepping into the stream of hot water, I let the abusing pelts bruise my skin. I wanted the pain. I deserved it. Placing both palms against the tile, I leaned into the force of the stream and closed my eyes.

I'd indirectly gotten the girl's brother murdered. I'd ordered the beating on her father, and the fucking Muñoz cartel killed Emilio's crew, delivering the wrong Lachey. Even if my men didn't pull the trigger, her brother had shed blood because of my orders.

I was also responsible for every Muñoz dick that wanted to violate her. I couldn't think of what would've happened if we hadn't gotten to her first.

She called me one of them. She called me a murderer. She was right. I was all those things. Yet, I'd never force myself on her. Unless she wanted me to. And God, did I want her to.

A soapy hand slid from the tile as I imagined her crawling on her knees to me, hands bound behind her. I'd make her wait. I'd make her ask for it…cry for it, even. When we both couldn't stand anymore, I'd grab a fistful of that bright red hair, jerk it back, and shove my cock down her throat.

She'd take it all, because of her insatiable need for me. More than anything, I craved to see my dick disappear past that smartass mouth. Then, I could remind her every time she told me to 'go fuck myself,' exactly how easily she swallowed it with a smile.

As the fantasy played out in my head, I worked myself into a frenzy. Images of her face flashed through my head as my breathing escalated. My eyes squeezed shut, and my grip tightened while thoughts of her tongue had me pumping at a furious pace.

I braced one hand against the shower wall as a groan tore from deep within my chest. "*Cereza,* fuck!"

Coming back down to earth, the visions in my mind cleared, and all that remained were stained walls and an unsatisfied cock. Sighing, I washed off and wrapped a towel around my waist.

I couldn't allow thoughts of her to consume me. I may be a murderer, but I wasn't a fucking rapist. Something had to give, or I'd spend the entire time in the safe house, jerking off to images of Eden Lachey's acid tongue.

BY THE TIME I GOT OUT OF BED THE NEXT MORNING, I WAS READY TO crawl back in. Sleep never came when my mind replayed the sight of Eden alone and bleeding in a concrete room. I'd tossed and turned, until I finally gave up and went in search of anything resembling a coffee pot.

What I found looked like it'd time traveled from 1983. The pot was stained, the filters were fuzzy, and I didn't even want to know what the hell still clung to the sides of the grounds bucket.

But caffeine was caffeine, and I needed a boost. Something told me our prisoner wouldn't be as pleasant as yesterday and may need some liquid energy of her own. Taking a sip, I grimaced and hoped she took her coffee with no frills. She was getting it tar black, just like my mood.

On the way to take it to the basement, I paused, hearing Mateo unlock the front door. It had to be him. Anyone else would've broken the windows or shot their way in. Still, I dropped the second coffee mug and molded my hand around the gun wedged in the waistband of my sweatpants.

I was sure, but I wasn't stupid.

My tensed muscles relaxed as Mateo's long hair popped in the kitchen door attached to a shit-eating grin. "*Hola, jefe.* You're up early." He raised a tray, and the smell of brewed Colombian coffee filled the room. "I brought brain food."

"Thank God," I exhaled, grabbing one out of the carrier. Taking a sip, I held in a groan of satisfaction and threw the remaining mug in the sink. I caught Mateo's eye as he watched the move, counting the cups before they shattered against each other.

"*Dos?*" He held two fingers up and shook his head with a smirk. "Taking the prisoner coffee doesn't exactly play up the fear factor, does it?"

I didn't appreciate what he insinuated, but I couldn't deny it either. "She has to drink, Mateo. We're not savages."

Mateo took a slow drink from his cup before answering. "She's hostile. I tried to give her food last night, and she walked away from it. The less you interact with her the better. She's throwing around accusations about the cartel and using our names." He glanced toward the closed door where she lay cuffed. "You've shown yourself once. Don't give her more ammunition."

"Too late for that."

The memory of her skin against my lips caused a crack in my hardened armor that I covered with a scowl. I couldn't let my men know Eden and I already had somewhat of a bizarre history. The insignificant conversations for months leading to my ill-timed decision to visit the cantina two nights ago were private.

From the look in her eyes, we'd both envisioned the ending to that night with me buried deep between her legs.

Jesus. I couldn't think like that. or I'd have to shower again.

Mateo paced. "The police raided Caliente early this morning."

His words knocked me out of my stupor and pulled me into full boss mode. "What reason would the police have to go to Caliente?" My eyebrow arched, and my hand stopped him mid-pace. "The cleaners already passed through, right?"

If our men hadn't gotten rid of Lachey and cleaned up the mess before the badges got there, we were fucked.

"*Si.*" Mateo nodded his head. "They found nothing. The alarms tripped, and Emilio had to go back not long after he left here." He glanced out of the small, reinforced glass window toward the isolated street. "They tried to rattle him, but he knows the rules."

I didn't like the way this was playing out. "There's only one way the police could've known Lachey was there, but it goes against everything cartels believe as a whole...despite our rivalry."

"You think the Muñoz Cartel called the cops and pointed them to Caliente?"

"Either they did, or they had someone do it for them."

Mateo's eyes widened. "Why? The cops could bust them just as much as us."

"Agreed." I ran my finger along my bottom lip, tapping it at the corner of my mouth. "Something doesn't add up. It was a ballsy move and not one I would've made without knowing it wouldn't backfire. Whoever made that call wasn't worried. The question is, what insurance policy do they have?"

"If you want, I can stay here while you—"

I nodded toward the door. "Thanks for the coffee, but you need to get back and check on the shipment coming in from the port." I clapped him on the shoulder and looked him in the eye to convey the seriousness of the situation. "I'm counting on you, Mateo. Without Nando, we're a man down. I need you to be my eyes and ears in Corpus Christi. Make sure that truck gets here."

"Of course, *jefe.*"

"I also need you to fill Nando's position. Look toward the higher soldiers. Someone's got to stand out as worthy."

He dipped his chin. "I'm on it."

The door closed quietly, the lock engaging along with the coded alarm. I stared at the cool coffee containers and cursed under my breath. Business came first and one unpleasant phone call needed to be made.

Sighing, I pulled my phone from my pocket and addressed my current problem before I opened the door to my other.

I fought a yawn as I dialed the number. He answered on the first ring, his voice holding a satisfactory mix of trepidation and anxiousness.

*This might be easier than I thought.*

"What do you want, now?"

"Brody, that's hardly an acceptable way to greet someone, don't you think?" I imagined him loosening his tie to breathe easier.

They all did.

"I'm at work, Carrera." His voice sounded rushed. "I'm going into court."

"Be late." I picked up my coffee, agitated from my conversation with Mateo.

"I can't," he snarled through what sounded like clenched teeth. "Talk fast."

"A few officers paid a visit to one of my men early this morning at his cantina. Do you know anything about that, Brody?" The man couldn't lie for shit. He had to be the worst assistant DA in history.

"N-no. Nothing, Val. I haven't heard a thing."

I knew he was lying. Brody Harcourt never called me by my first name. It was a human reflex to become friendly and communicate on a personal level when a man lied through his teeth.

"Nothing? Not a word around the office?"

"No, I told you, Val. It's been quiet. Nothing's come across my desk." He paused, and his breath became labored. "Why? What happened at Caliente? Something bad?"

My fingers tightened around my coffee. "I never mentioned it was Caliente."

"Well, I just assumed, you said cantina, and I know your guy, Emilio owns Caliente." He laughed nervously. "Simple process of elimination, Val."

*Goddamn it. Stop saying my name.*

This conversation was obviously headed nowhere fast. Harcourt knew more than he'd divulge over the phone. He needed some face-to-face encouragement to not be a rat bastard.

"Nothing happened. The alarm must have tripped and alerted the authorities."

He audibly swallowed. "Yeah, sure. That has to be it."

*Of course, it does, you lying motherfucker.*

Once I got Eden settled, and Mateo came back, I'd pay our fair ADA a visit and jog his memory. Until then, I'd humor his selective amnesia.

"Enjoy your day, Brody. Watch out for cars when you cross the road."

"What the hell does that mean?"

It meant absolutely nothing. I just enjoyed fucking with him.

"Traffic. I heard it's bad today. You're late for court." I disconnected the call in the middle of his string of curses.

Every man in the Carrera Cartel knew the penalties for lying. That knowledge prevented lies from being told amongst our men.

Unfortunately for Brody Harcourt, he'd find out soon enough why there was rarely a crack in our cartel family code of honor.

# Chapter Fifteen

## VALENTIN

An hour later, I still held the phone in my hand, my eyes shifting to the closed door that led down the stairs to the basement.

Mateo made sense.

Continuing to interact with her wasn't the smartest move, but I couldn't deny the magnetic pull she had over me. No matter how many times my brain told my body to shut up and turn away, I found myself facing that goddamn door.

I'd taken three steps toward it when the phone vibrated. Since only business associates knew my number, I didn't hesitate to answer in my native tongue.

"*Si?*"

"It's Consuelos."

Chris Consuelos had been hard to bring to control when I'd arrived in Houston six years ago. One night of Nando sitting across the street from his house in a tinted SUV cracked the Chief of Corpus Christi Port Security's shell before I could pull my phone from my pocket.

Nothing changes a man's attitude faster than an unspoken threat to his family.

I kept my gaze on the basement door. "Not a good time."

"Your boat never arrived, Carrera."

The edge in his voice gave me pause. "What do you mean, it never arrived?"

"Exactly what I said. The boat was never found, but the bodies of your boys washed up on the Padre Island National Seashore. There's no proof, of course, but if I was a betting man, I'd say they were intercepted not long after they left the coast of El Mezquital."

*Son of a bitch.*

Small shipments had been MIA here and there for months, but lately, the frequency had tripled. Stolen cargo was a nature of the business, and I'd learned to eat the cost, but I couldn't ignore it anymore. Writing it off as a coincidence wasn't an option.

With the weight of his words distracting me, I stepped away from the door. "What the hell happened, Consuelos?"

For the first time, fear crept into his detached voice. "I have no idea, but my guess is there's only one group with the *cojones* big enough to cross you."

*Muñoz.*

My hand tore through my hair as my fingers ripped the strands from the root. Scenes of what would happen when word reached my suppliers that Muñoz enforcers had intercepted their shipment flashed through my head.

"Do you realize what this means, Consuelos?"

"It can't be good."

"Good? These are the fucking Colombians, Consuelos. Suppliers don't send an IOU to collect a debt on ninety pounds of cocaine." I closed my eyes and cursed. "They wipe out entire neighborhoods."

"That sucks, man."

I opened one eye at his dismissal. "Don't be stupid, *pendejo*! If you think they don't know what you ate for breakfast this morning, you're an idiot."

His voice shook. "You mean…?"

"Update your insurance policy." I disconnected the call without another word.

Callous?

*Probably.*

But I had more pressing issues than Chris Consuelos's newly-soiled pants. I had hours to figure out how the hell to appease an eleven-million-dollar debt and smooth trade negotiations with my best supplier.

This feud had gotten way out of hand. Rivalry was one thing, but they'd fucked with my business one too many times.

I'd had enough.

Filling my chest with a calming breath, I released the death grip I had on my phone and started to dial the last man I wanted to talk to, when a high-pitched scream echoed from the basement followed by a clang of metal.

Warning that had built inside of me all morning exploded into a siren. Dropping the phone, I flung the door open and took the stairs four at a time, pulling my gun from my waistband.

Eden stood next to the iron bed, her cherry-red hair disheveled and wild, with a crazed look in her eyes. Bent over the mattress with her hands clasped together, she jerked roughly on the handcuff, snapping the metal into her wound with each pull.

Shocked at her ferocity, I stood with my gun pointed at her while she continued to jerk and pull, screaming like a wounded animal. Blood poured down her arm, and the food tray lay on the floor just under repeated marks and chips in the wall where she'd beaten into it.

I assumed it was to get our attention.

It worked.

Unfamiliar with unbalanced females, I tried reasoning with her. "*Cereza*, you need to calm down."

As if I were prey that had wandered into the lion's den, she shifted her eyes toward me with her chest heaving. "This *is* calm. Uncuff me…*now*." Every word she spoke dripped with disgust, spoken between clenched teeth.

"You know that's not going to happen. I don't want to hurt you, but I will if you don't calm the fuck down."

She paused a moment before turning her eyes away and continuing her maniacal screaming. The safe house was secluded in a rural area, but it wasn't soundproof. I had to shut her up.

Letting out a sigh, I shoved my .380 caliber pistol back in my waistband and sat down on the bed. "Sit down, *Cereza*."

At my command, she quieted, the fight seeming to melt out of her. Sinking next to me, her shoulders slumped forward in defeat. "I'm scared."

"I know." Her closeness raced my pulse, so I increased the distance between us. "I'm sorry about your brother. I know what it feels like to lose family."

"Did you kill him?"

"No."

She inched closer, her small frame shaking. "Who did?"

"Rivals."

I needed to move away from her. That'd be the smart thing to do. I shouldn't let her feel as if we were equals. I needed her fear to keep her on edge, but for some reason, I craved her closeness.

"Why?" The tremble in her voice gutted me.

I could give her nothing but honesty. "Bad blood."

She glanced up with tears pooling in her bright blue eyes.

"My brother died because of some vendetta between drug cartels?"

I couldn't explain. The less she knew, the safer she'd be. "It's more complicated than that, or you'd be dead, too."

Silence raged between us. Neither one of us moved as both of our eyes pinned to the wall in front of us. She folded one leg underneath her and sighed loudly. I wanted to relieve some of her pain, and I'd never wanted to relieve anything for anyone.

It confused the hell out of me.

I didn't know how to console her, but instinctively, my body turned inward. "Eden, I…"

With lightning speed, she shifted, catapulting herself into me. Something shiny glinted in her hand moments before it plunged into my left bicep with a searing burn I'd only experienced once in my life.

"Fuck!" Throwing myself backward, I landed on the floor three feet away from her grasp.

Curse words flew from her mouth as she yanked on the cuff, screaming like a woman possessed. I pulled my hand away from my injured arm, stunned to find blood dripping from my fingertips. Shifting my gaze back to Eden, my eyes landed on a three-pronged fork she held like a sword.

The bitch fucking stabbed me.

"Are you insane?" A newfound anger coursed through the same veins sympathy had just occupied.

"Come here, *Val Carrera*. Come tell me how complicated it is, Mr. Drug Lord. Explain it to my face, because I'm dying to hear it straight from your lying goddamn mouth!"

I'd had enough. She'd overstepped the line.

Jerking the handle of my gun from my pants, I threw it across the room and out of her grasp. Lunging at her, I secured her free wrist in a strong hold.

The stunt she pulled exerted all her stored energy, and in her weakened state, she was no match for me. Collapsing underneath me, I easily wrestled her to the bed and pinned her arms above her head. My own arm throbbed in pain, and after Consuelos's phone call, I'd been fucked with enough for one day.

"I knew I couldn't trust you."

Her eyes went blank. "Just kill me now," she whispered, her voice hoarse from screaming. "What the fuck are you waiting for? Aren't you the goddamn boss?"

"Yes, I'm the goddamn boss. You should fucking remember that. Men have died for less than the shit you just pulled." I didn't even know what the hell I was saying. She had me seeing red. I had no intention to hurt her, but I'd learned over the years that perception was power.

She turned her chin toward me and blinked. "Then do it."

"What?" I didn't know what I expected to come out of her mouth, but that wasn't it.

With her arms restrained, she used the only thing she had left—her legs—which I currently had myself wedged between. Thrashing, she dug her heels into my lower back. "Just do it, so I don't have to feel anything anymore or pretend like you give a damn."

I don't know what possessed me.

Our bodies pressed together, and heat radiated off her with a ferocity I couldn't deny. The fire in her words and the desire that had my balls in a vise since I'd laid eyes on her, all drove me against her mouth. S

he gasped the moment I licked the seam of her lips, and I didn't hesitate to dip my tongue inside. Still riled, Eden resisted for a few seconds, pushing her body away, and then against me.

Shifting her cheek to the side, she gulped in a lung full of air, her chest heaving. "Get off me!"

"Well, you might want to arrange a conference between your mouth and body, *Cereza.* There seems to be a miscommunication. For a woman who doesn't want me to touch her, you're pressing pretty close."

She fought against my hold on her wrists. "You disgust me!"

I loomed over her, my pulse roaring in my ears. "You're an insane, homicidal bitch!"

"Oh, you're one to talk. You murder people for a living."

I knew who I was, but her black-and-white assessment made me wince.

A vein throbbed against my temple as I lowered my face against hers with a snarl. "You tried to stab me, what does that make you?"

"A failed mission."

I should've walked away.

The heated sparring flipped a switch in me, and after one taste, my need for her shattered. Logically, I knew if I didn't pull away, I'd do something I couldn't take back.

But before registering the thought, I rejected it and crashed onto her lips again.

Tightening her fist, she attempted to punch me, but the stronghold I had on her prevented any movement. I had no forethought and no game plan. A riotous mix of lust and hate converged inside me, pouring both into a kiss that took both of us by surprise.

With a breathy gasp, she stopped struggling and moaned into it. Her body melted into mine, our tongues tangling at a furious pace.

"I should hate you," she whispered between frantic kisses.

"I know."

Bowing her back, she pushed her chest into mine, dropping her chin back and offering her neck. Wordlessly, I accept the invitation, diving in and sucking her skin between my teeth.

"I want to hate you."

Groaning, I released her neck and followed a path down her collarbone. "Then hate me, but God, let me have what I've craved for months."

At those words, something shattered inside Eden. Reservation died and both legs snaked around my waist, crossing at the ankles, and urging me closer. A long-drawn-out sigh ghosted from her chest on a whimper.

It was that whimper, breathless and sultry with a hint of remaining fear, that broke the hold on my resolve. Lifting my mouth from her chest, I took in the flush painting her cheeks and the want in her eyes. Her lips struggled to form words that never came.

They didn't have to. Only one made it past a whisper. "Val…"

The sound was my name. The meaning was fuck me.

Reaching a hand in my pocket, I pulled out a small metal key. Holding her cuffed hand steady, I turned the key, springing the lock free. Before she could react, I grabbed her free hand and crossed it over the other one, snapping the lock in place over both.

Glancing above her head, her eyebrows lifted, but my body lit on fire as I stared hungrily at her bare skin. Fusing my mouth to hers once more, I plunged inside, needing the taste of her more than I cared to admit.

With her arms bound above her head, her back arched even more and pressed her breasts into my palms.

I wasn't a man used to waiting for what he wanted. This moment would be no exception.

Hooking my fingers around the bottom of her tank top, I yanked it up and over her chest, taking her bra with it. The moment her round flesh sprang free from the lacy material, my cock hardened to a level that had me wincing in pain.

I'd never wanted a woman this much.

Anticipating the taste, I flattened my tongue and raked it over the sensitive flesh of her nipple. A low gurgling groan rumbled in her chest as she jerked on the cuff restraining her.

I wasn't particularly into BDSM, I just still didn't trust her.

"God, Val…"

Closing my mouth around the tip, I sucked vigorously, eliciting a wail from her tilted chin. Curses flew from her mouth as I divided equal attention to the other one. Satisfied she'd had enough, I resumed my descent.

By the time I reached for the button on her jean shorts, I couldn't hold back. Unzipping in a frenzied pace, I yanked them down her legs, taking the pathetic scrap of lace with them, just as I'd imagined doing that first night at the cantina.

Tearing off my own pants, I paused for a moment of clarity to grab a condom out of the pocket. Seconds later, I leaned over her and plunged two fingers deep inside her depths.

"Jesus, *Cereza*. You're drenched for me."

"Val!" She screamed, yanking on the handcuffs and twisting underneath me. "Stop talking!"

Growling, I removed my hand and lined the head of my cock at her entrance. With one last look, I closed my eyes and drove inside without reservation. A scream tore from her throat with the force of my possession, and she tensed, her walls clenching me tightly. The pressure sent blinding waves of red swirling across my closed eyes.

Fuck, nothing had ever felt this good.

There was no turning back. The need to fully possess her was too strong. With a primal groan, I plunged the rest of the way in, drawing another piercing scream from her lungs. I almost pulled back, but she wrapped her legs tightly around my waist, encouraging me.

That was all I needed. Taking control, I drove inside her repeatedly, each thrust harder than the last. Blind lust replaced common decency as I fucked her like a wild animal.

Her back slid against the metal rail of the bed, and I bit down on her shoulder as our hips collided. Our bodies moved in a chorus of furious movement that eventually pinned both of us flush against the bed frame.

I'd never fucked this hard. I wanted to fuck her harder. I wanted to fuck her unconscious.

"Val, God…"

"Do you want to come, Eden? Is that what you want?" Every word I spoke was punctuated by a forceful thrust that shifted her body backward.

She screamed as her inner walls clamped hard around me. "Yes."

"Then ask me, *Cereza*."

Her eyes widened, then darkened. "Fuck you."

A snarl plastered across my lips. "No. I'm. Fucking. You." On the last word, I threw her right leg over my shoulder and went deeper. The angle forced her back to bend over the rail, and her head to disappear behind her.

"Shit!" With a scream, she squeezed the life out of me as she convulsed. I held her through the aftershocks, still pounding into her as my mind went blank.

"*Queriéndote me acaba…*" Wanting you will end me.

As I exploded, my mind unscrambled, and I slowed my pumps until my body stilled. Resting inside of her, the frenzy ended, and clarity returned.

*Fuck. What have we done?*

Unable to look at her, I dressed quickly, and moved off

the bed, desperate to be anywhere else. She lay there naked and silent, her breathing shallow.

Picking up the fork that led to the fuck, I shoved it in my back pocket along with my gun. Without a word, I reached for her hands and unlocked the handcuff.

After what just happened, I couldn't bring myself to re-cuff her.

"I'll have Mateo bring you something to eat later."

Keeping my eyes focused forward, I closed the door to the sound of the metal cuffs hitting the wood with force behind me.

# Chapter Sixteen

## EDEN

They sounded like fireworks popping off in the distance—rhythmic in their cadence with an echoing thunder that seemed to immediately follow each one.

The moment I cracked an eyelid, darkness enveloped me. For a moment, irritation convinced me I'd left the television on full blast again. Groaning, I reached for the remote to quiet the intrusive sound when a jolt of lightning shot up my arm.

Confusion set in as my limbs itched with stiffness.

Then it all came rushing back in a hot haze of defeat and submission.

The finality of what happened, and my resolve to see everyone involved, including myself, dead for causing it, flashed through my head. Tears clouded my vision, and I curled up on my prisoner's bed, mulling it over.

Night had fallen, darkening my already burning self-hatred.

Not that the fire needed much stoking.

I just hoped that somewhere Nash turned a blind eye to the way I'd pissed all over his name.

Flinging myself onto my back, I counted eighteen water-stained dots on the ceiling before visions of Val's body slamming into mine had me squirming in place.

I knew it was wrong.

Every bone in my body knew it was wrong, but my mouth refused to say "no." Powerful physical attraction, coupled with admitted defeat, broke me. But what tore me up inside the most was that I wanted more than anything to hate him for it.

Instead, I hated myself because I didn't.

The only time I didn't feel like drowning was when I was with him. The correlation between the two made no sense, and I didn't care to think about what kind of fucked up Stockholm Syndrome I'd developed long enough to figure it out.

My father used to say that mistakes were life's necessary evils. Without them, there'd be no way for a person to see the error of their ways and know the right path for the next time.

Val Carrera was an evil mistake, but far from necessary. Righteousness wouldn't be a moral dilemma again. There wouldn't be a next time.

Rubbing my tender wrist, I thanked small miracles that Val didn't cuff me before he left. I had no concept of time without my phone, but I guessed it to be sometime after nine or ten. Refusing food and water had been a stupid move. All my body wanted was sleep to conserve energy after my pathetic attempt at utensil retaliation.

My whole life had been a psychiatrist's wet dream. At fourteen years old, I'd gotten caught with a senior behind the football field. My therapist called it "Impulsive/Undisciplined Child Therapy" and shoved antidepressants in my face.

I didn't need drugs.

I was just pissed I'd found out my father had been lying to me my entire life about my mother. She hadn't died. Three days after my birth, she decided being a mom was too much of a hassle and took off.

I didn't need drug therapy. I needed dick therapy.

Then, when I was twenty-four, after three years of changing who I was to conform to someone else's ideal, my husband sank a knife into my back and his dick into my best friend. I swore the day I found them I'd never put my trust in another human being and slept with as many men as possible.

My therapist called it "Detached Overcompensating Behavior Therapy" and shoved antidepressants down my throat.

I didn't need drug therapy then either. I needed dick therapy.

Lying in the small prison with four walls and a mattress, a sadistic chuckle fell from my chest. The one person that meant anything to me was gone. There was no therapist here to label me or shove pills at me, yet somehow, I'd still managed to find dick therapy.

Running my hands down my face, my eyes landed on small droplets of blood on the floor. I knew they weren't mine and reminded me that once Val's post orgasmic sex high wore off, he probably spent the afternoon figuring out the best way to kill me with the least amount of exertion.

A full body shiver ran through me. Even after sleeping for an hour, exhaustion had permanently set in. My body ached, and the pain in my arm radiated up my shoulder.

Cradling my elbow against my chest, I cleared the few steps from the bed to the door. Logically, I knew it was pointless; however, I still closed my fingers around the doorknob, jerking furiously.

*Nothing.*

"Val! Open the door. You can't keep me in here. Val!" Releasing the knob, I slammed my hand against the wood. "Val!" Pounding until my palm stung, a strangled cry tore from my throat as I slid to the floor.

Touching the St. Michael medallion, I closed my eyes, and leaned my forehead against the doorframe. Heaviness gathered in the corners of my eyes as a wave of fatigue threatened to pull me under again. Haze clouded my vision, and I welcomed the blackness, surrendering to it.

The peaceful calm had almost claimed me under when a *pop pop pop* from outside the bedroom wall jolted me back into consciousness. Fear paralyzed me as I recognized the sound.

They weren't fireworks.

I'd heard the same sound in a pantry closet while Nash took his last breath. Peace flew out the window and panic overtook me.

"Val!" Scrambling to my knees, I pounded on the door with renewed force. "Val, open the door! Please!" Tears ran from my eyes as I beat the door with both fists.

Several blasts ripped through the house, and the force knocked me back onto my palms.

Within seconds, the door flew open, and Val burst in, his eyes wide and wild. Dressed in black athletic pants and a thin white T-shirt, his unkempt hair dusted over his eyes as he bent down and hooked a muscular arm around my upper back.

"Get up!" he hissed. "We have to go."

"What's happening?" I felt myself panicking.

"We're under attack, no time!" Jerking me up, he pushed us both toward the door. In a daze, I resisted, staring blankly back into the bare room. "Eden!" he commanded.

He never used my given name. That got my attention.

I stumbled into the hallway, and Val's hand braced the base of my spine as men dressed in black clothing flanked us. It was too dark to get a look at their faces, and honestly, I didn't care to see them anyway.

Val's hand tightened around mine as he dragged me through the house. Suddenly, he moved it to my neck and shoved my face toward his chest "Keep your head down!"

My stomach twisted in knots. "Where are we going?"

"Somewhere else."

He sounded calm, and I desperately wanted to look in his eyes to make sure his eyes matched his voice. But his hold tightened, keeping me literally and figuratively in the dark.

"We've got you covered, *jefe*. There are four out front and two in the house. Stay down around the next corner. On my command, dive low and to the right into the car. I'm right behind you."

Ignoring instructions, my head popped up. "Emilio?"

Cursing, Val gripped my hair and bent me forward. "*Cereza,* get down!"

"Stop yelling at me!"

"Stop trying to get us killed!"

Heated taunts echoed from inside the house. "Where are you, you chickenshit? Face us and bring that *puta,* too, *El Muerte*!"

My heart pounded as he expertly maneuvered us around the corner and out a side door. Once outside, a blast exploded beside us, and Emilio let out a low groan.

Val paused, turning around. "What happened?"

With a hand on both of our backs, Emilio shoved us toward the car, his face twisted in pain. "Go! It's just a nick."

"Emilio…" Val called behind him, a sheen of sweat coating his forehead.

"Get in the fucking car before I kick your ass, Carrera." Clenching his teeth, Emilio held his side as his tanned skin turned a grayish-white color.

Without another word, Val picked me up at the waist and

threw me in the back seat of a dark colored sedan.

The pain on my boss's face etched in my mind, and despite the disdain I felt for him, I crawled toward the door. "You can't just leave him!"

Planting one foot inside the vehicle, Val propelled himself forward, knocking me onto my back. With the door closing behind him, the car lurched forward and peeled away from the house.

"Get off me!" I screamed, beating my fists against his chest.

"Stay down and shut up." Covering my mouth, he pressed his full weight onto me, pinning me where I lay.

As gunshots popped off in the distance, a tear rolled from each corner of my eyes.

I hated Emilio Reyes.

But even *I* knew that wasn't a nick.

THE BUZZING BECAME CLEARER AS THE ROOM CAME INTO FOCUS. Blinking repeatedly, I swallowed, my mouth feeling like I'd stuffed a bag of cotton balls down my throat. I attempted to find my voice as the buzzing morphed into voices.

"How the hell did they find us?"

"Don't know. Only the top level knew the safe house location. At this point, the only logical explanation is to start looking for a mole."

The sound of sloshing liquid filled the room as the voice switched back. "Fucking hell. I want everyone's house searched. No one is excluded, is that understood?"

"*Si, jefe.*"

With a fully functional brain, I shifted a gaze around the unfamiliar room. The guy who'd brought me food at the other

BLURRED RED LINES

house, Mateo, nodded as he exited the doorway, his eyes sagging from fatigue. A concentrated stare fell to my left, and with one glance, I quickly averted my eyes to the floor.

*Val.*

He sat in a chair four feet away from me, his hair disheveled, and a heavy five o'clock shadow covering his face. His hands cradled a half-emptied bottle of tequila between his legs. My lips twitched as multiple conversations ran through my mind regarding his disdain for assholes who drank tequila out of the bottle.

*I guess desperate times call for desperate assholes.*

Remembering the frantic exit from the safe house, I stretched, attempting to sit up and get a handle on my new surroundings. A sharp burn in my right arm caused me to cry out as I realized I was, once again, cuffed to the bedframe.

"You've got to be kidding me…"

Val steadied his eyes on the closed door in front of him and turned the bottle up, taking a generous drink. "Nope."

Drawing in a deep breath, I released it before speaking, reining in deep rooted anger. "Val, in the last forty-eight hours, I've been kidnapped, drugged, restrained, held prisoner, and shot at. Where the hell would I go?"

He shrugged, twisting the bottle in his hands. "Don't feel like getting stabbed with any more forks, thanks."

I darted my eyes to his bandaged arm and offered a fake smile. "You deserved it."

Glaring at me, he took another gulp from the bottle and resumed his stare at the wall.

Realizing the defensive approach was getting me nowhere, I tried another tactic and softened my tone. "After what happened in that room, I didn't think we needed restraints anymore."

His eyes darkened as the muscles in his jaw tightened. "That

155

was a mistake. It won't happen again."

While I'd already made the same promise to myself, somewhere inside it still cut deep to hear the words come from his mouth.

What we'd done had been born out of wrongness and hate, yet I'd never felt so alive. The guilt I'd felt afterward had been too overwhelming at the time to consider exploring what that meant.

Sex had always been on my terms since Davis left. For some reason, Val dismissing what we'd done pissed me off and immediately set me on the defensive.

I jerked on the cuff again, to express my irritation. "Then why bring me here at all? Why keep me alive? Obviously, I'm trouble for you and your little operation. You could have let them kill me back there and be done with me."

Val cocked his head to the side, assessing me. "I don't know. It'd make sense for a man in my position to have been done with you. It's not like I haven't killed before." He sat back in his chair, seeming to mull over his answer. "But you're different. There's always been something about you. Maybe I see myself in you." In a sudden shift of questioning, he pointed the mouth of the bottle in my direction. "What happened to you, *Cereza,* to make you so hollow?"

Taken aback by his personal question, I pressed my medallion between my finger and thumb, rubbing it while I stalled for time.

"Eden?"

"I'm nothing like you."

He chuckled and drank from the bottle again. "We're still alive, aren't we?"

*Alive and alone.*

Sighing, I turned my back to him. His penetrating stare

heated my skin just a little too much and confused the hell out of me.

My whole world had tilted on its axis and spun in the opposite direction.

Somehow, I'd landed myself front and center in the middle of the entire Carrera operation—the same men I'd believed were responsible for murdering my brother.

For hours, I'd wanted nothing more than to escape their hold on me. As I sat with the pathetic excuse for a weapon, waiting for the kingpin to get close enough to cause damage, a plan had started to formulate.

But maybe escape wasn't the answer.

I'd sworn to Nash and my father I'd find the men responsible and see them dead. What better way to do that than in the lair of the snake himself?

Val Carrera swore a rival cartel held the smoking gun. Did I believe him, or had a moment of sexual weakness blinded my judgment of the truth?

I had no idea.

But one thing was for sure, I'd never find out standing outside the lines of their inner circle.

Knocked out of my internal tug-of-war, the mattress dipped with weight as Val's hand dusted over my cheek, gently turning it to face him. "I promise not to let anything happen to you, Eden."

His slightly slurred voice washed over me with a deep cadence. Immediately, images of being together in the basement of the safe house raced my pulse as my body flooded with warmth.

His lingering touch quickened my breath, and I centered all thought on that one point of contact.

"Don't make promises you can't keep."

The words seemed to resonate something deep within him.

Furrowing his brow, he dropped his hand back to his lap and nodded softly. "You're right. I'll never make that mistake again."

*"There's always been something about you. Maybe I see myself in you."*

I wanted to ask him what he meant, but a wall blanketed his face, ending any further communication.

Somehow, I'd touched a nerve without knowing it.

Sighing, I reached over as far as the restraint would allow and grabbed the bottle from him. Silently, I drank long and steady. The warm liquid burned a trail of fire down my throat, and I welcomed every drop. Wordlessly, we passed the bottle back and forth until only a sip remained between us.

Enough time and alcohol had passed that liquid courage built inside of me. Draining the last of it, I tossed the bottle across the room and turned to face him, my head wobbling heavily on my neck. "Is Emilio dead?"

Running his hand through his hair, Val raised an eyebrow, smirking with delivered intent. "Do you care?"

"What kind of ridiculous question is that?" I moved to punch his chest, forgetting my arm was cuffed and performed a slingshot back against the bedframe. "Ow."

"Watch out for that."

"Wow, thanks for pointing out the obvious."

"It's a valid question."

I scrunched up my nose. "Huh?"

"Your question."

"What question?"

Groaning, he scraped his hand down his face. "The one you asked, *Cereza.*"

"You asked *me* a question." I had no idea what we were arguing about, but my stubborn streak kept giving me the thumbs-up and a high five.

"I didn't ask you any fucking question. This is why I should've left you there."

"A-ha!" I screamed, pointing my free finger in his chest. "I knew it! See? I told you that you were trying to kill me."

Val wrapped his fingers around my wrist and held it in a strong grip between us. "I never said that. Stop putting words between my mouth."

A loud snort rolled off my tongue as I fell backward against the bedframe again. "Ow!" I rubbed the back of my head and bit my lip to keep from laughing. "Oh, my God, you're drunk. I think you meant 'stop putting words *in* my mouth.' If I put words *between* your mouth, I'd be connected to it."

His fingers tightened against my wrist, and he pulled me flush against him. Danger glinted across his darkened eyes. "That could be arranged."

Overwhelmed at the intensity in his stare, I focused on the hold he had on my arm. Licking dry lips, I said the first thing that popped into my head. "Is Emilio dead?"

"No," he smiled knowingly. Releasing his hold, he sat back like I'd just jumped from his fuck list to his shit list in two-point-oh-seconds.

*Story of my life.*

Since the first flame had been doused, I might as well dance in the ashes.

"But I saw him get shot. You can try to tell me otherwise, but I saw it. I know what I saw."

"I'm sure you saw what you saw."

"So?" I waited for confirmation.

"So? We all get shot from time to time. He'll be fine. It was a flesh wound."

My mouth dropped open. "Do you realize how asinine you sound right now? People just don't get shot from time to time,

Danger. Not normal people, at least."

He wiped a hand across his mouth as if to hide an emerging smirk. "Danger?"

Shaking my cuffed wrist, I narrowed my eyes to hostile slits. "Don't get cocky. It's not a term of endearment. I can't stand you."

"You're not exactly my favorite person either, you know," he offered quickly.

The alcohol bottomed out in my system, and my mouth claimed the throne, taking ownership of my better judgment. "Then why don't you get out of here and go fuck yourself? At least you'd satisfy one of us."

The smug look drained from his face, only to be replaced by darkened fury. Before I could blink, his palm engulfed my cheek, bending me backward until our mouths and lips bruised in a punishing kiss. His free hand buried in my hair, twisting with a need barreling from somewhere deep within.

Once my alcohol-infused brain caught up with what was happening, my libido went into overdrive, kicking what reservation wasn't slovenly drunk behind locked doors.

Wrapping my unrestrained arm around his neck, I pulled him closer, lost in the feel of his hardness pressing heavy against my curves.

Rage and passion ran parallel with Val and me, and as we frantically groped each other, I wondered where the line lay between manslaughter and sex. As his hands ran down the length of my body and his lips whispered dirty Spanish in my ear, I questioned both our sanity.

Trailing his mouth down the hollow of my neck, he dove his fingers under the waistband of my shorts. *"Esta panocha es mía."* This pussy is mine.

"Who's *El Muerte*?"

The words came out of nowhere. From behind the locked door where I shoved her, my subconscious stood on the headboard, hands on her hips, eyebrow cocked, and armed with three words I had no clue I'd even verbalized until Val froze.

Swallowing harshly, he dragged his hand from my shorts and sat up, his face twisted with a mix of shock and loss. Pressing the heel of his palm in between his eyes, he inhaled slowly, counting to ten before answering.

"Why do you ask?"

"When we were running... I heard the men who shot at us scream for you to face them. They called me a *puta* and you *El Muerte*. I don't know much Spanish, but I know what a *puta* is." Something in his eyes drew me away from him and into the corner of the bed. "What I don't know is what *El Muerte* means. Val, I heard the men say it when they killed Nash, too."

Grabbing the empty bottle, Val moved off the bed and stood in the middle of the room, pinching the bridge of his nose with his thumb and forefinger. A confusing rush of guilt swept through me at the emotion wrestling inside of him. Finally, he dropped his hand and tilted his chin over his shoulder, his face a mask of blank resolve.

"*El Muerte* means The Reaper. The Reaper is me, *Cereza*. It's the name the Muñoz Cartel gave me. Unspeakable crimes have been committed in the name of *El Muerte*. Some I have been a part of; some I haven't. Men, who were determined to see me ruined, murdered the wife and child of Manuel Muñoz and carved the name in their foreheads."

The room felt half its size and lacked air. "Jesus."

Val's smile pulled downward. "No, *Cereza*...Jesus was nowhere near Guadalajara when Manuel Muñoz's family died. Just as I suspect that he turned a blind eye when your brother took a bullet to the head and had the same words carved in his skin."

Tears rolled before I knew they'd formed and a wounded cry tore from my throat. My hand clutched the St. Michael medallion hanging around my neck. "No…"

A hint of sadness hung heavy in Val's eyes as he nodded toward my hand. "I'd hold tighter if I were you, Eden. It's not over." Shuffling to the door, he flung it open and paused in the entryway. "It's only just begun."

# Chapter Seventeen
## VALENTIN

*Sometimes a man just needs to handle business.*

At least that's what I kept telling myself as I left Eden sleeping in the safe house the next morning and drove to RVC Enterprises. Keeping up appearances seemed a necessary evil and getting out of a house where she proved to be a constant temptation was essential to my sanity.

She knew about *El Muerte*.

That meant all bets were off.

Indulging in Eden Lachey had been the biggest lapse in judgment I'd ever willingly been a part of. Giving in to her weakened my authority within the entire cartel. Not only had I allowed her to see me lose control, my men could tuck away the dangerous knowledge that I'd protected her with my own life in the safe house.

She had no idea in that unguarded moment in the basement, she'd stolen everything from me.

My sanity.

My rationality.

My indifference.

I'd held her in my arms, knowing my world had just ended. I was completely fucked.

Sitting at my desk, I raked both palms down my face. God, I needed sleep. The last time I'd closed my eyes for a substantial amount of time... Shit, I couldn't remember when I'd closed my eyes. Every time I tried, images of her head thrown back as she violently came around me found me in a cold shower at three a.m.

I'd fucked hundreds of women. Not one of them mattered enough to think about after the door hit them in the ass on the way out of my bedroom.

Heartless?

*Maybe.*

But something in Eden Lachey's pale blue eyes haunted me. There was a hidden vulnerability that desperately wanted to be needed and needed to be wanted. She floated without belonging—one impulsive act away from self-destruction—and not giving a damn one way or another. She silently screamed for salvation and craved isolation.

She frustrated the shit out of me. Because she *was* me.

I had to live this way. My life had no choices, but I'd fuck some sense into Eden if it was the last thing I did.

Either that, or I'd be the cleanest motherfucker in Houston from living in my goddamn shower.

Scrubbing my face again, I let out a frustrated growl, shaking my head to focus on the problem currently screwing up the pipeline of my organization. Checking my phone, I verified no missed calls from Mateo. It was only a matter of time before the Colombians sent a collector for the eleven million I owed them. With the lost shipment, I had no product to move to compensate for the trade.

Fucked didn't begin to describe my situation.

The whole operation reeked of Muñoz involvement, but I couldn't figure out how they'd pulled it off with so many government officials on my payroll. They had a presence in Houston, but nowhere near the reach and infiltration the Carreras had for years.

Something else had to factor in. I just needed to find it.

And where the fuck did Nash and Eden Lachey fit into all of this? They should've been insignificant to someone like Manuel Muñoz.

Unless Mateo's theory proved to be right, and a mole had infiltrated my cartel.

The thought sent a sharp haze of red across my vision. I picked up the nearest object on my desk, which just happened to be a coffee mug, and hurled it against the closed office door.

"Fuck!" I'd just reached for my laptop when my phone vibrated. Anxious for an update from Mateo, I accepted the call without hesitation. "You'd better have good news."

"It depends, son. Is the *puta* still in your possession?"

I grew up hearing the man's rapid-fire Spanish barked in harsh commands to everyone from my mother to high ranking soldiers. However, the moment his broken English slithered through the phone, attempting to sound worldly and refined, I found the revolt in my throat almost palpable.

"I know you didn't cut your happy ending short to ask me that, did you, Alejandro?"

His low chuckle unsettled me. "You get *one*, Valentin. Another disrespectful comment will cost you a lieutenant. You're fond of this Mateo Cortes, yes?"

I remained silent. Responding would only jeopardize my crew and one of my best men. One-upping my father wasn't worth the risk. Mateo was the closest thing I had to a friend, and in this business, loyalty wasn't to be taken lightly.

Alejandro took my silence as compliance. "This woman, Valentin…she weakens you."

"I'm handling her."

"How? By shielding a cunt while Muñoz bullets hit your men?"

"Don't call her that." I gripped the phone, slamming my fist onto the desk with the other as I cursed myself for letting him provoke me into reacting.

"*Tsk, tsk, tsk,* Valentin. You fucked this woman, didn't you?"

I had to think fast. The moment Alejandro Carrera knew Eden mattered to me, she'd be a marked target.

The words boiled like acid on my tongue as I choked them out. "I wanted it, so I took it."

His laugh of approval chipped away at my soul. "*Bien*! This woman…she fought you, yes?"

I pulled at my collar, jerking three buttons loose to breathe as I lied. "Yes."

"My boy." The sense of pride in his voice swirled the coffee in my stomach and threatened to bring it back up. "Now, kill her."

I didn't cry out or protest. I wouldn't give my father the satisfaction of my begging. On some level, my subconscious expected the words to come as almost a natural progression of his pride in Eden's fictional rape.

I was literally the son of a sick bastard.

Instead, I placated him as my mind raced a hundred miles an hour crafting different plausible plans to keep her safe.

"Fine. But I need you to find out why the Muñoz intel seems to be always ten steps ahead of me, and why they're so interested in her. Before I take care of her, I need to know how she fits into their plan. Somehow, she's the key to their sabotage."

I had no clue what I was saying, but hopefully it bought me enough time to figure it out.

Quiet for what seemed like a lifetime, Alejandro sighed low to show his annoyance. "Very well. Gerardo will see what he can find out."

"Thank you, I—"

"But, Valentin, there are no promises. I'll put my top man on this, but whether he finds information or not…the *pinche puta* has forty-eight hours."

Before I could respond, the line went dead. As with most conversations with Alejandro Carrera, the last word always began and ended on his terms.

*Forty-eight hours.*

Grabbing the phone again, I dialed Mateo.

I hoped it was enough to buy a miracle.

STANDING OUTSIDE THE SAFE HOUSE, THE GUN WEIGHED HEAVY IN MY palm as I watched her through the window. Helpless and weak, she lay exactly where I left her six hours earlier on the bed, shackled with a defeated look painted across her gorgeous face.

Up until now, my life held no confusion. I counted clarity among one of my many virtues, knowing exactly who I was and which side of the law my foot planted on.

Gray areas didn't exist in my world.

Until her.

Flipping the cold metal over and over in my palm, sweat gathered on my brow as her worn tank top shifted and rode up her ribcage.

Indecisiveness festered in that gray area the moment Eden Lachey crashed into my life. Clarity ceased to exist, and the cut-

and-dried life of a criminal wasn't as easily separated from a conscience I thought I'd long since abandoned.

Fuck, why didn't she pull that tank top down?

I closed my fingers around the gun. Alejandro's voice echoed in my head.

*Forty-eight hours.*

My father's orders were never disobeyed. The moment the Mexico contingent of the Carrera Cartel came after Eden, her death would be slow and torturous. They'd violate her in ways that forced crimson streaks across my vision.

If Mateo gave her a loaded injection of M99, she'd peacefully fall asleep within seconds. There'd be no pain—only eternal rest. I'd make sure above all else, no one would take her dignity from her.

*What the hell?*

Stumbling backward, I fought a wave of nausea that barreled up my chest. Pressing the hand holding the gun against my lips, I puffed out my cheeks, willing the impending dry heaves back down my throat.

*I'm a monster.*

Did I seriously just contemplate poisoning Eden because it was the *humane* thing to do?

Unlocking the front door, I pushed my way inside, angry at the world for mind-fucking me. The moment I reached Eden, she sat up, her eyes wide with dark circles lining the bottom. Leaning over with purpose, I tightened my grip around the metal in my hand, knowing I didn't need forty-eight hours to make this call.

It was going on four days I'd kept her locked up. No one should have to endure that.

My father was right. This ended now.

Capturing her wrist, I avoided her stare, as I pinched the metal and extended my arm in front of me.

She gasped as one strangled word whispered past her dry lips. "Val..."

"It's time, *Cereza*." With a heavy heart, I inserted the key and unlocked the cuff. The metal clanked against the bedframe as it fell off her wrist and disappeared behind the mattress.

We both stared at it, lips tight, the moment taking both of us by surprise.

Finally, with no purpose for it, I let the key fall from my fingers and bounce on the floor. "I'm going to check on the stash houses. I'll be back in a few hours. You can go where you want."

Unable to take her incessant staring, I swallowed and reached for the door. Before I could turn the knob, she scrambled off the mattress, holding onto my wrist with both hands.

"Eden..." I closed my eyes, willing her to stop this game we'd been playing.

"Val..." Her voice broke, betraying a vulnerability I didn't expect. "Before you came back, I had a dream that you didn't..." She paused, her throat working hard to form the words. "I woke up, and no one was here. I was scared. It seemed so real."

"You've been through a lot; that's going to happen." I hated how cold my voice sounded, but I had to start distancing myself from her. It wasn't safe for either one of us to become attached.

A flash of irritation crossed her face. "No, jackass, it wasn't about me." As quickly as her anger rose, it faded, the memory shaking her confidence again. "I'm worried about you."

"Don't worry about me, *Cereza*." A genuine smile crossed my lips. "I've been doing this for a lot longer than you. I've got a few of my nine lives left."

Contemplating my dismissal with a scowl, Eden furiously rubbed her forefinger and thumb across the pendant hanging around her neck. Raising a questioning brow, I glanced down at the strong hold she continued to have on my wrist.

Still in deep thought, she sighed, releasing my arm and taking a few steps backward, a worried line cresting in the middle of her forehead. Giving her an obligatory nod, I turned once more toward the door.

"Hey, Danger…"

Glancing over my shoulder, I watched as, in a rash moment, Eden slipped the medallion off her neck and pressed it into the palm of my hand.

"Eden…no."

She shook her head stubbornly. "Take it. It's for luck. It'll protect you."

I raised an eyebrow. "Like it protected you?"

"We're still alive, aren't we?" she said, throwing my own words back at me. "Besides," she lowered her eyes, a smile playing on the corner of her mouth, "it hasn't been all bad."

Before I knew I'd moved, I crushed her against me, dragging my lips across her jaw. Closing my eyes, I inhaled the familiar scent of her skin. Fusing our mouths together, I drank from her lips like a starving man.

The woman had a way of being my verbal undoing.

And goddamn it, I was keeping her.

I kissed her once more and raked the pad of my thumb over her bottom lip. "I'm coming back tonight. This isn't over."

One corner of her mouth curled in a knowing smirk as she walked backward toward the bathroom. "I don't suppose you have anything I could change into while you're gone, do you?"

I never turned around as I closed the door behind me. "Why would I do that?"

"WHAT DO YOU MEAN THE TRUCK NEVER MADE IT?"

The flannel clad warehouse guard shrugged, stopping to take a long drag off his cigarette before answering. "I mean it never made it. It was scheduled to come in off Highway 59 from Victoria, when it just went away." He waved his hands in the air to simulate evaporating smoke.

I pinched the bridge of my nose, attempting to keep myself from reaching into my waistband and pumping an entire round into this asshole. "Eighteen-wheelers don't just vanish, Enrique. It's kind of fucking hard to get rid of an entire truck bed of shark bellies stuffed with cocaine. It's not exactly underpass transfer cargo."

He blew another smoke ring before stomping the butt out at the entrance to the stash house. "Don't know what to tell you. No truck, no coke. You can search the place if you want."

*"Odio mi vida!" Fuck my life!* Pissed at the second missing Colombian shipment in the past two days, I pulled my fist back and coldcocked the guy in the side of the face.

Knocked into the corner of the stash house, Enrique grabbed his face, wisely choosing not to retaliate. "Jesus, man, what the hell was that for?"

Shaking my fist, I swore as my knuckles throbbed. "For being a useless asshole. You're lucky I don't blow your dick off and make you smoke it."

Muttering to himself, he quickly made his way back inside and closed the door, intermittently glancing in between the blinds to see if I'd left. Just to be a dick, I stood around, sizing up the property, wondering what possibly could've gone wrong.

Only one word made sense. Muñoz. The root of all things fucked.

Shit with Manuel Muñoz was escalating, and interference of this magnitude called for a face-to-face meeting.

Resigned to what had to be done, I reached for my phone.

Instead, my fingers pulled a long chain from my pocket, attached to a small medallion with a porcelain top. Running my thumb over the smooth face, I studied the design. It depicted a scene of St. Michael attacking and defeating the fallen enemy torn. Surrounding the image were written the words:

*O St. Michael, give us your strength*

*To defeat our fears*

*And rise to any challenge*

She'd given me a medallion for protection. The irony wasn't lost on me.

Here I stood, rubbing the image of an archangel, asking it to give protection to a murderer doomed to hell. On a whim, I brought it to my lips and kissed the smooth finish.

No one had ever given me blind faith. I had no idea what to do with it.

Standing outside the warehouse alone, I could be honest with myself. She'd gotten to me a little.

Fine. Fuck, she'd turned me inside out.

I recognized the darkness inside her, and it called to me. Maybe it was wrong to fan the flame, but I couldn't stop myself. It didn't take much for her to transform from a tragic victim who begged for her release, to a cunning warrior, free falling into a world she knew nothing about, yet craved.

If we burned…now we burned together.

Swinging the medallion around my neck, I glanced at my watch and sighed. Ten-forty-seven p.m. It'd been a long drive to Corpus Christi, and it'd be a long drive back to Houston.

And there was still unfinished business waiting for me at the safe house.

Smiling to myself, I shook my head at the empty stash house and turned toward my Lexus. Lost in thought, I'd just reached for my keys when the ground shook beneath my feet and an explosion lit up the night sky, knocking me airborne.

I remembered feeling weightless before a searing pain crushed my skull and silence echoed into a dark hum of nothing.

# Chapter Eighteen
## EDEN

Mateo and Emilio sat at the small, wooden kitchen table, huddled together well after midnight. Their brows alternately raised and lowered as they talked in hushed tones. Occasionally, they'd glance over at me. Whether it was out of suspicion or concern, I had no idea, and, honestly, I didn't give a shit. My mind raced, trying to catch every third word that passed between them.

Mateo's hand brushed his mouth, as his other palmed his long dark hair. "Crew…there…now."

"Flames? Any survivors?" Emilio shifted positions, still holding his bandaged ribcage.

It didn't take a genius to figure out their conversation. Only one person's whereabouts would have their phones ringing off the hook and hands scrubbing their faces every ten seconds.

*Val.*

My eyes closed, attempting to block out what had been unfolding. As they whispered, I paced, absent-mindedly rubbing the tender ring around my wrist where the handcuff used to rest against my skin.

A war raged inside of me, and with every stride across thread-bare carpet, I chewed my nails to slivers.

Out of nowhere, a horrifying thought gut punched me. "You think he's dead."

Mateo raised an eyebrow, taking in my hardened stare. "We didn't say that."

"You didn't have to."

A tightened squeeze on his phone was his only response as he lowered his eyes.

From what I'd gathered in eavesdropping from my curled-up seat on the couch, a neighboring textile factory called in an explosion to the Corpus Christi Fire Department concerning an abandoned warehouse five miles off Highway 59. Mateo got the call from one of his crew members two hours ago, causing chaos to erupt at the safe house.

Within minutes, Emilio arrived, and men came in and out, all eyeing me up like I was some kind of black widow.

Maybe I was.

If the rumors were true about Val, the last two men I remotely had any sort of relationship with had been murdered.

I'd never recover from losing Nash. The memory of being in that kitchen would haunt me until my last breath, but the thought of Val walking into an explosion forced a reaction out of me I didn't expect.

He'd made me his prisoner. He indirectly had a hand in my brother's death. Yet, I found myself clawing at my neck for my St. Michael medallion, offering up a prayer for his protection.

Of course, my fingers scraped nothing but bare skin.

*"Hey, Danger..."*

*"Eden...no."*

*"Take it. It's for luck. It'll protect you."*

*"Like it protected you?"*

*"We're still alive, aren't we?"*

I just hoped it'd done its job. With Nash gone, and my father on the run, I realized the man who'd initially held me against my will had become all I had left. Whether morally right or wrong, I needed him. I didn't give a shit what anyone else thought. I never did.

Mateo's phone rang again, knocking me out of my introspective revelation.

"To the ground?" The lines in his forehead deepened. "How many bodies?"

Reality slapped me cold in the face. "Bodies?" Running to the table, I braced my palms against the edge. "Whose bodies? How many?"

Mateo dismissed me with a wave. "How long before the medical examiner can identify?" With a slow shake of his head, he sat back in the chair and raked a hand over his sparse goatee. "Send extra men and call me the minute you find anything. Search the car, search the area…fuck, search within a ten-mile radius." Ending the call, he cursed under his breath.

"Is he dead?"

A deeper voice called out to me. "Sit down, Eden."

Panic shifted my attention toward Emilio. "What do *you* know?"

"Don't stick your nose into business you know nothing about, Eden O'Dell," he bit out, refusing to look at me.

"Lachey."

"Whatever."

It took me half a second to lose my shit.

Nine days of physical restraint, fear, and hunger strikes simultaneously set me off. Pushing off the table, I lunged at him, my fists curling into his dirty white button-up shirt as I shoved my nose against his in a bold move.

"My last name is Lachey. You remember it, don't you, boss? You said it enough when you beat the shit out of my brother." Bottled up anger and grief exploded into an uncontrollable verbal tirade.

Val explained that their rival cartel orchestrated Nash's execution, and for some fucked-up reason, I believed him. Emilio didn't kill my family, but when I didn't know if the man I needed more than I cared to admit was alive or dead, rationality wasn't a high priority.

Emilio's eyes widened. "Get the hell off me, you crazy bitch!"

"Wrong answer." Letting go of his shirt, I slapped him hard across the face.

"Eden!" Mateo called my name as Emilio blinked rapidly— frozen—as if he literally couldn't process the concept a female had just assaulted him.

*Fuck, that felt good.*

I took a swing at Mateo, and he caught my fist midair, curling his fingers around its momentum.

"Tell me what happened, goddamn it!" I screamed, struggling against his hold.

"We don't know! A bomb went off at the stash house, leveling everything. The building is gone. A few beams are standing, that's all. We don't know if he was inside or not. All we know is his car was there, and it's fucking barbecued." Grunting, he grabbed my other hand as I fought against him. "Jesus, will you calm the hell down? Why do you even care?"

"I don't!"

"Could've fooled me. You're acting like a destroyed lover."

"Piss off, Mateo."

He narrowed his eyes. "What's with you and Val? He's

never given two shits about witnesses before. The man is cold as fuck. Who *are* you?" Without warning, he jerked me to his chest, his breath fanning my cheek. "Are you working for the Muñoz family?"

I pushed my forearms against him, digging my elbows into his sternum. "What? No! Get off me, Mateo. What the hell is wrong with you?"

"He's got a point," Emilio offered with a raised brow as he leaned against the table, his face darkening. "You conveniently get a job at my bar under an expired name, somehow escape a Muñoz hit, end up our prisoner—live better than our men, I might add—and the *jefe* refuses to let anyone get near you but him." A sneer coated his weathered face. "Either you've got a magic cunt or you're a Muñoz pump."

The room organized against me in a move I never saw coming.

Me? Muñoz? They had to be kidding. Still, their leader and friend was missing and, for all they knew, presumed dead. Clear thinking didn't seem to be taking precedence now.

I'd unknowingly become the third contestant in the Blame Game, and the two main contestants played rough and dirty.

*Well, game on.*

Dipping my chin, I bit down hard on Mateo's left wrist.

Cursing at a deafening level, he released his hold and stumbled backward. "You fucking bit me!"

"Don't call me a cunt. *Ever.*"

Shoving a finger past my face, he pointed toward Emilio. "I didn't! *He* did. Christ, you're insane, you know that?"

"I'm not a Muñoz anything. I'm a miserable bartender whose life got ripped out from under her by your cartel bullshit." I resumed pacing, as if I hadn't just turned Rottweiler on a drug runner. "I thought my life was shitty before. God, it was a goddamn Hallmark card compared to this. So, my husband stuck his dick in my best friend, and my father blew all our money on coke…sucks, right? Right. But this?" I threw my arms out, indicating the insanity of the situation. "*This* elevates suck to a whole new realm. This is…this is suck, blow, *and* swallow. This is a whole face fuck of fuck."

I had no clue what spewed out of my mouth. Fear for Val and rage toward their accusations, afflicted me with a sudden case of panic-laden Tourette's.

"Look, let's just all calm down, all right?" Mateo sighed, running his hand under the faucet. "My men will call back with an update, and then we can decide what to do."

I shot him a look. "What to do? Don't you mean, 'what to do with the pain in the ass, rabid bitch'?"

I had a million and one questions, and even more smartass remarks to back them up, but an impending breakdown shut me up. My nerves had fried to a crisp, and I'd worn a hole in the carpet with over four hours of pacing.

Honestly, I had no clue why either of them didn't just cuff me back to the bed and be done with it.

*I would've.*

I'd just shoved my fingers back in my mouth—going for round seventeen on what was left of my nails—when I heard the lock turn.

If a sound existed of breath lodging in one's own throat, it exploded in my ears.

No one moved, as all eyes focused on the doorknob. My heart pounded so hard I could see the thin fabric of Val's black T-shirt vibrate against my chest.

I had a fingernail sandwiched in between my teeth as the door opened.

The minute he stepped through it, all the air in the room

seemed to suck out with the momentum of his steps, choking the breath out of me. He paused in the entryway, our eyes connecting with a ferocity that almost knocked me off my feet.

He was dirty—filthy, actually—covered in soot and ash. His pants leg flapped open, torn up the side with a jagged rip. Blood poured down his tanned leg as well as both exposed arms. His t-shirt had burn marks, stained with the same scarlet patches as his limbs. The always-perfectly-styled midnight black hair fell shaggily over his ears and forehead. Cuts and gashes marred his perfect face, his bottom lip sliced at the corner, and a trickle of dried blood trailed from his right ear.

He was fucked up, but he was alive.

And we all stared at him as if a ghost walked straight through the front door.

# *Chapter Nineteen*
## EDEN

I opened my mouth, but no words came out.

In the distance, I vaguely recognized Mateo calling his name, demanding to know what had happened and that he see doctor. However, the noise faded into the background as his lips parted, and a labored breath fell from his chest.

The relief I felt scared me.

I'd always shook my head at the concept of Stockholm Syndrome. Who the hell could fall for someone who'd kidnapped and kept them prisoner from their friends and family? Those women were weak and stupid.

I rationalized that this wasn't Stockholm. Val had uncuffed me and walked out. I could've escaped.

Why didn't I?

*Weak and stupid…party-of-one, your table is now available.*

Obsession was a nasty little word.

I'd been obsessed with being who Davis always expected me to be, no matter how much it went against everything I believed. I swore after our divorce, I'd never allow myself to fall that deep under someone's control again.

"Val…" Before I knew it, I'd cleared the room. Flinging myself into his arms, I wound my hands around his neck, desperate to reassure myself he was real, and that I wasn't imagining him out of desperation.

As I clung to him, he stiffened, his eyes trained across the room. Eventually, he dusted a hand across my lower back, giving it a light pat.

*A pat? He freaking patted me like an obedient puppy?*

Slowly releasing him, I swallowed hard, my face flaming with embarrassment. Risking a glance up at his face, something shattered inside as I took in his tightened jaw, cold eyes, and emotionless expression.

How could I have been so wrong?

Backing up as if he were fire, and I'd just blistered a finger, I suddenly wished for my own clothes and a blanket. The inherent chill in the room froze the life out of me, and I folded my arms across my chest in self-preservation mode.

I had no clue what I hoped to accomplish with it now. I'd already tipped my hand.

"You look like shit."

*There we go. Change the tide with flattery.*

"Long day." With a quick nod of acknowledgement, he moved stiffly toward the kitchen table. "What do we know?"

A flicker of emotion passed across Mateo's face before official business wiped it clean. "Waiting for a report now, but it looks like a bomb. How about you tell *us*?"

"Hell, if I know," he said, palming the back of his neck and wincing. "One minute I was threatening to blow Enrique's dick off, the next I was eating asphalt. I blacked out and woke up three hundred feet away from my car…or what the hell was left of it, anyway. Two steps to the left and I'd probably fit in a Ziploc sandwich bag right now." His laugh came off dry as he eased himself onto the chair next to Emilio. "One of your men gave me a ride. I think it's a given where this is coming from. It's the second shipment in days to not make it to a stash house."

Emilio sat up, his hand still pressed to his side. "You're shitting me? Another Colombian drop is gone?"

Val nodded, his eyes glazed and tired. "I don't know how those assholes are getting inside information. They seem to know exactly when and where the drops are going to be made, and not only that, how the hell did they know I'd be in Corpus Christi tonight? For that matter, how'd they find the other safe house?" He glanced at Mateo. "Did you search for a leak?"

"Everyone checks out, *jefe*. Every lieutenant went to extremes, too." Mateo shot me a look before lowering his voice. "They went old country persuasion, if you get what I'm saying."

I got exactly what he was saying.

You didn't live in Houston your whole life without knowing a little drug cartel folklore. They were as much of an urban legend as Santa Claus and the Tooth Fairy. Except, these legends didn't just come down your chimney and take your teeth. They also took your family and life, splattering both across all four walls of your bedroom.

Old country persuasion meant the soldiers under each lieutenant most likely had a family member on their knees with a gun to the back of the head as incentive.

Nothing prompted action quicker than watching your flesh and blood die.

I knew that first hand.

"What about outsider infiltration?" Emilio mumbled with a sharp side-eye in my direction.

I held my breath.

I could hold my own with Dumb and Dumber; however, as

confusing as my feelings were for him, Val Carrera was a volatile man. By the way he shoved me aside like an outgrown pair of shoes moments before, that much was clear.

If his lieutenants convinced him I'd somehow betrayed him, the consequences could be deadly.

Val caught my eye and held it far too long for my liking. "Impossible. I screen all outsiders personally. No one has access to that information." He shook his head, effectively dismissing their suggestion. "From now on, no phone conversations about anything, am I understood?"

"Yes, *jefe*." Both men agreed.

"We communicate in person or not at all. No one gets shipment details but the three of us, or any details of my location. The next attack won't be a close call. It'll be an exact hit from either a Muñoz or a Colombian bullet." A strange look crossed Val's face as he directed a stare at Mateo. "If they succeed, by two witness rule, you're to take control of this cartel."

Mateo's eyes widened with dark undertones. "*Jefe*, that's not going to happen—"

"Yes, or no, Mateo? Do you accept, or do I need to find someone who can make a decision?"

Evidently, rank presided over friendship in cartel warfare.

"*Acepto.*"

"*Muy bien.*" Seemingly overpowered by sudden fatigue, Val rose from his chair and nodded to the two men. "That'll be all."

"But, *jefe*," Emilio protested, gesturing to his bloody limbs. "You need to see the doc."

*The* doc? Who the hell was *the* doc? Did they have their own?

*Must be the shithead vet with the endless supply of M99.*

"Yes, Emilio, I realize that," he commented, glancing at his tattered clothing. "But not today. It's got to be close to four o'clock in the goddamn morning, and I'm exhausted. It's nothing that can't be tended to in a few hours."

"Val…"

"Now!"

With a dip of their chins, both men rose from the table, and keeping their heads down, exited through the front door without another word.

*Interesting.*

I would've fought harder for him to see *the doc.*

Of course, after the cold shoulder and brush-off I got at the door, I was hardly in any position to push for a "how do you do," much less demand medical attention for a drug lord.

"Well, glad to see you're alive and in one piece." Antsy and awkward, I rubbed my damp palms down my legs. Risking a glance up, I caught Val eyeing my bare thigh.

In a bold move, I'd showered in his bathroom. Stealing his razor, I'd attempted to get rid of the small forest that had grown on my legs during my imprisonment. Rummaging through his bag, I chose a pair of black boxers, rolled down until they hung low on my hips, and a black button-down shirt that smelled of his cologne.

As pissed as I was right now, I'd kill for a parka and a poncho.

"Are you?"

"What kind of question is that? You think I want you dead?"

"Not many people would blame you." Pinning me with a deadly stare, he grunted as he reached behind him and grasped his T-shirt, pulling it over his head in one swift jerk.

"What are you doing?" The man was a master manipulator and knew how to push my buttons. Figuring out whether we were having a civil conversation or if he was trying to bait me proved impossible.

He paused, his bloody shirt balled in his hands. "I'm getting dressed for dinner at the White House, *Cereza*. What the hell does it look like I'm doing? I need to shower. Almost being blown up will do that to you."

I forced my stare away from his defined abs and narrow hips. "Right. Well, I'll leave you to it."

Blowing a rough breath out, I took two steps toward the room I'd been sleeping in, when a strong hand wrapped around my upper arm.

"Eden, wait. You know I couldn't let my men see that side of us."

Pride overrode the electricity from his touch.

"What? No friendly pat-down this time? Maybe you'd prefer a fist-bump, instead?" Smirking, I held out my fist in front of his bare chest, poised and ready. When he just stared at me, I pursed my lips, and raised it higher. "You just going to leave me hanging, *bro*?"

Lowering his eyes to glare at my clenched fingers, he mumbled a few low curses in Spanish before engulfing my much smaller fist with his own and jerking me into his broad chest. In a similar motion as when he opened the door, his arm snaked around my lower back, but this time, instead of a light pat, his large palm spread across my ass, gripping it tightly before lifting upward and hauling me flush against him.

"You know what I'd prefer, *Cereza*?" he growled, his voice laced with a tinge of threat.

"A shower?" Our lips, a whisper apart, grazed with each word we spoke.

Fire burned in his eyes. "For starters."

I opened my mouth to tell him to go fucking take one when he pinned our entwined fists to the side of my head and plunged his tongue past my lips. Startled, his incessant demands overpowered me as our mouths fought for dominance.

Gasping for air from his onslaught, my free arm wound itself in his disheveled hair, tugging at the out-of-place strands as I pressed my body closer against him. Simultaneous groans poured into each other as the hand clutching my ass gave an insistent shove inward, my stomach pressing hard against an impatient erection begging to be released.

Pants became moans as Val slid his lips across my jaw and down my throat. I arched my back, physically unable to get any closer, but trying regardless.

What the hell was happening to me?

Five minutes ago, he treated me like the lights flickered after last call, and he'd seen exactly what he had been about to take home and changed his mind. Now, he kissed me like he wanted to crawl inside me and hibernate for the winter.

Releasing my fist, his hand trailed by my lips then grazed the buttons at the top of my shirt, popping them one by one.

"I thought…" Swallowing hard, I groaned as he sucked the top of my breast into the heat of his mouth. "I thought…ah, fuck, I don't remember what I thought."

Leaning my head back, I gripped his hair hard, unable to contain the lusty whimper when his tongue trailed across the length of my chest.

"Eden…" His hands skimmed up my ribcage with fierce intent. I'd barely taken a breath when he fisted each side of my shirt below the collar and jerked outward, buttons flying in opposite directions as he raked his eyes down my bare chest.

Okay, so I didn't wear a bra. Maybe I had plans.

His eyes darkened right before lowering his mouth and latching it around a nipple. Chanting his name over and over, I all but threw myself in a full backbend, giving him access to whatever he wanted and more. Without warning, his hands slid under my ass again, lifting me around his waist until I wrapped my legs around his back and then claimed my mouth once more.

Without breaking the frantic kiss, he carried me back to the shower I'd left just hours earlier. Reaching inside with one arm, he turned on the water and set me on the counter. Within seconds, he had what was left of his shredded pants and my borrowed boxers on the floor.

The moment I laid eyes on him, standing proud and naked in front of me, my heart sped up and blood swooshed a pounding pace through my ears.

He was beautiful—all man, all hard, artfully decorated from head to toe in inked symbols and designs. Strong, muscular thighs and a toned hardened chest met in the middle at washboard abs that lead directly to the most impressive cock I'd ever seen.

And I'd seen a lot of cock.

The first time Val and I were together, it was angry. Somehow, we were punishing each other—a combination of resentment about our mutual situations and resentment over the fact that we even wanted each other in the first place. The whole thing had been so frantic and rushed, I never took notice of anything other than the fact that it felt like nothing I'd ever experienced.

Plus, he'd had me cuffed, and I couldn't touch him. So, that was the first thing I did.

He watched me through half-lidded eyes as I took him in my hands, stroking from the base to tip with slow, purposeful movements.

"What the hell are you doing to me, Eden?" he rasped, twining both hands in my hair.

"Meaning?" I asked, still pumping him.

"I'm a goddamn Carrera, and you're…ah, Christ…" He bit his lip and pulled the strands still wound around his fingers. "You're bringing me to my knees."

Val's eyelids closed, and a surge of power rushed through me, inciting an insatiable desire to literally bring him to his knees—by dropping to mine.

Sliding off the counter, I hit the bathroom tile, and his eyes popped open in shock. "Not yet," I warned. "But give me a few minutes and I'll do my best."

Focusing on my end game, I braced a hand on each ass cheek and took him in deep. His hand held forcefully to my hair as he threw his head back and groaned.

"Don't stop… Jesus…"

I'd never been one to enjoy a blow job, per se. It just wasn't my thing. Don't get me wrong, I wasn't a bitch in bed. I wasn't about to say, "thanks for the lick and tickle," and not return the favor. That was just rude.

But the power trip I had over this man fucked with my head.

Val's hands wound so tightly around my hair my eyes watered. His breath hitched, and with a growl, he rambled incoherent Spanish, finally breaking into broken English as he shook.

"*Dios mío…* Fuck, yes!"

If I didn't have a handful of ass, I'd fist pump the air.

"*Quiero hacerte el amor lentamente, Cereza.*" Pulling me up by my shoulders, he wrapped one arm under my ass and cradled the other around my head, lifting me into the steamy shower.

For half an hour, we soaped, washed, caressed, kissed, and touched each other. The one thing we didn't do was speak.

In any other situation, I may've felt awkward and used by the silence. But as he stared hard into my eyes, allowing me to wash his injuries, clean them, and inspect his bruises, I knew words weren't needed.

Something shifted in that shower as we built a level of trust and crossed an invisible line.

Tracing the cuts marring his skin, I trailed my fingers across his back, once again taking note of the massive canvas that told a very personal story I wasn't privy to. I knew if he wanted me to know, he'd tell me himself, but curiosity tore at me.

Deciding not to ruin the peaceful moment between us, I continued my inspection and nestled in front of him, his body ready for me.

Wrapping my legs around Val's waist, my mouth rounded for a silent scream as he plunged inside, thrusting as he cradled my face. The water from overhead poured into it, spilling from the corners the moment we both tumbled over the edge.

With a soundless union, I realized that life as I knew it was over.

As the sun broke over the horizon, I listened to Val's steady heartbeat, my ear pressed firmly against his heart.

We lay in the full-sized bed he'd been sleeping in since we arrived at the new safe house, our limbs tangled around each other, my cheek draped across another intricate tattoo scrawled across the width of his chest. It depicted skulls and knives and words in Spanish I didn't understand. It was gruesome and fascinating.

"How did you make it out of there?"

His arm tightened around me. "What do you mean?"

My eyes followed my fingertip as it traced a line down his stomach toward his navel. "Mateo said it was a bomb, Val. Nothing withstood the blast, but you. How in the hell did you walk away from that?"

I'd been afraid to ask the question up until now. Seeing him standing at the door in one piece had been enough at the time to quell any need for explanation, but lying next to him, the reality of what could have happened crushed me under its weight.

"Do you really want to know?"

"Is that a rhetorical question?"

"Would you've been upset if I hadn't made it back?"

Dipping my finger into the crevice of his belly button, I shrugged with mock indifference. "I wouldn't say upset, but arguing with myself isn't nearly as entertaining."

My cheek bounced as his chest rumbled with low laughter.

"*Cereza*, that mouth of yours, sometimes I wonder if..." He trailed off as if he'd spoken out of turn, his voice abruptly shutting down.

Lifting my head, I balanced my chin on his breastbone, staring into conflicted pools of molten chocolate. "Something wrong?"

Shaking his head, he sat up and leaned over the bed, fumbling with the few clothes we'd discarded in the adjoining bathroom.

Watching the intricate movement of his body as he twisted, and the way each defined muscle in his back contracted and tightened with the reaction of another, my skin flushed with rising heat. Sitting up, I tugged the sheet up to my neck and held it with a death grip.

My emotions swung on a pendulum, one minute screaming for his touch, the next, petrified and ashamed because I wanted it. No sane woman would willingly crawl in bed with a criminal.

A confessed murderer.

A drug trafficker.

A man capable of unspeakable things.

"Hey," Val ran a rough hand across my jaw and settled at the back of my neck. "Where'd you go?"

"Huh?"

"You spaced out there for a minute."

Val and I were explosive. Unable to keep our hands off each other, when we joined forces, the moment was enough to shake the foundation of anyone's psyche.

Which is exactly why I had to get away from him.

I promised myself I'd never blindly fall for another man, and I was falling hard for Val Carrera.

"I'm fine," I assured him with a half-hearted smile. "Just tired."

It wasn't a complete lie.

I watched as he settled back into bed, immediately wrapping his arms back around me in a protective hold. The instant feeling of security confused me, but I pushed it aside and focused on his tightly clenched fist.

"What's that?"

A slow grin spread across his face. It was the same devastating grin I'd watched for every time he'd walk into the cantina and sat at the far barstool on the left corner.

"Protection."

Rolling my eyes, I pushed away from his hold. "Again? Jesus, Danger…are you part machine?"

His eyes crinkled as a low chuckle rose to full-chested laughter. Grabbing me around the waist, I barely had time to think before he had me on my back, pinned underneath him as his knees rested on the outside of my thighs. With one palm pressed into the mattress by my head, he held his fisted hand high above my forehead.

"Not that kind of protection, *Cereza*…"

A flicker of something I couldn't put my finger on crossed his eyes. As I looked into them, I knew they'd seen more destruction than entire cities combined.

The cords in his neck tightened as he opened his hand, and

a long chain dropped from his palm, the rounded base swinging above my nose. "This kind."

I recognized it immediately.

"Oh, my God, that's my…?"

"I can't explain it, either. Every man near that stash house is dead. The building is gone, and my car is a pile of ash, but somehow, I walked away from it all. Moments before the blast, I pulled this out of my pocket by accident, and I remembered what you said about it protecting me."

The corners of his mouth turned down as he stared at the St. Michael medallion intently.

"I'm not a religious man, *Cereza*, but stupid as it sounds, something told me to put it on. Now, whether that something was my own paranoia, you inside my head, or this fictitious god I keep hearing about…I don't know. All I *do* know is I'm here with you, and those other men's families are burying what's left of them."

His confession grounded me. I couldn't speak as I stared at the medallion, swinging from his crooked finger.

Was it a sign?

Did I even believe in signs anymore?

What the hell did I believe?

"You made it back because you're indestructible, Val Carrera."

One corner of his mouth lifted in a private thought, meant only for him. "I made it back because I had someone to come back for, Eden Lachey."

His tenderness threw me. I wanted his anger as an escape and to prove to myself what we were doing was a temporary product of my confinement and grief. But as he whispered my name, I found my fingers sliding up the length of his arm, twining around the chain still dangling from his hand.

Val's eyes shifted, watching with a strange fascination. In a surprise move, he entwined our fingers, as the medallion enclosed tightly in between our palms. Lowering his body, he stared at my mouth a moment or two before brushing his lips against one corner, then to the other.

With his chest against mine, I felt his heart pound with either anticipation or fear.

I understood both.

With an unhurried calmness I'd never seen from Val, he cradled my cheek in his palm and delivered a slow, powerful kiss, exploring as he tasted, caressing as he licked.

No frenzy. No blinding need.

As his lips traced the shell of my outer ear, my mind raced, confused at this ruthless killer who held me as if I were the most breakable piece of priceless china in the world.

"What did you say before?"

Pausing, a hot wave of his breath filled my ear. "Before?"

I nodded. "In the bathroom… When I, uh… Well, you said it in Spanish." I had no idea what the hell I was saying. Random words short-circuited from my brain to my mouth, attempting to reconcile the shift in his behavior.

His fingers tightened around mine. "*Quiero hacerte el amor lentamente*. It means I want to make love to you slowly."

With five words in a language I didn't understand, I let go. "Then do it."

I'd never been touched as gently and reverently in my life.

Val took his time, kissing any and everything, making sure nothing felt rushed or impatient. He did exactly as he wanted.

He made love to me slowly.

Purposely. Passionately. Intensely.

He held me through our combined cries, his arms woven around me long after sleep claimed him.

But sleep hadn't come for me and wouldn't for a long time.

As we lay wrapped around each other, I realized with stark clarity, at that moment, Val Carrera was the most vulnerable he'd been since the moment I awoke, cuffed to a metal bed.

There couldn't have been a more perfect opportunity to escape to my long-desired freedom. I wasn't restrained. The door wasn't chained.

Get dressed and leave—it was that simple.

But it wasn't that simple. Because for all that had broken in me since walking into Caliente, I didn't want to.

Staring up at the ceiling, I silently cursed myself for becoming entangled with a man I had no intention of leaving.

# Chapter Twenty

## VALENTIN

The whole morning Eden and I kept our distance as we packed up what little we'd brought with us. A few stolen glances were all we allowed ourselves as my men cleared out any trace of our presence the past few days.

As a residence, the place was a piece of shit, but I'd be lying if I said leaving it didn't give me mixed feelings. It was the place I'd brought Eden to as a prisoner and was leaving as a willing companion.

I still had a hard time processing the thought or even beginning to rationalize it.

She had every opportunity to leave in the middle of the night. I awoke this morning, half-expecting to find the bed empty beside me. It didn't take but a moment to feel her warm skin still pressed against me, resting peacefully.

Well, as peaceful as one could be after all I'd put her through.

"Is that everything?" Tucking his gun into the waistband of his jeans, Mateo glanced from me to Eden, his eyes questioning but silent.

*Smart man.*

"Yeah, we didn't bring much," I answered, scratching the back of my head.

Eden snorted in front of me. "I didn't bring *anything*, warden."

Surprised at her outburst, I shot her a look across the room, ready for a fight, only to be rewarded with a secretive wink.

*Well played, Cereza.*

After the stash house explosion, Mateo thought it best not to remain in one place for too long. I couldn't have agreed more. In this stationary target, we were sitting ducks, weakened by the four walls surrounding us.

I was the boss of an entire stateside cartel, but up until now, I'd only given a shit about my own life. My own personal creed involved one simple rule—keeping my ass away from the wrong end of a gun.

In eleven days, my creed had been twisted beyond recognition.

Ushering us outside, Mateo climbed into the front seat of the black SUV. Two men followed suit and the rest dispersed into other vehicles as decoys, in case of an ambush. I made sure not to touch Eden unnecessarily, lightly pressing my fingers onto her shoulder as I guided her into the backseat.

I swallowed hard as she bent over. Her ass, now covered in the tiny white shorts I had one of Mateo's men borrow from his wife, pressed close to my face. The tight blue half shirt did nothing to calm my raging hard-on, which was growing by the second.

I'd asked for some decent clothes for her to wear. He brought me indecent with a side of torture.

I felt like a presidential caravan hauling ass down a highway toward nowhere. To the casual onlooker, we were nothing, but to me we were a glaring eyesore—a Muñoz flare just begging to be fucked with.

I had a bad feeling about the entire operation.

Mumbles from the front carried to the back, as I heard Mateo and Emilio exchanging a play by play of their communication with the other SUVs. I watched their eyes shift back and forth to each other, their hands intermittently wiping a brow or gripping the wheel and dashboard.

Instinct had me glancing at Eden. After exchanging the same apprehensive stares, she folded her legs onto the seat and slipped her hand in mine behind her bent knees, shielding the small show of affection from view.

Wisely, she kept her mouth shut.

After only eleven days, she'd learned quickly the three basic rules governing our cartel: *hold your tongue, never let anyone see what you stand to lose,* and *fear is a useless emotion.*

Out of instinct, I touched the medallion, still hanging around my neck. It lay hidden underneath my white button-up shirt and jacket. If my men saw it, I'd be done for, but something wouldn't allow me to take it off.

She'd given it to me, and as much as I'd never understood religion, I felt peace wearing it. Maybe it stemmed from it belonging to the woman sitting beside me, or maybe it truly had some mystical power I couldn't understand. Regardless, I'd put it on this morning the minute Eden and I got out of the shower.

The moment I touched the smooth porcelain face, I felt it.

I felt it, and Eden whispered it, breaking rule number one of my cartel code.

"Something isn't right."

Looking away wasn't an option when her eyes held such dreaded anticipation. "Keep your voice down."

"Something isn't right," she repeated, tucking a strand of

her shocking candy-red hair behind her ear. "Val, can't you feel it? Look at them." She slightly lifted our joined hands toward the front of the SUV, pointing to my men who were locked in deep discussion.

Breaking from her worried blue eyes, I shifted my gaze toward Mateo and Emilio, sharing phone screens, deep lines marring their foreheads. I'd never confirm her suspicions, but the same worry ran through my blood the moment we left the safe house.

However, I was the boss of this damn cartel, and I deserved answers.

"Enough with the whispering bullshit!" I shouted, my blood pressure rising with every sharp turn Mateo took. "What the hell is going on?"

"*Jefe*, there's something you should know," Emilio began as Mateo threw a scowl at him, jerking the wheel to the left.

Obviously, the earlier whispers concerned cartel rules one and two.

*Fuck.*

The car filled with tension, and an internal war raged within me between taking control as the boss and getting the one thing I've grown unable to resist the hell out of here.

As unsure glances passed between my two lieutenants, all I've known my entire life won the battle.

I dropped Eden's hand and gripped the back of Mateo's head rest. "Have you forgotten who runs this cartel, Cortes? I'm not dead yet. Until I am, you'll both stop the secretive whispering and inform me of every goddamn thing that happens. Now!"

Mateo's darkened eyes locked with mine in the rearview mirror. "Fine. My men confirmed suspicious activity around the—"

He never finished his thought.

Ear-shattering blasts shook the SUV, the impact rattling the windows and the frame. A flood of unresolved anxiety hit me from feeling the same damn thing not seven hours earlier. Instinct had me diving over Eden, covering her with my own body as the car rattled with the impact.

Mateo and Emilio cursed, fighting to stay in control of the wheel and shouting commands for me to stay down as they pulled their guns.

Several aftershocks hit, causing Eden to scream, her cries muffled by my own chest. My ears rang, the blast reengaging the deafness I'd experienced following the stash house explosion.

"Mateo, what the fuck?" I blinked through the clouds of smoke permeating the windows. As soon as I spoke the words, a second blast ripped any other words from my lips as the SUV took a hard right onto a side road.

He barked out orders, breaking rank in the chaos. "Stay down!"

"Val!"

I pushed up on my hands and knees and grabbed a handful of her hair, shoving it down onto the leather seat. "Head down, *Cereza*!" The blast seemed to have quieted, so I risked a look around.

Black smoke billowed from the horizon, a mushroom of explosion, leading the way for sirens gaining volume in the distance.

Mateo slammed his hand against the steering wheel and made another sharp turn. "Keep her down!"

"What the hell happened?" I demanded, watching the dark funnel cloud fade into the distance.

I'd had enough reactionary shit. I hadn't ruled most of the United States as the top importer, forcing any rival cartel that dared challenge me back to Mexico with an empty bank account and skeleton crew because I sat back and allowed myself to be challenged.

I'd been enthralled with a woman and let business get out of hand long enough. It stopped right now.

Mateo's jaw ticked as he cast a side-eye at Emilio. "They lit the safe house."

Fighting under my hold, Eden popped up, her wild hair wrapped across her chin. "What do you mean lit?"

Closing my eyes, I drew a long breath, knowing the blast was only phase one. "He means the safe house is gone."

"Gone?"

"Gone. As in blown to hell and back."

Disbelief coated her widened eyes. "But…we were just there."

"*Cereza…*" Raking my palm down my face, I willed her to stop talking.

"Oh, God," she stammered, her voice catching with understanding. "We almost… They tried… Oh, God!"

I wanted to touch her and reassure her we'd be okay. Instead, I stared at her blankly, then turned my head away in frustration. I couldn't tell her something that might be a lie.

"Are you sure? Jesus, you're sure?" Letting out a string of curses, Emilio punched the dashboard in front of him as he gripped the phone tightly against his face. "Is she all right? What hospital? Yes, take care of all the bills and make sure you talk to her. She knows not to say anything, but I want it reinforced, understand? *Bien*. Update in fifteen minutes, or I'll have someone's ass." Cursing again, he slammed his phone against the window, punctuating each hit with a new expletive.

I steeled my jaw. "What now?"

"They got RVC, too. About twenty minutes ago. My men don't know much—only that the bomb originated from the giant hole that used to be your office."

*She.*

"Janine? Is she…?"

Emilio shook his head. "No, she'd just punched in the code to open it up for a client who'd put in a call for a Saturday appointment. The blast knocked her out, and she's cut up pretty bad from the glass, but she's going to be all right."

We spent the rest of the ride in silence, the hard reality of the situation weighing on all four of us.

The Muñoz cartel just made a decisive move in a war I had to finish.

Something told me not all of us would make it through to the other side.

THE LAST THING I WANTED WAS FOR EDEN TO BE SUCKED INTO MY world.

Out of safe houses and places to go, we'd driven for forty-five minutes before making the reluctant decision to return to my own house. Miraculously, it still stood, unscathed from Muñoz artillery.

*For now.*

Mateo paced the floor, convinced we were all sitting targets. He was right. But I'd argued it didn't matter where we went. Unless we drove until the wheels fell off the SUV, eventually they'd find us.

I'd be damned if I'd run like a little bitch.

No Carrera backed down from a fight, and this would be no different. Fucking with me was one thing, but those bastards made it personal when they killed my men, put an innocent employee in the hospital, and endangered the life of a woman

205

who confused the hell out of me.

She sat curled up in the corner of my oversized, black leather couch, her knees hugged to her chest, staring off into the open kitchen. With her brows drawn and her lips pulled tight, I had no idea what she thought, but I had a feeling she hated me.

With good reason.

I brought her into this against her will. She still associated me with the death of her brother, and now, there stood a very good chance, we'd all die before the end of the day.

Not exactly the kind of guy every girl dreamed of bringing home to meet the family.

Then again, background info told me Eden's mom had split when she was born, her father took one of my biggest unpaid drug debts and left town, and my best cleaner did God knows what with her brother's body. There was no family left to meet.

But as much as I wanted her, as much as my body craved her, and her presence calmed the chaos, I knew the only safe place for her would be far away from me. The Muñoz cartel would take what they knew would hurt me the most. They wouldn't take pleasure in torturing me with physical pain. We'd all grown up with the same code and creed—endure until death but divulge nothing.

No, they'd never inflict direct pain on me. They'd do it through her. The longer I kept her, the higher the price on her head became.

Ensuring Mateo's attention remained on his phone and his incessant pacing, and Emilio remained outside talking with lower ranking men, I stole the moment to ruin the only good thing that'd ever been mine.

Taking a seat beside her, I clasped my hands in front of me to stop myself from touching her. "Are you all right?"

"Do I look all right?"

Attempting to lighten the heaviness in the air, I picked up a lock of her shocking flame-colored hair and rolled it between my fingers. Nodding to her white shorts and blue top, I somewhat managed a smirk. "You look like an extremely fuckable flag."

She rolled her eyes, dropping her head back against the cushion. "God, you're crude."

"What do you want me to say, Eden? I'm doing the best I can here."

"I want you to say we're going to be okay," she answered, rolling her chin toward me.

"I can't."

She remained quiet for a moment, and I didn't know whether to break the silence or let it ride as long as I could before I made her hate me. The decision was made for me when she abruptly sat up, rubbing her palms roughly down the length of her thighs.

"These are the men that killed my brother?"

"Yes."

"Fine. Then let's stop fucking around," she said balling her fists, her body taut. "Let's take the fight to them instead."

While on some sadistic level, the monster in me would love to see those Muñoz shits on the receiving end of Eden Lachey's barbed tongue, the suggestion made me laugh out loud.

When she turned her icy stare my way, I choked on my own amusement. "You're fucking serious?"

"Do I look like I'm joking? Why do you keep asking me stupid questions?"

"Because you keep saying stupid shit." I raked my hand through my hair. "No way, *Cereza*. You have no idea who these men are or what they're capable of."

Calm, almost *too* calm for my liking, she crossed her legs and sat back into the arm of the sofa, her elbows supporting her. "Oh, I think I know exactly what they're capable of, Danger. I watched it with my own eyes while hiding in a pantry. I saw them put a gun to the back of my brother's head and pull the trigger. I had to watch it all, because if I moved—if I screamed—if I said one goddamn word out of place, I'd be next."

Without a word, she wrapped an arm around my waist, resting her small hand above my lower back. My gut twisted at the images she created in my head. I hadn't stopped to think of what she'd been through. My entire life had been lived in a pantry. By the time I was sixteen, I had no idea how to ride a bicycle, but I could blow a man's head off from twenty yards away.

Our worlds were opposites, and I'd thought taking her had saved her life.

Seeing her hardened scowl and the determined bloodthirst in her eyes, I realized I'd ruined it.

AN HOUR LATER, THE FRONT DOOR SLAMMED OPEN AS EMILIO PULLED his gun, engaging all four deadbolt locks and punching in the security code.

Lifting my head from its propped position at my bar, I followed his movement with mild irritation. "Reyes, what the hell? This is my house, not a bomb shelter."

Checking the windows, Emilio's face held no amusement as he swung his gun from where I sat to the middle of the living room. "Move. Now!"

My blood ran cold. "Emilio..." I asked, drawing out every syllable to buy time. "What are you doing? Put the gun down." Shifting a glance toward Eden, her eyes widened, and I barely shook my head, indicating for her to stay still.

I had no idea what would go down in the next few seconds

and I didn't want her caught in the crossfire.

Moving quickly, Emilio turned his back to me, pointing his gun steadily at Eden. "I've asked you before, but now I want a fucking answer. Who are you?"

"Put the gun down, Emilio."

"Can't do that, *jefe*," he replied, his elbow straight and finger locked on the trigger. "Just got off the phone with one of my men. The gas station where we stopped to fill up the SUV just went up in flames. Convenient, don't you think?"

No, it couldn't be possible.

The muscles in Eden's neck tightened as she stared down the barrel of Emilio's gun. "And you think I jumped out while you pumped gas, dropped a few cell phone bombs out of my bra while in the ladies' room, and climbed back inside just for the hell of it?"

"How should I know what you crazy bitches do? From where I'm standing, all I see is the fact that every place you've been has blown the fuck up. Now, just how do you think that happened, huh? We,"—he waved the gun around the room, implicating the rest of us,"—are all Carrera men, sworn to protect and die for this man." I raised my eyebrows as he waved the gun in my direction. "You're an outsider who's caused everything to go to shit since I put you in my damn car!"

"Enough!" I yelled, moving to reach for my own gun.

I'd let this play out long enough. Emilio served as a high-ranking lieutenant, so I'd indulged his rant and let him blow off steam. But the way he spoke to Eden pissed me off.

Eden, however, had passed pissed off and turned explosive.

Before I could reach for my piece, she shot to her feet, boldly shoving him in the center of his chest with locked arms. "Don't you dare put this on me, Emilio Reyes! Don't forget that I watched you torment my brother right before you mutilated him.

You may not have pulled the trigger, but don't think I won't put a goddamn bullet in your head for what you did!"

I'd never seen Eden so callous and brutal. All the blood rushed south of my waistline, constricting my pants as I watched her transform before my eyes.

*Fuck, I wanted her.*

Emilio laughed, his eyes taking in her small frame and dismissing it. "You don't have what it takes, little girl."

Before anyone could move, Eden reached behind her and pulled something metal from the back of her shorts.

Splitting her stance, she raised both arms and pulled the slide on the top of the gun back, advancing the first shell into the chamber. "You sure about that? Why don't we find out?"

The minute I saw the gun in her hands, I recognized it.

All but falling off the barstool, I raked both hands across the waistband of my pants, shoving my fingers under my shirt, searching for the weapon I knew wouldn't be there. With one glance into her vacant eyes, I knew the small show of affection on the couch was a means to an end.

Karma certainly was a bitch.

"*Cereza*," I called out in a calm voice as I moved slowly toward her. "Give me my gun."

"This doesn't concern you, Val."

Two more steps, and I stood beside Emilio, yet her eyes never moved off her target. "I think it does when you threaten to shoot one of my men with my own gun."

"He cut my brother's fingers off while he screamed. I should blow his dick off in trade." Lowering the gun, she aimed it at Emilio's crotch.

Emilio backed up. "*Jefe*, this bitch is crazy."

I couldn't help but laugh. This was the life of a criminal. Point a gun in our face and we barely flinch. Aim it at our nuts and we tap dance like a motherfucker.

"Okay, Eden, you've made your point. Give me the gun." I held my hand out again.

"Go to hell, Danger."

The last thing I wanted to do was play on her already volatile emotions, but desperate times called for even more desperate measures.

I wasn't worried about Eden hurting my men. They'd seen enough gunfire and could protect themselves. However, the woman holding my gun didn't know the life I lived or the men who stood by my side.

In her world, it'd be reprehensible for a man to attack a woman for being angry. In mine, the only recourse for the stunt she just pulled would've been a bullet to the head.

The only reason she still stood was because Emilio inherently knew if he harmed her, the next bullet would land between his own eyes. However, he'd also taken a sworn oath to protect me with his life. If she turned the gun on me, even innocently, honor would force him to act.

So, I did what I had to do.

"*Cereza*," I whispered, stepping in between them. "It's not worth it. Let me deal with him."

"What the fuck?"

Ignoring him, I continued, staring into her flickering eyes. "Don't soil your hands for me."

Her hand shook. "I can't... Val, I can't just...do...nothing..." The trembling climbed up her arm, taking hold of her body.

Closing the rest of the distance, I held her cheek in the palm of my hand. "I'll do it. Stay who you are. Don't become me, Eden. This isn't you."

Turning her face into my hand, her finger slackened on the trigger. Seizing the opportunity, I grabbed her wrist, holding it toward the ceiling as the gun went off, blasting a round of sheet rock around our heads.

"Liar!" she screamed, twisting out of my hold.

Reclaiming a fierce hold on her, I shoved her to the carpet, both of us wrestling for the gun. Prying her fingers open, I pulled it from her hold and threw it across the room where Emilio picked it up and tucked it away. She kicked like a wild animal let out of its cage as I lay on top of her, holding her arms above her head.

"Get off me! I hate you! God, I hate you!"

"Well, you lasted longer than most of them."

The words were meant to hurt her enough to make her forget this fantasy we'd created between us.

Halting her struggle, she stared horrified into my eyes and whispered, "I hate you."

We lay there shooting daggers into each other's eyes as Mateo rounded the corner, emerging from my office, his face pale and dampened with beads of sweat.

"Mateo?"

"*Jefe,* I need you to come with me."

The monotony in his voice unnerved me. "What is it? Tell me."

Glancing from me to Eden, then to Emilio standing off to the corner, Mateo ran the pads of his fingers across his mouth and nodded. "It's your father."

A buzzing filled my head with warning. "What about him?"

"Alejandro is dead, *jefe.*"

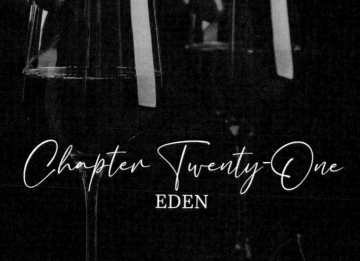

# Chapter Twenty-One

## EDEN

Together the words made sense, but with one glance in Val's face, I knew he hadn't begun to comprehend them.

"What do you mean he's dead?"

"Gerardo found him this morning." Mateo shook his head, the perspiration on his lips beading faster. "In his office. They cut his throat."

I knew the name.

Alejandro Carrera was infamous. Countless documentaries and true crime shows had been made about him and his ruthless reign of terror across the border. He was a monster and a coldhearted killer.

He also fathered the man I'd been sleeping with for the past eleven days.

Releasing his hold on me, Val staggered backward against the base of the sofa, looking as if someone slapped him across the face. "Do they know…? I mean…who…?"

"Val, you know the answer to that question."

No one spoke. The mood in the room teetered in between

shock and lethal reaction. Not daring to move, I watched Val for a reaction—any reaction.

Instead, he swallowed hard and nodded once. "Well, then. That'll be all, Mateo."

"*Jefe*—"

"I said, that'll be all!" Spitting fire at his newly appointed second in command, we all watched dumbfounded as Val climbed to his feet and turned down the hallway. "I'll be in my office. No one disturbs me unless we're under attack. That's a direct order."

Tracking his every movement, I followed him until he disappeared into a room off to the left and slammed the door. Biting my top lip in frustration, I made a move to follow him when Mateo stopped me.

"Let him go, Eden. He needs to do this his own way."

Dejected, I sat down amidst his pitying stare and Emilio's scowl, realizing the same truth that took form in the back of my head when we were in the SUV.

I couldn't claim something that didn't want me.

BY MIDNIGHT, I'D HAD ENOUGH.

Mateo and Emilio took turns keeping watch while the other slept. Apparently neither had gotten much of the latter in the last few days, the evidence rimming their dark eyes.

But sleep had no place on my agenda.

Val had been locked in his office for over six hours. One of the lower-ranking men had brought sandwiches and drinks to the house, and no one bothered to knock on his door to offer any.

When Val said to leave him alone, apparently his word served as gospel.

I'd given it as long as I could. I'd watched television, paced the floor, picked at a turkey sub while my stomach did flips. In the end, I couldn't stand the silence any longer.

While Mateo watched the front door and Emilio snored on the couch, I grabbed a ham sandwich and bag of chips. Pressing my back against the wall, I moved quietly down the hallway toward Val's office. Out of habit, I first tried the doorknob, not surprised when it didn't budge.

Raising my knuckles, I gave a soft knock. "Val? It's me." Before he had a chance to reject me, I added, "I know you're in there and you haven't eaten all day. Fine, don't talk, but at least take some food."

After a few moments, a slight commotion ensued from within, and I took a step back as the door cracked. Val's tired, frowning face emerged, his eyes cast down toward the plate in my hand.

"I hate ham."

He moved to close the door, so reacting on pure adrenaline, I shoved my foot in between it and the frame, catching it mid-slam.

"Oooof." Wincing as pain shot up my shin, I shoved the plate into his chest. "Okay, then eat the damn bread."

"Eden, I'm not in the mood to talk. Go away."

I'd been so focused on getting him to open the door, I didn't think beyond it.

Flustered, I said the first thing that came to mind. "Emilio pulled a gun on me."

Technically, it wasn't a lie. He had...

When Val had been standing there.

Val's eyes flared, and he swung the door open wide with a growl. "I'll kill him."

With catlike precision, I slipped under his arm and into the middle of his office. Turning to face him, I offered an apologetic smile. "Don't bother. I handled it hours ago."

"Eden, I don't have time for this." Swearing under his breath, he stomped back to his desk, flopping back into his oversized mahogany chair as it creaked with his weight.

His desk stood littered with papers and a bottle of half-empty tequila.

"Val, you can't just keep all this inside and not deal with it. Your father was murdered, for Christ's sake!"

"Shit happens."

"Shit happens? Excuse me, did you just say, 'shit happens?'" I tried to control my reaction, to no avail. "This is your father."

"He was an evil son of a bitch."

"He was your dad, Val."

Curling his lip into a sneer, he cocked his chin toward me. "He was my father. The man was no dad. No dad would've brought a young boy into this life."

"But, still…"

Swiping a stack of papers off his desk and onto the floor with a flick of his wrist, his eyes flashed with anger. "Still, nothing, Eden. You want me to say it? Fine, let's just put on the table how much of my father's blood runs through my veins." Propping his feet up on the edge of his desk, he spread his arms wide. "I'm glad the bastard is dead. Okay? There, I said it. He terrorized my mother, he destroyed my family, and he…" Trailing off, he glanced away.

"He what?"

"He ordered your execution."

I swallowed the boulder in my throat. "By whom?"

A sadistic grin crept along the seams of his mouth. "Me."

I staggered backward at his confession. As twisted as mine and Val's relationship was, something inside refused to let me believe he'd hurt me.

"Val…"

"Would I have done it?" His eyebrows shifted upward. "That's what you want to ask, isn't it?"

I nodded, my fingernails digging into my palms.

"I'd like to tell you no, *Cereza*, but I've got Carrera blood inside me. I don't know what I'm capable of."

"I don't believe that."

We stared at each other, our two opposing forces colliding with a ferocity neither of us could understand or rationalize.

On paper and in conversation, Valentin Carrera and I made no sense. We were a Hollywood script, destined for an Oscar night win. In real life, we were two people, incapable of walking away, regardless of the mutual destruction we caused.

Val's low laugh caught me off guard. "It doesn't matter anyway. Somehow, the damn Muñoz bastards know where we are every minute of every day. We go somewhere"—he threw his arms up—"*boom*, shit goes up in flames."

Risking rejection, I sat on the edge of his desk. "Could you have a traitor in your organization?"

"No. Mateo's cleared everyone."

I crossed my feet at the ankles, hunching my shoulders in a protective move. "What about Mateo?"

He pointed a finger at me. "Don't go there. Mateo is a good man, and I'll not have you wrecking his name within my ranks."

"You never know, Val. People aren't always what they seem."

"I never get it wrong."

My fingers curled under the edge of the wooden desk. "You got it wrong with my brother." Seconds ticked by before either of us spoke again. "Okay." I changed tactics by sliding off the desk. "Let's break down what we know." Walking around the edge, I moved his feet off the corner and leaned in, my palms flat on the surface.

"People blow up when I'm around." He smirked, his eyes swimming in the half bottle of tequila he'd consumed.

"Yeah, but why? We had to leave the first safe house in the middle of the night because we were being shot at, right?"

"Right."

"Why?"

"Because they didn't get a thank you note for a housewarming gift? I don't know, Eden…" Messing up his midnight black hair, he threw himself back into his chair as it protested with a loud creak. "Maybe because our families have tried to wipe each other off the face of the earth for decades."

"Yeah, but how did they know we were at that safe house? You have a lot of them, right?" Moving again, I stood in between his legs, and braced my hands on the armrests of his chair. "Then, you go to a stash house in Corpus Christi, and minutes before you leave, it blows up."

He eyed me curiously, a wrinkle embedded in his forehead. "Go on."

"Today, we leave a second safe house minutes before it, too, blows the hell up. RVC explodes, and after we stop for gas, it's lit up not long after we leave. How are they doing this, Val? It's not like they could put a GPS on your car without you or your men knowing about it. Besides, you've been in different cars each time."

Val waved a hand, effectively dismissing the notion. "No, our cars are checked daily for foreign devices. That'd be impossible."

I couldn't help but snort. "I don't know, then. Maybe your illustrious vet confused you for one of his usual patients and embedded a canine tracking chip under your skin."

Shaking my head, I pushed off the chair arms to move when

his jaw tightened, and he grabbed my wrist.

"What did you just say?"

"Val, I was kidding."

With his free hand, his fingers skimmed down his neck and pulled out the long chain attached to my St. Michael medallion. Holding the porcelain face up, he gripped it fiercely. "Where did you get this?"

I blinked, not understanding his tone. "My father gave it to me."

"When?"

"I went to see him after Nash…after I left the cantina. He seemed flustered and in a hurry. I was upset and ranted about finding Nash's killers and making them pay with or without his help. Before I left, he gave it to me for protection."

Val's eyes closed as if fighting to control his anger. "His exact words, Eden. What did he say?"

Thinking back, I struggled to recall our heated conversation.

*"Here. Take this."*

*"What is that?"*

*"Take it."*

*"St. Michael?"*

*"The Archangel. The guardian of souls who triumphed over hell. He was a spiritual warrior and the conflict against evil."*

*"It's a little late for a triumph over hell, Dad. I'm in it."*

*"Never take this off, Edie. You're a warrior, and so much stronger than your old man. You can win this war, but you have to be smart and vigilant at all times. Save yourself, Eden. Don't get involved with that man. They're watching you."*

*"What man? Who are you talking about? Stop talking in riddles!"*

"What did he mean, Val? Who's watching me?"

The conversation that didn't make sense eleven days ago

219

rang in my ears with the same confusion.

I'd barely gotten the words out when Val shot up from his reclined position and knocked me backward against his desk. With my elbows braced against the wood, and my breath lodged in my throat, I looked into chocolate eyes, glazed over with the blackest shade of fury I'd ever seen.

Ripping the medallion off his neck, he held it up between us like a dagger, his chest bent over mine in a position that scared the hell out of me. "Your father warned you not to get involved with *me*, Eden. He warned you my cartel would watch you."

"What are you saying?" I whispered, my voice thick with refusal to believe his words.

Raising his arm high, he let out a primal growl as he slammed his hand onto the desk's glass covering. The porcelain face of the medallion shattered, bits of it scattering across the desk and carpet. Scouring through the shards, his fingers picked up a small, circular, metal piece no bigger than half of my pinkie nail. Sliding his opposite hand up the side of my neck, he grasped a handful of my hair and forcefully turned my head toward the destruction.

"This is what I'm saying, *Cereza*." Holding up the small metal piece, he shoved it in front of my face, leaning his mouth against my ear, his words ground through clenched teeth. "This is a tracking device. A GPS microchip has been transmitting my location to Manuel Muñoz's intel." Pulling my hair back, my chin tilted upward to meet his icy stare. "Your father sold you out."

I tried to pull away from him, the first few seconds of his outburst not registering in my head. "No, you don't know my father."

"Neither do you."

"He's made bad decisions, Val, but he wouldn't feed me to

the wolves. He may be a drug addict, but he just tried to protect me. I'm sure he'd be as confused as me."

"Yeah?" Val raised an eyebrow. Releasing his hold on my hair, he pulled his phone from his pocket and handed it to me. "Prove it."

"What?"

"Prove it. Call him. See what he has to say."

"You know I can't do that. I've already told you he left."

Crashing his phone next to the shattered medallion, he pushed off me, and I exhaled the breath I'd been holding.

"My point exactly. Either your father sold you out, or you're both pawns in someone else's sick ass game."

Silence filled the room. "My family wouldn't turn on me."

Cold eyes shot my way, and his voice deepened to a low unexpected tone. "Now, see, that's the gaping difference in our worlds, *Cereza*. Mine would."

Grabbing the back of my thighs, Val lifted me onto the desk and reached between my legs. I started to protest when his fingers closed around the metal hook of his desk drawer and opened it.

Pulling out a pistol, he released the clip, examining the magazine before slamming it with the heel of his palm back into place. "Do you have some place you can go?"

"Why?" My tone flowed cautious, but inside, my heart pumped a furious pace. My hands gripped the desk again, still reeling over the knowledge I'd willingly given Val a wearable crosshair.

"I'm going to Mexico for a few days." He tried to keep the statement void of emotion, but his eyes tightened with every word.

An unexpected brick sank low and hard in the pit of my stomach. "You're going to take over the cartel, aren't you?"

Anger replaced the apprehension lacing his face as he tucked the gun into his waistband and slammed the drawer shut. "My father is dead. This is what's expected of me. It's my legacy."

Feeling overtook judgment. "What about us?"

No longer interested in pacifying me, his lips curled with a deadly smirk. "This was planned long before I tasted you, *Cereza*."

"Is that what you really want? Is that what your mother would've wanted?"

Bristling at my words, he turned his back to me. "You know nothing of my mother. This is all I've ever known. It's all I have left." Refusing to look me in the eye, he cast a glance outside of the darkened window. "I can't stop now."

Pushing away from me, Val stalked across the office and swung open the door while calling for Mateo. With my heart beating wildly in my chest, I listened to them make plans to cross the border into Mexico the following morning. Val instructed Mateo to arrange for them to stay at his father's estate before they met with the cartel in Mexico City. Vaguely, I heard plans for Emilio to stay in Houston and handle the day-to-day stateside operations.

With a final nod, Val reiterated his determination to settle his father's affairs and make his presence known to the cartel family.

As Mateo nodded in understanding, he left us alone once more to put the travel plans in motion. Disoriented by the gravity of what I was about to do, I slid off the table and took slow, purposeful steps until I stood behind him.

Gripping the wooden molding, I leveled a stare to the back of his head. "I'm going with you."

# Chapter Twenty-Two

## VALENTIN

A low sigh exited my chest, knowing the fight ahead of me. "No, you're not."

Releasing the doorframe, she barreled past me into the room, arms flailing. "What do I have left here? Nothing. I have a dead brother and a father that may or may not have betrayed me to save his own ass." Standing in front of me, she placed both palms flat against the edge of my desk, the dark blue of her shirt accentuating her ample curves. "I have my own score to settle with the Muñoz cartel, Val. I'm coming with you. If you leave me here, I'm dead and you know it. Are you going to let that happen?"

I knew this was coming.

In the past week, Eden and I had gotten too close. I'd disclosed information I would have never divulged to someone outside of the cartel. Women had never tempted me beyond the occasional fuck. Eden Lachey's pussy cast out snake charming voodoo magic that hypnotized secrets straight out of my cock.

Only one phrase could shatter the bond we'd forged.

"I ordered the hit on Nash."

The look on her face bordered on a slap as she stumbled back. "Are you trying to make me hate you?"

I shrugged, hating myself more with every lie. "It's a fact."

Eden's arms drew around her chest in a protective stance. "You didn't kill him."

"Does it matter? I've killed lots of people, and I'll kill many more."

Her features hardened, an invisible wall building between us. "I need to see the man who killed my brother, dead. Who is that, Val? Is that this Manuel guy?"

I remained silent, refusing to confirm her suspicion.

Rushing my desk, she bent her forearm, swiping everything to the floor that was left from my earlier tirade with a primal scream. "Answer me, goddamn it!"

"And then what, *Cereza*? Another one? And another? There are men who will always take his place and come after you. It'll never end."

She shook her head defiantly. "You won't let that happen."

"Won't I? I'm just like them."

"No, you aren't."

Having had enough, I charged into the room and shoved the chair out of my way, satisfied as it crashed into the wall.

Rounding the desk, I grabbed her hands, holding both in her face. "Yes, I am! I'm a killer. I sold the drugs that got your father hooked on cocaine, and my family began the war that got your brother murdered. Do you think we care about casualties like him? It happens every day in our world. In America, murder is just bad for business. In Mexico, it *is* business, *Cereza*. I can't be responsible for your life *and* mine."

Stubbornly, she held her ground, steeling her chin against my hold. "Val, if you won't bring me into this cartel, I'm sure I can find someone who will."

I flinched so quickly, if she hadn't been staring right at me, I'd have covered it.

Facing her, she held in a gasp as my laugh echoed around the empty room. "I'm sure the minute you walked out of this door, the Muñoz men would whisk you off your bound feet into the back of a van and ride away to parts unknown."

"Good." She egged me on, apparently tired of being on the outskirts of conversations.

The rhythmic tick in my jaw told her she'd succeeded in pissing me off.

Convinced she'd won the argument, she allowed a small smile to slip across her lips.

In seconds, I stood over her—the familiar scent of citrus and vanilla igniting and calming me in a twisted way. My hand found its way inside her hair and wound strong fingers around a bunch of candy-colored strands until my knuckles hit the base of her skull.

"Would you like to know what they'd do next, *Cereza*?"

She bowed her chin and violently shook it side to side. She had an idea what they'd do, and I'm sure she didn't need to hear me speak the words out loud—especially after what happened last night. I'd explored every inch of her body with determined, but careful intent.

Right now, the electricity vibrating off me was an exposed fuse, waiting to be lit with sparks of fury dancing around it.

She let out a pained yelp as I jerked her hair backward to force her eyes on me. "They'd rip your clothes off before you even got out of the van. They'd take turns fucking you until you passed out. Then, they'd torture you until you died a horribly painful death."

The corners of her eyes pooled both from the horror of my

words and the extreme angle of her head. The images I fed her detonated, shattering everything safe she had left in the world.

"Why?"

My eyebrows rose in question. "Why? You ask, why?"

She nodded as much as she could with her head immobilized.

"Because they're immoral sons of bitches who think women are nothing but available holes for them to fuck on command." Sweat rolled down my temple as it pulsed wildly beneath it. "And knowing you'd witnessed their hit, and you'd been here with me…well, that'd make destroying you a hundred times sweeter."

My fingers tightened again, and she lightly touched my arm with her free hand. "Val, you're hurting me."

I lowered us both to our knees and pulled her hair back again until she'd completed a full backbend. With her shoulders and head resting on my forearm, I brushed my lips against hers without kissing her. "And none of that will happen, Eden. Do you know why?"

She barely listened. Her instincts feared me and the vulnerable position I had her in, but our basic animalistic connection had her breathless with anticipation.

Eden opened her mouth to speak, but I cut her off by palming the back of her head. "Because…" I growled, my voice full of unreleased fury. "Nobody touches what's mine."

"What do you care?"

I dropped lower, our lips barely skimming. "I care, because they've wiped out my entire family, Eden. I care, because I'm tired of losing. I care, because once a man has had you, he doesn't share."

"Val…" Her body twisted at an unnatural angle, but her breathing had become so erratic, she seemed to hardly notice. Every inhale molded our chests perfectly and every exhale pushed logic further from our minds.

I moved a knee in between hers as my eyes roamed her body. The moment they locked with her half-lidded stare, I watched the blue in her eyes darken to the blackest night of a soulless sky.

"I won't share, *Cereza*. Not until I get my fill." Skimming her throat, I licked skin at the base of her neck. "And getting my fill might take a while."

"Fuck you. Just fuck you, Danger." With receding strength, she attempted to push me away. "Fuck you."

"I don't think we have time for three, but I'll see what I can do." Picking her up, I fused my mouth against hers and dropped her on top of my cleared desk.

With an open hand that I didn't see coming, Eden slapped me hard across the face. Reacting quickly, I captured her wrists in a strong hold.

"I'm not your fuck toy, Carrera," she seethed between clenched teeth. "You don't command me and take what you want."

"No?"

Shoving her fists into my chest, she climbed off the desk, offering one last punch to the center. "No. The only thing you'll get your fill of tonight is your own hand, asshole."

Stunned, I watched as she flipped me off on her way out.

# Chapter Twenty-Three
## EDEN

I'd barely slept. Not that the paper-thin mattress and jail-cell sized bedroom enticed any form of restful sleep anyway, but somewhere in the past few days, I'd grown accustomed to sleeping next to an asshole.

Rolling over for the hundredth time, I threw my arms above me, wincing as the healing skin on my wrist pulled with the sudden move.

From an outsider's point of view, I'd lost my mind. Hell, from my own point of view, what I'd been doing was not only counterproductive, it was damn near suicidal.

I'd been kidnapped by the most feared drug cartel in the United States. Once I'd come to terms with my captivity, I'd vowed to use it to my advantage, promising to an empty room to take every one of them down who'd had a hand in my brother's death.

Then Val barreled into my room and my world, screwing up everything.

*What have I gotten myself into?*

My behavior wasn't normal. Normal women didn't consider crossing the border with a known murderer just because of some stupid crush.

It was just a crush… Wasn't it?

Logic told me no future existed for Val and me. There couldn't be. Morality couldn't allow me to stand by the side of a man who remotely had a hand in what happened to Nash. The idea of doing so would be beyond disrespectful to his memory.

It'd be unforgivable.

A hollow burn spread through my chest as my mind catalogued the failed relationships in my life. Every man I'd ever trusted or loved had hurt me or deserted me. Davis left me, my father turned his back on all of us long before this mess ever started, and Nash was literally ripped out of my arms.

Maybe Mateo and Emilio were right. Maybe I was a black widow. For all Val's faults and reprehensible acts, the thought of harm coming to him tore a hole in my heart.

Everything inside me warned me to back out now and save both of us mutual destruction. But as I asked myself the silent questions, one answer rang louder in my head than any doubt.

I'd fallen hard for Valentin Carrera, and I was more conflicted now than ever.

My conscience knew he'd given the order to torture Nash, even though it wasn't my brother he'd targeted; he admitted it himself. However, there had to be some humanity in a man who held a part of me so strongly tied to him that I couldn't walk away. Surely, I hadn't fallen so far off the line between right and wrong that I couldn't recognize an irredeemable person from one whose soul seeped with evil?

Weaving my fingers through the metal bars in the headboard, I tilted my chin toward the ceiling, letting out a frustrated breath. "Damn you, Danger."

"If you're going to damn me before I get to hell, at least break down the list."

I jumped at the sound of his voice, quickly releasing the metal bars and pushing up on my elbows. He stood in the doorway, his left arm and hip bent as they both rested against the frame. A half-smile played on his lips as his body shifted forward.

An unstable surge of lust and emotion brewed inside me as I ran a heated stare from his messy hair to his bare toes. Clad only in a pair of draw string black sweatpants, the casual attire and bare chest threw me off.

Mesmerized, I mentally counted the defined rows of abs as they trailed down to the well-defined V that disappeared behind the low-slung waistband.

"I thought I locked the door."

"You did." He opened his mouth to argue further, then paused as his eyes lingered on my bare legs, exposed by my long T-shirt. "That's mine."

I glanced down at the oversized, green shirt and smirked. "The shirt or me?"

"Yes," he answered quickly. Moments of silence passed between us before Val exhaled and pushed off the frame, folding his arms across his bronzed skin. "I don't like the way things ended last night."

I lowered my eyes, playing with a rogue thread on the pillow. "Me either."

"Then let's fix it."

"Tell me about your mother."

Cursing in Spanish, he rolled his forehead against the door. "Can we not—?"

"Go back to your own room, Val." Hugging the pillow to my chest, I curled into a ball, facing away from him.

For some reason, I needed to know the human side of him. Before cartel life changed him. When he had a mother and a somewhat recognizable father.

A house.

A family.

Maybe a dog and friends who'd knock on the door and ask if he could come out to play.

To allow him completely into my life, I had to know if that version of Val Carrera existed. If he couldn't, or worse, wouldn't give me that, I'd walk out of his front door today and turn my back on him to save the last piece of myself from being lost forever.

Tears burned my eyes, and I closed them, willing the impending breakdown to stay forced behind closed lids. One rogue tear refused to obey and slipped through the cracks, trailing a telltale sign down the bridge of my nose.

Before I could get rid of the evidence, the mattress dipped with his weight and Val's hand gently wiped it away. Placing my hand in his, he shifted on the bed and pressed my palm between his shoulder blades. Swallowing hard, I slowly rolled over to face him. I had no idea what he was about to do, but the lull in the cadence of his voice demanded my full attention.

"Every word, every symbol, every color is for them."

"'Them'?"

"My family, *Cereza*." He traced my fingers over each symbol as he described them. "The number three on my left shoulder represents my family the day everything changed." Trailing the pad of my index finger horizontally across his upper back, he rested it against his right shoulder. "The number two is what was left when a young boy doesn't realize the difference between death and sleep." Moving my finger once more, he dropped it to the middle of his upper back, equal diagonal distance from the other two. "The number one represents me—what was left after the last one had been taken away."

Tears rolled harder as the block of Spanish in the middle of the inverted number triangle blurred. "Val, you don't have to—"

Moving my finger down the left side of his ribcage, he ran it around the petals of a wilted white lily. "This is for my mother. Her name was Liliana." Shifting my hand, it trailed horizontally over the sword which pierced through the petals and through another lily, smaller in size and shaded black on his right ribcage. "This is for my sister. Her name means dark little one."

A long pause followed his last explanation, and I watched his back rise rapidly as his breathing escalated. "Val, please stop. I don't need to hear anymore."

I didn't. The personal pain etched in each work of art painted on his skin ripped a new hole in my already destroyed heart.

"The bird with its talons on the sword is a phoenix," he explained as if I hadn't spoken. His eyes glazed over, transported to another time and place. "The phoenix rises from the ashes and rebuilds what was destroyed." The muscle in Val's jaw twitched as he ground his teeth together with repressed anger.

"And the Spanish at the bottom?" I heard myself ask, unaware I'd even formed the words.

"*La venganza es mía. Yo pagaré.*"

"What does that mean?"

Val hesitated a moment before finally turning his chin over his shoulder and pinning me with a pained stare. "Vengeance is mine. I will repay."

"I shouldn't have pried into your personal life." Touching him suddenly felt disrespectful, and I quickly removed my hand from his skin.

Staring through me, Val gripped a handful of the blanket and squeezed until his knuckles turned white. "My mother was a saint, Eden. She tried harder than any woman I've ever known to combat the evil she saw around her with the goodness inside of her."

"Was?"

"She's dead." His hand moved to my hair as he ran his hand down the length of it. "Close your eyes, *Cereza*. I'm going to tell you a story, and it isn't one of your American fairy tales that ends with a happily ever after."

# Chapter Twenty-Four
## VALENTIN

*Mexico City, Mexico*
*Twenty-Four Years Ago*

*I*lined all my toy soldiers up on the windowsill. My small fingers pointed a pretend gun at them, and I made the pashew sound as my finger gun knocked them down one by one.

"Valentin! Put those plastic men away. You need to come set the table for dinner."

Glancing over my shoulder, I watched her balance the baby on one hip and shuffle white breakable plates on the other.

I was a good boy. I liked to help. It made me feel strong.

"Coming, mamá." Sweeping the soldiers into my toy basket with one arm, I scrambled into the kitchen and took the plates from my mother. She rewarded me with a smile and ruffled my hair with her nails.

"You're such a big help, Valentin. Thank you."

"Of course, mamá." I carefully placed the dishes on the table, counting them to myself as I centered them on the red woven placemats. I hesitated, not sure whether I should make her angry by asking about him, but my curiosity got the best of my manners. "Mamá, why are there only three plates?"

*She buckled the baby in the high chair, and the smile dropped from her face. I didn't like it when she stopped smiling. She'd been doing that too much lately.*

*"Tonight, it will be just you, me, and your Tía Pilar, son. Now, go wash up before we eat."*

*Mamá taught me manners. I knew I should go wash my hands and stop asking questions, but I needed to know why he hadn't been home lately.*

*"Where is papá? He hasn't been home in weeks. Is it because I've been a bad boy? Have I asked too many questions?"*

*I should've run. I should've gone to wash my hands before she could get mad at me, too, but I stood rooted in my spot, just staring at her.*

*I missed my papá.*

*She sighed slowly and fell to her knees. I backed up, scared of what she might do. When papá fell to his knees, usually it was to belt me.*

*I didn't like the belt. It hurt.*

*"Valentin," she said, gently holding my hands. Mamá was always gentle. "Your father had to go away for a while."*

*Her words scared me. "But…but…who will be our papá?"*

*A small smile pulled at her lips, warmness radiating from her hands as they held mine. "He's still your papá. That will never change. He just got called away for a bit."*

*I could feel my lip quiver. I wanted to be brave for mamá. I tried to hide it. "When will he be back?"*

*"I don't know. But until he comes back, I need you to be a brave soldier. Can you do that for me, Valentin? Can you be my brave soldier?"*

*I thought about my toy soldiers from the window. I made them battle and win wars. They were brave because I made them that way. I missed papá, but I could be brave for mamá—just like my soldiers.*

*"Yes, mamá. I'll be brave," I said, shaking my head. "Until papá comes back, I'll protect you and Ana."*

*After dinner, I helped clean up the dishes for mamá and Tía Pilar like the brave solider I promised to be. I even cleaned up all my toy soldiers and got a bath all by myself.*

*Curled up in my big boy bed, I'd almost drifted off to sleep when I heard it.*

Pashew Pashew Pashew.

*Excitement rushed through me. Had my toy soldiers started fighting without me?*

*Climbing out of bed, I ran to my toy chest, and ripped off the lid. Confused, I stared down at perfectly placed soldiers, still in the box where I left them before bed.*

Pashew Pashew Pashew.

*My fingers tightened around my toy box as screams tore through the house, followed by men yelling words I didn't understand. I started crying because the noise scared me, then I cried harder because I knew I wasn't being a brave soldier.*

*Mamá needed a brave solider.*

*Reaching into my toy box, I grabbed the general and held him tight. He would protect me. The general protected all the army in battle.*

*He would protect mamá.*

*Opening my door, I rubbed my eyes as I walked down the hall. Men still shouted and I thought I heard Tía Pilar scream, but I couldn't be sure.*

*That was, until I walked into the living room.*

*At least five men in black held guns just like my army men, only their guns lit up my house. Tía Pilar lay sleeping on the floor in a puddle of red Jell-O.*

*I liked Jell-O.*

*I took two steps forward when mamá screamed.*

*"Valentin! Be a fireman, Valentin! Do as I say! Five alarm fire! Be a fireman now!"*

*I didn't want to move. The man had mamá pinned down on her back. They looked like they were wrestling.*

*I liked wrestling.*

*"Valentin! Go!"*

*I didn't like disobeying mamá's orders.*

*Nodding, I turned when I saw one of the other men in black pick up one of the guns and start to chase me. A funny feeling settled in the pit of my stomach.*

*Something didn't feel right.*

*"Valentin! Please! Be a fireman, now!" Mamá screamed again, and something in her voice made me run.*

*I ran fast as the man chased me.*

*My house was big. There were twists and turns and awesome places to hide. There was also a pipe that ran down the side of it. I'd gotten in trouble many times for climbing down it like a fireman. I liked to pretend I got called in the middle of the night to a huge blaze and was the only hero who could put it out. I'd open the window, wrap my legs around it and slide down, then hide out in the cellar until the 'fire' was over.*

*Or until papá stopped being angry.*

*Tonight, the fire was real.*

*Somewhere along the way, I'd lost the man in black. Opening the window, I heard mamá scream again then a loud blast. I wanted to cover my ears, but I couldn't and hold the window, too. So, I focused on jumping to the pipe and closing it behind me.*

*Once inside the cellar, I pulled my knees against my chest and covered my ears, drowning out the last of the screams until I fell asleep.*

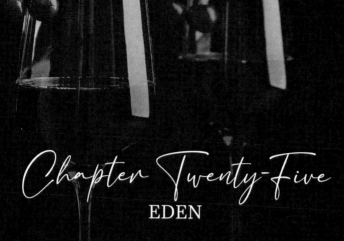

# Chapter Twenty-Five

## EDEN

Houston, Texas
*Present Day*

Tears rolled down my cheeks faster than I could wipe them. He'd painted a picture I'd never be able to erase from memory. My heart bled for the little boy, waiting in a dirty cellar for a mother who'd never come for him.

I fought to find my voice. "You mentioned a baby...Ana. What happened to her?"

"No one ever found my sister's body. I can't think about that, Eden. I never have."

Releasing the tear-stained pillow, I rolled over to face him, taking his hand in mine. "Why did you turn to cartel life after knowing what happened to your family, Val?"

Dropping his chin, the skin around his eyes bunched in a pained stare. "Why didn't you leave with your father after known criminals killed your brother in front of you?"

The question took me by surprise, as did the intensity of his gaze. In that instant, I understood him more than probably anyone ever had. The wall I'd built between us crumbled as the abomination I'd created in my mind of Valentin Carrera—*El*

*Muerte*—fell away, revealing only a man who'd loved and lost.

A man who'd sought revenge for a family member brutally taken from him.

*Just. Like. Me.*

Before I could stop to think about it, I pushed off the mattress and straddled his lap, the T-shirt riding the tops of my thighs. As if magnetic, his hands automatically pulled to my waist, resting low against my hips.

Hooking a finger under his chin, I lifted his darkened eyes to meet mine. "Take me to Mexico."

"Eden, I can't. Weren't you listening? I won't take the risk."

"Val, I'm not your mother, and you're not six years old." Forcing power into my voice, I took his face in between my palms. "Do you think I'm weak?"

"Of course not."

"Do you believe whatever this is between us is worth fighting for?"

Pulling away, he closed his eyes and drew a tired breath. "Eden, come on—"

"Do you believe we have something worth fighting for?" I repeated, enunciating each word.

Opening his eyes, raw pain shot through them as he held my face in a mimicking grip. "I can't go through the same thing again. It'll kill me."

"Me, too," I agreed, my voice shattering. "That's why you can't leave me behind. If we go, we go together. I have nothing left here, Val. The only two things I have to live for are revenge and you. If you leave, you take them both."

His breath came rough and heavy, and he closed his eyes again, tightening his hold on my cheeks as he pressed our foreheads together. "You're so stubborn, Eden." Pulling me closer, he tilted my chin, opening his mouth and brushing it repeatedly over the outside of my mine. "You're so fucking stubborn."

Fire raced through me as he traced my jawline with barely-there kisses, trailing them down my throat and back up again. Groaning, I threw my head back, reveling in the touch of his lips on my heated skin. As his tongue grazed the underside of my chin and raked across my bottom lip, need exploded within me, drawing from the powerful connection we'd forged with one conversation.

Trailing my hands down his chest, he swallowed my low moan as he captured my lips in a hungry kiss that I had every intention of drowning in. I welcomed it, pouring every ounce of fear for our combined safety into it—our tongues tangling in a battle of dominance neither of us cared to win.

"I need you, *Cereza*. But this time, this is on your terms— all or nothing."

The honesty in his voice, and uncharacteristic willingness to hand over power finally crumbled the last of my remaining walls.

Breaking the kiss, a small smile curled one corner of my mouth before it claimed his again. "I'm all yours."

With a low growl of my name, his hands bunched the bottom of my T-shirt and pulled it over my head, tossing it to the floor. Holding me protectively in his arms, he lowered me onto the mattress. His weight stole my breath, but I welcomed every theft.

As he made love to me, he groaned broken Spanish in my ear. I had no idea if the words were dirty or endearing, and honestly, I didn't care. All I knew was that Val and I had passed an invisible milestone in whatever was happening between us.

And tomorrow, we'd pass a real one into the border of Mexico.

"Eden, wait."

With a backpack full of clothes and supplies and one full of artillery slung over my shoulders, I paused in the kitchen on the way out to the SUV the next morning.

Val instructed me to pack light. That hadn't been a problem since he'd borrowed all of three outfits from his soldier's wife. Hopefully I'd have a moment in Mexico to at least buy something else to wear that halfway covered my ass.

"Did we forget something?"

Wincing as he set his own bags down on the barstools, Val shook his head and shoved his hands in his pockets. "No, I just…"

The vet made Val's much bitched about visit earlier in the morning, and other than a few stitches, antibiotics, tetanus shot, and temporary hearing loss, he'd miraculously escaped major injury.

Intrigued by his uncomfortable stance, I dropped my own bags and met him at the kitchen island with my hands on my hips. "You're *not* changing your mind. I'm coming with you."

"No, nothing like that. I don't go back on my word, Eden. Know that about me, if you know nothing else."

The veins in his arm bulged as his hand tightened around something in his pocket.

Narrowing my eyes, I leaned my elbows onto the bar and twirled the end of my ponytail around my finger playfully. "What's in the pocket, Carrera?"

The lines around his mouth deepened. "Look, I know all that stuff with your dad and the medallion had to have been rough to hear. You thought it was a genuine gesture. How were you to know you'd been used, right?"

"We don't know that for a fact, Val," I corrected, straightening as tension ran through me. "There's no proof he knew either."

"Right." He nodded, pity in his eyes. "Anyway, I know how much that thing meant to you."

"Okay." I eyed him cautiously.

"What I'm trying to say is… Well, I don't want you to feel like… Shit, here." Jerking his hand out of his pocket, he pushed his fist toward me and held it until I extended my palm. Immediately, his fist opened and a flat, gold link chain fell into my hand.

Curious, I held the pendant attached up for closer inspection. It was unlike anything I'd ever seen in my life. The top third looked to be gold, the sun dial looking top fanned above a woman's skeletal face crowned with flowing long straight hair. Her open-boned rib cage stood pronounced and melted into a rose gold cloak. In her hand, she held a silver scythe similar to the Grim Reaper. It was both terrifying and beautiful.

"What is this?" I whispered, unable to tear my eyes from it.

"*Santa Muerte* rosary," he explained, unclasping the hook and twirling his finger in a circle, indicating for me to turn around. "In my culture, *Santa Muerte* is very sacred, *Cereza*. In ancient times, sacrifices were made to the Lady of the Dead in order to receive a peaceful death. The tradition passed from generations and has changed into many different meanings. The basic request always remained the same; however, *Santa Muerte* can be asked for nearly every need, mainly protection from one's enemies."

Glancing down at the pendant resting against my chest, I ran my fingers across the cool metal. "But…*death*? Isn't that a little morbid? Especially since what we're walking into isn't exactly safe."

"The powers associated with *Santa Muerte* aren't all

negative, Eden. All men must answer to death. The greatest power in life is death. If we believe in that philosophy, then *Santa Muerte* has the power to turn the will of man in favor of one or the other."

Tracing the scythe, I tasted the name on a whisper. "*Santa Muerte.*"

"Protection," he reiterated, kissing my temple.

When I glanced up to thank him, he'd already reassembled his bags on his shoulder and walked out the front door toward the waiting SUV.

Closing my fist around the symbol, I stared after him, a feeling of inherent dread washing over me. "Protection," I repeated.

LIVING IN HOUSTON MY ENTIRE LIFE, I'D NEVER LEGALLY CROSSED THE border into Mexico.

I sure as hell hadn't done it at one-hundred-fifty miles per hour in rough gulf waters.

After almost losing my breakfast in a speed boat, hitting wave after wave with a choppy resistance that had me dry heaving in Val's lap, we docked off South Padre Island and took a waiting car down to Brownsville. I had no idea how Mateo and Emilio had arranged all the intricacies of the trip so quickly, but I knew not to question it.

In this instance, the less I knew the better.

Once in Brownsville, we easily walked across the border to another waiting car on the Mexico side in Matamoros. The entire trip took a little less than six hours, all said and done, but it felt like twelve. By the time the car pulled into a circular driveway, I could barely keep my eyes open.

"What time is it?" I whispered, dragging my head off Val's shoulder.

Turning his wrist, he squinted at his watch. "Six o'clock."

"Feels later." I yawned, stretching as I studied the modest house in front of us. "Where are we? This doesn't look like a drug lord's mansion."

Val chuckled and opened the door to the back of the SUV. "It's not, *Cereza*. Do you actually think I'd bring you to the middle of a battlefield?"

"What? You promised!"

Leaning in, he hooked his fingers under my chin and pressed his thumb against my lips. "I promised I'd take you to Mexico. I never said anything about throwing you to the wolves. Did I?"

Pouting, I shook my head.

"This is my house in Monterrey. We'll stay here tonight. Tomorrow morning, I have to claim my father's body, and tomorrow afternoon, I'll fly to Mexico City to his estate to handle business…alone."

"But, Val…" I dove for the door handle, sprawled across his lap, effectively stopping his exit.

"But, nothing, Eden. These are my terms. Accept them, or I'll put your ass on a plane back to Houston faster than you can shove it in my face again."

Deciding not to push the issue, I shot him a look and crawled back to my side of the car. Throwing the door open, I hoisted my backpack onto my shoulder and stomped to the front door, Mateo hot on my heels.

"Well? Are you going to open it, or do I kick it in?"

Mateo's eyes rounded as he bounced a look back to Val.

Hiding a smirk, Val tucked a semi-automatic in the waistband of his pants and twirled a set of keys on his finger. "That mouth of yours, *Cereza*… I'm telling you…one of these days."

"Rise and shine, Danger."

Val twitched once then fell back asleep, his bare ass uncovered by the blanket I'd just ripped off.

Irritated at his lack of response, I climbed onto the bed and straddled his back. Extending my arms, I curled my finger around the trigger and repeated myself.

"Val, wake up before I pop a cap in your ass."

Like a lightning bolt shot down from the ceiling, his eyes flew open, and he twisted his body until he lay on his back, facing the barrel end of his own gun. Slowly raising his palms, his throat bobbed with a heavy swallow.

"Eden," he said, drawing out my name slowly. "What are you doing?"

"What does it look like I'm doing?"

"It looks like you're aiming a gun in my face. Why don't you put it down, and we can talk about whatever's wrong?"

Pretending to think for a moment, I quickly shrugged. "Nah, I like this more."

His fingers wiggled, itching to grab the gun out of my hands. "I'm not fucking around, Eden. Give me the gun."

"I'm not either, and no."

"What is it that you want?" His eyes hammered into me as his nostrils flared.

Good. I'd been waiting for those words.

Slackening my elbows, I leaned into his chest, enunciating every word. "I want you to take me to Mexico City."

Taking advantage of my position, Val grabbed my elbows, flipping me onto my back and somehow wrangling the gun out of my hands at the same time. Unloading the ammo, he tossed the gun to the side of the bed and held my hands above my head.

*Well, that ended up the exact opposite as I intended.*

"What the fuck was that about?" he roared. "You think that shit's funny?"

No. I didn't think it was funny, but for some reason a chorus of laughter fell from my chest. As I fought for air, I shook my head in protest. "No, I don't. But how else was I supposed to get your attention?"

"Well you've got it now, speak."

"Teach me to shoot."

"What?" He pulled back, his eyebrows raising to his hairline.

"You heard me. Teach me to shoot. I know a little, but not enough to protect either of us if things get crazy in Mexico City."

Releasing me, Val sat up, collecting the discarded pieces of his gun. "You didn't seem to have an issue when you almost blew Emilio's dick off." Cursing, he rubbed his thickening beard. "Stop it with this shit. You're not going. Besides, waking me up with a gun in my face doesn't exactly make me want to do anything for you, Eden."

Changing tactics, I moved behind him, sliding my palms up his back and down the front of his chest. "Emilio brings out the violent side in me." A deep throated rumble let me know I was on the right track to getting what I wanted. "Oh, come on, Val, admit it. You got turned on seeing me hold it, didn't you?"

"No."

Pressing my lips against his neck, I drew circles against his skin with the tip of my tongue. "No? Not even a little?"

"Maybe."

"Just think what it'd feel like to see me shoot one, to stand behind me and feel me pull the trigger, Val. All that power. All that force squeezed in the palm of my hand."

Another groan and a shudder, and I knew I had him.

Grabbing his pants at the foot of the bed, he shoved one leg in before moving out of my hold. "Get dressed."

"Take a strong stance and a firm grasp." Val stood behind me and kicked my feet apart wedging his knee between my legs. "Hold the gun on your target. You want to let your finger barely touch the trigger and let it go limp."

Snickering, I rolled my chin over my shoulder. "You, um, *want* it to go limp?"

"Very funny." Smirking, he pointed to the cans he'd set up on wooden posts in a field outside his house. "Now, turn back around and focus."

Obeying, I extended my arms again like he'd shown me.

"Now, I'm going to cover your hold and pull the trigger with you."

With experienced precision, he held us both steady and shot accurately, blowing the can off the post in one shot.

"Wow," I breathed, genuinely impressed. "You're good."

"You have no idea." He grinned.

Through two more rounds, he shadowed me, instructing me on stance and follow-through. Finally, through enough whining on my part, he stood back and let me try it on my own.

The first time, I was crushed to realize I'd shot a migrating bird. Val laughed at my devastation, asking how I planned to shoot a man if I broke down over random fowl. Pissed off, I shot again, effectively deflating his tire.

"Eden, let's just call it a day. I'd like to keep my windows while I still have them."

I'd failed at most everything I'd ever tried. I'd be damned if

I was going to fail at this. That can was a dead man.

"Don't be a smartass, Val. Smartasses sleep alone."

"Always with the dick threats."

"Use what you know." Sighing, I gave him a pleading look. "One more time, okay?"

"Fine," he agreed, palming his neck. "One more, and then I have to get ready to leave."

If I couldn't show him I could hold my own, no way would he let me leave with him. I had to make this work.

"I can do this."

"Sure, you can."

The condescension in his voice boiled my blood to a level of wanting to turn his nuts into fertilizer. It didn't help that he stalked behind me like a hungry lion, just waiting to go in for the kill.

My hand shook as I tried to focus on the target, his pacing form distracting me out of my peripheral vision.

"Can you stop doing that?"

"As you wish." Sidling up behind me, he molded into my back, his chin settling into the crook of my shoulder. "Better?"

Rolling my eyes, I aimed the gun. "Much."

"Do I make you nervous?"

"No."

"If you go with me, there'll be distractions all around you, *Cereza*. Bullets could be flying from all angles, men shouting, and chaos erupting like you've never experienced."

As his whispers broke into hoarse rasps, I bit my lip to keep from laughing. "Do I make *you* nervous, Danger?"

"No, you make me want to hold you against the fence and bend you over."

My body temperature rose with the morning sun, and my palms became sticky against the grip. Squinting, I focused all my attention on the silver can sitting on the post.

"Shoot," he whispered in my ear.

With calm composure, I squeezed the trigger, hitting the center of the can and knocking it off the post and across the lawn. Shocked, I lowered the gun and turned my chin excitedly over my shoulder. "Did you see—?"

The rest of my words ended up in Val's mouth as he crushed my lips with a bruising kiss. Grabbing my hips in a strong hold, he shifted our combined weight as he turned us against the fence, taking the gun from my hand.

"Hold on."

"Val, someone will see us."

"No one's here," he mumbled, his lips in my hair. "They're all gone into town. I want you—*now*."

My heart rate picked up as he ruled my body with an expert touch. I couldn't hold back a lust-filled moan as his fingers released the button on my shorts, working them down my legs until they pooled at my feet.

A clang of metal and material rustled behind me while he fumbled with his own pants. Fire lit up every inch of my skin as his hand trailed up my spine, urging my head down as he pulled my hips back.

"Whatever happens later, I need you to remember one thing," he whispered hotly against my ear.

"What's that?" I groaned.

In a surprise move, his fingers dug into my skin as he drove into me, the unexpected invasion tearing through me in a heated possession. Screaming, I threw my head back, at the same time his fingers wrapped around my throat.

"You belong to me."

With unreserved intensity, Val plunged into me, each thrust claiming more and more of my identity. Intense friction drove me to the brink of insanity, my fingers slipping from my hold on the fence, only to be slammed back onto it by Val's.

"Yes," I moaned over and over until the word garbled in my throat, and I splintered apart in his hands.

A layer of sweat glistened between us, as with a roar of my name, he released a lifetime of fear into me, his body jerking with power.

Rolling his forehead onto my shoulder, he lowered us both to the ground, cradling me in his lap. Without hesitating, he enveloped me in a protective hold, his nose disappearing into my hair.

"What have you done to me?" he murmurs.

Shifting in his arms, a glaze hovered in his warm chocolate eyes before he focused on the clouding sky.

"What do you mean?"

One arm tightened as the other folded underneath his head. "I don't need anyone, but I can't breathe if your scent isn't in my lungs. I can't focus if your fire hair isn't in my sight. I can't enjoy a meal without your taste on my lips. I can't hear if your voice isn't fucking yelling what an asshole I am, and I can't feel unless your skin slides under my fingers. So, yes, *Cereza*, what have you done to me?"

I fought the smile that threatened my lips. Lifting my chin, I whispered in his ear, "I've strengthened you."

He arched an eyebrow and peered down at me, waiting for more.

"I've given you something else to live for other than anger and revenge. Just like you've done for me. I should hate you, Valentin Carrera. I should take your gun and put a bullet in you."

He stroked my cheek. "Then, why don't you?"

I glanced down at our entwined hands, the gravity of the words on my tongue constricting my chest. "I think I'd sooner stand in front of one for you."

With my head laying against his chest, I felt the catch in his breath and the rumble in his throat as he admitted the words in the language meaning the most to him.

"*Te amo, Cereza.*"

A tear slipped from the corner of my eye as I nodded. "Damn you, Danger. I love you, too."

# Chapter Twenty-Six

## VALENTIN

Mexico City, Mexico

The flight from Monterrey to Mexico City took an hour by private jet. Had it not been for the morbid nature of our destination, I would've found mild amusement in Eden's shock at finding my father's private jet waiting at Del Norte International Airport instead of the commercial airliner she expected. Even half-hearted, crude comments at joining the half-mile high club fell flat as both of us fidgeted with anticipation and anxiousness.

"Do you want me to go in with you?" Eden's red hair fanned around her face as we stood outside Mexico City's morgue.

A strike of irony hit me as people milled around the streets of Mexico's largest city. My father was an arrogant son of a bitch. He lived for notoriety and the thrill of hearing his name whispered in hushed circles. He traveled with an entourage, lived outrageously, and spent money as if every day were his last on this earth.

Yet inside the plain, nondescript building in front of me, that same man lay on a metal slab beside the rest of humanity.

Sometimes, death truly was the great equalizer.

Brushing a stray hair off her cheek, I shifted a glance inside the thick glass door and shook my head. "No. I'd rather you wait with Mateo at the cantina across the street. I need to do this alone."

I couldn't explain it, but even in death, I didn't want her near my father. Some irrational part of me feared Eden walking in that room would stir whatever evil lay dormant in his cold body and damn her to my fate.

"I can be quiet, Val. I'll just be there if you need me."

"I want you to listen to me, Eden, and I want you to hear my words, not your ego." Dropping the hand holding her cheek, I shoved it in my pocket to resist touching her again. "We aren't in Monterrey anymore. This is Mexico City. This is my father's seat of power and only six hours from Guadalajara, which is Muñoz territory. Eyes have been on us from the moment we got on that plane at Del Norte. Do you understand what I'm telling you?"

A flash of sadness swept across her face before hardened understanding melted it into a mask of cool indifference. "Of course, I do. Your father's men, as well as Muñoz informers, are watching us. We have to act like you're the ruthless asshole who kidnapped me, and I'm the petrified damsel in distress who fears for her life. Yeah, yeah. I've got it. You can't touch me, smile at me, or otherwise act like you give a shit. You're an emotional black hole."

"Eden—"

"No, I get it, Val." Attempting a quick smile meant only for me, she stepped backward before I could be tempted to reach for her. "Really, I get it. We'll do what we have to do."

"And then?"

Offering her wrist to Mateo, who stood at a respectable distance behind her, she held his eye until he sighed and grabbed it in a mock stronghold. "Ask me again when I've gotten justice for Nash."

Something I couldn't explain passed between us as her eyes flashed with promise. Then, as quickly as they'd warmed, they drained of all emotion, the corners of her mouth pulling into a frightened frown.

Glancing over her shoulder at Mateo, she pulled against his hold on her wrist, raising her voice. "Where are you taking me? I demand to talk to my father!"

Panic raced through me before Mateo's hold moved up to her bicep, squeezing it with gentle pressure as he urged her across the street. "I'm not putting up with your shit right now, lady. Either you walk or I drag you. Your choice."

My eyes shot between them as their stares connected and, with a slight tug from his hand, Eden purposely stumbled behind him, yelling obscenities about him hurting her.

Since I was six years old, I hadn't been able to form normal relationships like everyone else around me. When a neighbor opened that cellar door and found me hungry, thirsty, and soiled, I swore I'd never put myself in a position to lose another person I cared about. The moment my foot hit the dirt and the sun hit my face, the part of my soul capable of forming lasting emotional attachment died, and a will to protect myself encased it with revenge and hate.

Somehow, the two people muttering obscenities and dragging each other across the street managed to break through the barbed wire and revive what I thought could never be salvaged.

The ability to care again.

Somewhere along the way, Mateo Cortes became my friend, and Eden Lachey stole the heart I didn't know I still had. She made me want more than the life planned for me by a monster.

Gripping the door, I steeled my nerves for one last

confrontation with the man who'd caused it all, before I put the final nail in his reign of terror.

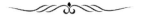

As the heavy metal door slammed behind the medical examiner, I stood alone in the middle of the morgue, a metal drawer pulled out in front of me, and my father's gray, lifeless cheeks reflected the flashing overhead fluorescent bulb from above.

*"Do you positively identify this man as your father, Alejandro Carrera, Mr. Carrera?"*

*"Yes."*

*"Very well. Would you like a moment alone?"*

*"Excuse me?"*

*"A moment. Would you like a few moments to say some words to your father, Mr. Carrera?"*

*"Oh. Sure. I mean, yes, I would, thank you."*

The exchange replayed in my head and a sadistic laugh rumbled in my chest.

A few words. How about a lifetime of words? A lifetime of beatings, blood, and being sold into a life no father should ever take pleasure in bringing a son into. The Carrera name stood for death and destruction, and it all stemmed from the man lying on a slab with a white sheet draped over his chin.

*"Why can't I see all of his face?"*

*"Mr. Carrera, as I'm sure you know, your father didn't die of natural causes. His throat was cut and it's not something we like to display to family members."*

Stepping closer, I reached out to lower the sheet before I could think better of it. In this cartel life, I'd killed many men and tortured many more. Blood, or the inside of a man's body didn't cause me to break a sweat. However, one look at the savagery inflicted upon the man who'd given me life shot a haze across my vision that blinded me for a moment.

*This is where I'll end up if things don't change between cartels.*

"Bet you never thought it'd end like this, did you, old man?" Not that I expected anything other than the hum from the overhead light, but I paused before continuing. "You promised her you'd stay away from Mexico City. She believed you. She trusted you, and look what you did to her. Look what you did to all of us. My entire fucking family is dead because you couldn't keep a goddamn promise. Do you know what it was like to hear them scream?" Rage built as memories flooded the tiny room. "I was six years old, you bastard! You only accepted me when I pledged to kill for you."

Fresh pain from the constant screams I heard every time I closed my eyes had me wanting to resurrect him, just so I could slit his throat all over again.

"I damned myself to hell just to get justice for the women you allowed to die. I dreamed of the day I'd be powerful enough to take you down and watch you crawl on your knees while I took everything away from you. Then I planned to kill you myself and run this goddamn cartel *my* way." Roaming a glance down his motionless corpse, a sadistic laugh tore from my throat. "Guess I'll have to settle for the last part."

"Mr. Carrera?" The door opened as the medical examiner stuck her no-nonsense ponytail through the crack. "Are you finished?"

With a last look at my father, I turned toward the door and smiled. "No, ma'am. I'm just getting started."

# Chapter Twenty-Seven
## EDEN

"Val's fine. Stop dissecting your burrito, Eden. It's dinner, not a science project." Taking a slow drink of his beer, Mateo tipped the neck of the bottle toward the sleeveless, short black dress I wore. "And you can't afford to skip any more meals."

Dropping my fork with a clang against my plate, I ran my hands over the loose-fitting material self-consciously. "Are you trying to tell me I look like shit, Mateo?"

"Woman, you've been on some sort of self-imposed hunger strike for a week now." Lifting an eyebrow, he shook his head and brought his own overstuffed tortilla to his mouth. "A strong wind could carry you out to sea."

"I had to exert some sort of control over my situation, you know," I argued, picking my fork back up and trailing it through a glob of guacamole. "Being chained didn't exactly lend itself to rational decision-making."

"Cuffed."

"What?"

"Cuffed. You said chained. You were cuffed not chained. You act like we had you hanging from a rafter in some dungeon."

"Whatever," I muttered, nibbling on a tortilla chip. It tasted like fried cardboard. My stomach churned, thinking of Val alone in the morgue with his father and raw emotions he'd kept bottled for years.

Sighing, Mateo finished chewing, then dropped his food back onto his plate, leveling an accusing stare at me. "Okay, truth or dare time, Eden."

The chip crumbled in my hand as I returned his stare. "Be serious."

"Oh, I'm very serious. Truth, or dare."

I didn't trust any questions Val's right-hand man could possibly have for me, so the answer flew out before thought could piece together his game plan. "Dare."

"Fine. I dare you to eat everything on your plate." A smirk coated his face as he sat back and crossed his arms for dramatic effect.

*Son of a bitch.*

The thought of even biting into my chicken burrito make my mouth water, and not in the 'oh my god, I'm salivating for more,' kind of way. No, a metallic taste filled every crevice, forcing me to swallow in more of a 'oh my god, I may just puke more than a drunk virgin on prom night,' kind of way.

However, a dare was a dare.

Steeling my nerves, I tried to hold my breath as I bit into the vile concoction, but chewing and swallowing apparently required oxygen and use of fine motor skills. Gagging on impact, I immediately spit it all out in my napkin.

"I can't do it, Mateo. God, I'm sorry. I just can't. I'm too worked up to eat."

His expression never changed as he simply nodded in

acknowledgement. "Truth, it is."

"No."

"Then I suggest you open that napkin and start licking, Lachey."

"You can't be serious."

"Try me."

If I had any clue where we were, or how to get back, I'd leave his ass just for being a dick. "Jesus, fine! Ask your stupid question."

Leaning his elbows on the table, his eyes studied my every move. "What's going on between you and Val?"

"Nothing."

"Eden…"

Pushing my plate away, I rubbed my temples as a headache brewed between them. "All right, there's…something. I just don't know what to call it, or label it, or…fuck, I don't know. Val doesn't want anyone to know, okay? He thinks it makes him vulnerable."

"He's absolutely right."

The gravity in his voice didn't lessen the ball of dread sitting in the pit of my stomach. "I don't want to hurt him, Mateo."

Crumbling his own napkin, he threw it in his plate. "Look, I'm not going to tell you what to do. Whatever you and Val do is between you two. That's none of my business."

"Thank—"

"But when it jeopardizes his life," he interrupted, folding his arms across the table, "That's when it becomes my business. I like you, Eden. I think you've been given a shitty deal in life just like him. Maybe in another time, you could've been good for each other."

My heart sank. "But now?"

"You're in Mexico City, waiting on a man who's identifying

261

the body of his father, one of the most notorious drug lords in the world, then he'll meet with that man's cartel to follow in his footsteps. You're not going to change him." He tilted his chin to hold my stare. "I want you to understand that. This isn't a game. You won't live happily ever after. If you step into this ring, be prepared to fight."

I heard every word of his literal and double meanings. The words he spoke hurt to hear, but I'd come to respect Mateo as a straight shooter when it came to the truth. This was no different. Whether I wanted to hear it or not, the truth he spoke couldn't be refuted.

Luckily, I'd reconciled myself to the fact that happily ever after was a lie fabricated by Disney and jewelry stores.

Standing, I glanced out of the window as Val exited the heavy glass door of the morgue.

"Come on, Mateo, it's time to find your ringside seat."

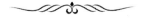

MY RINGSIDE SEAT TURNED INTO A BACKSEAT. AS IN THE BACKSEAT of the charcoal-colored Tahoe that Val and Mateo put me in before getting in their own car and heading to the meeting with Alejandro's top men.

I'd argued and pleaded until almost making a scene. In the end, I knew it was useless.

*"Val, you promised to take me. Don't end up lying to me, too."*

*"That's not fair, Cereza. I promised to bring you to Mexico. I promised to let you come with me to Mexico City. Not once did I agree to let you walk into a room of rapists and killers looking like an all-you-can-eat buffet."*

*As Mateo conveniently found something extraordinarily*

interesting on the side of a nearby building, Val leaned into the Tahoe, shrouded by the blessing of darkness, and kissed me quickly, but purposely. Resting my hands on his chest, I felt his heart beat wildly against my palm.

"How am I supposed to get closure for Nash if Manuel Muñoz is still walking around, Val?"

"We'll get him. Tonight, isn't the night, though."

"When?"

"Don't fear the enemy that hates you, Eden, but the fake friend that hugs you."

I raised an eyebrow, still pissed off at being left behind. "Have you been reading fortune cookies, Danger?"

A low laugh rumbled in his chest. "It's a famous quote. It means Manuel will be expecting me to retaliate right now. He'll be waiting for it—prepared for it, even. The risk of failure would be huge. Lulling him into a false sense of security, even convincing him I'd blurred the battle lines a little, is the key."

Then it hit me what he planned on doing. "Oh, my God. You're going to make them think you're burying the hatchet, aren't you?"

Another kiss, and he backed away from the Tahoe. "Interesting choice of words, Cereza. After Esteban Muñoz had my mother shot, his men carved out her heart and delivered it to him."

The one chip I'd eaten with Mateo threatened to come up as I slapped my hand across my mouth and mumbled through my fingers. "Val, don't go. Please, I don't have a good feeling about this."

Leaning against the doorframe, he nodded to Mateo. "I have to go."

"Val!"

"You'll have your justice, Eden, and I'll have mine."

*"YOU'LL HAVE YOUR JUSTICE, EDEN, AND I'LL HAVE MINE."*

Val's words echoed in my head along with my footsteps. The sheer square footage of Alejandro Carrera's estate was mind-blowing, but the ornate detail work in the framework above all the archways and molding indicated just what a self-indulgent, pompous asshole the man was. Mirrors covered every wall as if he couldn't walk two feet without stopping to admire himself. I almost gave myself a headache from all the constant eye rolling it involuntarily pulled from me.

Feeling stifled from the overwhelming presence of such a narcissistic man, I searched for an escape. I needed air, and I needed it now. I breathed a sigh of relief when my eyes landed on intricate brushed gold French doors that led out onto a terrace.

*Thank God for small favors.*

As I reached for the handle, a hand with thick, rough fingers grabbed me around my upper arm. "Miss Lachey, are you sure that's a good idea?"

Whipping around, my hand immediately flew to my leg, fingering the gun holster that sat nestled on my inner thigh. Once I recognized him, my eyes widened, then narrowed. "Jesus, Joaquin. You think you could wear a cowbell or something? You scared the shit out of me."

"A cowbell, *señorita*? I don't understand."

"Forget it," I said, waving a hand. "I'm just going to get some air."

"We have air here." Motioning around us with both hands, he took an exaggerated deep breath.

*Oh, great. Val left me in the care of a fucking comedian.*

Joaquin Salazar was a new soldier in Alejandro's army. He

was what Val explained was in limbo between something called a falcon and a *sicario*. A falcon was somewhat of a watchdog—the eyes and ears on the street—and the lowest ranking man in a cartel. One step up from that, a *sicario*, or a hitman, was part of the armed group who carried out the assassinations, kidnappings, and real dangerous shit for the higher-ups.

Joaquin had proven his worth in an attempt made on Alejandro's life near Guadalajara nearly six months ago but hadn't yet risen in the ranks enough to qualify for a place at the sit-down with Val and the other lieutenants. As a consolation prize, he qualified as my shadow.

*Lucky me.*

"Look, Kevin Hart, I realize you're just following orders, but if you don't get out of my face and let me walk onto this terrace to get some air by myself—you and me—we're going to have a problem. Do you get what I'm telling you?"

"Who is this Kevin Hart? Is he new? Mateo told me nothing of another guard."

Screaming in frustration, I grabbed the sides of my hair and gritted my teeth. "Go. Away."

"But, *señorita*—"

"Joaquin, do you have children?"

"No. Not yet."

"Do you want to?"

He blinked slowly before answering. "Someday."

"Then I suggest you leave before I tie your nuts in such small knots, you'll never shoot another load the rest of your life."

I'd never seen a man move so fast in my life. One minute he was there, the next—gone.

Men were so easy. One threat to the boys and they folded like a cheap house of cards.

Outside the walls of that monstrous house, I finally began to breathe again. Sinking into a plush outdoor recliner, I put my feet up and enjoyed the impressive view of the city lights.

The long trip, coupled with the stress of worrying about Val and what he'd walked into, finally wore on me, and my eyelids closed a heavy curtain over the world.

I had no idea how long I'd slept until a crash from inside woke me with a jolt of adrenaline. Muted voices carried through the house as my pulse picked up a furious tempo.

"Joaquin?"

Attempting to keep a level head, I stood up and tilted my chin over the railing.

Hell, no. Three stories down would not end well for me.

My gaze landed back on the French doors as the same sense of dread settled in the center of my stomach and burst into tiny shards of resignation.

Swallowing hard, I ran my hand up my thigh and used my thumb to unsnap the holder on the handgun Val had given me before putting me in the Tahoe. Holding it tight, with the chamber loaded and my finger on the trigger, I opened the glass door.

"Joaquin? Are you awake?"

# Chapter Twenty-Eight
## VALENTIN

Silence filled the room as all eyes stared blankly at me, then ping-ponged around from rank to rank, verifying they'd heard me correctly and hadn't hallucinated.

And I was very fucking serious.

"Is there a problem?"

"Hell yes, there's a problem," Guzman yelled, standing up and slamming his fist down on the worn wooden table. The table had seen many of these same meetings take place around it over the years. It'd seen arguments, deals being made, and even its fair share of bloodshed; the evidence still stained some of the crevices. "This is suicide, Valentin."

"For whom exactly?"

"For all of us," he bellowed, gesturing around the table at the dozens of men flanking him. "We served loyally under your father. We have a long-standing war with the Muñoz cartel. They killed your mother, sister, and aunt, for fuck's sake."

Hearing him speak their names did something to me, and I pummeled my fist onto his spread hand. "I know that, asshole.

You don't have to remind me. I was there, remember?"

With a howl, he pulled his hand back, recoiling into his chair. "You've gone soft, Carrera. You've been in the states too long. You don't remember what real life is like in the ranks."

"The only thing soft is your dick, Guzman. Now, sit down, and shut the fuck up, before you really piss me off."

Glaring, his eyes darkened as he held his injured hand against his chest.

"A little over the top, don't you think?" Mateo muttered under his breath beside me, his eyes questioning my actions.

"Probably," I conceded. "But the bastard has had it coming for years."

Gerardo Guzman had been my father's second-in-command for over a decade. When I joined the cartel at age sixteen, it was automatically understood within the ranks that, as the heir apparent, I'd one day inherit the empire. I could tell as the years passed, it bothered Guzman, but he wisely kept his mouth shut and his head down.

"Something else to say, Guzman?"

"No, *jefe*. Just like to stay informed."

If I wasn't hell bent on getting home to Eden, I might've pushed the issue with him. As it stood, I was just fucking tired. I wanted a warm bed, some good tequila, and to be nestled in between Eden's thighs. I had no time or energy to waste on bruised egos.

"As I said, there'll be no retaliation right now, but when the time comes, it'll be on *my* terms. Now, if there are no more comments, I'll explain why we're twenty-two million dollars in debt, and why…" I paused and looked each man in the eye before continuing, "…four buildings went up in flames, and we narrowly escaped all of them with our lives."

"We?" One of the newer lieutenants asked.

"Yes, 'we,'" I snapped. "As in me, two of my top lieutenants, and a prisoner. Shut up for a minute, and I'll tell you about her and why I think my father was so interested in her." Preparing myself for the bomb I was about to drop, I shot Mateo a side glance and curled my finger around the trigger of my gun under the table. "Then, I can tell you to fuck off if she interests you in any way."

"The fuck?"

"You heard me, Guzman."

A low rumble of voices milled around the room, and I waited for it to die down before I commanded their attention. "I'm speaking!" All eyes turned my way as silence replaced the incessant chatter. "Somehow Manuel Muñoz infiltrated a drug debt in Houston, causing my men to torture an innocent man. Afterward, Muñoz *sicarios* executed him."

"So? Innocent death happens." The new lieutenant snorted with annoyance. "What do we care?"

My trigger finger itched to shove it under his chin. "We care, because shit is different in America, you fucking idiot. Mistakes like that could bring down our whole operation." His jaw tightened in anger, but he stopped talking. "As I was saying, the innocent man's sister witnessed the hit."

The thought of Eden, hiding in the back of that kitchen as her brother died, filled me with indescribable anger, and I felt my entire body clench as the muscles in my neck twitched. Out of the corner of my eye, I saw Mateo rake his eyes down my stiffened form and take over.

"This girl, she's a close friend and employee of one of our highest-ranking lieutenants in Houston. By our own code, we had to act fast, so we took her before Muñoz guns could. Unfortunately, by a betrayal unknown to her, she'd been tracked by a GPS. In turn, Valentin's whereabouts were known at all times."

"And this *puta* is still alive, after all *that*?"

"Do not call her a *puta*!" I'd had enough. My nerves were shot, and the one thing I wouldn't tolerate was anyone disrespecting Eden. Pulling my gun, I grabbed Guzman by the front of his shirt and shoved the tip against his cheek. "You will never call her a *puta* again. Her name is Eden. However, you will refer to her as Miss Lachey, ma'am, or *señorita*, are we clear?"

"Jesus, fine." He raised his palms as my chest heaved. Releasing him, he sank back down into his seat. Glaring, he picked up the shot of tequila sitting in front of him and held it against his mouth. "Fuck, man, you'd think you had a hard-on for this chick or something."

Loosening two buttons at the top of my shirt, I drank my own shot glass sitting in front of me.

I needed to stay in control. I couldn't risk showing my hand too early to my men. My father ruled this cartel with an iron fist, and despite the fact he was a heartless bastard, every one of these lieutenants respected the hell out of him and followed him blindly. I needed the same level of loyalty from them to change the future of the Carrera name.

Letting them know I planned to bring an American into our world wouldn't win me any favors right now.

"I know you all want revenge for the attack on my father." A chorus of 'fuck yeahs' drowned out my speech, and I paused to let them have their moment before continuing. "And, trust me, you all will have your opportunity. If anyone has reason for a vendetta, it's me. The Muñoz cartel has murdered my entire family. No one wants their heads more than me, but when we ruin them, I want all of them. I want their territory and all their producers and suppliers. I want it all." Another round of 'fuck yeahs' and cheers echoed off the walls. "To do that, we have to be smart and bide our time. You all must trust me and my judgment to plan the end of the Muñoz cartel. The one question left is…are you with me, or against me?"

After a moment or two of silence, Mateo stood up, his gun in his right hand, crossed over his chest, and placed over his heart. "Allegiance until death. Carrera pledge to new *jefe*, Valentin Carrera."

Another man stood next. "Allegiance until death to Valentin Carrera."

Four more men stood. "Allegiance until death to Valentin Carrera."

One by one, every lieutenant stood and repeated the same words, until every eye landed on the only man still seated.

Finally, his eyes pulled tight at the corners, Guzman stood. "Allegiance until death."

I nodded in acceptance of their devotion. "One more thing. If any of you lay one finger on Eden Lachey, I'll see each of you hanged, beheaded, then spiked in front of your own houses. She's mine."

*Fuck it. They already pledged allegiance.*

I'D HAD ENOUGH TEQUILA AN HOUR AGO.

The men wanted to celebrate, and Mateo kicked me under the table when I opened my mouth to tell them to kiss my ass. A few bottles later, stories about my father had been told, and I'd lost count at how many times I rolled my eyes.

Glancing at my watch, I finally stood up. "We reconvene tomorrow. Dismissed, men."

Twenty minutes later, most of them had dispersed to local cantinas to continue the celebration. Mateo left to pull the car around, leaving me and Guzman outside the plain adobe building. Pulling my phone from my pocket, I'd just punched in the number to the new phone I'd given Eden, when a voice behind me snarled in my ear.

"I'll never follow you. This is my cartel, you spoiled brat." My knuckles cracked around the phone as his gun pressed against the back of my head. "You think you can just show up after six years and take what I've spent ten years kissing ass to claim? Fuck you, and your warnings."

"Pulling the trigger would be suicide, and you know it, Guzman. You were my father's second. You, above anyone, should've known how this would play out when he died."

"What I know, you over-privileged little shit, is that you'll get one thing you want."

I had to stall him. With a gun to the back of my head, he had the upper hand. My mind raced with any situation that'd end with my brains not being sprayed across the side of the building.

"And what's that, Guzman? Your dick, bronzed and on my mantle?"

His calm chuckle unnerved me. "You and your American *puta* will be together forever."

"How do you figure?"

He lowered his voice and leaned in close, the alcohol on his breath invading my nostrils. "Manuel Muñoz has probably slit her from throat to pussy by now."

It was as if a cold hand reached inside my chest, squeezed my heart, ripped it out still beating, and held it in front of my face. I couldn't breathe, fighting through a numbness that overtook any emotion I'd found in recent weeks.

"You're lying."

"Think so? It's a shame he had to rip that sexy, little black number to shreds when he gutted her. I'll admit, she looked hot in it. I must know, Valentin, is it true? Does the carpet match the drapes?"

I saw red. I didn't care about stalling. I didn't care about anything but getting to Eden.

"Motherfucker!" I landed a sharp elbow into his stomach, immediately getting rewarded with a forceful grunt as he doubled over. Taking advantage of his vulnerable position, I twisted and grabbed the wrist holding the gun. Regaining his footing, he cursed, slamming me into the side of the building. Still holding his wrist with my left hand, I grabbed his throat with the right. "What did you do to her, you piece of shit traitor? If Muñoz touched her, I'll see you both in hell!"

He coughed as a sadistic smile crept along his face. "You're not the only one who knows how to forge alliances, boy. You take from me, little Val, and I take from you."

The images in my mind swirled a torrid mix of blind rage and indescribable pain. Past and present raced toward one point in time and collided. The six-year-old boy in me, and the thirty-year-old man I'd become, converged and imploded as history repeated itself before my eyes.

Everything moved in slow motion. Guzman landed a punch to my stomach, causing me to loosen my hold on his throat. Gaining leverage, he wrestled the gun out of my grasp. Seeing the gun tucked in my waistband, he tossed it behind him, then aimed his own gun at my chest.

"Your old man fought me, too, Valentin. I wonder if I'll get the same pleasure in watching you bleed out?" Steadying his hand, he tightened his finger around the trigger.

Without a weapon to protect myself, I held his gaze and waited. The last thing I'd do on this earth wouldn't be giving this asshole the satisfaction of looking away while he killed me. An arrogant smile lifted the edges of his thick mustache as the gun went off, the blast echoing in my ears long after the shot rang out.

My last thought was of Eden. I wish I could've said goodbye. Without a doubt, I knew we weren't headed to the same place. She'd have everlasting life. I'd burn for eternity.

I waited for the pain…the blood…the coldness that told me I'd left this world.

None of it happened.

I ran my hands over my still dry shirt when I noticed blood seeping from the corners of Guzman's mouth. Frozen in the darkness, I watched as his eyes rolled back in his head moments before his knees buckled, and he dropped to the ground.

Tearing my fixated stare away, I glanced up to see Mateo standing behind him, his arm extended, and smoke still fuming from his gun. His eyes were a dangerous black with a depth of hatred I'd never seen from him.

"Mateo?"

"When we take our pledge, we do it with honor." Looking down at Guzman's lifeless body, he spit on him without remorse. "A man is nothing without honor. Death is mercy for a traitor."

There was more to say, but it'd have to wait for another time. Only one thing burned in my mind.

*Eden.*

"Car, Mateo. Where's the car?"

He pointed around the building. "Across the street. What's happened?" Following behind me, he nodded toward Guzman. "Should I call a cleaner?"

"Fuck it," I growled. "Let it be a message. Leave him for whatever wild animal gives a shit enough to eat him." Grabbing my gun off the ground, I hit the speed dial button to Eden's number and cursed as it rang repeatedly with no answer. "Damn it!" Disconnecting the call, I hit redial, and got the same result.

*"Jefe?"*

Bile rose in my throat as fear conjured my mother's screams from a place in my mind I never allowed myself to revisit. Eventually, her voice became Eden's, and I had to forcefully swallow vomit.

"Get me to the plane. They have Eden."

# Chapter Twenty-Nine

## EDEN

The gun shook as I pressed two fingers against Joaquin's neck.

*Dead.*

The bartender from Houston in me wanted to scream and cry as I stood over the young man whose throat had been slit. His only crime was protecting me.

However, the kidnapped woman in me, who'd lived through my brother's execution, fifteen days of captivity, shootings, bombings, and a volatile affair with the drug lord who arranged it all, shut my fucking mouth and took his gun.

I had no clue what happened inside the house, but common sense told me it had Muñoz written all over it. No civilian would have the balls to set foot on Carrera grounds, much less touch one of their men.

Pressed up against a corner wall, my breath came hard and heavy. Sweat rolled down my temples, and I forced myself to calm down enough to think when the realization hit me.

I was completely alone.

Joaquin was dead, Val and Mateo were God knew where, and I'd crossed the border into a nightmare.

"Eden Lachey…"

Squeezing my eyes shut, I crossed my arms against my chest with a gun in each hand and a layer of sweat building between the grips and my palms. The thick accent snarled with contempt as heavy footsteps moved around the living room.

"Come out, Eden Lachey. The longer you make me chase you, the worse it's going to be for you."

Stifling a scream, I pushed myself farther into the wall. As the footsteps moved closer, I opened my eyes and scanned the alcove for an escape route. Near panicking, I finally located a cracked door that led to a pantry the size of my dad's entire house. I'd run into it earlier in a self-guided tour of the estate.

Five hundred feet was all that stood between life and death.

I was prey, hunted in a fatal game of cat and mouse.

*I wonder if this is what Nash felt like before he died?*

Leaving the security of my dark alcove scared the shit out of me, but logic told me I was seconds away from being found. Needing a free hand, I shoved my gun back into my thigh holster and held the grip of Joaquin's with a sweaty grasp. Giving the *Santa Muerte* pendant a rub for good luck, I counted to three and pushed off the wall. My chest burned as I ran like hell toward the door, keeping a straight-line focus with a prayer on my lips.

With no footsteps behind me, my heart beat wild with adrenaline.

*Holy shit, I'm going to make it.*

Just as my fingers closed around the corners of the open door, my phone rang.

The phone I'd left in the pantry down the steps in front of me rang loud and repeatedly.

*No!*

Rapid footsteps pounded behind me.

Tearing the door open, I took one step when a rough hand grabbed me by the hair and jerked me backward until I lost my footing and tumbled against a hard chest. Terror shot through me, and I managed one scream before a dirty and calloused hand clamped hard against my mouth. Out of nowhere, his other hand ripped the gun from my hands the moment I took aim.

"Going somewhere?"

When Emilio took me outside my father's house, it was from behind. I never saw it coming and was unprepared for the attack. I never had a chance to defend myself or fight back.

If death came for me tonight, it'd be with blood under my nails.

Opening wide, I bit down as hard as I could on his fingers, immediately tasting blood on my tongue. Yelling loud, he shook his mangled hand, as droplets of blood splattered across the white walls. Seizing the opportunity, I quickly turned around and raised a knee, grazing the side of his nuts. It was enough to double him over and draw out a tortured groan.

With no time to wipe errant tears, I took the pantry stairs three at a time, praying I didn't stumble and fall. Part of me wanted to stop and look for the incessantly ringing phone to call Val, but I knew there wasn't time. Once my eyes landed on the door leading to the courtyard, I broke into an all-out sprint.

*Almost.*

Every Thanksgiving, Nash would invite his buddies over to play tackle football after dinner. Every year, I'd beg him to let me play. Every year he'd give me the same answer.

*"No, Edie. You're too breakable. Girls don't play rough sports like this."*

The year I turned sixteen, I'd had enough. Dressed in my sluttiest outfit, I talked Nick Tunstall into letting me play on his

279

team, in exchange for letting him see my boobs. It wasn't my proudest moment, but I had a point to make. I rationalized that the ends justified the means.

Nash had been half-right. It wasn't that girls couldn't play football; it was that they didn't play with huge, two-hundred-pound men. The first hit I took felt like what I imaged hitting a concrete wall at two-hundred miles per hour would feel like.

That tackle felt like a massage compared to a direct hit from a Muñoz henchman.

Catching me around the waist, the impact threw us both into the door. With his momentum behind me, I hit first, my chin smacking against the glass as it shattered. I didn't hesitate to turn, kicking my legs wildly in the air and searching out any part of his body to connect to.

"Stupid bitch!" With a roar, he swung his arm out and backhanded me across the cheek. The impact sent me sprawling against the door again. This time, the back of my skull connected with the glass with a sickening thud. As blurry vision clouded my line of sight, nausea crawled up my throat.

*I'm going to die right here.*

Clawing at my own leg, I blindly reached for my last hope. My fingers brushed the leather as he braced his forearm against my chest and pinned my arms in place. His gun settled against my temple and smiling a wicked grin, he cocked his finger. Shutting my eyes tight, I held my breath as he pulled the trigger.

*Silence.*

His grin widened. "Oops. No bullet in that chamber."

Tears rolled down my face as clarity came to me full force.

All the times I begged Val to kill me, I didn't want to die.

Readjusting his hold on the gun, the man with dead eyes and a thin mustache pressed harder against my chest. "I have a surprise for you, Eden Lachey. We're going on a trip…one that'll lead the rat to the cheese."

"A trip?" I croaked the words roughly, my voice hoarse from screaming. Before he could answer, the meaning of his words hit me.

They were setting a trap for Val.

"You're wrong," I swore, shaking my head as much as I could under the pressure of the gun. "Valentin Carrera doesn't give a shit about me."

Laughing, he adjusted his hold on the gun once more. "Nice try, bitch."

With brutality I'd never experienced in my life, he pistol-whipped me until I blacked out.

GASOLINE.

The stench of petroleum filled my nose way before sound did. It burned my throat and coated my stomach with a scent I could taste. Low conversation from above my head buzzed in my ear. The words sounded clipped and garbled as if I were in an alternate universe.

They were different. They were unrecognizable. They were Spanish.

Immediately, my body stiffened, and a searing pain shot from the base of my skull to the top of my head. Something inside of me warned my eyes not to open. It didn't matter if they listened or not, because they felt glued shut.

My wrists hurt with a familiar ache that reminded me of my arm being shackled to a metal bedframe. With concerted effort, my brain instructed my arms to move, only to be met with resistance.

Understanding the reason I couldn't move my limbs took

too much effort to care.

Everything seemed to move in slow motion, swimming underwater and against a strong current. Wherever I was, we were moving. With every jerk and jostle, I felt myself being transported from one place to another.

Soon, a loud rumble roared in my ears, followed by the sensation of going up…up…up…

Then, complete weightlessness.

I should've fought to wake up and look for landmarks. With all the transporting, I needed to remember useful information to give my location to someone who could help me.

But the harder I fought to open my eyes, the deeper I sank to the bottom of the ocean, the murky water closing in on me as the darkness claimed me once more.

"WAKE UP, YOU CARRERA *PUTA*. IT'S TIME TO GET ON YOUR KNEES. Surely, you're used to it by now."

Strong hands dug into my upper arms and dragged me across rough flooring. Bright light shone in my eyes, first forcing them open, then immediately commanding them closed.

*My head.*

Where the hell did they take me?

"Where…" Licking my lips, I tasted blood as they cracked and split from tension and dehydration. "What time is it? Where are we?"

"We're going on a boat ride, now shut up and walk."

The light extinguished, shrouding everything in an ominous cloud of darkness.

The hell *I* was going anywhere with these people. Digging my heels in the soft sod, my sudden movement caused a couple of them to stumble. Curses flew and another blow landed across my face. A new man grabbed my hair and dragged me across a river bed. The soft slosh of small waves crashing against the bank greeted us as my eyes landed on a small yellow blow-up raft.

"Oh, hell, no." Digging my heels in again, I shook my head violently. "I'm not getting in that thing. We'll sink."

Rough hands twisted in my hair, jerking it backward until I stared perpendicular to the night sky. "The only thing that'll sink is you when I shove this gun down your throat and throw you in the river. Now get in the fucking boat!"

As I stepped into the raft, a hard shove from behind had me sprawling face first onto the bottom. With my hands still bound behind me, I had nothing to break my fall but my already bruised jaw. Blood filled my mouth again, the taste almost becoming comforting.

At least I knew I was still alive.

Two men climbed in after me, and the rest pushed the boat away from the embankment. As the current took us away from civilization, Val and Nash entered my mind.

Regardless of what happened, I knew I'd see one of them soon. Which one depended on what happened in the next few hours.

# Chapter Thirty
## VALENTIN

The car had barely broken twenty miles per hour heading up the driveway to the estate when I couldn't take it anymore. Throwing the door open, I tumbled out, hitting the concrete with a jarring force that rattled my brain.

Once I caught my breath and got my footing, I took off on a full run toward the house. I knew Mateo called my name a few times, watching the movement of his mouth from my peripheral vision as he parked the car, but it didn't matter. The roar in my head took up all the space reserved for sound.

I reached the front door and prepared to kick it down, when I noticed it standing halfway open.

*They're already inside.*

Pulling my gun, I called her name the safest way I knew how. "*Cereza*? Where are the cans, baby? I can't see the posts, so you need to tell me." I waited for a response, listening for any signs of movement. "*Cereza*?"

Farther into the house, a metallic smell hit my nose, sending a violent chill up my spine.

*No.*

Out of the corner of my eye, a body lay on the floor swimming in so much blood, there couldn't have been any left inside of it. Instinctively, I closed my eyes, willing it not to be Eden. The moment I opened them and saw the militant style black pants and heavy black boots, I let out a sigh of relief, then felt like a shit for being happy about the death of one of my men.

But between one of my men and Eden, I'd choose death for my men over and over.

Leaning over him, I recognized Joaquin Salazar. Barely an adult, the loyal member of my father's personal team had proved his honor and willingness to protect our cartel with his life. It was the whole reason Mateo chose him to stay with Eden.

If a man like that had been gutted like a fish, what the hell had they done to a woman who'd been at the center of an international drug war?

*"Manuel Muñoz has probably slit her from throat to pussy by now."*

Within seconds, Mateo appeared by my side, gun in hand. "I've searched the upper floors and the pantry. They're not here."

"Where the fuck is she?" Conflicting emotions raged through me: relief at not finding her lying in a pool of blood and fear at what was happening to her at the hands of Manuel Muñoz.

"I don't know where they are, but come with me. I think I know how it went down."

Moments later, Mateo led me down into the cook's pantry. Shattered glass on the panes of the door indicated multiple locations of impact. They were too small to belong to a man. Blood splatter across the walls and the floor indicated a hard-fought struggle.

Sudden pride filled my hollow chest. She didn't go quietly or shaking with fear. Eden fought like a hellcat with everything she had inside her.

*That's my girl.*

Bending down, I traced a smear of blood that beaded on the cold tile floor. Somehow, I knew it was hers. Rubbing it between my fingers I brought my index finger to the left side of my white button down shirt and drew an 'x' over the muscle. Glancing down, the red from my fingers soaked into the white thread, staining the tiny lines a deep crimson color.

X marks the spot.

Cross my heart and hope to die.

Imprinted in blood.

Eden Lachey had branded her name on my heart and her soul in my blood for the rest of my life. However long that life lasted depended on the shape I found her in.

MATEO HADN'T SAID A WORD WHEN I REFUSED TO LEAVE THE PANTRY. Leaving momentarily, he climbed the stairs, retrieving his phone, and a few more guns. While out of sight, he'd called for a cleaner to remove Joaquin's body from the estate.

For the first time in a long time, a stab of remorse slashed a hole in the heart I couldn't believe still existed. Maybe it stemmed from the fact that Joaquin Salazar didn't hesitate to shift his alliance to me the minute I stepped off the plane in Mexico City. Maybe it came from his willingness to protect Eden with his life without any question.

Or maybe, the woman in question had managed to stitch together what had been destroyed for a lifetime.

When I first saw her, I thought Eden had been sent to save my soul. Losing her made me realize why I'd pushed her away. I was drowning in her, and she'd suffocate beside me. For the first time in my life, I'd put someone else's needs first and tried to do the right thing. Eden was no angel, but she was the closest I'd ever get to heaven. Marking her and caging her light had made me hate myself to the point of letting her go.

As her blood dried on my fingertip, I realized how blind I'd been. Eden Lachey had marked me long before I touched her. She'd branded me more than any tattoo and cut deeper than any blade ever had. She calmed my killer's soul and had become the bandage to a lifetime of chaos. The minute they took the woman I loved, chaos would be all they'd breathe until I had her back in my arms.

Regardless, I instructed Mateo to have Joaquin buried properly, instead of our usual destroy and dispose method. Eden would have my ass if she found out I'd done anything to the contrary.

I'd take whatever she had to dish out, just to hear it in person.

Two hours later, I still sat in the pantry, my eyes glued to the phone in my hand. Demanding all lieutenants abandon anything they were working on, I ordered them to pull all their best *sicarios* and disperse them to Guadalajara, Monterrey, Matamoros, and any other fucking place I could think of that they'd take her. Giving shoot to kill orders, I ran a hand over my wild hair, secretly hoping my men kept Manuel Muñoz alive long enough for him to beg me for death.

"Why hasn't anyone called?"

Mateo looked up from his phone, the lines in his forehead deepening. "They will, *jefe*. It's only been an hour."

"It's been two."

Turning my head away from his relentless stare, a glint from the overhead light caught a reflection from something shiny a few feet away. Pulled out of my destructive thoughts, I walked on my haunches over to it, and picked it up. Breath hitched in my throat as I recognized the top gold piece of the *Santa Muerte* pendant I'd given Eden back in Houston. It was jagged as if it'd broken off in a struggle.

Closing my hand around it, I brought it to my lips, praying it held enough power to still protect her.

And if we were lucky, *Santa Muerte* would answer a prayer and lead us to her.

*Lead us to her.*

A jolt of electricity shot through me as the fake metal all but burned my hand with the answer. Climbing to my feet, I pulled my phone from my pocket and activated the GPS application I'd installed days before.

"What are you doing?"

For the first time in hours, something besides loss occupied my soul, and I could feel my eyes flash with excitement. "Activating the tracking device."

"Uh, you destroyed it, remember?"

"Not that one, Mateo. *Santa Muerte*."

"I'm not following, *jefe*."

An actual smile tugged on one corner of my mouth, struggling to break free as I furiously punched numbers onto the keypad. "When Eden demanded that we take her to Mexico, I had a feeling she'd end up getting herself into some shit like this, so I pulled a trick out of Muñoz's own play book. I had one of your men implant it into a cheap ass *Santa Muerte* trinket he picked up at a street fair." I tapped it with my fingernail. "It isn't even real metal."

Mateo ran his hands over the top of his long hair. "Jesus, so you're saying…"

Punching the last few numbers, I turned my phone around and held it to his face. "I'm saying she's past Reynosa and heading up Highway 2. They're going back to Texas."

Hitting a speed dial number, I paced the room—the knowledge that Eden was alive and on the move spurring a fire in me.

"Who are you calling?"

"Reinforcements. I know where she's headed, but we need someone with connections to track down where they'll eventually hold her to prepare for the possible trap we'll be walking into."

"WHAT THE FUCK DO YOU MEAN, YOU TOOK HER TO MEXICO?"

"Just what I said," I repeated, reminding myself I needed his help and not to lose my shit on the assistant district attorney. "I had to go. She wanted to go with me, so I took her."

"Jesus…no one has seen her in weeks! We thought…we thought…goddamn it, you know what we thought, Carrera! I thought Muñoz had gotten to her, too. Her whole family is missing, for Christ's sake! I mean…damn, man…"

When Brody Harcourt's jerky speech and subject jumping connected in my disjointed brain, I growled deep within my stomach, and slammed my fist into the wall. "You fucking know Manuel Muñoz, don't you?" Brody grunted yet offered no further explanation. Cursing, I hit the wall again. "Goddamn it, Harcourt! Come clean or I swear to God, I'll blow the lid off everything for you. One call to the newspaper and your life will be over."

"You don't get it, do you, Carrera? My life is over regardless of what you do."

"What the hell is that supposed to mean?" What bullshit could the ADA have to compare to sending the only woman I'd ever loved into the hands of a sadistic killer?

*Even more sadistic than me.*

A resigned sigh crossed the line. "Manuel Muñoz came to me two months ago and threatened my sister's life. Man, she's only twenty-one and still in college. He swore he'd kill her if I didn't agree to find some way to get a tracking device on you."

Eden's St. Michael medallion.

*Shit.*

"What does Nash Lachey have to do with all of this?" And just because it'd been bothering the hell out of me, I added, "And how do you know Eden?"

"The guy I was putting pressure on to turn on you ended up flipping out on me. I tried to warn him, but he wouldn't listen. They killed Eden's brother to show him they could get to anyone at any time." He paused, his voice cracking as if unsure about delivering the rest. "Only the man freaked out and ran."

"And Eden?"

"Man, we used to fuck, all right? It meant nothing. Cherry never let it mean anything. I guess being frat brothers with her ex-husband ruined anything we could've had."

Fire filled my chest as my breathing came faster and harder. Images of Brody Harcourt in bed with Eden clouded my vision and a compulsive need to break every bone in his body took hold of me.

"You have nothing with Eden. Do you understand me, Harcourt? You never fucking touch her again."

"Fine, yes. Now, give me the access code to the app that's tracking her GPS."

Focusing on saving Eden, I gave him the information. "One thing I don't understand," I said, a thought hitting me. "Old man Lachey was supposed to get a permanent reminder from the Carreras to pay his debt. I never authorized a murder. How did Manuel Muñoz know what was happening that night at

Caliente?"

Silence filled the line for more than a few heartbeats before he finally answered. "You didn't turn your phone off, Val. You called me that day to threaten me to divulge info about Nando Fuentes' involvement with the DEA. I heard your whole conversation about roughing up Lachey. I passed along the info to help save my sister."

I could feel the muscles in my neck cording with unleashed tension. "So, during our whole conversation, you'd already flipped, you asshole?"

"He threatened my sister, Val. Surely, you can relate to family being targeted."

I knew what he was doing. The attorney in him tried to appeal to my human side, but with Eden gone, I no longer had one. "Yeah? Well, now he's going to rape and kill Eden."

"Man, don't say that."

"Was the run for the DA seat worth it, Brody?"

"Fuck you, Carrera. You don't live the kind of life you live and get to judge me. It doesn't work that way."

"*Santa Muerte*, Harcourt."

"What?"

"*Santa Muerte*." I imagined breathing in the deepest scent of citrus and vanilla when I clasped the rosary around Eden's neck. "I don't need to judge. We all stand face-to-face with death eventually, and *Santa Muerte* judges us all for our own actions. I've made peace with the sentence I'll be handed. What about you, Brody? How do you think you'll be judged when death comes calling for you?"

Before he could answer, I disconnected the call. As I stood there staring at the phone, the bombs of the conversation exploded at once, and I kicked it across the room. Watching my phone skid across the tile floor, it hit me.

Brody Harcourt heard the call about collecting the debt from Lachey.

Non-Carrera men came into the hardware store and freaked out Eden.

The scapegoat wouldn't take Muñoz's tracking device from Brody.

The bottom of my stomach fell out, and I scrambled for my gun. "Mateo! Gather whatever men you can in one room, now!"

This wasn't just a kidnapping. It was a sadistic, sick game.

And Eden was the star.

# Chapter Thirty-One

## EDEN

"*Edie, what the hell are you doing? Get down from there. You're going to break your neck!*"

Ascending one more branch, I plopped down and hung from my fingertips onto the jagged bark. "*Didn't you read the archives, Nash? There's no death certificate. God, how could I have been so stupid?*"

He tilted his chin, squinting into the afternoon sun. "*So, climbing a tree like a spoiled brat makes it better?*"

"*Piss off.*"

Chuckling, he swung his long arms and legs around the trunk and folded his muscular forearms around the thick branch underneath me within seconds. "*Look kiddo, so Mom took off. Yeah, it sucks, and she's a worthless piece of shit for it. But do you really think suspending yourself like some sort of monkey makes it any better?*"

"*I'm the one that caused her to leave, Nash,*" I whispered, my voice cracking as my arms started to shake from the tension.

Nash just smiled. "*No, you didn't. She left us long before you were born. She just walked out because she couldn't handle living with a living example of everything she'd never be."* For the first time since learning the truth that had devastated my world, a smile broke through the tears. *"Now, how about you get down from there before you pull your arms completely out of their sockets, and I have to miss football to take you to the ER?"*

A combination of a sob and a laugh escaped my lips as I dangled from my fingers, dropping toward a lower branch. *"Pain in the ass."*

*"Brat."*

OPENING MY EYES PROVED TO BE MORE AND MORE DIFFICULT EACH TIME I tried to do it. Beyond the crushing pain in the back of my head and above my eyes, the first thing I noticed was that I couldn't feel my hands or feet. After attempting to move them, a sharp tingling sensation shot through my limbs, causing me to twitch.

*Why do my arms hurt so much?*

I felt weightless and heavy at the same time, which confused me so much that I forced my eyes into submission. Everything was black on top of dark. I couldn't see my hand in front of my face.

Which was my first clue that things were very wrong.

A gravelly clanging had me swallowing the panic growing in my throat. I couldn't find my hand. It was tied above my head, along with the other one over a support beam with the floor barely dusting underneath my feet.

They'd hung me from the rafters by a chain.

Rope and metal cut into my already scarred and mangled skin so tightly that blood ran down my arms in wet trails. In a futile attempt to loosen the ties, I tried wiggling, which only twisted the chain. The chain's length had been carefully measured during my unconsciousness to make it short enough to restrict my movement, but long enough to prevent my arms from snapping.

The pain of everything I'd been through hit me in the awkward position, amplifying my injuries. Logically, I knew calling for help would be useless. However, regardless of how remote I knew the location had to be, I did it anyway.

"Is anyone out there? I'm an innocent American! Anyone? Help!"

"You're far from innocent...*Cereza*."

I froze at the hateful snarl of Val's private nickname for me. My eyes followed the voice to the far-right corner as a light flickered against a short, fat cigar. Thin lips wrapped around the end and sucked hard, puffing on smoke as the orange ember lit up his face.

Manuel Muñoz.

I'd never seen him in person, but Val had shown me pictures on the plane to Mexico City. He'd fought me on the issue, but I'd been adamant on knowing the face of the man who'd ordered my brother's death. Yet, seeing his picture, and seeing his face in person evoked two entirely different responses.

Val and Manuel grew up in the same country and were around the same age, but that was where the similarities ended. Manuel Muñoz's shaved head depicted scenes of war and bloodshed, with tattoos covering most his scalp. A dusting of facial hair hid what was probably once a handsome face, only now, it scowled with evil and hatred beyond anything anyone could imagine. But it was his eyes that turned my stomach. They were coal black and void of a soul or anything salvageable as a human being.

"You," I breathed with contempt.

A cruel smile teased his lips as he rose to his feet and stood in front of me. Inhaling a long puff from his cigar, he blew the smoke in my face and licked his lips. "We finally meet, Eden Lachey."

"Go to hell."

"In due time; first thing's first." Holding the cigar in between clenched teeth, he curled his hand and attempted to reach underneath my dress.

Screaming, I jerked and twisted as best I could, revolted at the thought of his touch, but also realizing they never checked my thigh holster. I needed to keep my only chance for survival hidden from view. "Don't touch me, asshole!"

"Calm down," he laughed, releasing me, and returning to his cigar. "I just wanted to feel the pussy that rendered Valentin Carrera's balls useless."

With my blood boiling, I forgot about my burning arms and swung my leg, landing a light kick straight to his dick. His face twisted in tortured pain, and he moved out of my trajectory, his body bent over and heaving. After moments of labored breathing, he straightened with a furious roar, and barreled toward me with a clenched fist. Holding my breath, I braced myself as bone cracked against bone, his knuckles driving into the side of my face with brutal force. Upon impact, my head snapped back as the chain swung above me. Spitting blood, I'd barely recovered, when he landed an even harder blow to my ribs, a sickening crack echoing in the silent room.

Coughing wetly, I held his stare. "You killed my brother, you son of a bitch."

"Not personally." He smiled, licking my blood off his fist. "That part, I regret."

I tried to hold in my rage like Val had taught me and stared at him with a cold eye.

*"Never show your hand, Cereza. Your next move is the only*

*thing you have that your opponent doesn't know."*

Returning my stare, Manuel paced around me like a wolf stalking its prey. "You've caused quite the international shit-storm, Eden Lachey."

"Well, as they say, go big or go home."

He laughed, baring his stained teeth. "I see why Carrera likes you. American women are—how do you say—lively."

"Fuck you."

"And then you say things like that and ruin a good conversation. Crudeness isn't attractive in a mate, Eden."

"Why don't you let me down from here and fight me like a real man?" I taunted, hoping to get a rise out him. Without many options left for escape, I grasped at straws.

He laughed again, waving the cigar in the air. "I have no interest in fighting. I'd just put a bullet in your head and be done with you."

"Then why am I still alive?"

"You've amused me." Taking another puff, he pointed the lit end of the cigar at me and raised a thick, black eyebrow. "I also know Valentin has a soft spot for you. We all knew you'd be the one to lead us to him. I enjoy torturing Carrera, and I love a good show. But, then again, this isn't my show."

That caught my attention. "No?"

"No."

"I didn't take you for a yes man, Manny." I managed a grin, despite my cracked and bleeding lips.

Returning my smile, his lips curved into a knowing smirk—as if he held a secret weapon about to be unleashed on the world. "Not a yes man…a partnership, *puta*."

For the first time, Manuel's eyes lit up with an emotion I could only describe as giddiness. I opened my mouth to ask him to explain when the door to the dank room opened, and a faint click of a light switch filled my ears moments before brightness flooded the four walls.

"Hello, Eden."

The moment my eyes adjusted to the shock of the light, they settled on the most beautiful woman I'd ever seen in my life. Almost as tall as Manuel, but with legs that seemed to extend well beyond her waist, she glided into the room, a halo of thick, shiny black hair flowing down her back. Her skin stretched flawless across her face, framed by deep set, penetrating, brown eyes that captivated me from the onset of their glare.

Her familiarity unnerved me. "How do you know me?"

"Marisol, this is Valentin Carrera's whore." Manuel motioned dramatically from the woman, back to me, then gave me a wink. "Eden Lachey, meet the beauty and brains of this operation—Marisol Muñoz, my sister."

AFTER OUR LITTLE INTRODUCTION, MANUEL AND MARISOL LITERALLY left me hanging while they called a family meeting in the corner of the tiny room. Satisfied with their communication, Manuel nodded and pulled out his gun, shooting through the chain above me. I cried out in relief and pain when I hit the floor. Without a doubt, I knew I had a few broken ribs and most likely a cheek fracture. The way my chest rattled from the wet cough, I wouldn't be surprised to find a collapsed lung.

If I ever made it to a hospital.

A heavy boot in my stomach had me flipping onto my back with stars in my eyes. "Get up." Manuel's hand jerked me roughly off the floor and onto my feet. "We've got a party waiting for you downstairs," he snarled, freeing my hands.

*Val.*

The logical part of me prayed I was wrong, and he was safe and out of their sadistic hands. Yet the weak and needy part of me ached to hold him again.

Turning over my shoulder, I threw a cold stare at Marisol Muñoz as her brother dragged me down the darkened hallway. "Why are you doing this?"

She looked at me as if I'd just asked her to explain quantum physics. "Money, darling. Valentin Carrera has it; I want it. You think I spent six years studying with my nose in a book at the University of Guadalajara to be stuck in an office somewhere?" A high-pitched laugh bounced off the walls. "Hell no. What this cartel has lacked since my father's death has been intelligent direction. No offense, dear brother."

Manuel shrugged and raised a quick eyebrow in her direction before snapping my arm toward a closed door.

"The Muñoz Cartel could never overtake Alejandro Carrera because the men in my family lacked strategic planning and intricate follow-through—something that required the long-term patience of a woman. You understand; right, Eden?"

"Sure," I replied, rolling my eyes in the dark.

As all three of us reached the closed door, the smile on her face morphed into an arrogant sneer. "The men in my family have always lacked patience for anything. They want everything now, now, now. But I told them, 'Bide your time and watch Carrera. He's not as inhuman as you think. Eventually, we'll find his weakness. When we do, take it. Carrera will come to us.' You're his weakness, Eden. We women, we're powerful creatures. In our lifetime, there will always be one man who will die for us." She stared at me and ran a painted red nail down my tangled hair. "No man is immune to our power—even the almighty *El Muerte*."

"I told you, Valentin Carrera—"

"Congratulations on being the woman who brought down the giant." Opening the door, each Muñoz sibling grabbed one of my arms and faced me forward. With a shove from each of them, I didn't even have a chance to touch the first few steps before I tumbled head first.

My toes barely grazed the tip of the fifth or sixth stair as I fell down the entire flight, darkness and light intermingling with intolerable pain. After what seemed like a never-ending fall, my broken body hit the concrete floor with a sickening thud as they slammed the door.

"Help…" It was all I could manage as the wet cough overtook me again, my mouth filling up with so much blood, I had to turn my head so as not to choke.

*I have to get out of here or I'm going to die.*

Crying out with every move, I dragged myself into a kneeling position, every pull of breath into my lungs, feeling like a hundred daggers stabbing me at once. As I crawled toward the center of the room, a voice broke the ragged silence.

"Eden…"

It took every concerted effort I had to lift my head and focus. The moment I did, the pain in my chest and limbs dulled compared to the searing, ripping apart of my heart.

"You," I whispered, wishing Manuel Muñoz had killed me when he had the chance.

# Chapter Thirty-Two
## VALENTIN

After pacing for twenty minutes in an alley behind the district attorney's office in Houston, my phone finally rang. "Harcourt, tell me you have it."

"I can do better than that," he replied, his voice anxious and short.

I rolled my shoulders in a futile attempt at releasing the knot of tension in my back. "I don't have time for this, Brody. I've been trying to find this house myself all fucking day, but according to everything I've researched, the damn thing doesn't exist." Glancing at my watch, I cursed the late hour. "Give me Eden's location and get the hell off the phone."

From five-hundred feet in front of me, the door swung open to a gray BMW. Black slacks emerged, followed by a crisp white shirt, a red power tie, and a pressed black suit jacket. A self-satisfied smirk planted across his face as he brushed back his annoying mop of dark blond hair. "How about I take you there myself?"

Gritting my teeth, I stomped past him. "How about you

don't?"

Slamming his door, Brody shed his suit jacket as he raced to catch up with me. "You need me, Carrera. I know where she is, and I need you. I can't go in there alone. I'll never make it out."

"You've got that right."

"Look," he said, placing a hand on my shoulder and stopping our movement. "She doesn't want me, man. I don't know what you've got going on with Cherry, but it's obvious you care about her. I may not like you, but that's enough for me. I just want her safe."

"She's mine." After his proclamation, I had no idea why I felt the need to stake my claim like a goddamn caveman, but the words just slipped out.

"Fine, she's yours. Can we go get her now?"

I narrowed my eyes, suspicious of his motives. "If you have no interest in her, why are you so dead set on walking into a massacre? You do understand this isn't the movies, right? These men are real. They have real guns with real bullets and a lot of people will die. I can't guarantee you won't be one of them. My only concern will be Eden."

Much to my surprise, he didn't flinch. "You think I haven't talked to Manuel Muñoz one-on-one, Carrera? I know exactly what kind of sick fuck he is. Let's just say, I'm hoping if I do this, you'll owe me one."

"How so?"

"If Muñoz makes it out of there, and I don't, I need you to promise me something."

"I don't make promises, Harcourt."

He continued as if I hadn't spoken. "I'll protect Eden with my life, no matter what. I'll even accept that she's yours, but you have to promise me, if something happens to me, you'll make sure nothing happens to my sister."

"No way."

"Please, Val," he begged, his eyes reddening with remnants of hidden fear. "She's an innocent. Her name is Leighton Harcourt. She's a senior at Texas State, and that bastard threatened to gut her like a fish."

*"Jefe, my bartender is an innocent. When I went back out, her car was gone. If they have her, you know what will happen."*

*"It's a shame he had to rip that sexy, little black number to shreds when he gutted her."*

Two separate moments in time collided with two different conversations from two different men as Brody Harcourt stood in front of me begging for his sister's life. Eden's face flashed before my eyes, and I knew I couldn't deny him or cause him the same fear I held in my heart.

Turning around, I motioned for Mateo. "Drive fast."

"ARE YOU SURE THIS IS IT?" RUBBING MY PALM ACROSS MY CHIN, I stared out the window at the modest half-brick, run-down house that sat in the middle of fifteen acres off Highway 90 and Lake Houston Parkway. I had my doubts Brody had tracked the correct address.

"Carrera, did you know I'd been working behind your back this whole time?"

The reminder pissed me off to the point of snapping his neck. "No," I bit out.

"My point exactly. I find out shit because people underestimate me. I made a call to the Texas Housing Agency. It seems that only structures with physical house numbers show up in a search." He held up his phone for emphasis. "No building permit, no house number. It doesn't actually exist per the state of Texas."

"So, how did *you* find it?"

Waving the gun Mateo gave him in his other hand, Brody flashed a wide smile. "Let's go get your girl."

"I don't—"

"*Jefe!*" Mateo broke in, wiping a layer of sweat off his brow. "Are we going to sit here debating how the *gringo* charmed some virgin receptionist in the attorney general's office, or are we going to go kick some Muñoz ass?"

Glancing at them both, I gave Mateo a quick nod, and we made our way to the door. No surprise, it was locked.

Mateo gestured toward the back while nodding to Brody. "We'll go around to the back and see if there's a rear entrance. You head off to the side and see if—" A loud crack broke our whispers as his side erupted in a mushroom of red. With his face twisted in pain, he waved his gun around the corner of the house. "Go! Jesus, go, now!"

My feet felt molded to the concrete landing. "Mateo, no!"

With mustered strength, he shoved me backward. "I said, fucking go! I've got this."

As I rounded the corner, more gun fire exploded. Mateo's voice screamed curses at Brody as he unloaded his weapon at the approaching forces.

Everything inside me told me to turn around and back up my friend. Then I heard it.

Her scream.

*Cereza.*

# Chapter Thirty-Three

## EDEN

*There's a fine line between love and hate.*

I'd heard that cliché all my life thrown around by half-interested adults who gave few fucks about either one. The idiom du jour served to placate me enough to remove my adolescent angst from blocking Monday night football and return to my room, where I belonged.

It wasn't until my heart blackened to a charred void that I understood the true meaning of the phrase. I found it amazing how much that fine line thickened while sweat dripped from the brow of someone I loved as I aimed a gun at his heart.

"Eden, you don't know what you're doing."

His image blurred although my hand held steady. "Yours is the betrayal I never saw coming. Congratulations." In my head the words sounded cold, despite the wetness that trailed from the corners of my eyes. Crawling to my feet, I paced the small space in front of him before I realized I'd uprooted from my spot. Keeping my breathing shallow, I focused on inhaling only when necessary. The run-down house reeked of dank mildew and death.

The number of deaths that would be added to the stench remained to be seen.

"I never wanted to hurt you," he implored, begging me to recall what we'd meant to each other. When I stared vacantly at him, he licked his lips and attempted to reach me on another level. "After all we've been through, it ends like this?"

"You've left me no choice."

"There's always a choice."

Hatred burned my eyes, incinerating the man reflected in them. "Fuck you."

His sigh turned into a cough, rattling his chest. A knowing smile curved his lips. "There's my feisty girl."

I waved the gun in the air—a stupid move on all accounts, but his play on my emotions ripped at my soul. "I'm not anything of yours. You sold me out. You made me believe we were on the same side." Tears rolled harder, ignoring my commands to stop and pissed me off. "The whole time you had an end game, you son of a bitch!"

*One step. Two steps. Three steps.*

If I pulled the trigger now, it'd be point blank range. I couldn't claim self-defense. True, it hadn't been his hand that'd pushed me off the step and sent me careening down a flight of stairs. But, in the end, it was his actions that brought me here.

And I wasn't the one looking down the barrel of a Colt 1911 .38 Super.

All this time I'd believed him. All this time I'd trusted him. In the end, I'd been a fool because all this time I'd been used.

"Eden," he pleaded, searching for a shred of the affection we'd shared. "I love you."

*There's a fine line between love and hate.*

Watching him grovel for his life, I suddenly understood the

meaning behind the phrase. When I loved a person, I saw them through rose-colored glasses. Everything was perfect...until it wasn't. I walked the line until I got knocked off and opened my eyes to the person I'd been blind to. My heart became torn, desperate to recapture the first untainted moments where the line was straight and steady. Before I knew it, hate filled the space where the love vacated, and my heart battled with my head.

Like an addict who promised one more hit would be the last, I knew it was a lie but told it anyway. I knew I couldn't stop. The cycle always repeated, and I hurt myself until there was nothing left but hate for the both of us.

*Unless the cycle ends.*

I thought the past eighteen days had hardened me to violence, so it surprised me when my chin quivered. Vengeance took my salvation, but apparently, a conscience still resided somewhere in the deep recesses of my mind. Maybe that was one thing he hadn't killed. Maybe that was the last shred of humanity I could hold onto as I burned in hell for the path I'd walked.

I would've done anything for him. He'd held me in his arms and promised to protect me.

I didn't bother to stop the lone tear as it rolled across my nose and fell onto my bottom lip, pausing briefly before tumbling down my chin. "I love you, too," I whispered as I unloaded the gun, my mask slipping as he stumbled.

*It's funny how sometimes the people you'd give your life for are the ones who take it.*

My breath came in shallow spurts as my hand shook. The last thing I remembered was kneeling, my eyes landing on my father, standing fifteen feet away from me with his shoulder turned toward the wall.

The part where I reached for the gun tucked in my thigh holster was a complete blur.

My father staggered against the wall, grabbing his chest with both hands, gritting his teeth as if in severe pain. "Edie! Oh, Jesus…why…?"

Coming down from the shock of pulling the trigger on my flesh and blood, a curtain fell over my emotions. No longer did the same heart beat between us. My own father sold me and Nash out to save his own ass. Val was right all along.

"You can stop the theatrics now, old man. I missed."

Opening one eye, he glanced down, and realizing no blood stained his shirt, he sighed. "Thank God…oh, sweet mercies."

"No," I said, frowning as I shrugged one shoulder. "Not God. Thank bad aim. If you'd had a can sitting on your head, I would've blown your dick off."

"Edie?" Taking a cautious step forward, he tilted his head as if seeing me for the first time. "What's happened to you?"

"I'm an orphan, you son of a bitch."

"No." He patted his chest as if that made things all better. "I'm here. We still have each other."

My arm extended, and he froze mid-step as I aimed the gun at his chest again. "You're dead to me." A laugh erupted, ending in a wet cough that burned my chest. "You know what's pathetic, *Dad*? I've been held captive by a man you made me a living beacon for, then warned me to stay away from."

Tears filled his weathered eyes. "Baby, I—"

"But you know what the most fucked up part is, *Dad*?" I interrupted, biting down on his name as if saying the word caused me physical pain. "Val Carrera has been the only man in my whole life besides Nash who has cared more about me than himself."

"Oh, Edie…you didn't…"

"Sleep with him? Is that what you want to ask me, *Dad*? Did I follow my usual open-leg policy and lay down with the enemy?" I smiled, the thought of our last morning together outside his house in Monterrey filling my mind. "You're damn right I did—over and over again."

In an instant, my father's face hardened, and his eyes frosted with an icy glaze. "Well, I guess once a whore always a whore."

Shifting slightly to the right, I pulled the trigger again. My father let out a blood-curdling scream that had me rolling my eyes. "Will you please shut up?"

"You shot me again! My own daughter!"

"I didn't shoot you. I shot *at* you." Shaking my head, I sighed at my own ineptitude and conscience. "For all you are, and the father you aren't, for some fucked up reason, I still can't kill you."

A commotion up the stairs pulled my attention away from my father and toward the door. With a slew of obscenities, Manuel Muñoz flew down the stairs, an entourage of men clamoring behind him. In the middle of him, Marisol stood sandwiched, a gun tucked in her perfectly manicured hand.

I backed up as fast as I could, but with broken ribs and a sprained ankle from the tumble down the stairs, Manuel easily caught up with me, jerking the gun out of my hand and grabbing me in a choke hold. "Where the fuck did you get a gun, *puta*?"

Clawing at his arm, I fought for air. "I... I…can't…"

"Let her go!"

Unable to turn my head, I rolled my eyes to the side as my father's clenched fists charged toward Manuel. I tried to shake my head and warn him to stay where he was.

"What the hell do you care, Lachey? She's been down here using you for a target practice."

"I'm warning you, Muñoz, take your hands off my daughter, or—"

Groaning, Manuel turned over his shoulder toward Marisol.

"You know what? I've had just about as much of the protective father act as I can take. You?" Marisol shrugged as Manuel raised his gun and pumped four rounds into my father's chest.

With the kick-back, Manuel's hold lessened enough for a full scream to tear from my throat as my father dropped to the ground in an explosion of angry red splotches that quickly soaked his shirt.

As Manuel readjusted his hold, I struggled to free myself.

*I'm next. I'm next. I'm next.*

The words repeated over and over in my head, until I swore I said them out loud.

With a kiss to my temple, Manuel chuckled in my ear. "Perk up, *Cereza*. The fun has arrived."

# Chapter Thirty-Four

## VALENTIN

The last thing I wanted to do was announce my arrival by shooting out a window, but once I heard her scream, I would've bulldozed my way in. With the commotion behind me, I knew Muñoz *sicarios* were minutes from pumping a few bullets in my back.

When gunshots rang out, I froze, glancing over my shoulder to make sure I hadn't been hit. Having been shot before, I knew sometimes the bullet tore through so fast, there was no way to know it had even hit until someone screamed, or blood stained a shirt.

The irony always made me shake my head. A bullet could rip through a man's skin, likely severing vital organs in the process, yet the only thing he'd feel would be the wetness of blood.

Once I knew the gunshots weren't meant for me, my heart constricted as another scream traveled up the stairs, leading from the basement.

*Eden.*

Without a second thought, I ran full force to the door where

I knew I'd find her. Tightening my hold on my gun, I kicked it open, ready to blow anyone's head off who dared get in my way. As I stepped one foot off the ledge, a gun pressed against my temple.

"Don't fucking move, Carrera." Ripping the gun from my hand, one of Manuel's enforcers smiled as he swung the tip toward the bottom of the stairs. "Only the hosts get party favors." Laughing at his own joke, he pushed the muzzle harder against my skull. "Now go...you're the guest of honor."

I half expected him to either shove me straight to the bottom or go ahead and put a bullet in my brain. He did neither. He just continued fucking smiling to himself as I slowly took one step at a time, making sure to stay aware of my surroundings.

The moment I hit the bottom, all hell broke loose.

"Ah, *El Muerte*, welcome. We've been anticipating your arrival. Sorry for the mess. One of our guests forgot his manners."

The familiar scent of spilled blood drew my attention to an older man crumpled on the floor in a pool of it. By himself, a dead man in a basement would mean little to me. However, as my eyes traveled back to the voice, I knew without question the dead man was Elliot Lachey.

My mouth went dry as my gaze landed on Manuel Muñoz, his forearm wrapped around Eden's throat. She struggled against him, her face red from lack of oxygen.

A murderous blinding rage shattered my hold on the humanity Eden had resurrected the minute I saw what he'd done to her.

Her beautiful face stared back at me, mangled and covered in too many bruises and gashes to count. Both her right cheek and right eye were swollen, and blood trickled from both nostrils and the corners of her mouth. We locked gazes and her brows furled as she fought for every rattled breath.

*Broken ribs.*

Her exposed arms and legs were covered in bruises and cuts, as if she'd been thrown around like a rag doll. Deep lacerations on her wrists drew my eyes, sickening me to the permanent reminder she'd suffered for me.

I held her eye, communicating without words.

*He'll pay. On the soul of my mother, he'll pay.*

"Let her go, Muñoz. This is between you and me. She has nothing to do with it." My mind raced, frantically trying to come up with workable scenarios where four against two logically came out in our favor. I kept coming up short, especially since the four were armed, and the two had nothing but the small pistol attached to my ankle holster. Unfortunately, with four guns drawn, one of them would put a bullet in Eden before I could reach for it. I wasn't willing to risk it.

"Hello, Val."

Who the hell was the woman? "Do I know you?"

"Probably not. But I've studied you for a while now, and I think I understand you more than most anyone."

"I doubt that," I shot back with full conviction.

Stepping out of the shadows, she ran a hand through her long dark hair, and I immediately took a step back. Something didn't feel right.

"I'm the one that ordered the hit on your new girlfriend's brother." She smiled and moved closer. "I'm the one who's been tracking you, turning all your allies against you." Pounding her chest with her palm, the light hit her eyes, highlighting flecks of glittered anger. "I'm the one who watched you long enough to know you had such a hard-on for your own lieutenant's bartender that it was just a matter of time before you fucked up."

A rock landed in my stomach. "You didn't get Elliot Lachey hooked on coke."

A wicked smile spread across her face. "Didn't I?"

"Oh, my God," Eden croaked, her voice hushed and strained from Manuel's restrictive hold. "It's you. You're the woman from the bar. You were sitting at the end the night Val came in. I remember because…because it was the night Nash was killed."

As if on rewind, my mind traveled back to the night at Caliente. Eden had just commented about the news broadcast of Nando's death when the two drunk assholes made remarks about her that made me want to blow their nuts off. Eden had been making conversation with a lady in the corner with long dark hair…*holy fuck.*

"You're Isabella Diego." Everything hit me at once.

*"There's one more thing."*

*"Make it quick."*

*"One of our new dealers, Isabella, let us know a repeat buyer in Maplewood has put four grams of our shipment up his nose. He's in for about ten g's and missed the last two drops…"*

I'd worried one of my high-ranking men had been a leak. Not once did I consider a street-dealing woman would take me down.

"No, not Isabella." She pulled her hair to the side and tucked the other behind her ear. "Marisol. Marisol Muñoz."

"Muñoz?"

"Yes, Valentin…Muñoz. As in Manuel's sister and Esteban's daughter. I've been away for many years while you've been in America. Too bad we won't be getting better acquainted."

"Mari! We've been here too long. It's time to finish this and leave."

My gaze reverted to Manuel, his hold still firm on Eden. I had no idea if Mateo and Brody were still alive, but I had to stall for time.

"I thought this was a party, Manuel. Where's your sense of

hospitality? Leaving so soon?"

One corner of his mouth lifted in a twisted smile as Manuel pressed the muzzle of his gun against Eden's temple. Catching my eye, he lowered his lips behind it and blew into her hair. "You always did have an overdeveloped sense of entitlement, Carrera." The moment his tongue darted out and licked Eden behind the ear, I almost forgot everything and gave in to the rage boiling inside of me. "I see why this one caught your attention, Valentin. Tell me, does she taste as good between her legs as she does behind her ear?"

"Motherfucker!"

"Manuel!" My head spun around to face Marisol, her face hot with anger. "We are many things, but you will not speak that way to a woman in front of me. Do you understand?"

"Fine," he muttered, lowering his eyes.

The exchange fascinated me—the tiny, younger sister commanding an iron rule over the much larger and callous older brother. But figuring out their dynamic was at the bottom of my priority list. Manuel still held Eden and showed no signs of letting her go. The fear in her eyes gutted me, and I knew I'd do anything to take it away.

"So, what do you want me to do with them, your highness?" Manuel shot back, a slight edge of resentment creeping into this voice.

"Dealer's choice," she answered with a wave of her hand. "You're the muscle in this partnership, not me. I have no stomach for it." Nodding to one of the guards, she walked away. He moved ahead of her, dutifully opening a side door I hadn't noticed when entering the room.

Her brother cocked an eyebrow, his eyes following her every move. "Where are you going?"

"Guadalajara," she smiled over her shoulder with one foot

out the door. "My work in America is done. *Adios,* Valentin." Giving me a wink and pursing her lips in a mock kiss, she left as the lieutenant closed the door behind her.

Using Eden as a human shield, Manuel turned toward me. "I guess there's just one thing left to do."

"Don't tell me there's cake," I offered with a well-timed smirk.

*Where the hell was Mateo?*

Throwing his head back, Manuel laughed with a roar. "No, but I've got a game we can play." Pulling his gun away from Eden's temple, he bounced it between her head and my chest, each word he spoke, punctuated by an aim of the muzzle. "Eeny, meenie, minie, moe..."

The moment his mouth formed the last word, I looked into the barrel of his gun. As I reached for my ankle holster, I heard Eden scream my name, but it melted into ripples of white, hot heat as pain shredded my insides like a warm knife through butter.

*I take that back... Sometimes, a man absolutely knows when he's been shot.*

Chaos ensued around me as multiple shots rang out, and shouting echoed in a warped bubble above my head. One word repeated on my lips as I hit the ground.

"Eden..."

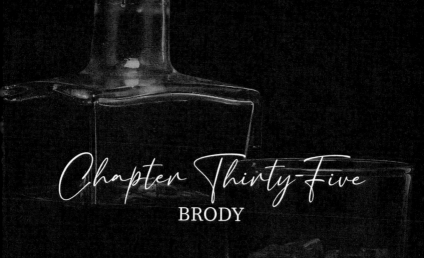

## Chapter Thirty-Five
### BRODY

**"You've** been shot!"

Soaked with blood and holding his side with a hard grimace, Mateo still managed to shoot me a disgusted glare out of the corner of his eye. "Yeah, and you're a fucking genius." Grunting in pain, he waved his gun across the street. "Get in the car."

"And leave you here? Have you been hoping for an early death or are you just really masochistic?"

Why I stood there instead of hauling my ass inside four panels of reinforced steel remained a mystery to me. What had happened in the last hour to alter everything I held sacred and cause me to jump head first into the inferno between life and death? Six hours ago, I sat in my orderly tenth-floor office where everything made sense and life had order. With one phone call and a snap decision, I'd found myself neck deep in a drug-war stand-off with bullets flying at me from all angles.

All because two women had found themselves on Manuel Muñoz's radar. One who had done nothing but love me, and one who had done anything *but*.

The irony wasn't lost on me.

Gunshots rang out in the distance, along with angry shouts in clipped Spanish.

"Shit!" Mateo coughed, blood pooling in the corner of his mouth and trickling down his chin. With another garbled curse, he smeared it across his cheek with the back of his hand while waving his gun at me. "We don't have time for this. I said get in the car, Brody. I got this."

The shouts became closer and more heated as Mateo wheezed and attempted to steady a shaking trigger finger. Boldly rolling my eyes at the second in command of the Houston leg of the Carrera Cartel, I grabbed his wrist and hauled his arm around my shoulder for support.

"Yeah, you really *got* this, don't you? You can barely breathe as it is. Whether you like it or not, lieutenant, you need me, and whether I like it or not, my conscience won't let me turn my back on you, Eden, or even fucking Carrera. So, how about you stop arguing and try working with me, huh?"

I expected an argument. When he simply nodded his head around the back of the house where Val had disappeared moments earlier, I raised an eyebrow. Supporting his arm, I stumbled around the corner with Mateo draped over my shoulder. I didn't take much time to consider why I wasn't more nervous about what we were doing. If I'd stopped to think about it, I'd realize we were walking into a mass suicide, and the thoughts I'd allow myself would probably be my last. I didn't have the years of gun handling expertise these men had. They'd avoided taking a bullet to the back of the head their entire lives. My target practice included weekend paintball with my fraternity brothers where I got my ass handed to me.

"Are you sure about this? My loyalty is with Val. Do

you understand what I'm saying?" Mateo dug his feet into the grass, causing us to come to a complete stop. He glanced up, his bloodshot eyes raising from his bowed head, serious and unwavering.

Steeling my chin, I turned away, the decrepit building in my line of sight. Somewhere inside those mildewed walls, Eden needed me. I was no idiot. I knew I'd lost her to Carrera. For a while, I would've fought to have had a chance at something real with her, but I wouldn't kid myself. A man didn't fight a Carrera on anything, especially something he considered his. Plus, I knew Cherry better than she knew herself. If she didn't want to be with him, even the almighty Valentin Carrera couldn't force her into it. Whatever existed between the two of them was something I didn't stand a chance in breaking.

And, I had to admit, without Carrera alive and on my side, there was no possibility in protecting Leighton on my own. I needed Manuel Muñoz dead, and for my sister, I'd die trying. I'd be damned if Leighton would pay the price for my choices.

Removing Mateo's arm from my shoulder, I steadied him on his feet. "Worry about yourself, lieutenant. I've got this." Plastering a noncommittal smile on my lips, I stalked past him, invisibility the least of my worries as we stood in the middle of a crossfire. I should've felt exposed and afraid for my life. Instead, I vibrated with a deep-seated need for a control I'd lacked for months.

I'd barely taken three steps when a crack broke through the air as loud as thunder and with the raw power of a storm. It reverberated in my ears, ringing out in an echo and shattering the window in front of me as if on auto delay. As a second shot ripped the wood paneling off the house two feet from where I stood, I gripped the gun in my damp palm, turning to either take a lucky shot or face my executioner when a blast exploded beside me.

*Holy shit.*

Reaching down, I ran my hand down my shirt, searching for a gaping wound, or at the very least, splotches of blood that signaled my impending demise. As my fingers scanned the rough fabric of my shirt, I swallowed as all they encountered was shaking panic and sweat. Before I could rationalize what had happened, or thank God for the fact I was still alive, a third shot rang out, pulling attention toward the man twenty-five feet in front of me whose chest had erupted in a cloud of red. As blood poured from both corners of his mouth, his knees buckled, and he dropped face first to the ground.

Mateo lowered his smoking gun and turned back to face me. "You okay?"

"What the hell just happened?"

"You were showing me how much you've *got this*," he mocked, displaying a wide grin.

"You know what?" I argued, throwing my arms wide. "That's unnecessary. You think you could show a little gratitude for dragging your ass—"

"My ass?" he interrupted. "I just saved your—"

A fourth gunshot cut him off mid-sentence, but this one came from inside the house. Neither of us spoke another word as silence surrounded the blast. Not a sound or a scream followed the fire, and I didn't have to look at Mateo to know we had the same concern.

*Someone was dead.*

Everything inside screamed at me to call out Eden's name, to have her answer me and know it hadn't been her on the receiving end of the bullet. I needed to know she was all right. However, survivalist instinct kept my mouth shut and turned my chin back toward Mateo. The look on his face told me he'd fought the same urge to call out to the man he'd sworn his life to protect.

I was a lawyer. I'd trained my whole life to be pragmatic and weigh both sides of an argument, choosing the best form of attack before going in for the guaranteed kill. But in the silence, practicality gave way to urgency as we both broke into a reckless run toward the back door.

# Chapter Thirty-Six
## EDEN

I screamed his name before Manuel ever pulled the trigger. I counted the rhythm of his words, and I knew where the rhyme would end. In a split second, I calculated the amount of time it'd take Val to reach for his ankle holster versus the short distance it took for Manuel to straighten his arm and release a bullet.

He didn't stand a chance.

In horror, I watched as Manuel shot Val in the stomach. Angry lines of red erupted below his ribcage and spread up his chest, soaking his shirt. He mumbled my name before he hit the floor, his hand instinctively covering his wound.

My body shivered, and almost as if I exited it, I looked down on the scene. While observing it from above, the dingy basement morphed into the chrome kitchen at Caliente. In one blink, Val's thick dark hair suddenly lightened, and one unruly piece flopped into his eyes.

I'd come full circle. For the second time, I watched my life bleed out in front of me.

Unable to take the crushing weight of the scene anymore,

everything converged, and the kitchen evaporated, leaving me alone in the basement with Manuel Muñoz and his guard. In a fit of desperation and rage, with nothing left to lose, I took advantage of his momentary slackened hold around my neck. Dipping my chin, I sank my teeth into his forearm and bit as hard as I could.

Letting out a primal howl, Manuel released his hold just enough for me to launch myself at him. With the surprise of my attack, and the sheer force of my will, I knocked him off balance and sent us both sprawling onto the floor. In the scuffle, he dropped the gun, the grip landing a few feet away. I scrambled off him and lunged for it.

"You fucking bitch!" Manuel clamped a tattooed hand around my ankle and dragged me backward on my stomach toward his chest. "You'll pay for that."

Movement out of the corner of my eye commanded my attention, but I forced myself to focus on getting the gun. In seconds, blasts erupted, with shouting and erratic flashes of light. Kicking Manuel's face, I howled through the pain and lunged again. Cursing, he jerked me backward, this time pulling me flush against him

"Time to be with your boyfriend." Pulling a knife from his pocket with his free hand, he pressed a button, popping up a six-inch blade, the edge serrated for maximum damage.

I refused to go out like this. Not without a fight.

"You first." Clenching my fist, I put everything I had behind it and landed the hardest punch I'd ever thrown against his nose. A cracking noise preceded a blood volcano spewing from both nostrils.

Before he could react, I threw myself off him and crawled to the gun, wrapping my fingers around it. Climbing to my knees, and shaking with adrenaline, I pointed it to his head. "It's over, you bastard."

Smiling through reddened teeth, he attempted to sit up. "You don't have what it takes."

"Wrong," I answered, my voice cold and calm. "All it takes is a lack of humanity. You took that from me when you killed everyone that meant anything to me." With an accuracy that would've made Val proud, I took my revenge on the man who broke my heart twice.

And then just to be sure, I shot him again.

"Eden…" Glancing up, I looked into Mateo's eyes, his brows drawn in concern.

"You've been shot," I blurted out, the reality of what I'd done starting to sink in. "Why are you standing if you've been shot?"

"Flesh wound," he answered softly. "Give me the gun, Eden."

Suddenly remembering where I was, I glanced around. "The other guard."

"Dead." Mateo assured me.

*Val.*

Dropping the gun, it clanged on the concrete as I crawled on my hands and knees across the room. Blood pooled all around him, and I slipped once, falling onto my side, the sticky warmth coating the length of my body. Pressing my palms into the puddles, I finally reached him, unsure of where to touch him first. He lay motionless, his eyes small slits that seemed transfixed across the room.

"Blood," I whispered. "There's so much blood." I did the only thing I could think of. I ripped his shirt open to find the source. Reality sobered every moment of the last few days as I cried out, covering him with my hands. A gaping hole to the right of his belly button continually pumped out fresh blood as it seeped between my fingers. "Mateo!" Screaming in sheer panic, I kept one hand on his stomach, while checking his face for signs of breathing with the other. "Mateo, I need you! It won't stop bleeding. God, I need you, please!"

As Mateo appeared at my side, pressing his balled-up shirt against Val's wound, a familiar voice called out from the top of the stairs.

"A car is on its way."

"Brody?" I blinked again to make sure I wasn't hallucinating. *What the actual fuck?*

Flashing a smile, he nodded toward Val's pale body. "Don't worry, Cherry. He'll make it. If not for anything else, but to kick my ass for this..." Raising his voice, he leaned over the railing and cupped his hand around his mouth. "Hey, Carrera, if you die, that means I get Eden, right?"

"Brody!" If I wasn't so focused on Val, I'd kick his ass myself.

Val's breathing was shallow at best by the time Emilio's SUV arrived. Lifting Val's shoulders, Mateo and Brody loaded his motionless body into the back. Unable to have Houston's assistant district attorney seen with criminals, Brody drove his BMW away from the scene, promising to see to it that the cops on Val's payroll would never file an official report from the hospital.

As Mateo climbed in the front seat, I took Val's face in my hands and dusted a light kiss across his lips. "I said I'd walk in front of a bullet for you, but you took one for me instead. It doesn't end like this, Carrera. You fight for me. You fight for us." Kissing him again, I traced the slope of his dark eyebrow as a tear rolled off my nose and landed on his cheek. "*Te amo.*"

Walking the floors in the hallway, I'd already bitten every nail I had until they bled. I'd abandoned the tiny waiting room an hour ago and paced the hallway in front of the nurse's station, garnering narrowed-eye glares after each pass of their desk.

*Fuck 'em.*

After the eighth pass, Mateo rounded the corner and gently steadied my shoulders. "Eden, why don't you go get something to eat? The doctor said he could be in surgery for another few hours."

"I'm not hungry."

"Okay, some coffee at least."

"I'm not thirsty."

"Nobody is thirsty for coffee, Eden."

I crossed my arms and rubbed my palms down the bare skin of my arms not covered by scrubs. "What's taking so long? If he was okay, it wouldn't take so long, right?"

Upon arrival at the hospital, the hospital personnel took one look at my battered, bruised body and blood-soaked dress and freaked. After refusing to shut up until I allowed a doctor to examine me, I gave in and filled out paperwork that I knew would disappear in less than an hour. They taped two cracked ribs, gave me a chest x-ray, stitched my face and wrists, gave me a tetanus shot, and prescribed a round of antibiotics. Even after much bitching on my part, they bagged my dress and handed it to me, offering either a hospital gown or a pair of ugly green scrubs.

So, here I stood, in army green scrubs two sizes too big.

"It's a good thing, Eden. As long as he's in surgery, it means we aren't getting bad news, yeah?"

Okay, that was one way to look at it.

Two hours later, exhaustion had won out and forced me back into the waiting room. As the clock ticked off the minutes, tears ran down my cheeks…the product of hours of bottled-up fear and anxiety.

Glancing at me quickly, Mateo said nothing as he took my hand in his and held it securely.

I'd never been one for public displays of affection, but I'd never been more grateful for anyone in my life. I felt like I stood balanced on the edge of a cliff, the balls of my feet teetering over the edge with every roll of my toes. One crack of a joint, and it'd be all over.

The door to the waiting room flew open, and I almost snapped my neck jumping to my feet. What I came face-to-face with was Emilio Reyes.

"Where is he? Is he all right? When can I see him?"

"Get him out." The words sounded like they came from someone else. A man. A heavy smoker. A demon straight out of hell.

"Eden!" Mateo scolded.

"What the hell is she talking about?"

"*She*"—I bit out through clenched teeth—"has finally been pushed too far. *She* has realized, regardless of the fact that you didn't pull the trigger, you willingly tortured her brother. And *she* lost every bit of reservation *she* ever had against shoving a gun straight up your ass and pulling the trigger when *she* killed a man tonight." I stalked forward as he backed up, swallowing hard. "So, I suggest you get out of my sight."

"You've lost your mind." Emilio shot a pleading look at Mateo, who shrugged and returned to the magazine he'd been reading.

"Have I?"

"You don't just walk into a cartel and start throwing your

smart mouth around—"

"Listen, you arrogant shithead—"

"The family of Valentin Carrera?"

With five words, the brewing argument between Emilio and me stopped cold. Stepping forward, I tucked a stray piece of hair behind my ear. "That's us."

The doctor nodded in acknowledgement. "Very well. My name is Dr. Kirkland, and I was the lead surgeon on your…" His voice trailed off as his eyes bounced between the three of us.

"Brother," Mateo answered, pressing a light hand to my lower back. "He's our brother."

The doctor raised an eyebrow and ran a disbelieving eye over my pale skin, blue eyes, and red hair.

*Good one, Mateo.*

Shaking his head, he continued. "Your brother suffered massive internal injuries to his liver. Those kinds of gunshot wounds are serious because the liver is highly vascularized and close to multiple large blood vessels. If a bullet hits one or more of the large vessels, a victim can bleed to death rather quickly. Even if a major vessel isn't severed, a liver laceration bleeds heavily, and it isn't always easy to get it to stop."

"What are you saying?" I whispered, a sharp ringing building in my ears.

The doctor offered a sympathetic smile. "Luckily, only a small part of your brother's liver was damaged, Ms. Carrera. The organ is highly regenerative. We were able to tie it off and repair surrounding damage."

"He's okay?"

Patting my hand, he tugged off his scrub hat and nodded. "He's sedated right now and will be in substantial pain when he wakes up, but yes, he's going to be okay. Give him an hour or so to recover, and you can see him one at a time."

In a hospital waiting room in Houston.

In a pair of ugly green scrubs.

I hit the floor on my knees and prayed for the first time since I was fourteen.

I THOUGHT I'D PREPARED MYSELF FOR WHAT I'D FIND WHEN I OPENED the door to Val's hospital room.

I was wrong.

Wires, tubes, bandages, and his beautiful, bronzed skin, now pale and ashen gray almost took me to the floor. Val Carrera stood as a giant among men. He spoke and people scattered. His name was murmured in quiet tones, for fear of conjuring the wrath of a killer.

But to me, he was neither a giant nor a killer. He was the man who'd crossed borders to rescue me. He was the man who almost gave his life to save my own.

Valentin Carrera was my hero.

Somehow, I forced my feet to obey and carry me to his bedside. For far longer than I cared to rationalize, I stood above him, listening to him breathe. In the dingy basement, I'd searched so hard for the slightest breath that the rhythmic rise and fall of his chest comforted me like nothing had since I ran out of Caliente.

Lowering into the chair beside his bed, the beep of the machine synced with my heartbeat as I held his hand and pressed my cheek against the mattress. "Hey, Danger. You scared the hell out of me. What was with the superhero act, huh? You told me you were a criminal and a bad guy—someone people should fear and run from." Rolling my lips inward, I pressed them against the skin on his arm as tears I had no idea I had left rolled down the other side of it. "There's no fear, Val. Only love. I'm not running from you anymore. I'm running toward you. Wake up and catch me."

# *Chapter Thirty-Seven*
## VALENTIN

"I'm running toward you. Wake up and catch me."

Why the hell did it feel like I was climbing a ladder in a lake full of quicksand? The higher I climbed, the farther I sank, with each step more and more difficult to take.

She was near. That much I knew. Either that, or I was fucking hallucinating her voice.

"*Cere...*" My voice broke, the inside of my throat feeling like I'd chewed and swallowed a handful of broken glass.

"That's it, Danger. Come back to me."

A surge of white light burned my eyes as I finally climbed to the top of the ladder. "*Cereza?*"

Her soft hand cradled my face, the familiar scent of citrus and vanilla immediately calming my nerves. "I'm here, Val. Take your time. Don't make any sudden movements, all right?"

I blinked, taking in the stark, sterile room. "Where am I? What happened?"

"You're in Houston Methodist."

"Hospital?" The word settled in the base of my brain as the

entire night came rushing back in a heated panic. Holding her forearm with my IVed hand and taking a strong grip on her cheek with the other, I winced at the intense pain that shot through me. "Eden, are you all right?" I forced myself to look her over. "If he hurt you, I'll fucking kill him."

She lowered my hands, a serious look crossing her face. "Calm down, Carrera. Mission accomplished."

"What the hell does that mean?"

Something had changed about her. She seemed calmer, wiser, a hell of a lot more self-assured, and maybe even a touch cocky. A hardness lined the corners of her mouth that wasn't there before I walked into that basement.

I always swore Eden Lachey didn't belong in my world. From the look in her eyes and the ruthless smile that curved the corners of her lips, I wasn't so sure now.

"What did you do, Eden?"

"Shooting cans is easy, Val," she said with a knowing glint in her eye. "You just hold the gun on your target, allow your finger to barely touch the trigger, and let it go limp."

As she threw my own words back in my face, I knew immediately what she'd done. I looked away, not wanting to hear her say it any more than she wanted to admit it.

She'd murdered Manuel Muñoz.

Still, her supreme smugness drove me to point out one glaring omission she seemed to gloss over. "Eden, Marisol Muñoz is still out there."

Acknowledging me with a curt nod, Eden intertwined our fingers, turning them so her palm faced up. "Marisol Muñoz won't be a problem. Call it women's intuition, whatever you want. She said it herself; she doesn't have the stomach for the rough stuff. She's a planner. Without an army, she's nothing."

"*Cereza*, she has an entire cartel."

She shook her head defiantly. "No, Manuel had an entire cartel. Why do you think she hid behind him the entire time? Do you seriously think all those men would pledge their allegiance to a woman who couldn't even stay in the same room to witness her biggest enemy's execution? I don't think so. No, she's in the wind."

Fuck, I loved that woman's mind. "You're kind of brilliant, Eden Lachey."

"Aw, you're just saying that because it's true." Flashing a devoted smile, she squeezed our hands.

"Get your ass in this bed," I commanded, pulling the sheet back.

Her brows pulled together as she glanced around at the wires hooked up to me. "I don't know, Val. The bullet tore your liver. You were in surgery a long time. I don't want to bruise anything."

"The only thing you're going to bruise is my ego if you don't get that hot ass beside me, *Cereza*."

Moving slowly, she snuggled in, taking care to keep her weight off me. I ran my fingers through her hair as she played with the frayed edges of my hospital gown. "Val, can I ask you a question?"

"Depends on what it is."

"Why was Brody with you? How do you know him, and how did you find me? I was out most of the time, but I know we were in a car and a plane, then a boat. Eventually we crossed the border to that god-awful house in the middle of nowhere. There's no way you found that by accident."

I debated on whether to tell her the truth, then decided what we went through in that basement had given us a clean slate. Lying to her would only taint it. Taking her questions one at a time, I explained my relationship with Brody Harcourt, and how he used his connections to track her to the rural house that didn't exist.

Reaching under the neckline of the ugly scrubs she wore, I pulled out the broken *Santa Muerte* pendant and tapped it. "GPS."

As she glanced down at the pendant in my hands, she shook her head and frowned. "You tracked me like a dog, too? What the fuck is wrong with you, Val?"

Raising a hand, I effectively silenced her. "You can be mad at me all you want, but I won't be sorry. You were volatile before we left, and I couldn't take the risk of something happening to you. Besides," I said, giving it one last tap, before letting it drop back down against her taped ribs. "It saved your life."

She sat silent for a moment. I watched her, waiting for the eventual curve of a smile that told me I was forgiven. Eden never stayed mad at me for long.

Yet, the longer the muscles in her jaw tightened, the more rattled I became. In any other situation, we'd argue, throw shit, hurl insults, then fuck the mad out of each other until we couldn't walk. That's just the way Eden and I worked.

But, lying in a hospital bed, with a newly-closed gash healing above my stomach, sex was off the table. I didn't know how to reach her, and I didn't like it. "Eden?"

"I'm still mad at you," she finally offered, running the pad of her thumb across the top of mine. "But I don't have a good argument for what you said. You're right. It did save my life, and I guess I should be grateful."

"Damn right you should."

She fought a smile. "Don't push it."

I studied her face as a piece of candy-red hair fell across her eye. Pushing it back, her gaze lowered to the wires protruding from my chest. If anyone had told me a month ago—hell, a week ago—I'd have made the risky decisions I did to be with her, I'd have laughed in their face. I'd been a man who built a reputation on fear and destruction. Emotional attachments had no place in my world and only served to weaken me. I'd never missed something I'd never had.

The second Eden Lachey stormed into my life, something inside me knew I'd never be the same. As volatile as our circumstances were, I knew she'd be the one to get in and make me question everything I'd ever known. After touching her for the first time, I vowed I'd never be denied the light she brought to my darkness or the morality she crossed with my wickedness.

For her, I would and did risk it all.

Suppressing a groan from the searing pain tearing across my abdomen, I twisted a hand around her hair and tugged her down to me. "Come here, *Cereza*."

"Val…" She pulled back gently, bracing a hand on the mattress. "You just got out of surgery. Do you really think that's a good idea?"

"What I think," I growled, impatiently, "is that you've been taken from me for too long. I'm owed this."

"Well, as long as you have a good reason." Laughing softly, she held her weight on her arms as she lowered her lips and gently pressed them against mine.

*Oh, hell no.*

Tightening my fingers in her hair, I forced her lips open and tasted every inch of her mouth. It was like coming home.

Breaking the kiss, she rested her forehead against mine. "Don't ever scare me like that again."

"Don't ever leave me like that again."

We stayed like that for a long time, neither of us speaking, until she glanced toward the door. "Mateo is probably pacing outside like a caged animal. I guess I should give him his turn with you."

"Wait." I grabbed her arm, holding her inquisitive stare. "You need to call Janine. We may not have a physical building anymore, but RVC is still an operational company for now."

Her eyebrows lifted in question. "Why would I call Janine?"

"To put your townhouse on the market. You've got to find a buyer before we leave."

"Leave? Where are we going, Val?"

She couldn't be serious. After all we'd been through, she had to know it'd come to this. "Eden, when I get out of here, I'm moving back to Mexico. My men need me there to run the day-to-day operations." I searched her face for signs of understanding. "I thought you knew this. In Mexico, you asked me if I came to take over the cartel."

"But I thought after everything happened with Manuel and Marisol...I just thought..."

"*Cereza*, we've cut off the head of the dragon, but it doesn't mean it won't grow another one. The Muñoz Cartel won't lay down and die just because Manuel did. This is my life and my legacy. I can't turn my back on it." Her blue eyes reddened as she dropped my hand. Warning sirens raged in my ears and my chest tightened. "Eden, I need you with me. I can't do this without you."

With tears spilling down her face, she wrapped her arms protectively around her chest. "I killed a man, Val. I sold my soul to get revenge for my brother. I got it, but I don't feel any better. I thought I'd have this weight lifted off my shoulders once Manuel was dead, but instead it's gotten heavier. It almost destroyed me when Nash died, and when I thought I'd lost you. I'd convinced myself I could eventually deal with it because everything was over, but you're asking me to live with that worry on a daily basis. I can't...I can't do that."

I couldn't think straight. I'd lay down my life for her, and she was walking away from me. As she pulled back, I grabbed her arm, my heart racing. "What are you saying, Eden?"

"My home is in Houston, Val. We can have a good life here."

"What life, *Cereza*? Who's left here for you? You have no family."

A sad look crossed her face at the same time as a dejected smile dusted her lips. "I am. I'm stronger than I was before, and I have you to thank for that. I've learned to depend on no one but myself and that will protect me for the rest of my life. The word family doesn't exist for me anymore, Val. Families protect each other no matter what the cost. For my father, the price was too high." Leaning down, she placed a gentle kiss on my lips again. "*Te amo*."

Moving off the bed, she walked toward the door and out of my life.

# Chapter Thirty-Eight

## EDEN

*Six Weeks Later*

"Thanks, Janine." Tucking the phone under my chin, I reached for a white wine glass from overhead. "Yeah, that's fine. I'll be by in the morning to sign the papers. I appreciate everything. Have a good weekend."

Dropping the phone on the counter, the hardware store flashed in my mind. Earlier in the morning, I'd cleaned out the last box at the store and turned the key, locking the door to my past and the last reminder of the cursed Lachey legacy. The new CEO and liaison at RVC Enterprises, Janine Banfield, worked relentlessly and found a buyer for Lachey Hardware who was willing to pay close to my full asking price. The money would be enough that I could take a little time for myself before selling everything else I owned.

I had no idea where I'd move, but my home held nothing but memories for me—some bad, some good, and some that still tore my heart in two. I needed a fresh start and sticking around constant reminders wouldn't allow me a chance to put what had happened behind me.

"Eden, are you going to pour that wine or dance with it?"

Shaken out of my thoughts, I shot an annoyed glance at Tiffany as she tapped her toe on the other side of the bar. Snickering, she motioned to the bottle of Kendall Jackson I hugged to my chest as I narrowed my eyes.

*Bitch.*

Tightening my grip on the bottle, I imagined it was her neck as I turned to the nicely dressed couple at the end of the bar. "Chardonnay, right?" A woman with way too much makeup nodded, and I over-poured on purpose.

*Screw this bar and their rules.*

Bending over, I shoved the bottle into the mini cooler as Tiffany tapped her toe behind me again.

"If you want to keep that toe attached to your foot, I suggest you stop."

Shifting her toe behind her opposite heel, she crossed her arms over her massive chest. "We're not supposed to be on our phones while we're at work."

Slamming the refrigerator door, I stepped in close and lowered my voice to a warning growl. "We're also not supposed to wear uniform sizes that fit a fucking toddler. Now get out of my face before I get that wine bottle back out and break it over your head."

With her mouth forming a perfect circle, Tiffany shook her bleached blonde hair and stomped off with her ass hanging out of her Lycra shorts.

*God, I hate these outfits.*

I felt and looked beyond stupid in the black booty-shorts and half-shirt announcing to everyone that I was a 'Naughty Irish Girl.' Besides, I was Scottish, not that anyone cared.

After leaving Caliente, I realized Nash had been right. I had no skills other than the ability to mix a Long Island Iced Tea in under forty-five seconds. After searching through every trash can in my house, I finally found one of the University of Texas brochures he'd stuffed in my purse and started the application for admission and financial aid. While I waited to hear if I got accepted, I got a job doing what I did best—slinging drinks. Only this time, instead of shaking margaritas in a Mexican cantina, I poured Guinness in the shittiest Irish pub in town.

Cashing out my bartender book, I nodded to Zach, the newest hire, who'd come to relieve my shift. He was a nice guy with a mop of sandy brown hair and a beard he tried hard to grow. Maybe one day he'd succeed.

"Hi, Eden. How's tips?"

"Shitty, as usual."

"Tiffany here?"

I rolled my eyes and pointed my thumb over my shoulder toward the manager's office. "Unfortunately, yes, and probably ratting me out for threatening to cut off her toes."

Zach laughed until I glanced up from grabbing my purse from underneath the bar, my eyes cold and serious. He swallowed uncomfortably, and a satisfied smirk coated my face.

"Enjoy your night, Zach. Don't do anything I wouldn't do."

"Uh, yeah. Sure thing, Eden."

Pushing the heavy, wooden door open, I inhaled the mild, seventy-degree, September weather. With a full chest and clear mind, I realized the exchange with Zach epitomized the new Eden Lachey.

The person that walked into the hardware store that June morning was no longer me. Even the way I reacted to situations and people had drastically changed.

I'd never again be anyone's victim or second choice.

I KNEW THE DAY WOULD COME, WHETHER I PRETENDED IT EXISTED OR not. I could tell myself as much as I wanted that I was prepared for it and could work through it. Keeping my mind occupied proved to be useless.

September second, my brother would've turned twenty-eight years old. Initially full of anger, the indignant side of me wanted to blow the whole day off and get drunk. By the time my car left the bar, I knew what I had to do, and where I was headed.

I walked out of the supermarket and ripped open the box of popsicles before I reached my car. Hitting the gas with a heavy foot, I rolled down the window and tossed all the orange and purple popsicles onto the highway, one by one, until only a box of red ones remained.

Holding the box tightly, I dropped everything on my way from the front door of my townhouse to the deck, not bothering to care where they landed.

One right after another, I sat by myself and ate almost the entire box until my lips were numb.

"YES, I UNDERSTAND. THANK YOU, OFFICER HELMS."

Placing the phone back on the glass table to my side, I shook my head at the reach Val had across the border and deep into law enforcement. Nash and my father's disappearances were classified as missing person cases, boxed and buried in files never to be reopened. As far as the Houston Police Department was concerned, my only family would be missing until the end of time.

Only, I knew their bodies would never be found. If they even still existed at all.

Still huddled on my deck, I faced the city lights and chased the red drip of the last remaining popsicle with my tongue as it ran down my arm. Shifting in my lounger, I hugged the empty box to my chest as my eyes clouded with tears.

*"I LOOK LIKE I'VE SHOVED MY HANDS UP A BABOON'S ASS, THANKS NASH." Holding my red-stained hands out for his inspection, I threw the dark red sponge in the sink and rolled my eyes at him.*

*Nash just grinned. "You should've come home and checked your mail instead of going to the bar with one of your ex's fraternity brothers."*

*"I was just blowing off some steam, big brother. I'm allowed after all I've been through, don't you think?"*

*Folding his hands in his lap, Nash seemed to take a moment to choose his words. "Be careful around Brody Harcourt, Cherry. I know him well enough, but I don't trust him…especially with my sister."*

*"Will you please stop calling me that?"*

*"No." He laughed, his resolve to tease me relentlessly obvious.*

*Plopping down in a lounger beside him, I stared out at the city lights of Houston from the deck of my townhouse. "What is it about me that makes everyone leave, Nash? First Mom, now Davis." Lowering my chin, a shudder shook me as I fought the impending breakdown I'd held in for so long. "I don't know what I'm doing wrong."*

*Reaching over, Nash grabbed the arm rest of my chair and dragged it over until it touched his. As he wrapped his strong arm around my shoulder, I rested my forehead against his chest, and breathed in his familiar Giorgio Armani cologne. "Nothing is wrong with you, Cherry Pop. You should never change to meet anyone else's expectations. If they can't love you for the amazing, strong, and adorably quirky person you are...fuck 'em. They aren't worth you or your time."*

*"But what about you? You're all I have left, Nash. If you ever left me, I don't think I could handle it."*

*Giving me a squeeze, he kissed the top of my head. "I swear to you, Edie, no matter where we end up in life, I'll always be here for you." Chuckling, he picked up one of my beet red stained hands and held it up. "Besides, there isn't any situation that can't be fixed by red dye number forty and a hug from your big brother."*

I WIPED THE TEARS AS THEY FELL AND BIT THE TIP OFF THE POPSICLE.

I'd have to settle for red dye number forty tonight.

Snapped out of my memory by the shrill ring of my phone, I dropped the melting popsicle on the glass table and glanced at the caller ID.

"Were your ears burning? I was just talking about you."

"With whom?" Brody asked, his voice curious.

"Nash."

"Cherry, have you been drinking?"

His concern for my sanity made me laugh out loud. "What's up, Brody?"

"I know it's late, but are you busy? Can I come over?"

"Look," I sighed. "We talked about this, remember? I like you, and you're a good friend, but just because he's gone doesn't mean I'm ready to see anyone else right now."

*Or ever.*

"Yes, I know that, Eden. You've made that perfectly clear on multiple occasions," he retorted dryly. "Besides, the last thing I plan to do is get on the wrong side of Val Carrera. Been there, done that, don't ever plan on it again."

My spine stiffened at the mention of his name. "We're not together, Brody. You know that."

"So you keep saying." He paused. "Does he know that? All I'll say is I feel sorry for the first guy you try to have a real relationship with, Eden. Emilio Reyes is still here running the stateside operations, you know. Plus, Carrera has eyes and ears everywhere. If you think he doesn't have them on you, you're nuts."

I'd heard enough. "You have twenty minutes. If you're not here, I'm going to bed." Moving the phone to disconnect the call, I pressed it back to my ear and added, "Alone." Then I hung up.

"Thanks for seeing me." Walking past me, Brody ran a hand through his dirty blond hair and sat on the couch, bouncing his knees up and down in his habitual nervous gesture.

"Please," I offered, after the fact. "Come in."

Brody shot me a hardened look, with his eyes void of amusement. "Eden, this is serious."

Scrubbing my hands down my face, I took a seat across from him and tucked my legs underneath me. "Fine, what's so important that it couldn't wait until morning?"

"You have to promise to let me finish before you flip out," he muttered under his breath. After I nodded and grew more and more suspicious of his behavior, he stood up and paced in front of me. "I've been searching for Marisol Muñoz."

"What?"

"You agreed to let me finish first."

"That was before I knew this had to do with the fucking Muñoz Cartel! Brody, have you lost your mind? This is like tap dancing on a land mine!"

Closing the distance between us, he wrapped his fingers around my shoulders. "In digging for information, I found a faked birth certificate, Cherry. Marisol Muñoz doesn't exist."

"What are you saying?" I whispered, afraid to hear the rest.

"Not only was there never a *real* birth certificate for Marisol Muñoz, but there isn't a death certificate on record for Adriana Carrera."

"No…" Shaking my head, I tried to pull away from his hold.

*"You mentioned a baby…Ana. What happened to her?"*

*"No one ever found my sister's body. I can't think about that, Eden. I never have."*

"Marisol Muñoz had to have a kidney transplant when she was fourteen. Her kidneys shut down because of a life-long battle with juvenile diabetes. The Muñoz family ran into a problem when none of her blood relatives were a match as a donor."

"That doesn't mean anything, Brody," I argued. "That happens all the time in families."

"Eden, both Esteban and his wife have type A blood. That means genetically they could only produce children with type A or type O blood." Pausing, he glanced at his hands before locking me in an intense stare. "Marisol Muñoz's blood type is AB. Adriana Carrera was born with type 1 juvenile diabetes. I have a friend in the Mexican Embassy. I had them run a comparison of the blood samples on record, on account of the unsolved murder of Adriana Carrera."

The gold flecks in her eyes. The thick dark hair. The refusal to degrade women.

I twisted harder. "Brody, no..."

"Adriana Carrera's blood type was AB. They matched, Edie. Marisol Muñoz isn't Manuel's sister. She's Val's."

# *Chapter Thirty-Nine*

## VALENTIN

### Mexico City, Mexico

"I think it went well, don't you?" Mateo asked, parking the car in front of the estate.

"Well, no one got shot this time, so I'm going with yes." Rolling his eyes at me, he opened the car door, and I broke a smile. It was one of the few I'd managed in the past six weeks.

Today marked the first time I faced the men as the official head of the cartel since the ill-fated meeting that ended in Guzman's death. Since returning to Mexico, I'd let Mateo handle the meetings with the lieutenants while I hid in the estate and healed from surgery. My men needed to see their leader strong and invincible, not in need of help just to walk to the bathroom.

Plus, I hadn't found much of anything to smile about after leaving everything that meant anything in Houston.

After all we'd been through, the last thing I ever expected was for Eden to walk away. The moment she left my hospital room, I knew it would be the last time I'd see her. A few days later, I was discharged, and I still hadn't heard from her.

Once across the border, I'd picked up the phone to call her, then realized I didn't have her number. The phone I'd given her in Monterrey was mine, and she'd either discarded it or simply stopped using it. For everything Eden and I had shared, there was so much more I didn't know about her. Normal couples would've known such things within the first few days.

I didn't know her phone number.

I didn't know her middle name.

I didn't know her favorite food or her favorite color.

I did know that I loved her, and with every week that passed, I missed her more, not less.

But it was time to come to terms with the fact that we'd both made our choices and move on.

"Did the shipment make it to Padre Island without any problem?" I asked, opening the front door to my new house.

"Right on schedule." Mateo nodded as he followed me inside. "We've appeased the Colombians with the new territories we picked up from the slack in the Muñoz holdings. I talked to Emilio a few hours ago. He says everything is running smoothly, and all stash houses should be filled and ready for delivery tomorrow."

"*Muy bien.*" I nodded and plowed a hand through my hair. "Tomorrow we need to set up an email account accessible for all the lieutenants. That's how we'll communicate for this next shipment we're moving by train from Mexico City to Houston. One email account, Mateo, and we all have the same password. That way we can eliminate all this traceable shit going back, and…" My words died on my tongue as I turned the corner into the main living room, and all thought blanked from my mind.

She'd never looked more beautiful. In a fitted sleeveless beige dress, she held folded papers tightly in her clasped hands as we stared at each other. The long, candy-red colored hair that I loved to wrap around my fingers was pulled up into a loose bun on top of her head. Large gold hoops reflected from her ears, and the *Santa Muerte* pendant I gave her hung around her neck.

I didn't know whether to pick her up and lock her in my bedroom or throw her ass out for putting me through six weeks of hell.

"Eden." It was the only thing I could think of to say that was safe.

"Hey, Danger." Unclasping her hands, she threw them out to the side. "Surprise."

"I think I have some…I need to go do the thing in the…they said I had to…I'm leaving," Mateo mumbled as he hurried out of the front door, closing it behind him.

"Did you take a wrong turn leaving Caliente?" Tearing my eyes away from her, I walked to the bar and poured a glass of tequila. I needed a drink to deal with seeing her again.

"Val, you know I don't work at Caliente anymore."

"How would I know that? I live in another country…*Cere*… Eden."

"Look, I didn't come here to fight with you."

Slamming the glass down, I turned over my shoulder. "Why did you come here? I assume it wasn't for a vacation."

Her fingers clenched around the papers. "I get that you're mad. I don't expect you to understand or forgive me for walking out at the hospital and not coming back. I'm not here to beg for your forgiveness."

Her words did something to me. For six weeks, I did nothing but imagine what I'd do if she walked through that door. I wished for it. Hell, I even prayed for it. But day after day, I lost faith in ever feeling alive again.

Now, here she stood, just like I dreamed she would. Except she wasn't apologetic and didn't need or want my forgiveness.

*Fuck that.*

Hitching my arm back, I threw the glass against the wall, shards and tequila exploding everywhere. "Maybe I want you to, *Cereza*." Stalking toward her, I gave up the fight not to touch her and roughly palmed her cheek. "Maybe I want you down on your knees, begging for my forgiveness."

Backing up, she grabbed my arm. "Stop it, Val."

"I mean, you're so good at it." I continued backing her up until her ass hit the wall. "Being on your knees, that is."

An impending storm of rage flashed through her eyes as she dropped the papers in her hand and slapped me hard across the face. For half a heartbeat, we stood there staring at each other, chests heaving, and jaws clenched. Then, as if a dam broke, our mouths crashed together in impatient fury. There was nothing slow or soft about our kisses. Our tongues fought for dominance as teeth clashed and lips plundered.

Without asking permission, I jerked her dress up around her waist and wound the string that rested by her hips around my hand and pulled hard. A satisfying rip filled my ears as the material tore in half.

"Val," she moaned, half encouraging me, half protesting.

I didn't care one way or the other. I was too far gone. "Beg me, *Cereza*."

"Fuck you."

Shoving two fingers inside her, I pumped them hard and growled again. "Beg me, *Cereza*."

Gasping, she threw her head back against the wall and groaned. "Fuck me. Forgive me, and for God's sake, fuck me."

I released my pants with one hand while continuing to thrust mercilessly into her. I felt her release the moment she clenched around my fingers. Moaning, she slammed her palms against the wall above her head and panted for air.

"Jesus!"

"Don't move," I demanded. Kicking her legs apart, I grabbed the back of her thighs and lifted her onto my cock. "No man will ever love you like I do, *Cereza*." Driving into her hard, I bottomed out as she screamed my name. Holding us both still, I took full possession of what belonged to me. "S*erás mía para siempre*," I commanded hotly into her ear. "You're mine forever, Eden Lachey."

"THIS ISN'T WHY I CAME HERE," EDEN MUMBLED, CRADLED IN MY LAP as I sat leaned against the wall.

Eventually coming down from the high of simultaneous orgasms, we'd finally caught our breath, too exhausted to move. I couldn't remember anything feeling as good as holding her in my arms at that moment. It was as if the anguish of the past six weeks faded away the minute I buried myself inside her. I didn't care what she had to say. Eden wasn't going back to Houston. I'd chain her to the bed again if I had to.

"Okay," I said, burying my nose in her hair. "I'll bite. Why did you come here?"

Climbing off me, she reached for the papers she'd dropped earlier and knelt beside me. "I have something to tell you, and I don't know how you're going to react."

"You're freaking me out a little, *Cereza*. Just tell me."

She blew out a heavy breath. "Okay, so, Brody came over two days ago."

"I don't like where this is going," I growled, my skin feeling like fire.

*I'll fucking kill Brody Harcourt.*

"Oh, calm your inner caveman, Danger. It was innocent. He came over to talk about you."

"Me?"

"There's no easy way to say this, so I'm just going to put it out there, and we'll deal with the fallout." Rubbing the back of her neck, she caught my eye and held it. "Marisol Muñoz isn't Marisol Muñoz."

I leaned away and studied her determined face. "That makes no sense."

"You told me your baby sister's body was never found after your family was attacked."

"Eden, I don't want to talk about…"

She placed a hand on my chest. "That's because there was no body."

"Huh?" I had no idea why she brought up such a painful subject, but I wanted no part of it. "Look, this is a part of my life I don't want to talk about, all right? The past is the past." Pushing off the floor, I buttoned my pants and headed back to the bar.

"That's just it, Val; the past isn't the past. Your sister didn't die that night. Esteban Muñoz was one sadistic fuck. Think about it. What would hurt your father more than murdering his wife and children?"

Her words started to sink in, and my hand gripped the glass so hard I worried it might shatter in my hands. "It can't be."

"Esteban Muñoz took Adriana and raised her as his own daughter. He raised your sister to hate her own family and plan their deaths." I felt her behind me before her hands touched my back. "I saw it in your eyes in that basement when you looked at her. You felt a connection with her, but you didn't know why, and it confused the hell out of you. Now you know."

I swallowed hard, forcing the vomit I knew would eventually rise back down. "What are the papers in your hand?"

"Faked birth certificates, real birth certificates, blood records, and hospital records. A paper trail of proof that Brody dug up supporting what we've found. Esteban's wife only gave birth once, and that was to Manuel. She's your sister, Val."

Turning, I met her stare, allowing her to see the fear that rolled through me. "If this is true, what will happen to her, Eden? This is all so farfetched, and she doesn't know. All she knows is her entire family is dead now. What if she's unsavable?"

Eden smiled knowingly. "She's a Carrera. She's not unsavable."

I swallowed hard and grabbed her hand. "She ordered the hit on your brother. How would you ever forgive her for that?"

"One thing at a time, Danger." Sighing softly, she buried her chin in my back. "Look, yesterday I thought I'd never see you again. That plan worked out well, huh?"

"I'm worried any goodness that might have been inside her has been eaten away by Muñoz influence." I'd lived with the death and destruction of both our families my whole existence. I had no idea how she'd return from a lifetime of that kind of mind control.

"You both have your mother's blood, as much as your father's, Val. Give her time. She'll find herself and seek you out. When that time comes, we'll deal with it and be there for her."

"What about you, *Cereza*?" I asked, turning and snaking my arms around her waist. "What've you found?"

A smile broke out across her lips as she wrapped her arms around my neck. Pressing her lips against my ear, she whispered with the strongest conviction I'd ever heard from her.

"Home."

# *Epilogue*

## EDEN

*Two Months Later*

"**V**al!"

He sank his teeth into my shoulder as my body tumbled over the crest. Panting, I struggled to focus on his face as I grabbed it between my palms and brought his lips to mine. After a devastating kiss that found us both exhausted and collapsing in bed, he rolled to the side and scooped me in his arms.

"So, *Cereza*, how does it feel to sleep with the most powerful man in Mexico?"

A full-chested laugh escaped before I could stop it, causing him to raise an eyebrow. "Oh, please, Carrera. Do you really think you hold all the power around here?" The cocked eyebrow raised even higher, and my smile widened. The confused look on his face was priceless. "Come on, get dressed. We're going to be late."

He watched as I threw the covers back and opened the closet. "We? Where do you think you're going?"

Adrenaline rushed through my veins as I met his stare, ready for the next step in my life. "We have a meeting."

As the last man walked out of the room, Val returned to his seat beside me at the head of the table and placed a shot of tequila by my folded hands.

I shot a side-glance at him. "*Añejo* tequila? Straight shot, in a stem glass, not a highball, room temp, and if it hasn't aged at least three years, shove it up the owner's ass?"

"Warm house tequila, in a dirty shot glass. Cartel special."

"Ah, big spender."

Glancing around the room, he sat back in his chair. "So, was this your plan all along? World domination?"

With Mateo's help, I'd finally figured out how I could be with Val and still keep my identity.

*As equals.*

I refused to be his dirty little secret or the little woman waiting at home for him to maybe come home, or maybe not. If what we had was going to work, I had to be in on every decision, every strategic move, and every dangerous situation he put himself in.

Sitting beside him at this table.

Bringing my idea to Mateo, he'd grinned and arranged my ambush of Val's scheduled meeting with his top lieutenants, demanding their compliance by assuring Val's approval. I knew Val would never agree with a partnership if I'd asked straight out. He was too protective, and if I started asking for his approval for my actions now, not only would that set a precedent in our relationship, but it also wasn't how Val and I worked.

Better to ask for forgiveness than permission.

Lowering my lids, I picked up the shot and downed half of it and shuddered. It was eighty proof piss water.

From beside me, Val let out a low chuckle. "All you Americans are alike. You never take time to appreciate the finer things in life."

Holding the glass by my cheek, I shot him an annoyed look. "You just said it was shit tequila."

"Not the tequila, *Cereza*," he said, his eyes deadly. "What's at the end of it."

"Oh, my God, there's a fucking worm?" Slamming the glass on the table, I pushed my chair as far away from it as I could and scrubbed my tongue with my palm.

His laugh growing louder, Val picked up the glass and shook it, as something made a *ting ting* sound at the bottom. Curious, I snatched the glass out of his hand and peered inside. Immediately, my heart raced with disbelief and apprehension.

It couldn't be real.

And yet, there it was, right before my eyes—large, round, brilliant, and very wet.

Taking the glass from my shaking hands, Val dug a finger inside and pulled the ring from the bottom, shaking off the excess tequila. Holding it up, he took my hand in his. "Eden, you're everything I thought I never wanted. I don't think there's anyone else like you in the world, and for the sake of humanity, I hope I'm right. The minute I saw you, you got under my skin. You make it impossible for me to make sound decisions when you're around, and you disrupt every aspect of my life."

"Is this your idea of a proposal, Danger?" I whispered.

"I'm getting there," he smiled. "With all that said, I wouldn't change a thing. I meant it in Monterrey when I said I couldn't breathe without you. I can't, *Cereza*. You're my air, and I need air to exist. I need you to exist. So, what do you say? Will you marry me?"

In that moment, I thought of Nash. "There's no one to walk

me down the aisle or give me away."

"Eden, no one needs to give you away. When I walked into that bar, you became mine. Your heart, your eyes, your smile—they combined to give everything to me, and we've belonged to each other ever since."

"I don't belong to anyone, Val." Touching his face softly, I reached in his waistband and pulled his own gun on him. Smiling, he never flinched before pulling another one from inside his ankle holster. Raising an eyebrow, I glanced between our weapons. "This is supremely fucked up, Danger."

"I agree. But you have no idea how turned on I am right now."

"You're such a pig."

"Ah, but this is the hallmark of how we operate, *Cereza*. We fight hard and fuck harder. Isn't that the key to a lasting relationship?"

"We're some seriously fucked up individuals."

"You still haven't said yes." Thinking over his words, the night he walked into Caliente popped into my mind. "What are you thinking, Eden? You have a strange look on your face."

"That night at Caliente. It was the worst night of my life and also the best." My mouth twitched as I mulled over the words I'd just uttered. "I don't think I'll ever be able to reconcile the whole dichotomy of it. I'm not the same person I was when you sat down on that barstool. I've done things I never thought I'd do, but I don't feel remorse. What does that make me?"

"Answer me and I'll tell you."

"Tell me first," I demanded, shaking my head defiantly.

"Eden, I was destined to run my father's empire. I'd be here with or without you. I've never needed anyone. I've never wanted anyone because a soul was easier not to have. Stoning my conscience and heart made it simpler to rationalize this life, but you've become as vital to me as my legacy. There's no distinguishable factor between them anymore. One can't exist without the other. I'd be a broken man."

"Val—"

"Listen to me, Lachey. Most of the world doesn't see what we see and that's all right for them. But the moment I saw you, *Cereza*, there was a fire in your eyes that matched your hair—a hunger for the power you lacked. Power that'd been continually taken from you. I offer you power and more. I never want you weak. I've seen what happens to weak women who aren't informed and aware." Holding up the ring, he grasped my hand. "Being my wife means being my partner. Not just in stupid meaningless vows people say every day, but in the true sense of *our* world. The world that's now yours. My equal. My love. My salvation."

"What about your precious heirs? Don't you need a true bloodline to run an empire?"

"I need *you*, Eden. The rest we'll figure out along the way. Stop putting everything in a box."

There was nothing I could say to that. *Well, almost nothing.* "Yes."

And just like that, I closed the door on Eden Lachey forever.

I MARRIED VALENTIN CARRERA THIRTY DAYS LATER ON THE GROUNDS of our heavily-guarded estate. There was no fanfare or extensive guest list befitting the head of one of the most powerful drug cartels in the world. Just like us, it was private and discreet, with only Mateo and Val's secretary Janine standing by our side.

After an impressive full cartel gun salute, he slung me over his shoulder, dismissed everyone with a wave of his hand, and threw me onto our bed. His hands trailed my sleek, white dress up the length of my legs, and he paused at the apex of my thighs as his hands brushed against my white elastic thigh holster. He lifted a sleek eyebrow as he traced his fingers over the metal fastened within its confines.

"Is this your old, new, or borrowed?"

I winked. "It was a wedding gift from Mateo."

"Remind me to kick his ass later."

I ran my hands through his thick, midnight black hair. He'd slicked it back for the ceremony, but I loved it when it was wild and dangerous—just like him. "Be nice. You know as well as I do, anything could've happened today. You're telling me you weren't armed?" His lip twitched in a half smile. "That's what I thought. Mateo just wanted me to have protection, too."

Val's hand tightened around my thigh. "Speaking of which, now that we're married, there will be no more birth control, Eden. What happens, happens. I want to feel every inch of you with nothing separating us."

Releasing the garters from my elastic thigh holster, Val slid it down my leg and tossed it and my gun to the floor. I groaned impatiently as he chased his fingers back up the length of my leg with his lips. The minute he passed my knee, I meant to moan something enticing and dirty.

Unfortunately, that wasn't what came out.

"About that heir thing…" He froze, with his mouth on my inner thigh. Glancing up through thick eyelashes, he waited for me to continue. Swallowing the lump growing in my throat by the minute, I took a deep breath and smiled. "Well, with Nash being gone, and neither of us having any family left, I decided to listen to you and stop putting everything in a box."

"Oh?" He smiled.

"Except for one thing. I left this in there."

Digging under the pillow, I handed him the rectangular box and held my breath. It rattled as he shook it and I smiled nervously. "So, how would you feel about a daughter running the empire someday?" The horrified look blanketing his face first scared me, then irritated the hell out of me. Narrowing my eyes, I peered at him through tiny slits. "Really?"

Full chested laughter overtook him as he rolled over and took me with him. "If she's anything like you, she'll run more than this empire. She'll run the world."

Holding my head between his hands he kissed me long and hard, glancing from the box to my face. "Really?"

"Really."

"We're going to fuck this up, *Cereza*."

"Probably," I agreed. Frowning, I ran a hand down his chest. "I don't think I've ever really thanked you."

"For what?"

"For kidnapping me. You most likely saved my life, and I repaid you by stabbing you with a fork. It's a wonder you didn't kill me yourself."

"The night's still young."

"We're bringing a kid into this, Danger. Are we doing the right thing here?" Panic seized me at the thought of our child enduring the life Val grew up with.

Eyeing me closely, Val brushed a piece of hair from my face. "Do you regret being here, Eden?"

I didn't hesitate. "Not a moment."

"Then neither will he or she. Family isn't what's around you. It's what surrounds you. My mother showed me that every day of her life. I think you'd agree—so did your brother."

"I miss him, Val."

"And you always will, baby. Just like I'll always miss my mother and the person my sister used to be. Maybe someday she'll remember where she came from, maybe not. What's important is we don't stop living just because they did."

Pulling his face down to mine, I dusted my lips across his. "How'd you get so smart?"

"Someone once told me I was an emotional black hole. I may've done some light Googling."

IN THE MIDDLE OF THE NIGHT, I WATCHED MY HUSBAND SLEEP. NO ONE would ever accuse Valentin Carrera of sleeping peacefully, but in the sanctuary of our bedroom, we let down our guards and let trust rule the night.

Wrapping the blanket around my shoulders, I realized that I barely thought of my old life anymore. Although we both lost our entire families and still mourned our slain loved ones, the ache they left would've eventually destroyed us. Ironically, the catastrophic events that their deaths set in motion created a love we found in each other, easing the ache and filling a void neither of us knew existed.

Some people were raised to see only two sides of a world—good or evil. You either stood on the side of righteous or damnation. I discovered life wasn't predictable and people weren't necessarily all pure or all malicious. Perceptions changed when cultures and survival were on the line.

Val said we fought hard and fucked harder. I supposed that was true. My emotions ran at heated fluctuations when we were near each other. He angered me and loved me like no one ever had or ever would.

My father's favorite quote referred to the fine line between love and hate. He'd tell me not to confuse or blur it. I should recognize the difference and turn my back on the latter.

*I disagree.*

Val Carrera taught me that life didn't necessarily run in clear shades of black and white. Gray areas clouded a side of people they had no idea existed—a side capable of unspeakable acts when thrust into darkness. In those gray areas, love and passion ran volatile in two people whose paths were never meant to cross.

Hearts.

Hatred.

Blood.

In this life we'd chosen to live, the blurred line between love and hate was sometimes stained red.

# Acknowledgments

I've run out of people to thank, so, thank you to Pinot Grigio for keeping my glass filled and my laptop from flying through the window.

Catherine Wiltcher, I'm not even sure what to say at this point except that "person" who sprouted horns and a tail two days before deadline? That was my twin sister, Dora. We keep her in a kennel downstairs. Not sure how she got loose, but I apologize for the sixty-four messages she sent you at four a.m.

A huge apology to my family for being MIA the last four years. In case you wondered, I was upstairs the whole time. Thanks to whoever brought me water, Cheetos, and Febreze.

Crystal, what can I say that I haven't already said in nineteen acknowledgments? Thank you for not complaining when I asked you to Google things in the name of research that probably have both of us on some kind of FBI watch list. Thanks for always being by my side, for championing this series, and for not being afraid to tell me when I've done your man wrong. Thanks to you, Val got his groove back. You are now and forever, Mrs. Valentin Carrera.

Thank you Ginger Snaps and Alina Kirshner for making me seem like I'm fluent in Spanish and Russian. Spoiler: I'm not. Because of you both, Val and Ava's dialects are authentic. You are my translation goddesses.

Thank you so much to KC Fernandez for your mad proofreading skills and your insane attention to detail. Simply put, you saved my ass. I'm not sure how I managed to rope you into my inner circle, but good luck getting out of it now.

To my incredible beta team, Carrera's Guerreras, thank you. You never complain when I roll in at the last minute with either a paragraph or seventeen chapters, or when I post them at two a.m. and type in all caps, *WHERE ARE YOU* because I forget that normal people sleep. Thank you for your love and support, and for telling me when something really sucks. Love you, Crystal, Sarah, Sienna, Ronda, Sheri, Tami, KC, Tiffany, Amy, and Melissa.

To my editor, Mitzi Carroll, thank you for your dedication to this series and for always making room for me when the manuscript is a week later than I promised.

Many thanks to Danielle Sanchez and the staff of Wildfire Marketing Solutions for your help with this release and for being my sounding board. I'm so blessed to be a part of your team.

To my reader group, Cora's Twisted Alpha Addicts, and my street team, Cora's Twisted Capos, thank you for being there every day to make me smile and give me the push I need to keep the words flowing. I couldn't imagine the book world without you.

Mom, thank you for seeing the stars, grabbing one, and holding it for me until I believed in myself enough to know I belonged among them.

Lastly, to the bloggers, readers, booktokers, and bookstagrammers who have read and shared this series over the years, a very heartfelt thank you. As always, without you, I'm just a chick with a laptop.

# About the Author

Cora Kenborn is a *USA Today* Bestselling author of over twenty-five multi-genre novels, including the Carrera Cartel Trilogy.

While best known for her dark and gritty romances, Cora infuses sharp banter and a shocking blindside in every story she writes. She loves a brooding antihero who falls hard for a feisty heroine who stands beside him, not behind him.

Although she's a native North Carolinian, Cora claims the domestic Southern Belle gene skipped a generation, so she spends any free time convincing her family that microwaved mac and cheese counts as fine dining.

Oh, and autocorrect thinks she's obsessed with ducks.

*Join her newsletter for updates and get a **FREE** ebook.*
www.corakenborn.com

# Author Library

## CARRERA CARTEL
### *(Dark Mafia Romance)*

Carrera Cartel: The Collection
(*w/bonus novel*)
Blurred Red Lines
Faded Gray Lines
Drawn Blue Lines

## CORRUPT GODS
### *Spinoff of Carrera Cartel*
### *(Dark Mafia Romance)*

Corrupt Gods Collection
(*w/bonus chapters*)
Born Sinner
Bad Blood
Tainted Blood
City of Thieves
Bullets and Thorns

## MARCHESI EMPIRE
### *Spinoff of Carrera Cartel*
### *(Dark Mafia Romance)*

Torched Spades
Tortured Hearts

## LES CAVALIERS DE L'OMBRE
### *(Dark Mafia Romance)*

Darkest Deeds

## BRATVA'S MARK
### *Spinoff of Les Cavaliers de l'ombre*
### *(Dark Bratva Romance)*

Illicit Acts
Wicked Ways

**LORDS OF LYRE**
*(Rockstar Suspense Romance)*

Fame and Obsession
Fame and Secrets
Fame and Lies

**STANDALONES**
*(Dark/Romantic Suspense)*

Sixth Sin
Cast Stones
State of Grace

**STANDALONES**
*(Contemporary/Sports Romance)*

Shallow
Playboy Pitcher

**STANDALONES**
*(Romantic Comedy)*

Unsupervised
Swamp Happens: The Complete Collection

**STANDALONES**
*(Paranormal/Dark Urban Fantasy Romance)*

Cursed In Love

Made in United States
North Haven, CT
17 February 2022

16205246R00226